D0759944

# THE STARS ASKEW

BOOKS BY RJURIK DAVIDSON

*Unwrapped Sky*
*The Stars Askew*

*The Library of Forgotten Books* (collection)

# THE
# STARS ASKEW

## RJURIK DAVIDSON

TOR

A TOM DOHERTY ASSOCIATES BOOK
NEW YORK

THE STARS ASKEW

Copyright © 2016 by Rjurik Davidson

All rights reserved.

A Tor Book
Published by Tom Doherty Associates, LLC
175 Fifth Avenue
New York, NY 10010

www.tor-forge.com

Tor® is a registered trademark of Tom Doherty Associates, LLC.

The Library of Congress Cataloging-in-Publication Data
is available upon request.

ISBN 978-0-7653-2989-9 (hardcover)
ISBN 978-1-4299-4512-7 (e-book)

Our books may be purchased in bulk for promotional, educational, or business use. Please contact your local bookseller or the Macmillan Corporate and Premium Sales Department at 1-800-221-7945, extension 5442, or by e-mail at MacmillanSpecialMarkets@macmillan.com.

First Edition: July 2016

Printed in the United States of America

10  9  8  7  6  5  4  3  2  1

*To the memory of Jolyon Campbell and*
*Michael Arnold—taken too soon*

*If we roused the peoples and made the continents quake . . .*
*began to make everything anew with these dirty old stones,*
*these tired hands, and the meager souls that were left us,*
*it was not in order to haggle with you now,*
*sad revolution, our mother, our child, our flesh,*
*our decapitated dawn, our night with its stars askew.*

—Victor Serge (1890–1947), "Confessions"

# PART I

# MORNINGS

*The cataclysm broke the world, but the death of Aya brought the age to a close.*

*The overseer, Panadus, roved from god to god, for he had lost his center, like a distraught child.*

*"What shall we do? Where shall we go?" Panadus asked. "This, our world, our utopia—gone."*

*Few responded, for the cities had been smashed, the palaces thrown down, the pleasure gardens spoiled. The forests had burned, and mountains had been thrown into the sea.*

*Alerion stood aside, his haunted eyes darting to-and-fro. His anger was unabated, but his despair was yet greater.*

*In the end, the gods chose to leave. The Aediles begged them to stay and rebuild the world, but the gods would not hear them.*

*So Panadus led the gods away and they abandoned the world.*

*Only Alerion chose to stay. Bereft and alone, he traveled to Caeli-Amur to revisit the scene of his greatest triumph. Yet his will was gone. Without his greatest enemy, Aya, Alerion was broken.*

*As his vitality leeched from him, the Aediles caught the last of his strength and bound it into a prism. And so the last of the gods was gone.*

*And Aya laughed from the Other Side.*

—The Legend of Aya

# ONE

A revolution is a festival of the oppressed. Caeli-Amur was alive with color and energy. Demonstrations coursed along the thoroughfares. Chants reverberated among the buildings. Everyone seemed involved in that carnivalesque atmosphere. In the crisscrossing alleyways, hardy washerwomen debated the new world; in the redbrick factories, committees discussed the conflict between the vigilants and the moderates; on street corners, avant-garde theater acts performed bizarre agitprop. At the university, students held endless parties, breaking into orgies or fisticuffs before returning to their dwindling stocks of flower-liquors and their nasty Yensa fudge. Love affairs were begun; hearts were broken; new ways of living invented. Life itself seemed to have taken on a new intensity, and time itself expanded so that each moment seemed to last forever. And yet, everything was moving at such a pace!

In the grand Opera building's northern wing, the moderate leader Thom pressed a letter into Kata's hand, his eyes wild. Barrel-chested, his beard sprouting in all directions, the second-in-command of the moderate faction possessed an artist's sensibility. He was nowhere more at home than in the Quaedian Quarter's galleries and theaters. Kata had always liked his unrepressed romanticism, and he was popular with the citizens. His strengths were suited to the moment of liberation.

Now, in the Opera, Thom's passion seemed to have taken a dark turn. His eyes were those of a haunted man. "I was meant to meet Aceline here earlier but was held up. Take her this letter. Guard it though." He turned his head, eyed Kata with a piercing sideways glance. "I must attend to something, something . . ."

As she slipped the letter into her jacket pocket, Kata felt a cold rush over her skin. Thom often acted extravagantly, but there was something different about this request, a desperation she had never noticed before.

Kata had become a go-between for various moderates. She spent most of her days scurrying up along the alleyways, across the white-topped cliffs, from Opera to factory to university. Most important, she carried letters between Thom and the moderate leader, the bone-white, childlike Aceline. It was a lowly role that suited her.

Thom grasped her arm, pulled her back. "Be careful."

"What *is* it?" asked Kata.

Thom adjusted the large bag that hung from his shoulder. A shadow crossed his face as he looked at it. "Go."

Then Kata was on her way, through the corridors, past the stream of people, and out into the square, where Dexion waited for her. The minotaur was like an image from ancient times, standing against that background of the red sun setting over the ocean. For a moment the rays blinded her, and all she saw was a magnificent silhouette: a creature too large to be a man, its bull's head outlined against a ball of fire. Kata was mesmerized by his explosive energy, the scent of his spiced hide. The inky blackness of his eyes always captivated and frightened her, but occasionally his joyfulness would shine through and she would breathe again.

Small groups watched the immense creature carefully, turning away quickly if he glanced in their direction. An old man kneeled in supplication—many of the older citizens still worshipped the minotaurs. Even farther away, a group of young women watched Dexion in awe, yearning to approach him yet held back by fear. In the corners of the square, shadowy figures lurked, looking on from under dark hoods. Kata thought of the black market, of the demand for minotaur parts, of the sound of a saw cutting through horn and bone, of her own dark past.

"Aceline is at Marin's water palace," she said.

Dexion's eyes gleamed. Still young for a minotaur, he was forever ready for new adventures, which pleased Kata no end, for the minotaur's exuberance helped bring her out of her bleak moods. He was a good, if unreliable, companion.

Together they charged along the streets, cutting across the unused tram tracks and over the tiny bridges that spanned the canals running between Market Square and the Northern Headland, where Caeli-Amur's famous water palaces and steam baths were built. A stench drifted over from piles of refuse banked up against the walls.

The sound of a protest march resounded in the streets ahead. First they heard chanting echoing between the buildings, drums setting the march's rhythm. "Down with the Houses, down with the hoarders! Bread! Bread! Bread!" The protest turned a corner onto the long and narrow Via Trasta. For Kata, such marches were a joy, for she found herself dissolved into them, at one with the other demonstrators and their passions, calling out spontaneous slogans, the energy surging into her from the seething mass. There was something intimate about a march, and for that reason they were frightening, too.

Yet there was an increasingly strident tone to the recent demonstrations and open-air meetings. The blockade by the remnants of the Houses was taking its toll. House Technis had been crushed, but Marin had withdrawn its ships to the Dyrian coast, and the House Arbor villas to the south were refusing to ship goods—corn, wheat, grapes, anything—to the city. Varenis had joined the blockade, and Caeli-Amur's machinery was slowly breaking down without the parts that would normally come from that great northern city. Now some of the marches bordered on riots; there was always some desperate cause, some grievance to be heard. A dark presence lurked in the free air.

Now the crowd pressed up against the walls of Via Trasta and reached a boarded-up bakery, where it milled around, engaged in conversation with lots of gesturing, and then a couple of men came forward and began levering open the bakery's shutters. There was a crack of wood accompanied by splinters falling onto the ground.

A distressed-looking man burst from an alleyway between the buildings and rushed up to them. "Citizens! Please! There must be some kind of order!"

A woman in the crowd yelled back at him, "Hoarder!"

By the time the shutters had been broken open, Kata and Dexion were close to the doors. Several in the crowd glanced at the minotaur, alarmed, and for a moment Kata wondered whether she should intervene. But what would she do? This was no way to organize a city, but the citizens must be fed.

In any case, the tone of Thom's voice urged her on, so she pushed through the milling crowd, Dexion beside her.

A squad of black-uniformed vigilant guards rushed down the street. Kata glanced back as the guards reached the crowd and pushed their way through to the bakery.

The baker cried out, "Finally I—" but a second later one of the guards had the man's hands behind his back. He protested, "But I'm the owner!" The vigilant struck him anyway, and the baker slumped to his knees.

Kata pulled at Dexion. "Come on."

Had it been just weeks since the seditionist movement had overthrown the three Houses? Events moved at a breathtaking pace. The Insurgent Assembly (though they had risen to power, they still called themselves seditionists—it seemed old habits die hard) was nominally in charge. Already it was divided. On one side, the cold Northerner Ejan led the vigilants, determined to use force against any resistance. On the other, Aceline and her moderates argued for freedom for all to express their opinions and take their own actions.

Kata aligned herself with the moderates. Like so many, the city's transformation had reshaped her, too. After the overthrow of the Houses, Kata had begun to learn about friendship. It was the moderate leader, Aceline, who had opened her to this strange and frightening possibility. Kata approached it like a cat entering a new room, ready to flee at the slightest danger, but Aceline sat patiently, allowing Kata to come to her at her own pace. Together they spent long evenings discussing the philosophy of the seditionist movement. They both felt that the movement itself should embody the kind of values they hoped to bring into being—a world of justice and freedom.

Kata was a seditionist at heart, living in a city that finally belonged to them.

Great pillars adorned the façade of Marin's water palace of Taium. Its many domes rose above them like a collection of bubbles in the corner of a soapy bath. The entry hall was equally wondrous. Water coursed along channels to each side of the entryway. Glorious mosaics decorated the walls, depicting minotaurs standing on the rocky island of Aya and looking far across the ocean toward the Sirens singing back at them from Taritia.

Inside the water palace was a maze of corridors and pools, rocky open-air gardens and long halls filled with great spheres. Apparently, a complex of rooms in the center of the palace could be filled with superoxygenated water, allowing the bathers to swim through worlds of imagination and fancy, breathing water as they journeyed. The notion of total submersion filled Kata with horror.

As Kata passed from room to room, great clouds of steam drifted around her, at one moment obscuring everything, the next revealing half-naked figures laughing giddily at their newfound freedom. Once the sole province of the upper echelons of the Houses, Marin's water palace was now constantly filled with seditionists, members of the Collegia, thaumaturgists liberated from the yoke of the Houses, and workers who had never been allowed in such a rarefied building. The once-stratified world was mixed up, and since one group of social rules had been shattered, why not others?

A long-haired woman bumped into Kata, then drunkenly staggered toward the archway that led to the steam rooms, renowned as a place for easy sex. Just beyond it, a group of students lay semi-comatose, arms and legs draped over one another, half-empty bottles of flower-draughts loosely gripped in their hands or toppled over beside them. Kata was both attracted to and repelled by these libertines. She pictured joining in but crushed the idea the moment she had it.

Kata's eyes roved the place for Aceline's lithe figure and close-cropped black hair. Aceline had been coming to the water palace recently, which surprised Kata, for Aceline was a moderate in all things: philosophy, politics, personal predilection. Still, House Technis had captured Aceline just before the revolt and subjected her to the terror-spheres in their dungeons. Who knew what nightmares she needed to escape from? Despite their newfound friendship, Kata did not dare ask her about it yet. But if Aceline needed the louche attractions of the baths, Kata could not judge her for it.

The minotaur shifted his great bulk and looked longingly at the baths, half obscured by steaming air. Linked by thin channels, they formed a labyrinth of connected baths—some circular, others square or octagonal.

"Oh, go on," she said.

Dexion's eyes blinked rapidly in excitement. In seconds he had dropped his clothes onto the floor. He leaped, seeming to hover for a moment in the air above one of the pools, while the other bathers' eyes widened in fear. They screamed, grimaced, and tried to push themselves away through the water, but Dexion crashed into it and drenched them before they could escape.

Kata passed through an archway, heavy wooden doors and exquisite crimson circular patterns disappearing and reemerging in the roiling mist.

At the end of the corridor, a half-hidden figure lurked. Kata moved closer until she caught the young man's profile: a fine nose and lustrous shoulder-length black hair. Walking close to the wall, Kata stopped beside the young man and examined the frigidarium beyond, where citizens plunged into the icy baths, laughing and giving cries of pleasurable shock. Others staggered from the cold waters and ran through another archway, toward a great central complex containing the water-spheres.

"So, Rikard," Kata said. "Ejan has you spying on his opponents, does he?"

"*Spying* is such a cruel word, don't you think?" Rikard turned his brown eyes to Kata. He had just recently passed over the cusp of adulthood and had a newly grown, soft, thin mustache. His father had died in the tramworkers' strike against Technis, and Rikard had joined the seditionists not long after. Now there was a steely cast to his high cheekbones and thoughtful eyes.

A couple embraced in one of the nearby baths. They dropped beneath the waters, then burst up again, calling out in joy.

Kata said, "Have you seen Aceline?"

"Taking a message to her, are you?" Rikard asked nonchalantly.

Kata smiled grimly. "Always at work, I see."

This time Rikard shrugged and raised his eyebrows rapidly, a half-humorous gesture he liked to disarm people with. "Tell me the message, and I'll tell you where she is."

Kata checked Rikard with her shoulder. "Don't do that, Rikard. You're too kind for such bargaining." When Rikard didn't reply, Kata changed the topic. "All this space devoted to quick pleasure—Ejan must hate it."

"The new order is fragile. The Directors, officiates, and subofficiates of the Houses—they all wait up in their mansions in the Arantine and here on the Northern Headland, out in their country villas or on the Dyrian coast. All the while, their agents are among us, encouraging this dissoluteness, weakening us by the minute. Just when we need discipline, the seditionists indulge themselves. Flower-draughts, hot-wine, gorging on food—look at them. How different are they from those who came before?"

Kata looked on. "Don't they have the right to celebrate their freedom?"

Rikard pushed his hair back with his hands. "You call this freedom?"

Kata knew if she could establish some rapport with Rikard, he might help her. She tried another tack. "We look alike, you know. We could be brother and sister."

Rikard pressed his lips together, the closest he came to a smile, and ignored her attempt. "Not all of us are uncertain about what should happen. We're not all like you moderates."

"Certainty can be a dangerous thing."

"No! It's uncertainty that is dangerous. Audacity is what made us victorious. That's what I don't understand about you, Kata. You're a woman of action. Every part of you screams it. You grew up on the streets, fought your way up and out. Your soul and your allegiance to the moderates will always be in conflict."

"I liked it more when you used to stand silently as if you were mute." Kata smiled. "Can't we go back to those days?"

Rikard pressed his lips together again. This time, the edges of a smile *did* appear. Dark and brooding, romantic—already he was a favorite among the young women of the city. Rikard seemed unaware of this—or, perhaps, like the cold-blooded leader Ejan, he had cut off that personal part of himself. For Ejan—and perhaps for Rikard—the seditionist movement was the four points of the compass.

"Come on, Rikard. This is serious. I need to find Aceline."

"She's in one of the private rooms along this corridor. I didn't see who she met, though. Come, I'll show you." They retraced Kata's steps along the corridor and stopped before a closed arched door. So it seemed Rikard *had* been spying on Aceline, after all. Kata kept the accusation to herself.

"They're probably . . ." Kata let the sentence drop away.

Rikard shrugged and knocked on the door. No response came. He knocked again. "Aceline?"

When there was again no response, he finished her sentence. "Enjoying themselves too much."

Kata placed her ear against the wooden door and heard what sounded like a single knock, followed by a groaning sound. Images sprang to Kata's mind of Aceline writhing with whomever she had met that day, her pretty face distended into a leer, groans escaping from her lips. But the sound also brought thoughts of violence to her mind.

Kata turned the handle, but the door held fast. "Aceline—it's Kata!" She knocked insistently. Anxiety gripped her. She turned to Rikard, who shook his head. They threw their weight against the door, but it didn't budge.

Kata said, "Wait. I'll get Dexion."

Dexion had dried himself and was half dressed when she found him. He rapidly threw on his remaining clothes and followed her.

Kata pressed her ear against the door again. There was a slight thudding clunk—perhaps someone banging against a table—then all was quiet.

She stood back and nodded at the minotaur. He placed his immense hands against the doorway, which groaned briefly. There was a crack; shards of wood burst into the air; and the door broke open.

One quick look into the room and Dexion stepped back, his nostrils flaring.

A few feet in front of the door, the body of a short heavy man was sprawled facedown, the smell of burning flesh drifting from it. A second man lay on his back in the middle of the room, the skin of his face seemingly melted, white froth around where his mouth had once been. His arms lay above his head as if he were stretching. Both wore black suits, the traditional uniforms of the thaumaturgists.

In the corner, Kata caught a glimpse of Aceline's black hair, her skin whiter than ever.

Kata raised her fingers to her lips. "Oh no," she said. "Oh no."

Grief gripped her heart like a ghostly hand, for Aceline's eyes were rolled back in her head. Death had taken her into the land of light.

Kata had cried only once in the last fifteen years. She did not cry now, though grief seemed to press her from her insides, threatening to erupt at any moment.

Rikard turned and whistled. A moment later a grubby little urchin was at his side. "Ejan. Immediately." The guttersnipe took a brief look into the room, his mouth as wide as his eyes. Rikard grabbed him by his torn jacket. "Keep that trap shut."

The urchin nodded—mouth still agape—and sped off through the mist. A couple, arms thrown around each other, staggered toward them along the steamy corridor.

"Come on." Rikard stepped lightly into the room. "Close the door."

Dexion forced the damaged door back into its frame, jamming it when it wouldn't fit.

Kata surveyed the scene. The door's latch lay shattered on the ground. On the left side of the room, a large bath was cut into the stone floor. On the right side, three massage tables were lined up against the wall. The three bodies lay in between: the two men closest to them, and Aceline up against the far wall, near the edge of the bath.

Kata stepped gently across the room to Aceline's body. She

avoided looking at the dead woman's empty staring eyes. She needed to focus, to reconstruct events.

"Look." Rikard knelt beside the shorter man. He pointed to the ground near him. "There's some kind of burned black powder on the floor."

"Here too." Dexion pointed to a place nearer the center of the room, close to the thinner thaumaturgist. "His face has been completely melted." Dexion's nostrils flared again with distaste.

Kata knelt beside her former friend and noticed several tiny black specks on the skin between her nostrils and mouth. A thin deep red mark encircled Aceline's neck, bleeding slightly in places. "Aceline was strangled." There were no cuts on her hands, though. It was almost as if she'd given up without a struggle.

Kata felt a familiar pressure building within her. She took a flask from her bag and swallowed some of the medicine that kept her seizures at bay. Without the precautionary medication, the fits came at moments of stress and left her incapacitated for hours. Now her mouth was filled with the pungent taste of dirt and ul-tree roots. She gagged, steadied herself, and returned the flask to her bag.

Delicately, using the edge of her knife, she lifted as many of the black specks from under Aceline's nose as she could. She looked around hopelessly for a vial, then placed the knife carefully onto the nearest massage table. Then Kata began to scrape some of the blackened powder from the floor with her second knife, until she had recovered a thick curl.

Rikard pushed his hair back with his hand. "The thaumaturgists must have killed each other."

"I suppose they knew the same thaumaturgical formulae," said Dexion. "A burning conjuration. Like two gladiators who strike at the same time, each mortally wounded the other with the same spell."

Kata agreed. "They probably dispatched Aceline first. One held her down; the other did the strangling. But afterward they fought. It must have been this one I heard falling when I pressed my ear to the door." Kata pointed to the heavy thaumaturgist near the entrance. "Maybe he was making his last effort to escape."

Kata took in the rest of the room. A glorious mosaic depicting one of the Eyries of the Augurers decorated the far wall. The rocky pinnacle rose into the sky, breathtakingly thin against an azure sky. Through a window, an Augurer could be seen seated in the center of a room, her wild hair waving in the air. With one black and piercing eye she stared toward the viewer as if inviting them in, as the line of Augurers had invited citizens of Caeli-Amur and Varenis since the time of the ancients. Around the pinnacle, the griffins circled in the sky, their feathered wings beating against invisible drafts, their eagle heads rearing up proudly.

The mosaic covered the arch of the roof above, the tiles there becoming first the light blue of the sky, then the dark blue of night. On the wall behind them, the mosaic depicted Caeli-Amur, a thousand little glittering lights in the night. At its center stood the door with its ruined latch.

Leaving Dexion and Rikard to guard the room, Kata slipped out and searched for an attendant. There seemed to be none working—perhaps they were gone for good—so it took her a few minutes to find a storeroom, which had already been ransacked, presumably after the uprising. She snatched two vials, returned to the room, carefully dropped the tiny specks into one vial, and screwed its lid back on. Kata then scraped the blackened powder from the second knife into the second vial.

There was a rattle at the door, and Dexion opened it. Ejan strode into the room and surveyed the scene with his usual Olympian cast. Tall, glacial-eyed, and with white-blond hair in a city predominated by olive-skinned and dark-haired people, it was ironic that he had become the preeminent seditionist leader. He stood out, and he used this fact to his advantage. Kata had never liked the man's calculating, machinelike mind. She felt that if she ever touched him, she might find his skin cold like ice. The vigilant leader built those around him in the same mold: a collection of lieutenants ready to take any action. Even those who had begun with a touch of softness, like Rikard, soon took on the harness of a hammer.

Ejan's bodyguard, Oskar, stood behind him, straight like a flagpole. Scars from the House wars ran across his arms, and a long scar ran in a jagged line from forehead to chin on the left side of his face. Kata knew him immediately as a pragmatist, one of the philosopher-assassin schools that had remained aloof from events, mercenaries for hire. Oskar possessed the same cold distance as his employer.

At the rear of the group, the wide-eyed waif edged around the door and looked at the bodies with amazement. For a moment Kata felt as if she were in a play, some surrealist tragedy: enter the leader, enter the assassin, enter the urchin. Each would play his role.

Ejan turned to Oskar. "This must remain secret. The city is already teetering precariously; if the citizens discover Aceline has died, who knows what vengeance they might take? We'll take the bodies back to the Opera and bring the embalmers in."

"Wait," said Kata. "There may be answers here we haven't yet discovered. They'll be lost if we move too quickly."

No one moved. In the silence, Oskar sized up Dexion. Sensing his gaze, Dexion let out a soft and deep grumble, like the growl of a lion. Oskar's eyelids twitched once before his impassive and dark stare returned.

Kata stepped closer to Ejan. "You can't stage-manage everything. Aceline deserves recognition. Her death is not only a personal matter, it is a matter for the entire movement. For the city. If we suppress it, how can anyone judge the truth of things? Freedom requires knowledge."

"The dead don't have rights," said Ejan. "You know that people are already carrying out private vendettas. Our guards can barely keep the peace. Once Aceline's murder becomes known, mobs will wreak vengeance on the city. Is that what you want?"

There was truth to his words. In these overheated days, who knew what the consequences might be? But the seditionists had to rule in a new way. Kata shook her head. "We can't continue the secrecies and lies of the Houses."

"And who are you to make this decision, Kata? Who do you represent?"

Kata froze. She had no authority over Ejan, an acknowledged leader of seditionism. Kata remembered the great demonstration on Aya's Day, which had led to the overthrow of the Houses. She recalled the way he and his troops had placed themselves at the head of the march, a symbolic position gained as much by audacity and assertiveness as by anything else.

But Kata was only a foot soldier with a lifetime of crimes to make up for. She hated to think about the biggest betrayal of them all, informing Technis of the location of the seditionists' hideout just before the overthrow of the old system. How many had been captured or died because of her? Aceline was one of them, Maximilian another. She couldn't bear to think of it. A foot soldier was all she *wanted* to be.

Ejan turned to Rikard. "What do you think?"

Rikard took a breath. "I suspect these thaumaturgists are House agents. Blocking the grain supply and moving their ships up to the Dyrian coast surely isn't enough for them, so they've begun a campaign of low-intensity warfare. Trying to decapitate the seditionist movement to leave it weak and confused."

"Find out who these thaumaturgists are and who they represent," said Ejan. "I want to know what occurred here."

Words tumbled from Kata's mouth. "I'll work with Rikard."

Ejan shook his head. "You'd only be wasting your time."

"I'll pursue it on my own, then. Aceline was . . ." Grief swept over Kata again. She looked at the tile floor, which blurred from the tears swimming in her eyes. She blinked.

"Was?" Even Ejan's inquiring look was unnerving.

"She was my friend, and you have no control over me. I'm sick of people telling me what to do, Ejan. I'll do it whether you like it or not."

Ejan tilted his head to one side and eyed her calculatingly. "All right, then. You'll work together, and report to me."

"I'll report to Thom. He is the leader of the moderates now," said Kata.

Ejan shrugged and turned from her as more seditionists arrived, wrapping the bodies in blankets and treading over the floor with great dirty boots.

Rikard spoke softly to her, as if he might disturb the dead. "Shall we find out what Thom knows about this fatal meeting?"

# TWO
⟨⟨⟨⟩⟩⟩

Twilight fell, and the cool autumn winds blew in from the ocean, swept through the narrow streets, over the white cliffs on which so many beautiful buildings were perched, and up the mountain that overlooked the city. A melancholy air settled over everything as if the city itself were grieving for Aceline's death.

As they approached the Opera, Kata tried to shake off her sadness. Dexion had returned home, where he'd agreed to meet the little urchin, Henri. Kata was sorry that the minotaur was not there to help her process Aceline's death, but she knew he would only ever be a fellow traveler. He would accompany her if he were interested, but otherwise, he'd find his own entertainment.

She still held Thom's letter in her pocket. She could almost feel it, heavy and pulling at her, but she would not open it in front of Rikard, for he would report directly back to Ejan.

The great entry hall of the Opera was a bustle of activity, just as she had left it hours before. Behind a large reception area stood seditionist intendants, yelling over the groups of people pressed up against the long table, begging for help.

"Food parcels in the morning."

"Yes, yes, we're reopening the trade routes shortly."

"Blame Arbor—don't blame me."

People scurried in all directions in the northern wing. Many of the seditionists now lived in this labyrinth of rooms and halls, and Kata and Rikard passed dorm rooms with dozens of makeshift beds, some only piles of rags covered with a sheet. In other rooms, circles of seditionists sat in meetings. Kata caught snippets of discussion.

"They say the New-Men are building a train line east, across the Etolian range."

"What have the New-Men to do with all this?"

"Maybe they'll help us deal with Varenis."

"No one can deal with Varenis. Varenis does all the dealing."

In the editorial offices, the young militant Olivier sat at a large desk, poring over proofs of the new issue of the moderates' broadsheet, the *Dawn*. Paper lay strewn around him, all over the table and on the floor, much of it cut up or scrawled on.

One of the new generations of seditionists, Olivier had been a leader of a university cell before the overthrow of the Houses. Possessing a subtle mind, he had quickly become chief editor of the broadsheet and every day turned out article after article with metronomic efficiency. Kata liked the complexity of his thought but knew he wasn't a man of action. Olivier was at home with the word, not the deed.

Rikard crossed his arms in a gesture of passive hostility. As lieutenants within their factions, the young men held identical positions. Yet they came from different backgrounds. The son of a tramworker, Rikard had a suspicion of the soft and educated. To Olivier, Rikard no doubt seemed like most of the vigilants: inflexible and lacking theory, unable to discern the subtle interplay of ideas and people and events.

Oliver looked up from the sheet and dropped his pen. His bloodshot eyes were like dying coals in a fire. Like most seditionists, he stayed up late and rose early. They all tried to hold on to events the way a rider holds on to an unbroken horse.

Rikard clasped Kata's arm before she could speak. "No details. Remember what will happen if people find out."

Kata shook the vigilant off. She tried to summon the words, but nothing seemed adequate. Finally she settled on, "Aceline has died. In Marin's great water palace, together with two thaumaturgists."

Olivier's face drained of its color; his eyes seemed redder than before. He was an innocent when it came to death.

Rikard stepped close to Olivier. "No one must know."

Olivier stepped around Rikard and spoke to Kata. "How did she die?"

Kata collapsed into a chair, felt despair once again. "Strangled."

Olivier raised his arm, pressed his face into the crook of his elbow, rubbed his eyes against his forearm.

"Where's Thom?" said Kata eventually.

"Gone," said Olivier. "I asked him if he was going to the baths, but he shook his head. He had a strange stare—suspicious, you know. I stopped him, but he shook me off. At first I thought he was simply his usual emotional self."

"What made you think otherwise?" asked Kata.

"That look in his eye, as if I might be an enemy."

"Where does he sleep?" asked Rikard.

Olivier looked to Kata. "He has a hidden crib somewhere in the Artists' Quarter, I think. He used to joke that it was his hideaway, where no one could find him. That's where he designed most of his lithographs. So it's a workshop, I suppose."

"Find out where it is, Olivier. Ask everyone. Now that Aceline is gone, he's the leader of the moderates. Without him—" Kata stopped, aware of Rikard beside her. "We need to find him." This time Kata took Olivier by the arm. "Aceline's death must be kept secret, at least until we've found Thom. Things are bad enough in the city."

Olivier glanced briefly at Rikard, then back at Kata. "You know who stands to benefit most from this: the vigilants."

Kata spoke with a certainty she didn't quite feel. "It's the Houses who stand to benefit the most. We've overthrown them. But they still wage war on us, even without their palaces and their networks of organization and power. Arbor and Marin are starving us. Where are the grain carts? The fishing boats?"

The truth was, the entire seditionist movement was teetering on the precipice. The longer the crisis continued, the greater the calls to repress House activities. Soon Ejan would have a majority of the Insurgent Assembly, and would let loose violence against its enemies. The tragedy was that Ejan was right. Soon they *would* have to use force. There was no other choice. It was a question of timing, of trying every other possibility first. But the thought of it sent shocks through Kata's body. For, in Ejan's mind, anyone who disagreed with him in some way was an enemy.

"Is this to do with the book?" asked Olivier.

"What book?" Kata frowned.

"The one Thom has been carrying with him. Didn't you see it?"

A creeping feeling ran over Kata. She remembered the way he had looked at his large bag when he had passed her the letter. "His sketchbook?"

"No. It was an old book. There was something sickly about its cover. I only caught a glimpse, but I knew immediately there was something perturbing about it. It had that sheen."

"That sheen?"

"The sheen of thaumaturgy."

Deep in the labyrinth of the south wing, vigilants rushed around, a mirror image of the moderates in the north wing. The three corpses lay on tables in a side room, where baths had been filled with ice to help preserve them. Two elderly men stood over the bodies, cocking their heads as they examined them. On a cart nearby lay all the tools of embalming and preserving: cruel-looking knives and scalpels, bowls and long thin tubes.

One of the anatomists turned to Rikard: "We'll have to get the blood out of them quickly, but thaumaturgists—they usually have all kinds of inner decay. You think that the worst of it is the outside." He gestured to the warped and knobby bodies, so common among those who used the Art. "But the real changes are running wild in the organs."

Kata forced herself to lean in and examine the two dead thaumaturgists. She gagged at the sight of their blistered and burned faces, the skin melted unnaturally.

She steeled herself and turned back to Aceline, averting her eyes from her former friend's face. The welt around the tiny woman's neck was red and raw. She looked closer: a tiny blue thread was lodged in the skin—a piece of the material that had been used to strangle the woman. Kata turned to the nearby cart, took a pair of tweezers, and gently removed the thread, which she placed in a vial she took from the embalmer's tray. The thread might have come from a strangling scarf, used most commonly by philosopher-assassins connected with the secretive Arcadi sect. These scarves were weighted, allowing the assassin to whip them around the neck of the victim from behind. And yet, they had found no such scarf at the baths.

The doors burst open behind Kata and Rikard. A large bald man strode into the room, the dramatic entrance and the force of his personality drawing everyone's attention. The irises of his eyes were an icy white, a trait common in the Teeming Cities far to the south. Kata had seen the thaumaturgist Alfadi before: he was the former prefect of the Technis thaumaturgists but had refused to attack the seditionist forces at the decisive moment of the uprising. Instead he had bravely led the thaumaturgists through Technis Complex's great double doors and into the surrounding square. There he had embraced Ejan as the seditionists looked on. That was the moment everything had changed.

Like most of the thaumaturgists, Alfadi now lived in the Marin Complex. Unlike most, his loyalties were clear: he frequently came to the Opera building to speak at the Insurgent Assembly. Kata was glad to have him on the seditionists' side.

Kata had never seen him up close, though, and now his presence—fueled by the uncanny power that resided within him—dominated the room. He was one of the few thaumaturgists who did not have any outward signs of the Art: none of the warping or sickly gleam that affected those who invoked its powers. Whatever changes it had made to him were chillingly hidden inside.

Alfadi stood eerily still, his eyes settling on the bodies of the thaumaturgists. He looked slowly at the old men, then across to Kata and Rikard, who stood fixed by his piercing gaze. There was a measured quality to the man, but as he looked back at the melted faces of the thaumaturgists, a hundred little muscles seemed to give way. He reached out, his hand hovering over their bodies. "We'll bring them back to the Marin Palace. Someone will recognize them."

In the background, one of the anatomists held a tube in one hand and whispered to the other anatomist, "We'll start the drainage on the fat one. More blood."

Alfadi drew a deep breath. "You must be Rikard and Kata. Ejan told me he'd put his best people on this, that I should help in any way I can. What do you know?"

"We're looking for the new moderate leader, Thom," said Rikard. "He might have more information."

Alfadi's eyes fell on Kata. "Aceline was a friend of yours, wasn't she? You poor thing." The man smiled gently and reached out to Kata. His hand was soft, its touch gentle. There was a sudden darkness around his eyes, then he stepped back. "I'll send a message once we've an idea of their identities."

As the former prefect left the room, Kata glimpsed two black-suited thaumaturgists waiting in the corridor. The sight of them reminded her of the days when thaumaturgists had struck fear into the citizens. *Perhaps they still should,* she thought.

"This one has a tattoo," said the younger anatomist, who had stripped the larger thaumaturgist and was examining his warped body. Above the man's heart was crude art depicting two hands clasped together.

"This one too," the second anatomist said.

"Does anyone know if it has a meaning?" said Rikard.

No one seemed to know, so the anatomists continued with their work. Kata watched with horror as one of them started to massage the body.

The embalmer grinned. "Breaking up any circulatory clots he might have."

Kata and Rikard sat at a table at the corner of a tiny plaza. The eatery that served them was full of talking customers, both inside and at other tables on the square outside, though the spiced breads were exorbitantly priced.

The long hot summer had given way to a cool autumn, and a gentle night breeze caressed Kata's face in coy gusts. Once winter settled in, it would be too cold to eat outdoors, but even at this late hour, citizens were on the streets. Some made their way to a staircase that climbed to a first-story bar that overlooked the plaza. Excited chatter drifted through the cool air and down the alleyways. Others passed in little groups, still debating.

Kata examined Rikard. She had to admit, the vigilants were dedicated, even if she didn't like their certainty, Rikard's cold calculations, the abstraction of their ideas. In the vigilants' minds, if people had to die, then so be it. There was a purity to Rikard, and a consistency, but was the world itself consistent and pure?

"Olivier was right," she said. "Ejan would gain much from Aceline's death."

Rikard took a bite of bread. "Olivier is a fool. Ejan thinks only of the seditionist movement, only of the new world we're building. If the Houses and their agents joined us instead of resisting, think of the things we could achieve."

How simple it would be, if Kata could reach out and shake some sense into Rikard. She sighed. The world was not simple, and truth not easy to achieve. That was the point of being a moderate: to recognize that complexity, to realize you might need the input of others to see the world as it actually is.

She engaged after all. "But when does that resistance simply become an excuse for carrying out repressive measures? At what point do you turn necessities into virtues? Your black-suited guards remind me too much of the Houses."

Rikard's lips twitched. "Surely, you overlook the stylistic improvements. I mean . . . black leather."

Kata closed her eyes. "How could I miss that?"

Rikard offered Kata a piece of the spiced bread. "Why would two thaumaturgists meet a seditionist leader in secret? Who were they hiding from, if the Insurgent Assembly is the highest power in the city?"

Kata took a bite of the bread, struggled to get it down, placed the rest back onto the plate. Recent events had killed her appetite. She put her hand into her pocket, ran her fingers over the letter that lay within, then put her hand back in her lap.

Rikard crossed his arms to keep himself warm. "Both thaumaturgists have the same tattoo on their chests."

How much should Kata share with the vigilant? Should she tell him of the letter? "Yes, but what does it mean? We'll take the contents of the vials to a philosopher-assassin I know. She may be able to identify them for us. In the meantime, I'm going home. It's late."

Kata returned to her apartment to find Dexion on the floor with the street urchin Henri. The two threw their dice at the same moment. When they rolled to a stop, Henri barely flicked his eyes at them before wordlessly putting out his hand.

Dexion groaned and pulled out several coins from a pocket. "That's it—this is the last roll. After that, you'll have bankrupted me! You'll have to pay for everything now."

Kata sat at the table and pulled the letter from her pocket. She watched Henri's devilish little eyes, alight with joy.

"No! No, no, no, no, no!" Dexion groaned again. "That's it—this is the last time, I tell you. The last time!"

After Kata filled them in on her day, Henri pocketed the remaining coins and said, "I might be able to find Thom." The urchins had complex networks throughout the city. It was true: they might know where a man as famous as Thom hid himself away.

"I won't have you involved in this affair," said Kata. "Someone has died. It's not safe, and you're not an adult."

"It's just a few questions." Dexion tossed his bull head, stretched his neck. The scent of the spices rubbed into his hide—ginger and cloves—drifted over to her.

There it was: her anger again, at herself, at the world. "It's never only questions."

Henri shrugged and turned to Dexion. "I'll give you one chance to win these back. What have you got?"

Dexion closed his huge black eyes slowly. "Let me think . . ."

Kata watched them for a moment. She then looked down at the envelope in her hand and slowly unfolded the letter within.

*Armand,*

*I know you believe the prism will be crucial for your task in Varenis, but surely it would be of more use here? Both of us agree on this. Remember that those who control the thaumaturgists control Caeli-Amur. Stay here, and it will make their task far easier. Without it, it will take too much time to reinforce our position, though our best plan should be realized by the Twilight*

*Observance. Should you carry the prism north, given the support for the seditionists, we will be forced to be even more secretive and patient. If necessary, we will wait for your return, but I beg you to reconsider. I await your reply.*

*D*

Later that night, as Kata lay in her bed on the top floor of her apartment, she listened to the boy and the minotaur arguing, and thought about the letter. She had known an Armand who had been an assistant to Boris Autec, the Director of House Technis. She remembered his calmness. He had always seemed honorable to her. But what had happened to him? Had he been killed in the assault on the Technis Complex? Kata closed her eyes. After the uprising, there had been chaos. Seditionists, citizens, all stomping through the Palace, seeing the great halls, the library, the section whose rooms moved around one another like some complex puzzle—a mobile maze built for the protection of the powerful. Vigilants and moderates had both rifled through the files. Kata had been among them, desperately shuffling through papers, looking for her own records, files that would condemn her as having been a House spy. She hadn't found them, and even now the terror of their being discovered weighed on her. Whoever possessed them could destroy her in a moment.

Kata pushed away the thought. She reasoned that Thom had found the letter in Technis Palace, and that it was from a third party—a certain D—who worked with Armand. Perhaps D had commanded the thaumaturgists to kill Aceline. What powers, she wondered, did this prism possess? And what, she wondered, were Armand's plans for it?

As she considered the possibilities, she felt Henri slip into the bed, as he was wont to do occasionally. He turned his back to her, and she threw her arm over the little boy. He coughed and shuddered a little. *That damn cough,* she worried. He seemed to have it constantly. She'd have to have it seen to.

In no time, Henri was asleep. Sometimes he kicked out at whatever enemies he fought in his dreams. At these times she clasped him closer, and he relaxed. She knew those dreams only too well, for they visited her, too. They always had, ever since she had been on the streets as a child, just like Henri. As always, his presence calmed her, and soon enough she, too, drifted into sleep.

# THREE

When he looked back later, Armand couldn't be sure exactly when he knew someone was following him. The knowledge had started rattling around in his unconscious well before he arrived at the roadhouse at the edge of the small town of Scaptia a week after fleeing Caeli-Amur.

Exhausted from the ride, Armand didn't so much sit as collapse into a rough wooden seat in the roadhouse, his head tilting back, as if any effort were too much. For some time he looked blankly across the dingy hall. In one corner, a group of merchants leaned toward one another, discussing news of the revolution. Varenis had begun a blockade, and their group would be the last to make it to Caeli-Amur, they said. Other traders had been halted at the Palian Wall. Varenis's grip on Caeli-Amur was tightening.

"Be happy about it," roared a merchant, whose beard was huge and wild like a mountain man's. "Think of the profits we'll make." He slapped his hands on the table to emphasize his point, and his beard shook with the reverberations.

"Until Caeli-Amur runs out of money, that is."

Another struck the table. "What will become of me after that?"

Armand's attention drifted. He thought about the following day, when he would take the road near the Keos Pass. Wastelanders had been streaming away from their homes, escaping the wasteland site where the forces of Aya and Alerion had clashed almost a thousand years ago. There the two gods had twisted time and space. Now there were rumors the site was growing inexplicably, engulfing everything around it. Armand shuddered at the thought of that strange zone, where the air warped under peculiar physics and creatures emerged, horribly changed.

Even now a small group of wastelanders sat in a corner. One leaned back against the wall, seemingly weary. Hundreds of small tentacles wriggled energetically on his forehead. Beside him, a woman stared balefully through eyes that had dropped low around her nose. Her face had grown goatlike and terrible. They were headed to Caeli-Amur, it seemed.

Only then was Armand suddenly aware of the shadowy figure watching him from the corner of the room. The man's head was turned toward him, but his hood dipped deep over his eyes, obscuring his features. Armand felt a chill rush down his spine. Armand had been riding north alone, occasionally passing carts headed south. One cart had been carrying wool for the weavers in Caeli-Amur, and a handsome young man sat on the bales, carving a piece of wood. After the cart had passed, Armand had glanced back, his eyes following the young man. Yes, with his red lips and large brown eyes, the young man was dashing indeed. *In another life, at another time,* thought Armand. As he turned to watch the cart pass, Armand had barely registered the hooded figure behind him at the edge of his vision.

Now, sitting in that lonely roadhouse surrounded by strangers, the reality of the situation struck him. The seditionists had sent a philosopher-assassin after him. Of course they had, for he had been seen rushing through Technis Palace by several officiates. Everything had been mad in those moments after the suicide of Technis Director Autec, with intendants crying in the corridors of Technis Palace, subofficiates trying to hide in cupboards or beneath desks, officiates spitting recriminations at one another. Officiate Ijem had used the sphere to connect with Varenis, but the Director had promised only damnation for the officials who had failed to contain the seditionists. Officiate Ijem had run from the room, laughing absurdly—he was always laughing—about how the seditionists would slaughter them.

Armand had used the chaos as a cover to steal the Prism of Alerion, the lists of seditionists compiled by House Technis before its overthrow, and the maps of the tunnels beneath Caeli-Amur. When the letter from his supporters arrived, begging him to leave the prism in the city, he slipped it into a pocket and ignored it.

Then he heard the seditionists were in the building. Dashing to the stables, Armand took the most valuable horse, a snow-white beast he had called Ice. Using the maps, he slipped through the underground passages, beneath the city, and to the road north. It was only then that he realized the letter of support had somehow fallen from his pocket. He cursed and railed, but there was nothing he could do.

Ijem or one of the other officiates had clearly talked, and now a killer tracked Armand from the opposite side of the common room. The assassin would catch him alone on the road, tomorrow or the day after, and slip a razor-sharp stiletto between his ribs.

Armand touched his bag, still hanging over his shoulder. Beneath its worn leather, he could feel the bulging of the prism, said to contain the spirit of the god Alerion himself. Armand shivered at the thought. The prism was the only item able to halt the deleterious effects of thaumaturgy. While all other thaumaturgists were warped and broken by their use of the Art, whoever controlled the prism could avoid that fate. He would have to guard it jealously. With the prism in his possession, Varenis would back him as the liberator of Caeli-Amur.

Armand slipped away from his table and climbed the stairs up to his room. He slid the bolt on his door into its hole and examined it for a moment. *Would it hold firm?* he wondered.

He spent the night sitting against the wall, expecting the assassin to silently unlock the door and slip the bolt aside with some delicate skill. He sat there running his hand compulsively over his ring, which had once belonged to his grandfather. Occasionally he looked down at the ideogram that hovered oddly in the air above its labyrinthine face. He'd worn it since his father had died, but he'd never known its use or function.

Despite his fears, the night passed quietly. Well before sunrise, Armand slipped from the roadhouse and rode rapidly to the northern gate of Scaptia. Though he hated to do it to the poor animal, he drove Ice more quickly than before.

What had these poor creatures done to be caught up in the sordid world of people and politics? These fine animals were more simple and noble than humans; they did as their nature demanded;

they were incapable of the cruelty, mendacity, or vindictiveness of the kind of mob rule that had helped seditionism take hold in Caeli-Amur. It was clear to Armand that seditionist freedom meant tyranny: tyranny of the mob, tyranny of the lowest forms of culture. The more equitable things became, the more the crudest sensibilities ruled. What did they seek out as entertainment? The sordid spectacles of the Arena, cheap ale and dirty drugs, immoral sexual escapades. All things beautiful and delicate would be drowned by these base tastes, this recrudescence of sewerage.

The horse continued, uncomplaining, and by midmorning the rugged hills to the west gave way to the Keos Pass. He thought of taking the road that branched left through the pass, and approaching Varenis the long way. The assassin would not expect such a turn, but Armand knew it would be a foolish plan.

As he rode into the afternoon, the site came more and more into focus. Weird light refracted off the horizon. Its undertones were gray, but luminous greens and violets flickered on the surface. Closer to him, shimmering pools hovered above the landscape like ethereal lakes. Nearer still, he glimpsed bubbling puddles of dark violet and viridian liquids. At the edge of the site, or perhaps within it, he could see the ruins of a town shimmering and wavering, the windows of haunted buildings black and empty. Some of the buildings had crumbled; others stood resisting whatever bizarre forces were at work on them.

Armand came to another roadhouse near the wasteland site. He considered riding on, but thought of his brave horse, Ice, and decided against it. That night the hooded man from the night before slipped into the common room and sat in the corner. Armand once again fled to his room, anxiety slipping around in his stomach like a cold snake. So the days passed: Armand setting off early; the figure following him but never able to catch him on the road, for Ice was too fast and strong. Armand retreated to his room as soon as he saw the figure, whose face was always hidden in shadow, until Armand felt there might be no face there at all, just a chasm of darkness. Once Armand caught sight of a red beard and a straight nose. He became even more terrified, for now the shadow took on a real and deadly form.

With the Keos Pass behind him, the road wound between two chains of ever taller hills. Some three days from Varenis, he stopped Ice for a moment after the road curled gently around a slope. Before him stood the immense Palian wall. Its half-ruined grandeur rooted him to the spot, and he felt the wonder and glory of the ancients. The wall rose up forty or fifty stories, sections missing from its upper reaches that had been blown apart during the war of the gods. High behind the wall, little clouds rushed across the blue sky, and Armand got vertigo from the contrast of the towering wall and the stratosphere behind.

Vast cracks ran from the wall's crumbled edges toward its base. It looked like a giant cracked plate, but he brushed the absurd idea aside. Built into cliffs on each side of the valley, two ancient deserted towers rose at least twenty stories higher than the wall.

Armand rode through the gigantic gate, past a checkpoint guarded by Varenis's troops. Cyclops auxiliaries to the troops camped nearby sat around a fire. One stared at him with its single beady eye, and Armand averted his gaze.

A few minutes later Armand pulled his weary horse to a standstill. He dismounted and gazed over the vast plain of Al-Varen, all the way across to Varenis.

The first sight of Varenis—sometimes simply called "the City"—is said to represent one of the momentous events of a person's life. In front of Armand lay the vast plain, littered with farms and villas, waterways and crisscrossing canals. On the western side of the Etolian Mountains, the rain fell heavily, and the landscape was lush. Shrouded in smoke and fog, Varenis rose like some mystic's vision shimmering in the light at the center of the plain. Its suburbs rolled out around it like lava from a volcano, steaming and smoking. Farther in, Armand could glimpse buildings fifteen, twenty, thirty stories tall, walkways and train lines cutting in between them like threads of a spider's web. And finally, covered by smoke and soot, barely visible at the City's epicenter, stood the Twelve Towers of Varenis, impossibly tall. There was one tower for each of the legendary Sortileges, the thaumaturgist rulers who hovered above the cityscape like hawks over their prey.

The sight of Varenis filled Armand with hope. Somewhere in that massive metropolis lived Karl Valentin, who had once been Armand's grandfather's protégé. When Armand's grandfather had been exiled from House Arbor, Valentin had chosen not to remain in his home city of Caeli-Amur. Instead he moved to Varenis, where he had made his name. Armand's father had told him, *If ever you should visit the City, you must see Karl Valentin at the Department of Benevolence. He will look after you.* Armand hoped Valentin would be his passage into the Directorate that ruled over Varenis.

Armand glanced back to where the assassin was passing through the checkpoint beneath the wall.

Armand remounted Ice and whispered, "Let's go," into the horse's ear.

It took Armand a day to cross the plain, the assassin ever behind him. Finally the outskirts of the city drew near: slums punctuated by wealthier sections composed of large town houses. Looking back, Armand saw that his pursuer had closed on him. The decisive moment was at hand. Armand kicked Ice into a gallop. Over his shoulder, he saw the assassin race after him. Fear shot through Armand: his aching arms shook, his legs trembled. Ice dashed past buildings, sped around carts and pedestrians.

"Hey! Look out!" cried a pedestrian.

Ice galloped farther and longer than Armand could have hoped for, until they were deep inside the city. When he looked back, the pursuer had been left far behind. Finally Ice slowed to a walk and Armand breathed out. After the long harrowing journey, he was safe from the killer.

Before long, the streets were filled with steam-trams and rickshaws ducking in front of one another, fighting over space. Every now and then, a train on one of the tracks curving through the sky would burst out of a tunnel. Moments later the train would plunge into another tunnel like a serpent going into its hole. Ice became jittery but held his nerve. The road rose up on tall columns, passed into a building, and became some kind of arcade, storefronts on both sides offering spiced soups, designer clothes, alcoholic berry-drinks, and takeaway flower-liquors. It emerged from the other side as a walkway once more, hundreds of feet above the city.

Rickety-looking elevators climbed up the sides of the buildings or descended into holes below the ground, for the buildings had lower levels extending deep beneath the surface of the earth: Varenis's famous Undercity. Everywhere, chimneys spewed out smoke and soot, and the very ground beneath Armand's feet seemed to vibrate from the churning of faraway engines. The entire city seemed to Armand like some gigantic creature, puffing and heaving and shuddering and rumbling, its populace like minuscule blood cells passing along its vast circulatory system. His head swooned with vertigo from the size of it all; his stomach lurched with a fear that this creature might devour him.

Onward he rode, closer and closer to the Twelve Towers, moving through the crowds who hurried this way and that. Whole flocks of them passed like birds; no one had any interest in him at all. The crowds frightened him as much as the city itself, not only their cold indifference—the way their eyes slipped over him as if he were nothing—but the sheer variety of them. They were garbed in all kinds of unusual and gaudy colors—purples, lime greens—and patterns that disoriented the eye. Others had shaved heads or strangely asymmetrical hair colors and styles.

Now and then the walkways would open up onto tiny squares—some perched on top of buildings—housing verdant gardens filled with trees and stones coated in moss and lichen, where lovers sat beneath tiny arbors or crossed miniature bridges over delicate ponds. This sudden beauty in the bustling city surprised and encouraged Armand. As he rested briefly in one of the gardens, a torrential rain began. Many of the people around him threw hoods over their heads and began to rush along the streets. Others opened umbrellas, which Armand had only ever seen in that strange image brought to Technis by one of the officiates returning from Varenis. A daguerreotype—that was what the officiate had called it.

The Department of Benevolence was housed in a giant gray block that rose up, massive and monolithic, on one side of the Plaza of the Sun. Armand left Ice in one of the long rows of stables and entered a cavernous hall, its roof lost in the darkness above. Far away, a man worked behind a massive desk set on a dais, stamping papers, moving them from one side of the desk to another, and periodically reaching up to open one of many cylinders, which descended on wires from the gloom above like spiders. From these he unrolled papers, which he added to his various piles or signed, stamped, and sent back up one of the cylinders.

Armand's footfalls echoed around the reaches of the room so that he seemed to be surrounded by a hundred invisible figures marching beside him. "Excuse me," said Armand.

The man shifted his pince-nez on his nose and continued to work.

Armand waited a moment then cleared his throat. "I'm Officiate Armand Lecroisier from Caeli-Amur. I've come to speak with Controller Valentin."

The man looked down at Armand over his pince-nez. He had the air of a schoolmaster disturbed by an irritating child. "I don't care if you're one of the Sortileges themselves. One cannot simply walk into the Department and demand an audience with the Controller."

"I am an officiate of House Technis," said Armand brusquely. "Valentin is a friend. He is expecting me." He immediately regretted adding this plaintive coda, which made it sound as if he had lost his nerve.

The man looked coldly at him. "Wait." The man then took a blank sheet, picked up a quill, wrote something on it, and pulled a cord above him. Immediately a cylinder dropped from the darkness. He placed the paper within it, pulled yet another cord, and the cylinder whizzed off into the shadows above.

The man then returned to his work.

Eventually another cylinder dropped from above. The man opened the metal container, pulled out the paper within, read it, stamped it, and gestured into the darkness to the right. "Elevator Nine."

An attendant in front of Elevator Nine opened the grate as Armand approached. The elevator rose for a long time, the attendant standing stock-still beside him, like a statue. Armand smiled to himself: it seemed that people knew who they were in Varenis, *what* they were, and—like this attendant—were happy. The problem with much of the new world was the ceaseless mobility, the shifting social strata. People became lost in the tumult, consumed with anxiety and distress at the uncertainty of it all. And there were those who called for even greater freedom of movement! Seditionism was the nadir of this line of thought. The gods knew Armand had felt that anxiety himself, even as he had reached Varenis. But he still wondered if he would find his rightful place with Valentin above.

# FOUR

The attendant led Armand along a narrow walkway that jutted
out into the Varenis sky. At the end of the walkway, a lone square
room afforded a magnificent view of the Plaza of the Sun. Standing beside a vast desk was a gray-haired man, his face warm and
inviting. Despite his perfectly cut suit, his slicked-back wiry hair,
and his closely shaved, rugged face, he had the look of a long-lost
uncle who would adopt everyone as his own. A deep red birthmark on one side of his face gave his good looks a unique spoiled
quality.

"Armand Lecroisier, the grandson of my oldest and dearest
friend?" He shook his head in disbelief.

"Yes, it is I," said Armand stiffly.

Valentin smiled brilliantly and embraced Armand warmly. "Armand! Why, yes, you look just like him when he was young. I'd
never forget that nose, and you've the same tall, willowy build—
like a wading bird. So aristocratic, I always thought."

"Too few recognize such traits now. Those born to rule ride
alone and bereft, while the masses rise to positions they could never
fill. The world is turned upside down, in Caeli-Amur at least."
Armand stood back from the embrace.

"Yes, yes, you speak the truth. We're worried, you know. There
is consternation about events there, much debate about how to respond. Still, it's wonderful that you're here. Now we will have an
eyewitness, and you'll be terrific support for our policies. Come, sit
down." Valentin led him to a series of couches in a semicircle, with
a view of the Twelve Towers standing in a massive square, over-
shadowing everything. Armand placed his bag on the floor beside
him, feeling suddenly vulnerable without it.

"Tell me about everything, Armand. The Houses overthrown? That seems impossible." Valentin gestured widely with his arms, inviting Armand to unburden himself.

The words tumbled from Armand's mouth as he recounted events in Caeli-Amur: the strikes and demonstrations, the clashes at the university, the rise of Director Autec, and finally the disaster of Aya's Day—the entire sorry sequence of events leading up to the overthrow of the old system.

"Together we will convince the Director to send Varenis's legions," Armand said. "We must dig this rebellion out before it has a chance to take root."

"Ah, yes. Well, my dear boy, things are more complicated than you might expect. You see, there is no Director at the moment. The last one . . . well, his failure to foresee events in Caeli-Amur has resulted in his removal. In two weeks the Council of the Directorate will meet to decide on its nomination for a new Director. Our task is to ensure that the nominated person is one of our friends."

"Oh," said Armand. He had focused so much on reaching Varenis, he hadn't thought about the difficulties he might face here.

Valentin stood up and walked to the vast window. Armand followed, stopping a few feet behind the Controller. The Department of Benevolence was one of nine huge identical buildings surrounding the plaza. Each had a single ninth-story room that jutted out over the square like an overhanging cliff, a mirror of the one in which Armand and Valentin stood. Valentin gestured to their right. "Our enemy, a man called Zelik, sits over there. He's the Controller of the Department of Violence."

In the center of the plaza, the Twelve Towers rose high into the sky, their black stone slippery looking in the afternoon light. Though they were even more ominous than the Department buildings, Valentin didn't mention them. Perhaps they were so much a part of his worldview, he took them for granted.

Armand stepped next to the Controller. "I have people in Caeli-Amur. They are gathering our forces and waiting for me to return.

And I have something that . . ." Armand hesitated before mentioning the prism. He would need to be certain of his security first, even with his grandfather's old friend.

Valentin cocked his head and eyed Armand closely. "That?"

"I have the power to win over Caeli-Amur's thaumaturgists when I return."

"That *is* interesting." Valentin glanced back at Armand's bag, which still lay on the floor beside the couches. He waited for Armand to explain further. When he didn't, Valentin gestured to a circular building nestled in the very center of the plaza, in the space surrounded by the Twelve Towers. "The Director's office is there. The center of things is not always the most comfortable place. We must gain a majority on the Council and win that position, Armand. But we should not rush too quickly to war. It would be better to pursue a policy of economic pressure, to continue the blockade and negotiate with the seditionists. We can insist they install one of our representatives as one of their highest powers. Pressure and politics—that is the way to avoid unnecessary bloodshed."

Armand assessed this unexpected position, so contrary to his own plans. "The thing is, Valentin, you don't understand the nature of these seditionists. They're driven by"—Armand searched for the right words—"abstract ideas. Philosophy of the most idealistic kind. They let the mob rule. All kinds of brutal actions can be justified by this ideology. You can't negotiate with them. They're like a gangrenous limb. You must cut it off."

Valentin put his hand on Armand's arm. "Grandson of my dearest friend, let me be honest with you. Our factional opponents, the belligerents, argue for such a policy throughout the Empire. For them, Varenis must rule with an iron fist. But if we examine those places where such a policy has prevailed, well . . . things have not gone well for the conquered. Look at the barbarian tribes of the north and west: driven from their lands, those who resist thrown into the bloodstone mines in the mountains. It will be the same with Caeli-Amur. The belligerents mean to enslave Caeli-Amur, to strip it of its wealth, to bring its art and culture back here to Varenis. They do not intend a return to the days of the Houses, but to turn Caeli-Amur into a colony. But we could pursue a more humane policy. In exchange for lifting the blockade, we would insist the seditionists allow us to buy up their industries. We force them to accept an ambassador to their city. We install a military force inside the city to defend our investments. If we become the city's greatest power, the legions might not be necessary at all. . . ."

Armand saw that there was reason in Valentin's arguments. Varenis's empire stretched north and west. It did not conquer only to allow its new colonies freedom. He had thought that Caeli-Amur was large enough to assert its independence, but of course that was most likely pure idealism.

At that moment a younger man—in his early thirties like Armand—appeared at the end of the walkway. His hair was shaved on one side of his head, a black-and-green tattoo of a sea serpent writhing on his bare skin. The rest of his hair was greased back like a wing. The man's face was gaunt, his eyes large and froglike, unblinking. There was something baleful about his gaze, mixed with the hungry look of ambitious young men everywhere. He raised his hand in greeting, as if the whole situation were routine and quite uninteresting.

Valentin greeted him. "Controller Dominik."

"Ready for Bar Ikuri?" Dominik spoke in the clipped accent of Varenis, so different from the more mellifluous tones of Caeli-Amur.

Valentin raised his hand to his face and covered his birthmark for a moment—a long held and unconscious gesture, it seemed. "Not only ready, but we now have a trump card, Controller Dominik. This is Officiate Armand from Caeli-Amur. Tonight he will help us convince Controller Rainer. Won't you, Armand? Rainer is the fulcrum on which our plans rest. He is the decisive vote on the Council, and though he has been flirting with the belligerents, now we have you, Armand. Do you think you might be able to use your powers of persuasion?"

Armand looked at Valentin's rugged and genial face. His father and grandfather had always spoken of Valentin as scrupulous and high-minded. Armand would simply have to trust him.

"I hope I'll be of some use," said Armand.

"Of that I have no doubt," said Valentin. "But you must be careful. Don't speak too much, and do not give away too much information. Remember, you are our secret weapon. Promise me, then, that you will defer to me."

"I promise," said Armand. "When are you meeting?"

"Oh, not for several hours. Let me recommend a rooming house for you, and then you can meet us at Bar Ikuri in the Spires." Valentin scribbled a name on a piece of paper and passed it to Armand. He stepped back and smiled warmly. "The grandson of my old friend. Splendid."

As he left the building, Armand relaxed, his body emptying of tension of which he had barely been aware. The flight from the terror of the seditionist uprising, the long journey from Caeli-Amur, only Ice to keep him company, the strange hooded pursuer, the hours of disorientation in the vast city of Varenis . . . Now he had hope.

Armand wanted a hidden place to stay, and it would still take some time before he trusted Valentin, so he ignored his recommendation and searched for a rooming house in an area called the Kinarian Pocket, a labyrinth of streets that climbed and descended up over archways and down into subterranean arcades. Tiny bars and rathskellers were scattered here and there. Some of the coffee shops were only holes in the wall, mantelpieces on which to place the coffee. Varenis was larger than Caeli-Amur—its buildings rose massively into the air, the crowds thicker and more impersonal—but this very fact seemed to lead to miniaturization: the exotic gardens, miniature bars, the rooms themselves seemed tiny and compressed.

Eventually he found a little rooming house called the Long Rest, hidden away at the end of a cobblestone cul-de-sac, lit by overhanging red and gold lanterns. He didn't exactly find its name auspicious, but it seemed appropriate. Armand tied Ice to the post outside and took a few short steps beneath ground level to access the entrance hall.

From a little cubicle in one corner of the hall, the owner looked up over dirty spectacles. He introduced himself gruffly as Tedde. As he showed Armand to his diminutive room, Tedde warmed up, pointing out the built-in wardrobe he had installed himself and the new sleeping mat that stood in for a bed. They boarded Ice in stables at the very end of the cul-de-sac. Tedde looked around the dusty stables. "We don't have much use for them. But he'll be safe enough here."

Armand stroked Ice's neck. "It's not much, is it? Not much at all."

Once back in his room, Armand took out the Prism of Alerion and held it in his hands. The hexagonal prism was the size of a child's head. The crystal, unmarked by the years, was smooth and cold. The thing seemed heavy now in his hands, though he had noticed that at other times it seemed lighter. Unlike the scrying ball back in Caeli-Amur, which had an intricate mechanism of cogs and wheels at its center, the prism instead contained a misty swirl of fog, occasionally billowing into shapes that suggested something alive and sentient. Armand rarely took it out, for it had a hypnotic quality. Too often he found himself staring into its depths blankly, all thoughts having left his mind. From these fugues he would jolt out suddenly, his heart racing, uncertain of the amount of time that had passed. There was something frightening about the thing, and he avoided it as much as he could, even though it nagged at his thoughts, seemed to be calling to him to look into its foggy heart.

He wrapped it in a jacket and placed it in his carry bag, wondering whether he should carry it everywhere, or if he should hide it here, in his room. With some effort, he pulled up two of the floorboards and hid it beneath them. He replaced the nails that held the floorboards in place, and shifted the sleeping mat back over them. It would be safe there—for a while, at least.

Armand ventured out with Tedde's bony eight-year-old daughter, Hedy, a cheerful girl who would not stop asking him questions about Caeli-Amur. She hoped to visit one day. She had never seen the ocean, she said. She imagined it to be the most amazing thing in the world, all that water.

"That's it," Hedy said, pointing across to a needle-thin tower among dozens of others—one of the Spires, as the area was called. High up on several balconies, revelers laughed and talked.

As if some voice in his head warned him, Armand looked back in the direction they had come. A couple wandered toward them. Some small animal scuttled along the side of the walkway. In the shadow of a building, Armand caught the glimpse of a figure, just a shadowy form engulfed in darkness. Fear struck his heart once more.

"I have to go." Armand hurried away, but the figure did not follow him. Once he was in the elevator, he laughed at himself. His imagination had surely got the better of him.

In the tower, an elevator carried him up to an entry hall, its walls glowing the soft blue of the patterned and luminous lichen that covered its walls. The concierge led Armand across the floor, past a circular bar. The tables and chairs all seemed like organic shapes: rounded corners, legs that bent and curved like the stems of plants.

The walls were covered in brilliant green and blue lichens in flowing patterns like waves on the sea that gave off a faint light.

In an isolated section away from the main floor, three men lounged on long chairs made from some kind of sponge. Valentin and Dominik reclined near each other. Another huge man with a shaved head sat a little away from them, exhibiting slightly more energy and vigilance in his posture. His delicately trimmed beard—sculpted so its edges were sharp and geometric—suggested a man of fastidious habits. Yet there was something of the bon vivant about him; he gazed at his drink the way a lover gazes at their amour.

The concierge gestured toward Armand. "Officiate Lecroisier from Caeli-Amur for you, Controller Valentin."

Valentin looked up warmly. "Ah, here he is!"

The corpulent man spoke with exaggerated politeness. "Welcome, Officiate Lecroisier. I'm Controller Rainer from the Department of Satisfaction."

"A busy department, I'm guessing," said Armand.

The others laughed politely, and Armand realized that the joke was probably well-worn.

A second later Armand sat, holding a thin flute of blue flower-liquor as if he were part of the Directorate himself. The liquor was sickly sweet, unlike the wines he was used to in Caeli-Amur. He grimaced as he sipped it. Everything in Varenis seemed exaggerated: too sweet or too sour, too large or too small, too dark or too light.

Valentin smiled genially. "We've just been convincing Rainer here that we should pursue a policy of appeasement toward Caeli-Amur. These seditionists are well organized, are they not, Armand? We can't simply walk into the city and take it without a savage engagement."

Armand blinked, feeling unsure of his footing. "Really, it is the tyranny of the mob that runs wild and free, and then there's a small highly organized group that has taken advantage of these affairs—hard, cold, calculating types. But it's true: they will not give up without a fight. Who would have thought they could have overthrown the Houses? And Caeli-Amur is surrounded by walls, so any assault would result in grievous losses."

"Rumors have spread that they have the thaumaturgists on their side," said Valentin. "Again, another reason not to jump hastily into war."

"Rumors," Rainer said obliquely, eyes twinkling and a smirk seemingly planted on his face. It was unclear whether he was suggesting that there weren't any rumors at all, or that he disbelieved them.

"The Department of Satisfaction should take more interest in external affairs," said Valentin.

Rainer shifted his huge bulk. The sponge beneath him squeaked. "Oh, we're happy to focus on the roads and the railways—people respect, first and foremost, everyday things done right."

They broke into laughter for some reason Armand couldn't fathom. Dominik laughed a little too loudly until Valentin gave him a withering look.

Valentin then said, "You're a clever man, Rainer. You know where the truth lies, and now you've heard what Armand has to say. The capture of Caeli-Amur would bring about too much bloodshed. Varenis cannot afford to pay such a cost. Think of the drain on our resources. Already the legions are overstretched, fighting the barbarians in the northwest."

Rainer touched his finely shaped beard and said in a serious tone, "But that's not what it's really about is it, Valentin?"

"Of course that's what it's about. I'm a patriot." Valentin's eyes narrowed with a flash of anger.

"You're not even from Varenis," said Rainer.

"The Empire allows all its subjects equal status." Valentin took a sip of his drink, then looked away as if he were bored.

"Let's not play these games." Rainer finished his own drink and looked at it longingly.

There was silence as Armand tried to gauge the direction of the conversation. Things had become hard to follow, the words spoken with inflections he could not comprehend and filled with mysterious import. He thought about revealing his possession of the prism. That would surely sway Rainer. And yet a feeling of vulnerability kept him silent.

Valentin's birthmark took on an uncomfortable redness. "Anyway, you're partly right. I was born in Caeli-Amur. I still harbor a care toward it. I miss it, even. You should journey there, Rainer—I'll take you one day. The white cliffs, the vast sea, the cafés and philosophy . . . it would be wrong to ruin all that with war."

Rainer shifted himself onto his side and faced Armand. "So, Armand, tell me. Are these seditionists corruptible? Can we starve them first and then buy them off later? Would the golden coin light up their idealistic eyes? If so, Valentin might just have me on his side, after all. We would share the profits, wouldn't we, Valentin? The Department of Benevolence and Satisfaction united."

Armand pressed his lips together momentarily. He felt Valentin looking at him expectantly. He tried to form the words, but Armand could not lie; he simply didn't have it in him. Perhaps it was one of his failings, but principles were all one had. "Starvation might work. They might compromise, but I think there is little chance of corruption among their leaders. They are bound too closely to their ideals."

Rainer looked at Valentin triumphantly. "You see."

Valentin closed his eyes slowly, perhaps in disappointment.

Armand leaned forward, seizing the chance to speak. "Varenis has perfected the art of keeping all things in their right places. The reason is simple: you have one central authority, the Directorate, which is able to mediate between competing factions. In Caeli-Amur, the Houses were forever at one another's throats. A benign central authority like the Directorate is what we must impose on Caeli-Amur."

Rainer shook his head. "No, it seems to me that the belligerents have more reason on their side." He stood up. "It's nice that you bring these"—he glanced at Armand—"exotic provincials as garnish, but until you can offer me something of actual value, well . . . until then."

Rainer heaved himself up from his chair, took one last look at his empty glass, and ambled away.

"He was our only chance, Valentin!" said Dominik. "The others are unmovable. They've built their reputations as belligerents. It's him or no one."

Valentin sighed. "We'll have to get him another way then. I suppose that's it, then."

"Shall we find some Trid-Girls?" Dominik ran his hand over the side of his head with long hair. "I feel like—"

"Not tonight, Dominik," said Valentin. "It's my party in a few days—you will come, won't you, Armand? Why, yes, you must!" Valentin rested his clenched hand on his knee. "You simply must."

"I'm sorry I failed you, Valentin," said Armand. "Failed us."

Valentin put his hand on Armand's knee. "Not at all, my boy. You spoke your mind. Rainer isn't a lost cause yet. He'll be at the party. We can convince him there."

They went out to the walkway and said good-bye. Armand immediately looked for the figure stalking him, but there was no philosopher-assassin in sight. He knew he had imagined the whole thing.

As he walked away, he heard Dominik whisper to Valentin, "You're not really going to adopt this man, are you?"

"Why not?" Valentin said. "His grandfather and I were the best of friends."

Dominik laughed cynically. "Yes, yes, of course."

# FIVE

Maximilian knew he was in the clutches of a dream. Still he twisted, turned, reached out. The tall robed figure was chasing him through a dark forest. Winter had stripped the trees of their foliage, and they now appeared as ghostly sentinels surrounded by ominous fog. Panic gripped him. He stumbled along overgrown paths, brushes clawing at him, roots tripping him, but he knew he had to continue on, for the thing behind him was a horror he could not face. It meant annihilation.

Exhausted, he finally tripped. The dark robed figure stood above him, a wicked knife in its hand. Max looked up from where he lay. Fear froze his limbs. Beneath the figure's hood, Max saw his own face, cold and dreadful.

Every night it was the same. Even when he knew it was a dream, he felt the same fear as he ran, the same horror at seeing the figure stand over him; he felt the same agony as the figure slipped the knife under his skin and drew out his bloody and still-beating heart.

Max had first seen these terrible images in the terror-spheres of House Technis's dungeons. Then he had been awake, his mind providing the material for the sphere to work on. The visions had stuck with him, sunk deeper into the recesses of his mind, only to burst forth each night until he awoke in the morning, disturbed and fearful.

Like now, as he rolled onto his back and stared up into the darkness of the cavern.

*Good morning,* a voice said in his head.

—Go back to sleep—said Max to the voice.

*I awake when you do, and sleep when you do. If you want me to sleep,*
*you need to go back to sleep.*

Max clenched his teeth. Was the voice really the memory of
the joker god Aya that he had somehow allowed into his head
in the Great Library of Caeli-Enas, the Sunken City? He knew now
there had been no gods: the ancients had been people, just like the
rest of them. After the cataclysm, they had seemed as gods to those
remaining in the broken world.

Max shielded his reflections from the voice, but he felt it prob-
ing at him, trying to uncover those thoughts. He slapped Aya away.
—Leave me alone.

The voice retreated to a marginal place somewhere inside him.

Max sat up and looked around the Communal Cavern that had
been the seditionist hideout before House Technis raided the place.
In the lamplight, the place was dark, shadowy. To one side, doors
opened like black maws in the gloom. One of the geometrical
rooms inside had been Max's workshop, where he had taught others
thaumaturgy; another room had housed Ejan's workshop, where
he had built explosive devices. All that was left was strewn across
the ground, like flotsam on the shore after a storm: ragged clothes,
broken glass, bloody stains where seditionists had died.

Max could barely remember the sequence of events: dragging
his air-cart along the watery boulevards of Caeli-Enas, crabs scuttling along the cobblestones, fish darting around his feet, and the
leviathan—the thought of it sent shudders into him—waiting there
for him, spying him with its hundreds of roving eyes, ready to wrap
him in its deadly tentacles. Then the conversation with the sentient
Library beneath the oceans; the deal he made with Aya to escape
the underwater world. From there the memories became even more
fragmented: snatches in the ultramarine and emerald of the underwater world; bursting from the waters, gasping for air under the
glittering lights of Caeli-Amur; staggering back to the seditionist
base, this awful second personality in his head. Kata had looked
down at him—Kata! The thought of her charged him with surprising emotion—then the House Technis guards had arrived, and he'd
been dragged off to the dungeons.

*Don't forget: I provided you with the knowledge to swim through the water,* said Aya.

The headache grew like a little tumor in Max's head. His memories were half ruined. At times they weren't even his own. Every now and again pieces of him broke away and merged with Aya; at other times, fragmentary memories from times long gone flashed into his mind, and he realized they had come from Aya.

—I wish I'd never allowed you into my head, not for all the thaumaturgical sciences in the world—Max thought.

Aya laughed. *You're only saying that. Who wouldn't want me inside them?*

Nearby, Max's oldest friend, Omar, lay asleep, his scarred face like that of a small injured animal. Both of them had been in bad shape after the raid, and at first Max could not leave Omar's side. Once the worst had passed, Max's mood had kept him in the hideout. Some part of him feared rejoining the seditionists, facing up to the failure of his mission to the Sunken City. He had dreamed he would be a leader of the overthrow of the Houses, but it had occurred without him. How stupid he had been! He saw now that his arrogance had blinded him to real events, to the real structures of power. Defeat lay heavy on him, and yet he was still committed to seditionism: he still cared for the lost and the dispossessed. He cared for slaves taken against their will, for the orphans in the factory quarter, and for the workers broken by brutal conditions. These things still filled him with anger, and now that his egotism had been stripped away, that anger burned more purely.

Max picked up a pouch of florens that the seditionists had hidden in the cave before the raid. He counted them briefly: there were enough to last several weeks, even with the inflation that had gripped the city in the face of shortages. He then left Omar and walked along the pathway to the city, emerging high up on the mountain on which the city was perched. Max drew a deep breath, amazed once more by the sight. For a moment it seemed like nothing had changed. Two headlands reached out to either side like arms reaching out into the sea. By the docks, far away, he could spy the Opera building and Market Square. Beyond them, the wide blue ocean sparkled in the light, a multitude of whitecaps as far as Max could see. Out there beneath the waves lay the Sunken City.

Caeli-Amur had changed subtly, though. There was less smoke pumping from the factory quarter that lay between him and the Northern Headland. There were fewer steam-trams on the busy streets. He sensed some molecular change in the atmosphere, a tension that hung over the city and the figures moving around it.

Aya said, *Look at the smoke pumping into the air. You've ruined the city.*

Max felt Aya searching around in his memories. In a panic, Max walled them up.

*How am I supposed to learn anything about this world if you won't let me know what you know?*

—I don't want you shuffling around in my head, picking out this and that as if my memories are a chest of bric-a-brac.

*I wanted to learn more about Iria—things you might have learned as a child but have forgotten.*

—I've told you all I know.

The notion that there might be things in Max's mind he'd forgotten perturbed him. The idea that Aya might discover them perturbed him even more.

According to legend, Iria had retreated from the world after the other gods' victory over her lover, Aya. In Sentinel Tower, hidden away in the mountains, she had eked away her final years, having chosen mortality rather than the eternal life of the gods. The pain, they said, was too great for her to bear.

*Tell me again,* said Aya.

Max drew in a deep breath. —She's gone. All the ancients are gone.

He felt Aya's grief. Like Max, Aya was also caught in the sense of the inexorable passing of time, the feeling that things could never go back to the way they were.

Aya possessed the language of the unified theory of thaumaturgy. For almost a thousand years this language had been lost, and thaumaturgy had been fragmented, each discipline developing on its own. But this forgotten primary language—this mathematics—

functioned in all of reality: both the land of life and the Other Side, the land of death. The language had its own costs, but it allowed the thaumaturgist to use the Art without the Other Side flowing into them, distorting them.

And that was something Max needed. He had risked too much for it—he would brook no opposition from the second personality in his head. The question was: How could he access it without Aya's consent?

They arrived at the great, black, steaming, clunking tower, and climbed the dark stone steps, ready to take the cable car down to the Opera in Market Square.

Hundreds of golden globes danced on the Opera's entry-hall ceiling. As Max entered, they froze. A second later they descended as one toward him. Floating down, they changed color to a bright gold, illuminating the hall in a flood of light. When they reached him, they began to spin around him, a whirlwind of dancing, flickering lights circling him.

The hundreds of citizens who had been milling about or lining up in long queues stared at the lights, which now pulsed with energy.

*Hello, my little ones,* said Aya.

"Get away." Maximilian waved his hands at the lights, some of which playfully danced around his hands. "Away."

Aya pushed an equation up toward Max, who grasped it and invoked it silently. The lights rushed back up to the roof, where they resumed their dance, this time slightly less energetically.

*Not even a thanks?*

—Are you always this narcissistic?—said Max.

*I might ask you the same question.*

Wide-eyed citizens parted in front of Maximilian as he strode to the main reception desk. He recognized the old pinch-faced Antoine, working as one of the intendants behind the desk. Antoine had been one of the first generations of seditionists led by Markus. These older types had been surpassed by the following generation, who had been swayed by leaders of the three new factions: Aceline, Ejan, and Maximilian. After Markus had been expelled from the seditionist group, the other older ones had broken and drifted aimlessly, or aligned themselves with one of the new factions. So history had marched on. Antoine had sided with Aceline, but like most of that older generation, he had lost a sense of his own ideas, a sense of certainty.

Antoine's awestruck face seemed even more pinched as he stared at Max. "We all thought you had disappeared in the Technis dungeons!"

"Who? Kata? Oewen or Ariana? Clemence?"

Antoine shook his head. "Ejan will explain it all, Max. Come with me."

Max felt his stomach tighten with uncertainty. What had become of the group he had built?

Antoine took Max to the head of one of the other desks in the hall. The crowd watched Maximilian, apparently wondering who this man was.

"Papers. Now," Antoine ordered the man behind the desk. He hurriedly put together some papers. "Sign here. Fingerprint."

When they were done, Antoine led Maximilian into the south wing, through the maze of corridors. They passed seditionist guards rushing to-and-fro. Two old men lurked at the doorway of a room, smelling of chemicals. As they passed the room, Maximilian caught a momentary glimpse of three bodies. Two wore the suits of thaumaturgists. The third, from the fragmentary glimpse, appeared to be a teenager, his back turned so that his face was obscured.

Antoine rushed Maximilian past the scene and into a large room. At one end of a central table sat the Northerner Ejan, stone-faced and cold as a knife. Even Ejan's clothes were stiff and creaseless, as if they'd been pressed that very morning. Before him lay an illustration of a disturbing mechanism. At first it appeared to be a massive bolt-thrower, or perhaps a military machine—a scorpion, perhaps. But its purpose was even more grisly. With the swing of a frame, you could lock a person into it, and the mechanism would drive a shaft the size of a tree trunk directly through the person's body. At the top of the illustration was written *The Bolt*.

Explaining the contraption to Ejan was the head of the Collegia,

Dumas. His bulldog head seemed to have grown even thicker, his jowls hanging even farther to the floor, the lines around his eyelids even redder. Max remembered the man with distaste, for the Collegia—half-criminal collections of small traders and shopkeepers—still used slaves. For Max they would never be real allies. They would oppose the Houses when it suited them, but never consistently, never from the point of principle.

"It will be quick, humane," Dumas said.

Ejan looked up, his eyes registering the slightest shock at the sight of Max. "A general without an army. How did you survive?"

Maximilian sighed and sat on a nearby seat. "I'm not sure I did, Ejan, but I'm not here to fight. I just want to know where my supporters are."

Ejan smiled ever so slightly. "Maximilian, after you ventured on your mad journey to the Sunken City, your group fell apart."

"Not all of them, surely. Kata? Where is she?"

"Many of them were arrested by Technis before the overthrow. Some were driven half mad by torture. The rest dispersed, gone. Oppositions cut across new lines now. I do hope you'll join us vigilants. We're pressing the insurgency all the way, revolutionizing every part of life, binding the thaumaturgists to the decisions of the Assembly."

Dumas sized Maximilian up. "Opponents must be eliminated, you understand."

Ejan leaned across to Maximilian and clasped his hands in an awkward attempt at affection. "We need everyone on our side. There are those who argue for moderation, for discussion. But you cannot allow discussion to occur when the very basis of our rule is threatened."

Max shook Ejan's hands away. "Ejan, I always hoped we'd be allies. You frightened me, though—your certainty, the cold equations you do in your head. I had hoped you would grow into a brother, but you have moved in the opposite direction. Not toward warmth, but to ever more abstract ideals—ideals above all else, am I right? Touch is not something that comes naturally to you, Ejan. You should have someone else do your convincing for you, someone with softer hands."

Ejan sat back, unmoved. "Don't you make those same equations in your head, Maximilian? We overthrew Markus and the rest of the old guard. Events passed them by. Make sure the same doesn't happen to you."

Max stood up, angry now. Ejan was right: he, too, made cold calculations in his head. But who didn't? The trick was to keep yourself anchored to life, to people, to warmth. To realize that those calculations are simply in *your* head, not in the world itself.

Max looked away and down, but in that direction were only the designs of the Bolt. "An instrument of murder, no doubt."

"A terrible instrument, isn't it?" said Ejan. "We never wanted this, did we? But have you seen the citizens, hungry on the street? Have you seen the saboteurs, striking wherever we are weak? They force our hand."

"They brought it onto themselves," said Dumas. "They have blockaded the city, attacked us from within. I designed it so it is almost painless. Like a rapid blow."

"Killing one's opponents is a sign you've already lost the battle," said Maximilian.

Ejan shrugged. "You would prefer us to starve, then? Is that what you plan to do?"

To this, Max had no response.

"See, you find yourself doing the same cold calculations in your head. Once we starve, then the Houses return and drench the city in blood. There is no middle road. It's either one path or the other."

"Either way, we've already lost."

"Either way, *you've* already lost," said Ejan.

As Max walked dejectedly through the corridors, Aya said: *Oh, I like him.*


The Quaedian was Maximilian's old stomping ground. Once, he had thought of it as his quarter, and again he found the dynamism that had attracted him: new theater companies announced their avant-garde productions; half-drunk bohemians spilled from tiny galleries displaying ever-popular Vorticist art. He dodged past the red-wine–stained grins of avant-gardists, ignoring their calls to join them.

He stopped on an overhead walkway and watched the street below. Beneath him marched some members of the Order of the Sightless. The apocalyptics wore blindfolds and held themselves together with a small network of chains.

*What strange people.*

—They believe the world is reaching some second cataclysm. That things will fall apart. That some end is near.

*If only they'd been around before the war. Then we might have had some warning.*

Max reached out for Aya's memories of his battles with Alerion, but the mage kept these safely cordoned off. Both of them were aware of the precarious nature of their situation; at any stage the balance might be upset and their personalities might merge with each other. If they let their barriers down, they might lose who they were and dissolve into some incoherent split personality.

On the street beneath the walkway, Max saw Kata walking alone in black shirt and dress, her black hair flowing to her shoulders. His heart clamped in sudden emotion. "Kata! Kata!"

The woman stopped, looked up, her face impassive. She did not reply. Something was wrong with her, but Max could not tell what. She looked gaunter than Max remembered, her eyes a strange pale color—yet darkness hovered around them.

Again he called to her. "Kata!"

But Kata picked up her pace and skipped down a side street: she was running from him. Max scrambled over the balustrade and prepared to jump to the street below.

*We'll break our ankles on the cobblestones.*

Max hesitated, leaped anyway. He hit the cobblestones, and a sharp pain drove up his right leg from the ankle to the knee. He fell to his side, clutching it. He scrambled to his feet, tested it out. It wasn't too bad, after all.

*You really like this woman.*

Max ignored the voice, ran to the side alleyway, and continued. He reached a crossroads and looked down the side street to where a group of old men sat on wooden crates and drank coffee silently. Max looked the other way, where the street was empty.

*You'll never find her in this maze of streets.*

Max rushed on to another side street, where three women were pasting up posters advertising a play called *The Story of X: A Narrative of Everyman.*

In the opposite direction, an open sewer ran along the street; the smell of dank water was overwhelming. As he ran on, Max became aware of doorways passed, open staircases that led into apartments and tenement buildings, side alleyways. When the alley opened into a tiny square where a washerwoman hung clothes from a low line, Max despaired. "Did you see a woman pass this way? Black hair and clothes?"

The woman scrunched up her face and shook her head.

Max sat on two small stairs before a closed and rotting door. Now the loss flooded fully into him, a blackness that seemed to fill his limbs with lead. Why had she run from him? He had lost everything: his seditionist group, half of his body and mind. Even Kata had fled from him.

*Oh, I see now. You don't just like this woman. She is more than that to you.*

—You're right—said Max. —No, you're wrong. I don't know what I feel for her. Anyway, there's no room for such feelings in the seditionist movement. Everything must be subordinated to the cause.

Aya laughed. *That's the spirit.*

Now anger flooded through Max. —We can't go on like this. I would rather die than have you chatting away like an imbecile forever.

*That's melodramatic. But I've been thinking: there might be a way of freeing me from your mind,* Aya said. *Perhaps the Aediles still have the technology.*

—The Aediles disappeared after the cataclysm—said Max bitterly. Max knew the myth. After the gods had warred, leaving the world shattered and ruined, the Aediles had despaired. They had called out to the universe for a new force to bring order to the city. They spent their nights invoking powerful equations until they summoned the strange Elo-Talern, who had ruled over the city like shadow puppets, hidden from the light. The Elo-Talern had become myths to frighten children, strange creatures who were said to secretively influence the Houses, though Max could not be sure what part they had played when the seditionists and the Houses had come into conflict on Aya's Day.

*Then their technology will still rest beneath the mountain somewhere.*

Max's despair lifted for a moment. He would be free from that other cold and distant personality lodged in the recesses of his mind. The thought filled Max with savage excitement.

# SIX

Max passed the still-sleeping Omar and continued along a route he'd traveled before, into the heart of the ancients' underground domain. He walked down that strange corridor leading to hundreds of hexagonal chambers filled with strange skeletal cadavers lying on beds, tubes plunging into their orifices, others piercing their veins. Those corpses seemed like a symbol for the ancients themselves: strange, mysterious, dead.

—If we succeed in freeing you from my mind, I want you to teach me the prime language—said Max.

*And what do I receive in return?*

Max thought rapidly. —If you don't agree to teach me, I won't let you free.

*You know, it would take you years to master the prime language. To join the Magi requires decades of study, of practice. It requires a journey into the dark lands, for you cannot understand the language without knowing both its sides. You would have to give up everything else. Your seditionism, your Kata.*

—They no longer need me. They never did.

Maximilian did not remember the way, and so he put himself at the mercy of the ancient mage, for this was Aya's world—a world of strange spaces and weird technology. They continued down, down into the mountain on a central elevator and into a vast ruined complex, a melancholy pleasure palace of empty ballrooms and baths, fountains and broken amphorae, rooms filled with chessboards and dice pits for two-knuckled jolly. On and on they went, deep into the heart of the mountain.

———

The vast circular door was covered with intricate inscriptions. At the sight of it, Max's anxiety intensified, and the muscles in his body felt tense and ungainly. They were about to pass some deeper threshold.

*Let me control your hand,* said Aya.

Maximilian hesitated. He feared losing even part of himself.

*Do you want to pursue this course of action or not?*

Max released some part of his mind. It was like forgetting something for a moment, knowing the knowledge is somewhere within you but you can't quite retrieve it.

As Max let it go, Aya picked up his hand and moved it across the door in a complex configuration. Suddenly the door lit up and hummed with uncanny power; silver ideograms descended its face like snowflakes falling in winter. The door slid open, revealing a vast hexagonally shaped hall. Max felt Aya's feeling of revulsion and surprise alongside his own feeling of horror, for the perspectives of the hall were impossible: the farthest walls seemed closer than those nearby. Staircases and walkways crisscrossed the space like spider's webs, reaching up to places that appeared to be other floors but now were deserted.

But this was not what horrified Max. No, his heart thumped rapidly at the sight of the strange creatures, long and thin like a fusion of spider and human. There seemed to be too many vertebrae in their wiry bodies, and their long horselike faces were composed of too many gaunt planes to be human. Some were robed, others half naked, their shriveled breasts and tiny genitals absurd and horrific to see. One group lay upon chaise longues, clasping tankards, their dead eyes staring at the roof. Over their robes and the floor, foodstuffs and liquid had spilled. Most had dried to dull yellows, reds, and oranges, but those that still retained a vestige of their former moisture were luminescent. Elsewhere, bowls of gray deflated fruit rotted slowly. Yet another group lay on pillows, their limbs draped over one another, tubes attached to the insides of their elbows. Still more lay facedown or sprawled at unnatural angles, as if they'd crashed to the floor in some terrible and deadly rain. These were the Elo-Talern, shadowy creatures of legend who at one point controlled the Houses but who had long ago retreated into the darkness, letting the Houses live as they wished.

Across all surfaces grew lichens and molds in the most extraordinary colors: luminous greens, bright oranges, wild purples. In places, these had grown to monstrous proportions, towers and massive lakelike carpets. An entire corner of the hall was buried beneath a sea of crimson mold. Elsewhere, only the shadowy forms of groups of these spidery creatures could be seen beneath their horrid lime-green blankets. None of the creatures had escaped the mold's abhorrent embrace. Here a blue mold covered an arm like a glove. There a cadaverous back was clothed in a green lichen cloak. Yet elsewhere one creature lay half covered by a pink blanket, as if a wave had flooded over the creature's friends, the high tide marked by his own sternum and the bridge of his nose.

Max felt limp, as if he might collapse to the ground. When he saw that some of the creatures had roving eyes and that others moved their limbs weakly, a shiver ran across his skin.

Against a nearby pillar—its sides chiseled with ancient faces—one of the creatures sat propped, its chest heaving. The creature stood shakily, like some hideous and furless newly born deer. It haltingly staggered toward Max.

The thing called out, its voice the sound of sand streaming over glass. "Ah, you've come, you've come."

As it approached, Max was filled with the desire to flee. Instead finding that he still had the use of one arm, Max quickly invoked an invisibility conjuration. He spoke the word, drew out the ideograms with his hand, and felt himself disappear from vision. The world gleamed with strange power—everything except the creature. To Max's amazement, the creature's appearance did not change. He saw now from the withered breasts that it was a woman.

The Elo-Talern stopped walking and stared briefly. An orange mold had grown over her left arm, up her spindly neck, and over the left side of her face. The mold covered one eye and seemed to plunge into the creature's mouth. Max pictured mold growing in the creature's lungs, slowly choking her.

The Elo-Talern laughed a horrible laugh—almost a cackling cough. "Forget your puny tricks. You think you can hide from me?"

Max let the conjuration fade, and the world once more became prosaic. Already he had begun to feel weak and nauseated—the consequences of using the Art without the prime language. Max had learned that only the prime language stopped the Other Side, the world of death, from seeping into the thaumaturgist and warping them, sickening them.

The Elo-Talern flickered, and in her place stood a decaying skeleton, all rotten bones and meat. Another flicker, and the vision disappeared.

*Let me talk to her.*

—Tell me what to say, and I'll say it.

*Let me have control of your speech centers. Now.*

The Elo-Talern stepped close to him, now more certain on her feet. Her spidery hand shot out and grasped Max's jaw. He felt its wetness as well as its strength. The eyelid hidden beneath the mold slid like something under a sheet.

"You're not who I was expecting. Are you a messenger?" She craned her head close to his, one eye blackly menacing, the other half visible beneath the layer of mold.

With this, Max relinquished control of some part of his mind and, with a slight panic, felt himself mute. He realized that along with the power of speech, he needed to allow Aya control of his face and jaw muscles. He let them go slowly, as one would a rope after a long period of gripping it. He felt them slip away, as if through his now open fingers.

*And your body. I have to be able to gesture—just while we speak to her.*

Max released the remaining parts—arms, body, legs—and drifted away into the deep recesses of himself. There he floated without anchor on a dark sea, watching events from afar.

Aya knocked the Elo-Talern's hand away and smiled broadly. "Well, Drusa, I see you've been looking after yourself."

The Elo-Talern stepped back, uncertain. Now her voice took on a shaky tone. *"Who are you?"*

"It's I—Aya. Drusa, don't you recognize me?" Aya laughed.

"Aya died almost a thousand years ago. He's gone."

"I stored myself in the Library of Caeli-Enas before I fled across the seas. I died, but now I am reborn. I inhabit this body for the moment, but I must escape it. I must have a new one."

The creature laughed horribly, a cackle barely distinguishable from a cough. "But really, who are you?"

Aya invoked the prime language and pulled the Elo-Talern toward him like a puppet. When her ghastly face was almost close enough to touch his, he stared into the creature's slowly comprehending eyes. "Drusa. You were always one of the kindest of the Aediles. I liked your raven hair, your strong face. Before Alerion came down upon us with his troops, it was you who helped the children escape the city. What has become of you?"

The Elo-Talern tried to move but couldn't. "It's not possible. You died. You died, didn't you? Yes, but you saved your mind. I remember that now, before you left. You— Why did you leave us, Aya? We trusted you. You seemed so confident. Now look at us. Look at *me*."

Aya released her, and she staggered back. "Help me escape from this body. The man who inhabits it is filled with the everyday desires of this time, these people. I find it—grubby."

Again, Max felt Aya's terrible distance from humanity. He knew this was the eventual cost of using the prime language. Even with Aya's momentary invocation of it, he felt a little wedge between him and the world.

"Everything is destroyed. All is lost. Look around you." She gestured to the bacchanalian scenes of death. "That's all that's left of the ancient world. The gravities failed, and look." She indicated the bodies scattered around. "The dehumidifiers are broken, and the mold creeps over everything. There are no technologies capable of what you ask here anymore." She halted, cocked her head as if thinking. "There is the Library in Caeli-Enas."

Aya shook his head. "It was losing power when I left. Even if the waters haven't already flooded it, its Core would probably not survive extraction. What about Sentinel Tower?"

The Elo-Talern straightened her head again. "Iria always kept it hidden."

"I know where it is," said Aya.

Drusa blinked out of existence for an interminable second, re-appeared in a slightly altered position. "You do, but the landscapes have changed. . . . Still, if you could find the Sentinel Tower's Core, Aya, we could restart things. Bring us that, and we will be able to help you. Return with the Core, and we will free you from this body. And we might even be able to save ourselves. From the mold. From everything."

Aya sealed the door behind them, the ideograms fading out of existence.

—It's time now to let me have my body back—said Max from his place in the darkness. When Aya did not respond, a rush of terror engulfed Max. —Aya, let me have my body back.

Aya walked on, unperturbed.

Max flooded forward. With all his strength, he reached for the controls of his body. He grasped some of them, felt implacable force striking back at him. His strength slipped. For a moment he felt like water against rocks.

Max's body stopped, fell to its knees as the internal struggle went on. The face contorted as one personality took control then lost it to the other.

Max felt a blow, then another. His grip loosened. Another blow, and again he floated on a black sea of nothingness. He scrabbled up like a drowning man desperately trying to reach the surface, but he could not grasp on to anything. He felt he was drowning. The terror of nothingness gripped him, like those moments of sleep when he tried to awake and yet could not. His eyes wouldn't open, for he had no eyes.

*This body is mine now*, said Aya. *It is you, not I, who will be vacating this vessel.*

Alone and drifting, Maximilian was surrounded by leaden feelings of anger and betrayal and fear. He felt he didn't exist.

As they passed through the corridors, Max slowly began to hear as Aya did, and then also to see. About halfway back through the deserted pleasure palace, voices echoed softly along the long empty corridors. They may have been near, or perhaps they were far, but Aya had no desire to meet them. He took a step into an empty room: once-scarlet rugs hung, their patterns hidden by an age of dust, or else collapsed to the floor in piles.

The whispering voices came closer, and closer. "The Elo-Talern created the prism, after all. You'd think Elo-Drusa would know how to operate the damned thing."

"Maybe the Sortileges?"

"The Sortileges or the Gorgons—but it was created here, then the cataclysm came down before anything could be saved. It's either Drusa or Thom."

"Armand shouldn't have taken it," said a second voice. "Too risky. But what can we do?"

Max thought he recognized the second voice. Yes, its husky tones reminded him of before the overthrow. "When was it?"

Then the men flashed past the room. Curious, Aya afforded a quick glimpse. One of the men's faces was obscured, but he radiated power. Max immediately recognized the second man's deep-set eyes: they seemed like little points of light down a dark tunnel, as if he had not slept in days. He was the seditionist Georges, one of Ejan's group. Max barely knew the man. In fact, before the overthrow of the houses, Georges had seemed nothing but a shade of gray, a mediocrity drifting among the middle ranks of the seditionists. He seemed to have few notable skills; Max couldn't remember anything about his past. He was no orator, no theoretician, possessed no thaumaturgical skills. He just seemed to drift around, doing Ejan's bidding. Exactly who or what Georges exactly was, Maximilian didn't know. And now, seeing him in this vast and empty pleasure palace . . .

"Do you think he trusts us?" said Georges.

"He's a fool. He lives in the old world of tradition. He doesn't understand the new world."

"We need him as much as he needs us, though," said Georges.

"Sadly true."

By the time the men spoke again, their voices were far away and came only as inaudible whispers, carried along the corridors.

When Aya returned to the seditionist hideout, Omar had packed a shoulder bag with a pot hanging on it. He had neatly folded the blankets on his straw mattress, as if he were leaving it for someone else. As Maximilian watched from his dark place, something about this moved him. Again he felt as if an age were coming to an end, and it filled him with sorrow.

Omar stood, threw the bag over his shoulder. "So, this is it."

Aya watched the little man, saying nothing.

"I know it's hard for you that I'm leaving. You think I'm betraying the seditionist movement. You think I'm giving up on building a better world. But I see it differently. Something within me has changed. I want to help in my own small way. Back at the Dyrian coast, I can help out at the library, perhaps. Work a little on the oyster farms. Lead a simple life."

Max felt a terrible sense of loss flood into him. *Events were irretrievable,* he realized. The weight of history crushed everything. He tried to say something, but he didn't have the capacity. He struggled to move his tongue; Aya fought back, pushing Max ever further down into the blackness.

"Won't you say something?" said Omar.

"There's nothing wrong with little people finding their place in the world. Great events are not for everyone," Aya said.

"Perhaps your struggles are ineffectual," said Omar. "Have you thought of that? Have you thought that perhaps leaders are simply carried along on the flow, like flotsam on a rushing river?"

Aya laughed. "You would be surprised."

Omar stepped forward to embrace Aya, but the mage held his hand out. To Max, this gesture seemed like some metaphor for Aya's relationship to people. Like all Magi, he was always and increasingly at a distance from the truly human.

Omar's face showed the strain of grief and rejection. Max tried once more to speak; with a powerful surge he rushed up to take control of the body, which twitched and convulsed, before Aya dealt Max a blow and sent him plummeting down the well of nothingness.

"I see you're still repressing your true feelings, Maximilian. Well, I'll still consider you a friend, even if we may never see each other again."

Omar turned, picked up a nearby lamp, and walked away into the darkness toward the tunnel that would eventually lead him outside. In the blackness, Omar soon became simply a silhouette, with a little burning light bobbing beside him. With each step his outline faded into the surrounding dark. *So people slowly fade from history,* thought Maximilian. He yearned to run after Omar, to give him a decent heartfelt farewell. But Aya looked on with ironic distance.

*Now we must prepare for our own journey,* said Aya. *As soon as we can, we leave for the Sentinel Tower. Then I can free you from this body.*

—Free me?

*Well, yes. I think I might need it awhile. It's perfectly good, you know. The curly hair is a bit annoying, granted, but I'm starting to quite like it.*

—This is wrong—said Max.

*I think you'll find it's all a matter of perspective. Think of it this way: at least you'll still be you, sort of. I think. You might not have a body, but you can't have everything, can you?*

# SEVEN

Someone always seemed to be watching Kata. Wherever she walked in the city, passersby stole quick glances, seditionist guards assessed her. Here in the tiny alleyways of the Quaedian, the feeling intensified. She felt—or imagined—a thousand eyes constantly fixed on her. The city was full of spies and philosopher-assassins, and Kata sensed dangers closing in around her. Perhaps the D who wrote the letter might have his—or her—eyes on her even now. Meanwhile, Rikard was ever watchful behind her, and she still didn't trust him.

Kata had left the two vials of material with a philosopher-assassin for analysis the day before. Now she returned to the tiny alleyway, Rikard stepping lightly after her, Dexion's huge bulk moving behind. The minotaur had been bored and decided wherever they were going was the cure to this ailment.

Here the streets became so narrow that Kata, Rikard, and Dexion could only walk single file. As they strode on, Kata examined the tiny apartments, the garrets and rooming houses. Thom's workshop would be hidden somewhere up there. Kata was plagued by the fact that Henri might well be able to discover its location if she asked. One of the waifs had surely worked for Thom, but she would never be able to find that child. Of course Henri knew the patterns of power on the streets, where to find each gang or lone urchin, but when she asked him, he refused to name names. There was a kind of urchin code, not unlike that of the philosopher-assassins. Even with their bitter territory wars, they wouldn't betray or name one another. Her only option would be to ask Henri to make the inquiries in her place, and that was impossible. She would not endanger him.

She knocked on an absurdly narrow door. The squarish matri-archist called Greta let them in, looking up over her spectacles in alarm at Dexion as he squeezed through the doorway. Greta's short gray hair and eyepieces lent her the air of a scholar, but Kata knew that they obscured the fact she had killed more than twenty men in the House wars.

A trapdoor hidden beneath a brilliant red carpet led to her small underground workshop. Dexion came last, the ladder creaking under his weight. The workshop's walls were covered with shelves packed with bottles and vials of brilliantly colored liquids and powders, jars and vials, siphons and funnels. Kata had known Greta since Technis had hired them both to poison a Marin officiate. He had died cruelly on the deck of a cutter headed for a holiday at the Dyrian coast. Apparently, his wife and children had looked on as he collapsed, frothing on the ground, kicking out and smashing his head on the deck in his death agonies. Kata had called on the matri-archist several times since for her expertise in chymistry.

Now the squat woman hunched over the glass plate under the powerful magnifying glass on the workshop's central table. "You'll have to see it—amazing."

Before Kata could step forward, Greta turned quickly and pointed at Dexion, who hovered close to the ladder with Rikard. "Don't touch anything!"

"I never—" Dexion slowly placed a round bowl back onto the shelf, as if nobody would notice.

Irascibly, she turned back to the magnifying glass, spun the wheel on the side of the instrument, and nodded to herself.

"Look," she said to Kata. "These are the grains from Aceline's nose."

Kata placed her eye to the microscope, and the tiny particles came into focus. Magnified, they appeared as mechanical mites with six tiny metal legs, intricate latticework constructions of cogs and wheels, hundreds of tiny eyes in their black heads. "Ancient tech-nology."

Greta nodded. "Brain mites—extremely rare. They climb up through the nose and are used to drain someone's memories, or to add new ones. They come from a storage machine, which you need to access the memories. Gods know where you might find one."

Greta turned to the second vial, scraped the black smudge onto a plate, and sprinkled a fine yellow powder onto it. It began to smoke. "This is the remains of bloodstone, used in some thaumaturgical conjuration."

From behind them came a crash. Dexion stood rooted to the spot. Between the fingers of one huge hand he held the glass stopper from a bottle. At his feet lay the remains of the bottle, smoking liquid spreading out in a puddle around it.

Dexion shrugged, as if to say, *Who, me?*

"Out—you men, out." Greta pointed to the ladder. Rikard didn't need further encouragement. He scaled the ladder and disappeared up through the trapdoor.

"Perhaps I should clean . . . ," Dexion started.

Greta's eyed him unforgivingly. He turned like a chastened child, the ladder again creaking dangerously as he climbed into the room above.

Greta returned the mites to a vial, passed them to Kata. "Come back if you need more help, or if you find one of the mite machines. I'd love to see it."

Rikard and Dexion had been leaning against the alleyway wall, waiting. At the far end of the alleyway, a group of urchins were playing dice against the wall, laughing and cheering, but Kata felt their little eyes glancing at them surreptitiously.

Dexion said, "Well, that went well, didn't it!"

Kata looked at him for a moment.

"Anyway," he added, "I don't think you'll need any more of my help today, so I'll be off. But you should ask Henri to find Thom. It's the quickest way."

Kata stood fixed to the ground, aware of Rikard listening in beside her. "There's more to the murder than Aceline and two thaumaturgists. The mites were used to implant memories in Aceline or, more likely, to retrieve them. So what did she know? There are too many unanswered questions to risk Henri."

"All right. All right." Dexion stood a little straighter, as if a weight had been lifted off his shoulders. "I think I might go to the Arena. There are still fights happening there. I might even take part. Become a gladiator."

He turned and happily walked toward Via Gracchia. The waifs scuttled away from him, staring wide-eyed as he passed.

When he was gone, Rikard said. "Who is Henri?"

"No one." Kata looked away from Rikard's piercing brown eyes.

"If you have a way of discovering where Thom hides, you had better use it," he said. "Individual lives are insignificant at this point."

Kata pushed the young man back against the alleyway wall. She was suddenly aware of his face close to hers: the minute imperfections of his skin, the soft hairs of his mustache. "Individual lives are never insignificant. Every life has a weight. Henri is an innocent."

Rikard's head tilted back, and he stared at her coldly. "There are no innocents. There are ignorant people, and ones who stand aside, and they're just tacitly supporting the strong. You and I both know it. You must do your duty. We have to protect the city, no matter what the personal cost. After all, Aceline was your friend, wasn't she?"

Kata let go of him. "Don't you have any heart, Rikard? There *are* innocents."

When they got back to the Opera, word had come from Prefect Alfadi that the dead thaumaturgists had been identified, so Kata and Rikard headed quickly toward the Marin Palace. Citizens clutched the jostling sides of the tram as it chugged its way along Via Trasta. The steam-trams still moved despite the fall of the Houses, some tram drivers continuing to work out of some notion of civic duty, and relying on donations from the citizenry. Others lay immobile in the tram depots, for supplies of spare parts had stopped coming in from Varenis. Just like the factories, the trams were grinding slowly to a halt.

"At least Alfadi is on our side," said Rikard.

"You mean the side of the vigilants. Anyway, how do you know?"

"After the overthrow, Ejan had me examine the Technis files— well, as many as I could. There are rooms and rooms of them, you know. Each file contains everything they knew about that person. Alfadi was born out in the rocky mountains inland from the Teeming Cities. He was a village boy but was adopted by the Priests of the Dead, and there learned some of their primitive sorcery. Turns out he was outcast for liaising with one of the princesses of the Pyramids down there. Well, that was the official story—the priests were meant to be celibate. But the real reason was that the Head Priest feared Alfadi. Alfadi was too talented. Alone and exiled, he drifted for several years. He seems to have disappeared from view before he took the long journey by galley to Caeli-Amur. He'd heard about thaumaturgy and was quickly brought into Technis, rising through the ranks to become prefect. The other thaumaturgists respected him, so when he left Technis Palace after the overthrow, they followed him."

"A village boy from beyond the Teeming Cities. That was a long time ago."

"He understands we'll have to crush the villas soon enough," said Rikard. "Expropriate the grain. And to do that, we have to ensure that the thaumaturgists are loyal to the Assembly. They must become militarized, bound to us by force if necessary. Ejan will propose a motion at the next Assembly to resolve the situation, and Alfadi will support it."

Kata shook her head. "Didn't the thaumaturgists join us so they weren't bound by force to do the Houses' bidding?"

Rikard brushed back his black hair. "You sound just like one of the philosopher-assassins on Via Gracchia, Kata. Always debating, to what end?"

Kata tensed. When he searched through the Technis files, had he found hers? Did he know about her past, that she had been hired by Technis to spy on the seditionists, that she had betrayed them? An icy feeling settled into her.

Rikard grabbed Kata by the shoulder. "And you haven't told me the message you had for Aceline on the night of her murder. You've kept it from me."

Kata hesitated. "Thom wanted me to fetch her. He didn't tell me what it was about."

Rikard stared at Kata impassively. "That's not what you said on that night."

Kata felt her skin begin to itch. Her entire face felt like it was about to break out in a rash. "Yes, it is."

Rikard leaned in close, his eyes challenging. "You don't trust me, do you, Kata?"

"We're seditionists together," said Kata. "We serve the movement, don't we?"

"Do we?" asked Rikard.

Unable to continue the lie, Kata turned toward the Marin Palace. "Look, we've arrived."

# EIGHT

Where the Arbor Palace and Technis Complex had gardens, Marin had elegant water features, fountains and delicate interconnected pools and canals. Shrimp scuttled along one stony bottom; bright red crabs hid beneath equally red stones brought from Numeria; golden fish drifted between columns of kelp and seaweed. In another pool, gray fish floated weakly on their sides, giving the occasional flap of their tails. Many of these had chunks of flesh taken from them. The fish seemed to have become cannibals.

A group of three black-suited thaumaturgists were attempting to scoop blue and yellow fish from one of the rock pools with a long-handled net.

"That way. That way!"

"Quick—no, wrong direction. Push them against the wall there."

"Yes!"

A thaumaturgist pulled up the net, two fish flapping in it. One of them caught sight of Kata and Rikard. He shrugged. "Have to eat. Suppose these will all be gone soon enough."

The water palace rose high above Kata and Rikard, constructed of white marble, blue-and-yellow mosaics of beautiful ships on the wall. High up were great balconies where House Marin officials must have once overlooked the city. At several places in the wall, waterfalls cascaded from fissures: crashing water plunged into the moat that circled the massive palace.

In the grand entrance hall, falling sheets of water formed liquid walls, rushing into channels of water that disappeared through archways. Gondolas were moored against the hall's far wall. Around a circular desk stood a group of thaumaturgists.

One of the thaumaturgists called Detis had been instructed to wait for them. Like many thaumaturgists, he gave off a sickly sheen. As they came closer, Kata saw that soft greenish patches seemed to drift beneath Detis's skin, catching the light and occasionally shining softly through it.

He led them to the gondola and paddled them beneath an arched tunnel and into the heart of the palace. The canal joined with others in a network of crisscrossing waterways that connected the many halls and rooms. Every now and then the delicately tiled walls of the tunnel became translucent, revealing great tanks filled with sea creatures: little clouds of orange and yellow fish, massive spider crabs the size of small children, huge mollusks attached to the glassy surfaces, their meaty interiors gray and brown. Occasionally, larger and more ominous creatures drifted in darker waters beyond.

All the while, Kata was aware of Detis summing up her and Rikard, assessing them like an accountant concerned over numbers. She returned the favor. He had the look of all thaumaturgists: superiority mixed with desolation at the losses the Art had exacted from him.

Deep inside the water palace, Detis brought the gondola to a halt before a wide platform. Waiting for them by the berth was the thaumaturgist Alfadi. Again Kata was struck by the whiteness of his eyes and his impressive presence. He moved like a retired athlete, confortable with his bearlike frame.

"Look at this place. This is where the Director worked," he said.

At the far end of the room, a gigantic delicately curved desk—itself a fish tank—stood on a dais. The floor of the room was nothing but a glassy surface covering a prodigious pool. Beneath them floated a round creature, something like a massive cephalopod. Strong tentacles—some powerful and thick, others long and thin with stingers on their ends—emerged from its body. But the thing that struck the most fear into Kata was its hundreds of ghastly eyes, packed together in two clusters and filled with malevolent intelligence. She knew the creature could take on the illusion of someone she loved, or something she hated, and for a moment she thought she saw Maximilian floating helpless in the water beneath. But then all she could see was the creature's baleful eyes, rotating disturbingly.

Alfadi looked down at it. "Terrifying, isn't it? I wanted to get it out of here, but it turns out it would be too dangerous to move. The whole place has a kind of deadly beauty to it, doesn't it? There are trapdoors in this floor beneath us. Apparently, during the overthrow of the Houses, the crowd fed the Marin Director to the leviathan. Brutal, really, but . . . well, I suppose it was war."

As they crossed the room, the creature gave a kick of its tentacles and floated beneath them, a dreadful image mirroring their movement below. To Kata's relief, Alfadi led them away into a comfortable side room, perhaps used by the Director's intendant. There were soft chairs and a chaise longue made from a spongy material.

Alfadi and Detis took seats, leaving the chaise longue for Kata and Rikard.

"The two dead thaumaturgists worked for Marin, so I barely knew them. They were my men, though, liberation-thaumaturgists: Ivarn—the skinny one—and Uendis, the heavy one. They wanted thaumaturgists to be bound to the movement and directed by it. Detis was the one who identified them." Alfadi gestured to the second thaumaturgist.

A green patch of color resembling some strange butterfly slowly drifted beneath the skin of Detis's face. "They were like brothers, always together. But in recent days they seemed to retreat to themselves. They became skittish, wary. Their eyes darted, as if they were expecting an attack."

Kata did a rapid calculation. It was still possible one had turned, or was a double agent. "Did you see them on the day of the murder?"

"Yes. They slept in the common room with all the others. In the afternoon they came in and collected some papers. I was just entering the room when I heard Ivarn say something to Uendis—and I remember the secretive way he said it. He was talking about a man called Armand, who was some Technis official. 'If what Aceline says is true about the Prism of Alerion, almost all will follow Armand. He'll use the prism and win over most of the thaumaturgists. No other motivation can overcome the desire to avoid the consequences of using the Art. It's already happening, can't you see? There are groups here, in the Palace . . .' Then he caught sight of me and said no more."

Mention of the prism struck Kata like a blow. She tensed on the chaise longue. "What is this prism?"

Alfadi leaned forward, elbows on his knees, white eyes lit up. "After Alerion defeated Aya, he himself was broken. The Aediles were said to have captured what was left of his spirit within the prism."

Kata nodded. "So this prism survived somehow, somewhere."

"Survived for nearly a thousand years." Alfadi's white pupils seemed to burn into Kata.

"Can we see where these thaumaturgists slept? Perhaps there is more information in their belongings?" said Rikard.

Detis pointed to a pile of clothes to one side of the room. "I've brought their possessions, but there's nothing of interest."

Having learned all they could, they returned to the gondola. Before they followed Detis on board, Alfadi reached one hand out to each of Kata's and Rikard's shoulders. His touch was warm, his face open. "Let me know if I can help."

As they passed along the canal beneath one of the narrow tunnels in the Marin Palace, Detis stopped paddling and let the gondola drift, occasionally bumping against the stone walls. The thaumaturgist turned and Kata tensed, ready to draw the stilettos she kept hidden in sheaths beneath her shirt.

The darkness seemed to bring out a sickly glow to the patches on Detis's face. "Ivarn and Uendis were certainly not agent provocateurs. They were seditionists like many of us, dedicated to a new world. They were moderates. They believed thaumaturgists should be free, like any other person—free to join the movement or not, as they see fit."

"Why didn't you say this before?" asked Rikard.

"This place is haunted. There are eyes and ears everywhere. No one is safe. Not even Alfadi: he feels secure, but I think there are people watching him, too. Ivarn and Uendis came to me a day before their deaths." Detis whispered the words rapidly. "They talked about secret meetings in the canals beneath the city. Someone here had accessed the Marin treasury. Chests filled with florens were exchanged. I wanted to tell Alfadi, but he's too trusting. He's never really understood the Caeli-Amur way, you know. He speaks to the wrong people. He—"

At that point, the still-drifting gondola emerged into the entry hall. Detis fell silent under the watchful eyes of the other thaumaturgists. He moored the gondola, and the three of them crossed the floor.

When they reached the open air, Detis looked behind him and whispered to them, "Ivarn and Uendis talked too much as well. Too many had heard their rumors."

He turned, but before he had taken two steps, Rikard grasped him, turned him around. With a rapid pull, he opened Detis's suit and the shirt beneath. Buttons bounced onto the ground. An image of two hands clasping was tattooed on the thaumaturgist's chest.

"What is this?" said Rikard. "What does it mean?"

Detis pushed him off, his face frozen in a frightened leer. Aghast, the thaumaturgist turned and rushed back into the Palace, leaving them standing there.

"How did you know he had a tattoo?" Kata asked Rikard.

"Instinct. There was just something about him."

Kata blinked as she assimilated the information. "Why was he hiding that from us, do you think?"

Rikard's face was now set with cold anger. "You would know why someone hides something from another."

"What do you mean?"

This time Rikard grabbed Kata by the shirt. "What is this Prism of Alerion? What are you hiding from *me*?"

Kata looked at the young man guardedly. She knew whatever she told him would reach Ejan. Could she risk telling him of the letter? But what if Ejan himself was mixed up in the murder? *No,* she thought. *Surely not.*

"I don't trust you," Kata whispered.

"Then I suppose I shouldn't tell you what I know either," said Rikard.

Kata's mind lurched toward a compromise. "Let's make an

agreement. Neither of us tells anyone—including Ejan—of our discoveries without the other being present."

Rikard's usually calm face dropped. He let go of her shirt, took two steps away from her. She had never seen him so agitated in her life. He looked back at her, his face a study in conflict. Something gave way. "All right."

From her pocket, Kata produced the letter from Armand. She hesitated a moment. She still didn't trust Rikard, yet she handed it over to him. "Thom gave me this in the Opera about half an hour before I saw you."

Rikard shook his head. "That's impossible. That's what I was about to tell you. Thom was in that room with Aceline and the thaumaturgists. I saw him enter perhaps half an hour before you arrived. Between the mist, the revelry, the half-naked couples, and of course that minotaur who causes so much ruckus wherever he goes, I'm not sure when he slipped out."

Kata shook her head. "He sent me from the Opera. It took me half an hour to reach the water palace. Are you saying he was there at the same time?"

Rikard took the letter from her. "Perhaps it was an hour. Time stretches and distorts in the baths. That would have given him time to return to the Opera and give you this letter."

Kata shook her head. "But why would he send me to her if he were going himself?"

Rikard spoke with certainty as he opened the letter. "Thom is a liar, then. We shall find him and extract the truth. Otherwise, we'll catch him at the Insurgent Assembly in two days."

The young man's tone frightened Kata. Her stomach churned from the fear that she had now put Thom at risk. Thom, who was passionate and erratic. Thom, with the huge heart. Thom, who was now the leader of the moderates but was not cut out for leadership. Ejan could not break Aceline, but perhaps he could break Thom.

"How do you know he'll appear?" asked Kata.

"He sent a letter to Olivier saying he had a revelation for the Assembly, a dark truth that would unhinge things. Ejan intercepted it before it reached Olivier."

Kata shook her head. "That's unforgivable."

Rikard tilted his head back, as he did when he felt uncomfortable. "We wanted to find Thom's hideout."

"And did you?"

"No—the letter came from a courier who had been given it by an urchin. The trail was lost."

Kata stood wondering what dark truth Thom would reveal. She wondered if perhaps it was a secret about Ejan himself. With each day that passed, the less Kata trusted the vigilant leader.

# NINE

Armand stood on the balcony of Valentin's apartment, looking down over Varenis. The multiform towers decreased in size until they merged into the suburbs. Beyond that lay the farmlands surrounding the city. Farther still were shadowy forms of black on black, the hills that marked the beginning of the Etolian range, beyond which lay Caeli-Amur. A pang of grief struck Armand. Caeli-Amur: he missed its squares and plazas, the eateries on the Thousand Stairs and the bars and cafés along Via Gracchia. What visions he had for it: visions of a new order, where it would take its place next to Varenis.

Valentin threw his arm around Armand and looked out onto the metropolis. "Look at the great city. It's a long way from Caeli-Amur, isn't it?"

Armand had to admit the sight was awe-inspiring. "I miss my home."

"I felt the same way when I first arrived. I could barely understand this place. I yearned for the sight of the sea. I wished for the spiced breads, the baking sun, the white cliffs, even the philosopher-assassins. There is little room for philosophy here in Varenis, or for the other slow things in life. There was a reason this place was Alerion's base. It's the center of the world: fast, cold."

The two cities had come to resemble the two gods. Varenis, powerful, forward-looking; Caeli-Amur, creative, unpredictable. Caeli-Amur had always lived under the shadow of the larger city, just as Aya had lived under the shadow of Alerion.

Valentin took his hand. "Your grandfather's ring!"

Armand looked down at his beautiful piece. Forged from steel and platinum, white ideograms circling a knife's width above the face of the ring. "Watch."

Armand took the ring from his hand, placed it in his palm. At this, the ideograms stopped spinning and pressed themselves down into the metal. As it lay there, it appeared to be nothing but a ring with delicate engravings.

"Do you know what it does?" asked Armand.

"Not even your grandfather knew. There are some ancient secrets that are forever secret. It reminds me of him, though. Your grandfather took me under his wing, you know. My parents had been killed in the Second House War, and he looked after me. One time I'll never forget: two officiates' wives and their entourage had retreated to one of the pleasure villas south of Caeli-Amur in the midsummer. Those villas, how beautiful they were! Sculpted gardens and long cool pools. But the workers had been complaining about the subofficiate who managed the place. They'd handed in a list of demands, which had come to me. I'd ignored it. They were workers; what could they do? Then word came from the villa: the workers had revolted, were holding the wives and their entourages captive. I'd ignored the worker's demands, and now, in the hope of keeping this a secret, I hired three philosopher-assassins to suppress the upstarts. At first we killed the rebels silently. But how was I to know that one of them had been a gladiator, unable to fight due to old injuries, but battle hardened and coldhearted? By the time I entered the villa's atrium, the women had been slaughtered. The gladiator paid for it with his life, but it was too late. I was ruined. Your grandfather should have exiled me. But what did he do? Instead he took responsibility. He protected me as he would his own child. He suffered for it, no doubt, but we survived that time. I'll never forget that loyalty. What a man he was, your grandfather. I've always hoped to live up to his standards. Loyalty, honor, truth— the old principles."

"They are my principles too," said Armand, who felt close to the old man now. Valentin had taken Armand under his wing and showed him how the Department of Benevolence functioned. In return, Armand had discussed the ways of Caeli-Amur, and they had examined maps of the city. Valentin had asked detailed questions about Caeli-Amur's industry, its transport networks, its former methods of organizing. Much of its food came from House Arbor's farms to the south and Marin's fleet. From Varenis came important components of its technical machinery. Valentin, it turned out, owned a number of these parts factories in Varenis—and the tram corporations that ran them—which put him in a perfect position to use this leverage. Later they discussed Armand's role as ambassador. Valentin had set up several accounts specifically for Armand's use, which helped Armand feel more secure.

Now on the balcony, Valentin pulled Armand close to him. "We must return this world to the old ways. It has drifted too far from its anchorage. You and me, hey?"

Armand drew a breath. "Are the belligerents here this evening?"

Valentin cocked his head for a moment. "They couldn't miss it. That's the thing about the Directorate—one authority, one culture, one group. Don't let the belligerents know you're here though, or you'll be in danger. Rainer won't betray you unless he has sided with them irrevocably, and he hasn't. We'll keep you as our secret weapon." He tapped the side of his nose and raised his eyebrows conspiratorially.

"I'm sorry I didn't support you more strongly at Bar Ikuri. From now on you can count on me." Armand thought about Alerion's prism. Perhaps this was the time to reveal its existence to Valentin?

He was about to speak of it, when Valentin gestured behind them. "Come on, let's enjoy the party!"

The apartment was filled with hundreds of guests. Black dresses with complex hooped structures seemed the fashion among young women, while both sexes seemed to wear their hair in strange half-shaven styles like the young Dominik's. The older guests wore more conservative styles—suits and scarfs—but still with unusual cuts: here, long arms, so that the hands were half obscured by the sleeves; there, a buttoned collar that stood up from the shoulders like a little circular wall.

A waiter offered Armand a plate of delicate rice balls with fish and a yellow paste arranged just so on top of them. Armand took one, placed it into his mouth whole. The burst of flavors was like nothing he'd tasted before, the salty fish melding with a spicy paste that made his eyes water. He couldn't tell if he loved it or hated it—which was exactly how he felt about Varenis.

Valentin passed him a blue drink in a long flute. "Flower-liquor."

Valentin turned and waved at a woman. She wore a dress with a cleave at its front so deep, it reached almost to her waist. She moved with a studied languor, a mannered sensuality, her hips shifting from side to side, her legs almost crossing over each other with each step. Age had eroded her glamour, so that she stood on the borderline of parody—an aging minx. A touch too much powder on the face, a little too much leg, pendulous breasts heaved up to the sky by a corset. She had the look of a woman whose beauty regime had precisely the opposite effect of what she'd intended.

"Here he is!" said Valentin to the woman. "Armand Lecroisier, grandson of Gerard!"

The woman leaned in and kissed his cheek. "I'm Valentin's wife, Olka. You'll have to forgive me. I've just been to the thaumaturgists— for my skin."

"Your skin?" She had an odd complexion, as if her face were slightly overripe and sweating.

"Yes, they can help with aging, you know—but it's expensive, of course." She turned her head coquettishly.

"Ah, there's Controller Randes—I really must speak with him." Valentin turned and walked away.

Olka pressed her lips together and eyed Armand as if he were a curious object. Her eyes roved over him. "You're a little thin, aren't you? Gangly, really. But your nose gives you a certain character." She touched him on the arm.

Around him, the world began to shift a little. The stars above them shone a brilliant white, and Olka's eyes were an emerald green he hadn't noticed before.

A waiter took Armand's empty flute and passed him another. "The Controller insists."

"Flower-liquor!" She smiled at him. "Oh, Valentin is a rascal, isn't he? Be careful with that. It breaks down the barriers in your mind!" Before Armand could mention anything, she said, "Come, let me show you something."

She led Armand through the throng. He was bustled to-and-fro as the crowd pressed around him, but Olka grabbed his hand, throwing comments left and right. "Hello, my dear" and "Oh, look at you!" and "You're always so delightful!"

She led him into a wing of the house that jutted out over the city. To each side of the corridors sat steaming baths filled with revelers holding flutes of liquor high, away from the water. The angles of the room seemed to be shifting, as if space itself were distorting. The revelers drifted away and yet somehow didn't move as the pools themselves stretched.

She led him farther on, into a circular chamber that was entirely covered by an orange-and-purple carpet of fungi. It was composed of thousands of little stems that quivered at their approach, starting with those closest to them, rippling away like the water of a pond, then rippling back and reaching out toward them. Was the carpet moving, or was it the effect of this strange flower-liquor Valentin had given him?

"Pleasure-fungi, from Taritia! You'd never believe it. Of course, this wing is a terrible luxury—all this space in a city with hardly any room for its inhabitants. But then again, why else have a husband who is a Controller?"

She looked at the circular room. "You don't even need another person. I hate to think how much time I spend in there. . . ." She looked at him lasciviously, her face leering at him like a lizard's, and then away. "Oh, you're much too young for me." She looked back at him, assessed his expression, and shook her head with finality. "You must let me introduce you to some of the women here, Armand. Believe me, you'll be exotic to them. You've got that odd little accent. You could bring them in here. . . ."

"I, really—no, I really don't think I have time."

"Oh, you're just so delightful, Armand. I could just roll you up in a blanket and carry you around with me." She touched the side of his face. "So beautiful. So lovely."

Back in the central room, Armand spied Rainer lying on a chaise longue, surrounded by a group of young and slight women whose hair was more intricately sculpted than any he had seen, and dyed unlikely colors: bright and gaudy emeralds, golds, sapphires.

"Ah, our friend from Caeli-Amur," said Rainer as Armand approached. "Let me introduce you to Yuki, Siki, Amori, and Kandi. They're Trid-Girls."

Armand nodded, though he had no idea what Trid-Girls were.

"Delightful, aren't they?" Rainer ran his hand over his bald head.

One of the Trid-Girls gave Armand a sultry look through her eyelids. Another inspected Armand curiously. He realized that despite their different-colored hair and singular intricate tattoos of geometric and fractal shapes, they were identical. The upturned noses, the chiseled cheeks, the perfect skin—they could have been identical siblings.

"Waiter!" Rainer called out. A waiter arrived and passed Armand another glass of flower-liquor. He took it, politely. He wanted to make Rainer comfortable.

"You know," Rainer said, "I don't understand you. Why haven't you sided with the belligerents? After all, they would prefer to descend on Caeli-Amur with the legions and install a new power immediately, without all these politics Valentin is planning."

Armand took a sip of the drink. "No city survives such an attack. Not really. Didn't Peroloa resist the legions, only to be burned to the ground?"

Rainer leaned forward. "The Perolese were suicidal, and their city was built of wood. At least this way, you'd have some say in the outcome. The belligerents"—Rainer nodded toward a group of men standing in the corner of the room—"might welcome you, you know. You might be their man in Caeli-Amur. Certainly not independent, but . . ."

Armand looked over at the group of tall regal suited men, more conservatively dressed than most. He thought of talking to them but interrupted the thought. Valentin was his grandfather's old friend. Loyalty—that was one of the first principles. Anyway, as

Rainer admitted, they would never allow a free Caeli-Amur, only an occupied one.

Rainer nodded. "Well, it's all a sideshow anyway."

Armand looked at the fat man. "How do you mean?"

"Why, the position of Director, dear Armand. That is the main attraction." Rainer smiled knowingly. There was something unnerving about the smile—it was the smile of a man who was safe in his position.

Armand moved to sip his drink, noticed it was already finished. Then Rainer was handing him another. It would be rude to refuse. He needed Rainer on his side. But how many had he drunk? He could barely make out the revelers' faces, which seemed like floating plates detached from their heads.

But now he was back on the balcony, looking in on the central room, where Valentin was whispering to a dark-suited man, one of the belligerents. Armand staggered back inside, but when he arrived, Valentin was gone.

The world shrank into him, so that there was no past and no future. There is only the present: a hand grasps him, pulls him aside into a narrow alcove. Before him stands the great behemoth Rainer, his cheeks both a rosy red. "Valentin: he's not to be trusted."

To Armand, it seems as if the man's face is composed of a million flowers, shifting and moving, blooming and shrinking. He tries to pull himself together, but it is no good.

"Self-interest, that's the currency of Varenis." Rainer's face flashes in prismatic color. "You think there's a central authority, and there is. There are departments. There is a rigid structure. There is a bureaucracy. But how does a bureaucracy work? Politics, that's how. You think this place is different from Caeli-Amur? It is. There is stability here that Caeli-Amur never had. We don't need violence or repression to control our population, because we have them all trapped in our complex web. There *is* no opposition here. There *cannot* be. All rivers are directed through controlled channels. They all lead to the same thing. Absorption."

"Why do you tell me these things?" To Armand, it's as if they are enclosed in their own little bubble.

The huge man shrugs. "Something you said the other night

moved me. You don't fit in here. Don't think I won't stab you in the back like anyone else. I understand chess is a popular game in Caeli-Amur: think of all this as an elaborate chess game, and you'll know where you are."

"And what piece would you be on the chessboard?"

"Me? Why, a minotaur, of course." Rainer's laughter is like a cascading waterfall.

"And me?"

"Don't be a fool." Rainer looks across the room. "I know you'd like to think of yourself as a Gorgon, but you're not."

An image of a Gorgon flashes into Armand's mind, an image from children's tales: snakes sprouting from a woman's head, roving eyes beneath, long canine teeth like those of a wolf, red with blood. The Gorgons had sided with Alerion, when the gods had warred. They were natives of Varenis, strange creatures of unfathomable motives and alien desires. He looks around and sees them now, Gorgons slipping through the party, laughing, serpents slithering terrifyingly on their heads. Blinks rapidly: no, there are no Gorgons; it is just a flower-liquor image.

"What part do they play here, the Gorgons?" asks Armand.

"They oversee practical affairs on behalf of the Sortileges, who are too busy with their research to take interest in the petty affairs of politics. So the Gorgons perform the ritual of ascension when a new man rises to Director. The Director must stare into one of their faces without trembling to show he is not afraid of the challenges that await him. The trick, they say, is not to picture yourself failing, for then you'll think of the consequences. Once *they* enter your mind . . . well, you can't help but tremble."

"What consequences?"

Rainer ignores the question. "If they approve of you, well, they say they go easy on you. Before the test and after it. They're fickle. They have favorites. Some say you can buy their favor, for the right price."

Armand grabs Rainer by the shoulders. "I have maps. I have lists of seditionists. I have something else, something even I could not imagine possessing. It's not for me, you understand. It's for the greater good. I have Alerion's prism, the prism into which he was bound as he died!"

Rainer stares at him, frozen in disbelief. Armand is filled with an uncertain feeling. He planned to keep these things secret, but some part of him wanted to share them, to say to the world, *Look!* Now, as he gazes at Rainer's face, changing with feverish curiosity, Armand realizes his terrible mistake.

"Let me introduce you to the belligerent leader, Zelik." Rainer pulls Armand toward a stooped man surrounded by a group. For a moment Armand thinks Zelik is a weeping willow, but then he is again a man, gesticulating as he speaks.

Armand shakes Rainer off, ashamed. "No! I can't. I won't."

Rainer reaches out again, and Armand slaps his hand away violently. Before Rainer can say anything, Armand rushes away into the party.

Olka presses him up against the wall. The night fragments like shards of glass—he doesn't know which piece fits where. All he knows is her hands are roving over him, touching him on the stomach, the leg, *there*. To his horror, he feels himself harden.

"Oh, you're too much. You're too much," she says.

In the center of the room, Valentin puts his arm around Armand. "Too much flower-liquor, huh? Well, I wouldn't worry. But why not have another?" He passes Armand another flute.

Later Armand vomits in the street as rain pours down around him. The street is slick with water, which courses over his hands. The rain never seems to stop in Varenis. When he looks up, he fancies he sees a figure looking down at him from an arched walkway several levels above him.

"Who are you? What do you want?" he yells. He looks down at the gray ground beneath the coursing waters. That's what he needs to hold on to, something solid. When he looks back up, the figure is gone.

When he enters his room—the walls shifting with color and light—Armand lifts up the floorboards and takes out the prism. He staggers along the corridor, to a side door that leads into the stables.

Ice, who is resting on the ground, raises his head.

"Ice." Armand places his hand on the horse's shoulders, rubs his face against the horse's neck. Armand lies down in the hay next to the creature, feeling its warmth beside him, the prism in his hand. Finally he sleeps.

When Armand returns to his room in the morning, he finds the door broken open, the mattress torn apart, the floorboards pulled up. He closes his eyes. The night before he told Rainer about the prism. This is the result. Armand curses himself. What a fool he is.

# TEN

After the break-in at the Long Rest, Armand slipped through the streets—dodging around corners, rushing up and down stairs and walkways, dashing on and off steam-trams—until he was certain he was lost in the city. He found a second rooming house, though he had kept Ice in Tedde's stable. He carried his valuables with him, including, of course, the prism. If whoever had attempted to steal it—perhaps it was the belligerents, perhaps the philosopher-assassin who had trailed him from Caeli-Amur—tried again, at least he would be prepared.

He sent a note to Valentin that he would be away for several days, but that he could be reached at the Long Rest, though he still did not tell his friend about the prism.

Valentin sent a note back, telling him to stay out of sight for a while. Three days before the ascension, when the Gorgons would confront the Controller's nomination for Director and test him in some strange ritual of nerve and will, he sent a second note. It read: *You must meet me in the Undercity immediately.*

This time, as he scurried away from the Long Rest, Armand looked back to see a group of men running toward him. Their asymmetrical haircuts bounced as they ran, their faces grim with repressed violence. The belligerent watchmen came at him like dogs slavering for a wounded animal.

Fear gripped Armand's stomach; he clenched his teeth enough for them to squeak. He found a nearby walkway. Indifferent pedestrians barely noticed as he dashed past. This time the belligerents would capture him and the prism. He would be broken in some prison or on some torture machine. The walkway ran straight and long between buildings. Several more curved above and below him.

Another group of men approached slowly and malevolently in front of him. Armand was trapped. Despairing, he looked down at the walkway below. He might leap, but he would surely die from the fall. Behind him, the first group of men rushed closer, grins fixed to some of their faces.

When a rope dropped beside him, he stared at it blankly. Looking up, he saw a figure silhouetted against the glare of the sun, itself hidden behind smog that hovered around the buildings. He grabbed the rope, wrapped it around one foot, and closed his eyes. A second later he was being winched up. He felt the vast spaces around him seem to expand. Terror gripped him. His arms and legs began to shake. He let out a whimper, then a cry, for Armand was afraid of heights. Moments later he heard the cursing of the men below him. Someone dragged him onto the walkway above. Arms grasped him, dropped him onto the ground.

A woman said, "Get out of here."

He could not stop trembling. Only after a few moments did he dare open his eyes to see a crowd of Varenisians looking at him oddly. His savior was gone.

He scrambled away and ran until he was certain he had lost his pursuers, then he caught the train to the Undercity.

Valentin waited by the fungus forest that ran by the lake. Great white treelike flora grew here, oranges and purples on the tips of their branches. As they walked, Valentin's eyes continuously darted left and right. His handsome face was now gaunt and unshaven.

Eels moved beneath the water of a lake. Armand looked out over the underground expanse to where classical buildings lined the walls of the cavern, their many-columned façades overlooking the smaller suburb rising from the cavern floor. Narrow streets cut between six-story buildings; restaurants and bars nestled around a train station. Carts and rickshaws hurried along roads and walkways rising up to the many tunnel entrances dotted around the cavern walls. Bursting from the mouth of a tunnel nearby, a train rattled across a bridge over the lake and descended toward the

THE STARS ASKEW ✲ 99

station in the middle of the suburb. Armand marveled at the place, but he had little time to wonder, for he knew things were coming to a head.

As Armand and Valentin walked through the strange underground forest, the Controller despaired. "It's over for us, Armand. We're ruined. Rainer has betrayed us. He suggested he would support me, but he is the *second-in-command* of the belligerents. Wheels within wheels, Armand. His so-called vacillation was just pretense to draw us in." Valentin grabbed the hair at the back of his head in despair. "We're ruined. Young Dominik has disappeared. Picked up two days ago."

Armand sucked in a breath. "Picked up by whom?"

"Internal Affairs, of course. Perhaps they'll release him. Perhaps he'll be sent to the camps. All those years I struggled to get to where I am, only to be thrown out now. It will be worse than Caeli-Amur. I might be sent to the camps too. Do you know what they're like? Slavery in the mines in the Etolian range, or in the freezing forests to the north. They work you until you break. Then they throw you away." He looked behind them again. "Did you see that? Did you see that shape?"

Armand looked behind him but saw only trees.

Valentin closed his eyes. "People have been following me for days."

Guilt washed through Armand. "This is my fault. I should have trusted you, but I was afraid. Here. I have something to show you."

Armand opened his bag and felt the prism, which seemed light and warm today. Gently, he lifted it out. The mist inside it seemed to have grown, to envelop the entirety of its insides. It churned quickly now, as if it knew that the future was uncertain.

Valentin gasped. "Gods, what is it?"

"It's the Prism of Alerion. The Elo-Talern gave it to House Technis's Director in Caeli-Amur. He was meant to use it to win over the thaumaturgists, but by that stage, he was a broken man. This was what the thieves were looking for at my rooming house."

Valentin took a step backward, his eyes darting. With a trembling hand he reached out to touch the prism, but the mist pulsated suddenly and he drew his hand back. "The Prism of Alerion. No, it's not possible. Is it? No."

"I assure you, it is," said Armand.

Valentin's eyes filled with a savage desire. "But how did the thieves know it existed?"

"I told Rainer."

"Rainer!" Valentin put both hands to his face. "Why did you tell Rainer?"

Armand shook his head in shame. "I thought I could win him to our side."

"Oh, this explains everything. He'd already made his decision by then. I knew it in my heart. But this changes everything. We must bring the prism to my apartment." Valentin grabbed Armand by the shoulders. "The prism is our path to power. Now we . . . . With the prism, we can win back the thaumaturgists of Caeli-Amur. Yes—they will be ours! Yes, it's perfect. We can unveil it at the ascension."

"But—the numbers will still be with the belligerents."

Valentin smiled. "Oh, at the moment, yes. But we can bypass the Controllers altogether now, approach the Gorgons themselves. I'm sure they will have an interest in this."

"Wouldn't they want the prism themselves?" asked Armand.

"We'll use that against them. We'll promise it to them some time in the future, after we've regained Caeli-Amur. Bring the prism to the ascension as proof, and there we'll have our victory over the belligerents."

Armand did not understand. "But the belligerents will still have the numbers."

"But the new Director will need to pass the Gorgon's tests." Valentin smiled slyly. "I think we may have a way now to ensure he doesn't."

As they walked back to the train station, Valentin said, "Why don't you give me the prism now? I'll take it immediately to my apartment. It will be safer there."

Armand thought about this. "I have promised myself I must keep it safe. I will bring it to the ascension, but I feel better if it's in my hands. Still, I'll collect my things and come to your apartment as you suggest. It will be safe there. Again, I'm sorry I kept it from you."

"We won't be the ones who are sorry." Valentin threw his arm around Armand. "This will be our triumph."

As they boarded the train, Armand fancied he saw a familiar figure standing at the far end of the platform: the philosopher-assassin who had been trailing him. Was it the same figure who had rescued him earlier, or was it a killer? This was the red-bearded man, he thought, not the woman who saved him. The figure seemed to be shaking his head. Armand craned his neck back through the door, but the figure was gone.

Back at the Long Rest, Armand stood in the foyer, settling affairs with Tedde, who glanced again and again at the guards from the Department of Benevolence lurking in the foyer: hulking men wearing helmets that fully enclosed their heads, grates over the mouths, eyes, and ears. Each had a miniature bolt-thrower strapped to his arm. Valentin had assured Armand he would be safe with them.

"Of course I'll take care of Ice for you," said Tedde. "Until it's time for you to return. He'll be all right with me. I've no use for the stable otherwise."

"Soon I will ensure you are able to build that restaurant you hoped for," said Armand.

Tedde laughed, embarrassed. "Oh, I don't know about that."

*Tedde is a good man,* thought Armand. A man who knew his rightful place in the world. He was the sort who held society together so that all might find happiness, whatever caste they were born into. The world needed more like him.

"But where are you going?" asked Tedde.

"To stay with the Controller of Benevolence."

"Well, I'd be wary of those sorts." Tedde eyed the guards once more. "From what I hear, it's a cruel world up there at the heights."

"He's a friend," said Armand. "A friend of my grandfather from years back."

"Well, you're welcome back here whenever you like."

Armand left with the guards. They marched him to a private

carriage: a long vehicle dragged by a separate steam engine, something like a personal steam-tram. As it took off, Armand saw the group of belligerent ruffians hulking in a side street. He was happy to see the last of them.

When Armand arrived, Valentin stood on the balcony of his apartment, overlooking the vast city. He turned and waved, a smile breaking out like sun from behind a cloud. Armand joined him, looking at the insectlike figures on the walkways beneath them, the trains periodically bursting from tunnels, climbing over high bridges, disappearing once more.

"You are worried about the ascension," said Armand. The thought of it oppressed him, too. The ceremony would occur in the Room of Pools. All the Controllers would attend, as would a circle of dignitaries, men and women of industry, foreign leaders, bureaucrats from the Departments, Armand himself. The chosen member of the council—in this case the leader of the belligerents, Zelik—would step forward for his trial. He would need to look into the Gorgon's face without flinching. Visions of the scene leaped into Armand's mind, each one worse than the one before.

Valentin nodded. "The Gorgons have agreed Zelik will fail. Then I will claim the right to become Director. All we must do is show them the prism. Later we will allow them to use it once, under supervision. But we will need to assert our ownership of it," said Valentin. "You have it with you, yes? Yes, of course. But there is so much that could go wrong. I could still fail the Gorgon's test. Possession of the prism is no guarantee against that. Then you'll be on your own. I wouldn't trust Dominik—he's been released, you know. He's full of ambition."

"You will be strong. Think of all the years you've spent leading up to this moment. Think of all the sacrifices. All the actions you've had to take. Some noble. Others pragmatic."

"All the betrayals . . ." Valentin stared over the city as if the past were being conjured before him now. He broke from his reverie. "Come, let us eat. Then sleep, in preparation for tomorrow."

That night Armand awoke to a form standing at the doorway of his room. He started and sat up, fear running through him. Had the belligerents sent their agents to raid the apartment? Perhaps it was Internal Affairs.

The form stepped quietly into the room. "It's just me."

"Olka, what are you doing?"

She ran her hands over his chest gently.

"I can't— Valentin."

"Oh, he doesn't mind. He's asleep." Olka's hands touched him, leaving little trails of fire across his skin. He shuddered at the intensity of it.

Olka whispered in his ear. "I know what men like. I know how to make them shiver."

Armand felt himself harden, against his best wishes. Her hands strayed beneath the sheets, over his stomach, and lower. No, he didn't want this.

In the darkness, she was only a shadow, a hint of movement.

"Please. Valentin is my friend."

"He would want you to." Her hands felt him, now aroused. "He can't satisfy me anymore. He lets me do whatever I want. Anyway, after the ascension, you'll be too busy for me. You'll forget me, leave me trapped here in this apartment. This might be our only chance."

Armand was breathing faster now.

"Come. I can't do this here. There's somewhere more exciting." She pulled him up, led him along the corridor to the circular room, and pulled him down onto the quivering pleasure-fungi that rippled around them. Armand could not help himself, for now he was driven by the urges of his body, which pushed all thoughts of consequences away. The orange-and-purple carpet moved beneath them, gently massaging their bodies, pressing into their flesh like a thousand tiny caressing hands.

Olka whispered to him, "Oh, you're just too much, Armand. You're just too perfect. Such a pity, such a pity." All the while the carpet rose and fell. At first, bits of the fungi broke off and slithered over them, rejoining itself on the other side, until it covered them totally, like a blanket. Armand's body was overwhelmed with sensations it could scarcely assimilate. If felt as if their skins were connected to each other through the carpet, and Armand's senses expanded and lost their form. He became one with Olka, somehow.

He could feel the pleasure and desire coursing through her, and yet the feelings were his.

"You're too much," she said. "Such a pity. Such a pity."

Armand halfheartedly picked at his breakfast in the morning. At any other time he would have devoured the delicate strips of seaweed and meat, but the bulk of it remained untouched. Valentin didn't even bother with his.

When Olka had eaten her breakfast, she turned to Valentin. "I'm just ravenous this morning. I can't say why." She smiled almost imperceptibly. "You don't mind if I try yours?"

Valentin pushed his plate across to her and looked at Armand. For a split second his face seemed to crack, revealing a cold-eyed and desolate one underneath. Then it was gone, and the kind old one returned. *Valentin must be terrified by the thought of the Gorgons,* he thought.

Valentin said, "Afterward, Armand, I'll meet you in my office. We'll plan things from there. Perhaps you should go to Caeli-Amur as an ambassador for our plans."

Armand nodded. "A good idea."

Some hours later the Ritual of Ascent began. A grand passage led beneath the great plaza to a large subterranean hall, the Room of Pools. They marched in in solemn procession. The meeting of Controllers had occurred earlier in the day. It had been a formality: Zelik was nominated for the position of Director.

Armand and several hundred others filed toward the seats, which ran in concentric circles around the room. The wide circular hall magnified the merest sounds of the crowd as they moved nervously in the outer seats. At the room's center, a dark pool of water surrounded a small marble island connected to the rest of the room by a thin walkway. The place was lit by patterns of lichen on the domed roof, which threw off unusual colors: greens and purples, slowly changing and shifting. Pearl-flowers dangled on long stems from the roof, like clusters of little stars throwing off brilliant white light.

Valentin and the Controllers stood in formation at the end of the walkway. Valentin directed Armand to a seat close to him.

When all were seated, the pearl-flowers seemed to dim, and a soft rumbling sound rose from deep below.

"It's time," someone said as the willowy belligerent leader, Zelik, walked carefully onto the island. He stood in his closely cut black suit, looking every bit a Director: calm, prepared. He threw his head back, called to the ceiling, "Gorgons, I have come to announce my claim for the position of Director." The sound of his voice resonated in the perfectly shaped room. It joined the rumbling sound, filling Armand with dread. Slowly, the sounds died away, leaving an ominous silence.

A moment later the perfectly flat waters in the pool began to churn. Something moved beneath, rising slowly and ominously. The room was filled with tension. Members of the crowd shifted uncomfortably, the sound of their rustling amplified. The waters roiled more, now in three distinct parts of the pool. Armand could see a form beneath the water in the disturbance closest to him.

A head broke through the surface, and an icy fear ran through Armand. He wanted to move but could not. Instead he stared as water flowed from the slippery scales of the gray serpents that sprouted from the head of the Gorgon. The writhing of the snakes drove terror into his chest: the way they wrapped around one another, curling in and out, now showing their white bellies, now flicking out red forked tongues. From the water, three of them emerged, surrounding the island, stepping gently up to the island's shore. Armand's eyes flittered from one to the other. He caught a glimpse of their eyes, the elliptical pupils horizontal, like a goat's; their powerful musculature; the claws at the end of their hands.

Above, the pearl-flowers retreated up into themselves, leaving the room darker still.

Around Zelik the Gorgons circled, in some intricate dance. The Controller kept his head, but Armand could see his chest rising and falling rapidly, and knew that the man must have been caught in the vise of fear, just as he was.

One of the Gorgons, this one with a wide flat face, stopped before Zelik, turned to face him head on. At that critical moment time seemed to slow to a crawl. Silence reigned in the cavern.

Zelik began to shudder, just barely discernibly.

The Gorgon leaned in closer to him, face-to-face, and the snakes leaned forward and slithered over Zelik's head, engulfing him. The belligerent leader grabbed the Gorgon by the arms. His thin body shook unnaturally, his entire face hidden by the covering of serpents. Its face was pressed against his now in some horrific kiss. More and more Zelik's body shook, until finally he fell backward, blood pouring from his mouth in gushes. Armand thought he saw the bloody stump of Zelik's tongue flittering around in his mouth. But then Armand's focus shifted to the Gorgon, standing above the Controller, blood dribbling over its chin. It grimaced in intense joy, showing its canine teeth. It turned to look across at the congregation of Controllers and officials. For a moment Armand fancied it looked meaningfully at Valentin.

Everything sped up again. Valentin stepped across to Armand, his face gripped by some kind of desperation. "The prism. Give me the prism."

Armand brought the prism forth from his bag, and Valentin held it before himself, stepped across the walkway to the Gorgons. "Zelik has failed to pass the test. Hence I stake my claim as Director." Now he stood before the Gorgon and looked into its face. There was a slight smile twitching on its lips. It seemed to whisper something to him.

"As a gesture of goodwill, I give you the Prism of Alerion." Valentin passed the Gorgon the object, whose misty insides seemed to burst into excited activity. "Use it wisely. Use it well."

The Gorgon leaned in to Valentin, smiled. Within seconds the Gorgons were dancing around Valentin, who stood beaming at their center, raising his hand in triumph as the chamber resonated with the chant of his name. "Valentin! Valentin!"

Armand drooped involuntarily to one side. What had just happened? He stumbled to his feet, fell backward to the floor. Valentin had given away the prism—the realization smashed into Armand like a catapult stone.

Events moved at a strange pace: drawing out like some never-ending dream, then lurching forward crazily like some out-of-control machine. Armand's mind was a tumult. Like a churning river, thoughts coursed around one another, washed one another away. He found himself staggering along with the rest of the procession, back along the walkway beneath the plaza. Excited discussions seemed to burst into the air around him.

Two helmeted guards grabbed him by the elbows and helped him along. "You're sick, sir. We'll bring you back to the Department."

They left him in Valentin's office, looking over the plaza, and he tried to assess the scale of Valentin's betrayal. He rehearsed what he would say, ran over it again and again. And yet, deep down he felt his vulnerability and helplessness. What did he have now that would protect him? At least he was insignificant. There would be little point in punishing him.

When Dominik entered the room, followed once more by guards with the grated helmets, Armand remained still. "Where's Valentin?"

"I am the new Controller of Benevolence. Valentin is Director, don't you know?"

The suited men continued to walk toward Armand, who tensed.

"Valentin said to meet him here. Will he be here shortly?" Armand was disturbed by the cruel smile on Dominik's face.

"I think he just might," said Dominik.

"I'm here, I'm here," came Valentin's voice. When he stepped into view, his face gleamed with victory.

"Valentin . . ." Armand's words failed him. He had rehearsed what he would say, but it scattered along with his hope.

Valentin crossed his arms. "Now, Armand, it's time for a bit of truth, isn't it? Yes, a good dose of truth. See, Armand, I hated your grandfather."

"You loved him," said Armand.

"It was his idea to make the assault on the villa. I told him no. I tried to stop it. It was madness. Of course, workers will kill their hostages. What other power did they have but the power of preemptive revenge? But your grandfather wouldn't listen. No, he had the arrogance of the elite, you know. He thought he knew better than everyone. But when it went bad, he tried to blame it on me. On me! Where were his precious principles then? Where was the truth and loyalty, Armand?"

In a softer, broken voice, Armand repeated, "You loved him."

Valentin's birthmark deepened in color. His handsome face was barely recognizable now. "It didn't matter. We were both thrown onto the streets. I was exiled from Caeli-Amur, but he was allowed to stay. I kept my thoughts to myself, but I promised one day I'd have my revenge, and now I have, Armand."

"But why?"

"I considered ruining you from the first, but you gave those little hints about the prism. I sent my guards to raid your hotel, but it wasn't there, was it? But I bided my time, and now, this. Do you know how sweet revenge is? It's a return to order. The universe must be brought back into balance, mustn't it? Yes, it must."

Armand's mind was racing. He tried to gather his thoughts, but they rushed at him from all angles, like wasps protecting their nest. Only when the suited men were next to Armand did he realize the terrible extent of events. A second later a hood was over his head. Strong arms grasped him. He was forced into a jacket of some sort, its long sleeves strapped around him, pressing his arms to his side. He didn't cry out—there was no dignity in that. Instead as he was led away, he was filled with a despair as black as the night. Tight-lipped, he held his nerve, not allowing the bitter emotions to well out of him. *Poor Ice,* he thought. *Left in the stable at the Long Rest. At least you have Tedde to look after you.*

# ELEVEN

Maximilian watched as Aya bought a sturdy horse, complete with bridle, saddle, and saddlebags. He watched as Aya purchased bags full of spiced bread and dried meats, and he watched as Aya picked out a long knife and scabbard, which he strapped around his waist. He watched Aya buy blankets, then watched as Aya rode south from Caeli-Amur, out past the walls and the scattered slums pushed up against them. Indeed, he could do nothing but watch, a disembodied soul lost in his own body, a body someone else used now. He struggled to hold on to something in there, some control of his functions, but it was like grasping mist. So he lurked in the basement of his own mind, a creature dispossessed and raging. At times he fell into that basement filled with defeat. At other times he schemed to take back his functions, though he wasn't sure how or when he would. The feeling of powerlessness was complete.

The best he could do was see and hear, and absorb whatever stray thoughts and feelings Aya let drift away. So he knew they were riding southwest, toward the ancient city of Lixus. Once, the Sentinel Tower had been hidden in the mountains to the north of Lixus.

From a low rise, they looked down on the water-parks to their left, their magnificent gardens crisscrossed with canals, dotted with white marble statues rumored to move around at night. The main road headed south to the fishing villages that ran along the coast. Another, more ancient, road ran southwest, into the rolling green hills. Here Aya stopped for a moment, confused.

*The old ruined road—that's the one to Lixus, isn't it?* Aya said.

—You expect me to tell you?

Max remained silent. He sensed Aya dredging through his own

memories, but they were fragmented things, and the land had changed.

In frustration, Aya kicked the horse, and they took the southwest road, through the rolling hills and glorious villas overlooking the fields and vineyards below. Greenhouses dotted the land in between lines of olive trees, and laborers worked on orchards. Others moved through the more exotic fields of furnace trees, candle-flowers, and fire-roses, which, clearly at the end of their reproductive cycle, had burst into flame some time earlier, leaving only the blackened remnants of their flowers.

These flora had once been destined for the Arantine, or else exported to the voracious Varenis, the Dyrian coast, or even across the sea to Numeria. Now nothing was heading up to Caeli-Amur, and Max saw the workers piling bags and barrels into storehouses.

Soon enough they came to a barricade built from sturdy logs and broken farm implements. To one side it pressed up against a hedge; to the other, a stone wall. Rough-clothed rural workers milled around, chatting quietly; a small fire burned to one side, thin smoke floating up at an angle, carried by gentle winds. The golden sun glinted off several swords and spears, but most of the workers held pitchforks and rakes. A gap between the barricade through which travelers might pass looked like it could be easily closed. They were prepared for violence, it seemed.

One of the men spat ul-tree root on the ground as Aya approached. "Escaping Caeli-Amur, huh? They starving up there yet?"

"That's what you'd like, isn't it?" said Aya.

Several more of the ramshackle force milled around, eyeing Aya suspiciously.

"What I'd like is for them to pay us for the grain, for the work we do. We used to get at least some recompense, you know, but now—nothing. We need boots, coats—winter is coming, but the factories aren't producing much back in the city, are they? They sure ain't sending anything down here. Now, the question is, what do *you* want, mister?"

"I'm headed south."

"Ain't nothing south, mister, unless you plan on heading all the way to the Teeming Cities." The man took another bite of ul-tree root, which he held in his hand like a stick.

"There's Lixus."

"Suppose that's true. There's even an Arbor outpost down there, you know, but we ain't heard nothing from them." The man laughed and spat out the ul-tree root again, leaving a black stain on the ground. "You wanna pass, it'll be five florens."

—That's highway robbery—said Max.

Aya tossed him the coins and rode through the suspicious group. Farther on, he found a fine roadhouse in which to stay, with polished floors and delicate wines served in grand crystal glasses. The food was cheap, for there was plenty of it here among the villas, and the conversation of the former House agents, who came down from their villas for the evening, revolved around the crisis: How long would Caeli-Amur last before they capitulated? The entire population of the area—rich and poor alike—seemed committed to the blockade.

*Seems even the poor are going to betray your seditionists,* said Aya.

—Just because you're poor doesn't mean you're on the right side—said Max.

There were plenty back in the city who identified with the Houses, worshipped them. They hung pictures of the Directors on their walls, read gossip about the parties and soirees. It was their little taste of glamour, of a better life.

*That's not what's happening here. They have real concerns. You heard the man at the barricade. They need boots. They need coats.*

—We all have to make sacrifices.

*Well, that's convincing.* Aya laughed. *I'm sure they'll be happy to hear that when winter comes in. It's not long now, is it, before the biting cold.*

The following day the landscape began to change. Fewer and fewer villas dotted the hills or shaded the valleys. In places, rocky ridges had driven up from the ground. They formed yellowish cliffs that blocked any passage. The land became wilder, and copses of ancient wiry trees became more frequent. Great beds of vines covered the ground and crept over decaying walls.

*We should be closer to the coast. Have we gone the wrong way?* As Aya spoke, a fragment of his memories sank down to Max. The image of Lixus, its towers and minarets packed closely together, formed from gleaming white marble. They rose high into the blue sky, walkways gracefully curving between them. There, white toga-wearing figures promenaded, debating the latest developments of philosophy. The wondrous harbor was packed with silver-sailed boats, some heading out over the whitecaps of the azure sea. The sun was sinking over the western horizon, the sky on fire with streams of crimson and orange and vermillion, bending and wavering. The beauty of it struck Max deeply; he marveled at the world of the ancients once again.

But with the memory came needles of pain, driving into his mind. The headaches became stronger the closer he felt his mind come to Aya's. He noticed Aya pulling back with the same discomfort.

*Remember, this journey is for your own good. We'll return the Core of the Tower to the Aediles, free you from my body, and we will find happiness in our own way,* said Aya.

Aya may have gained control of Max's body, but he was still an outsider in this country, a fact that gave Max limited power. Max could use it to his advantage, and he hoped the surprises in store would allow him to seize back his body. That was his only option, for the thought of Aya "freeing" Max from his own body wasn't one he liked contemplating.

By the third day after leaving Caeli-Amur, the villas had been left behind, and the road had become rough and worn. Few people passed this way, if any. The rugged ridges had become more common, and they were covered with wild wiry trees and thick bushes.

In the afternoon they spotted a lonely figure walking with the aid of a staff far along the road. Soon the man came into closer view. He wore a simple blue robe tied at the waist, and a thick bandage wrapped many times around his eyes—a member of the Order of the Sightless. A small bag was thrown over his shoulder, probably containing the barest essentials, for most apocalyptics lived ascetic lives. Material possessions were denials of the coming disaster, which would sweep so much away. By denying themselves such goods, they were saying the apocalypse would make all such concerns obsolete.

Hearing the sound of the approaching hoof falls, the figure stopped and waited. As they drew level, Aya stopped the horse, looked down at the figure curiously.

"I have no valuables, stranger." The figure stared straight ahead but seemed to be listening closely. "I am a pilgrim, headed for the Teeming Cities."

"You'll have to pass through Lixus first. It's not too far from here," said Aya.

"Yes, I suppose that's true." The Pilgrim's voice was calm, unruffled.

"Well, we may as well continue on together for a while. The company I've had until now has been pretty awful." Aya kicked the horse, which headed off slowly beside the Pilgrim. "The sooner we arrive, the sooner we can relax in comfort."

"I guess that's true. An officiate rules the place: a strong man named Karol," said the Pilgrim. "I knew him once."

"Oh, there's some luck. It's good to find friends after a long journey. Were you close to this Karol?"

The Pilgrim reached out and placed a hand on the horse's hide. He seemed to like the warmth, or the feeling of the beast moving. "I worked with him at Arbor, before the overthrow of the Houses. I had been a subofficiate in charge of the gardens. Karol was a star then, on the rise. He was Director Lefebvre's favorite, so he didn't bother much with me. Still, he liked to come out into the gardens to think. Sometimes I met him there, because it was my job to water the plants and feed them when necessary. I tended the great theater built from vines and furnace trees too. But my favorites were the blood-orchids, though you'd do well to beware their lashing petiole. Like a whip, it is. They would drag you close, if they could, and suck you of blood and organs. They were planted in their very own garden, behind the palace. When I arrived, they would lean toward me, as if they wanted to step from the earth and greet me. They couldn't, of course. I loved those plants, you know. You come to know them, and when you speak to them, they respond. Some of them let out little trills. Others are quieter, but they grow under your careful care. When you speak to them, they grow a little more lustrous. They are sensitive creatures, see—like people, in that way. I think Karol understood that. Of course, this was before things changed."

"Nothing lasts forever, does it?" Aya's tone was suddenly melancholy.

"You're right friend, nothing does. Ruination came. When the people stormed the Arbor Palace, they trampled the candle-flowers and tore them from the walls. They stomped on the vines with no care at all. They hacked at the tear-flowers in the garden. They piled the portraits into a bonfire. I begged them not to. I fell to my knees before them, and they struck me down. The apocalyptics had been right: we are at the end of things. Our only hope is to fall prostrate, to recognize our insignificance, to give up our petty interests and desires, to beg forgiveness from the universe. This is the message I will bring to the Teeming Cities. I shall spread word of the coming apocalypse."

Max felt uncomfortable at the story, which rattled against his convictions, challenged his views. But history wasn't perfect. People searching for a pure revolt, morally clean, without compromises, were pedants who wanted nothing at all. Still, it was painful to hear.

"You hope to convince them that the world will suffer another cataclysm?" said Aya to the Pilgrim.

"Convince? No. I don't think they will listen. Like everywhere, in the Teeming Cities people are caught up in the needs of everyday life, their little affairs. It narrows their vision, like blinkers on a horse."

The joker god returned. "That's the spirit."

The apocalyptic nodded earnestly. "Sometimes you do what you must."

They continued in silence for a while, the sounds of the horse's hooves falling on the uneven road, the wind softly brushing Aya's face, the smell of the wild in the air. Far away, Max thought he heard a sound: a soft booming, carried on the air. But as he strained to hear, the sound drifted away.

"And you?" said the Pilgrim. "Why do you travel south?"

"My love lived there once. Out in the wilderness. I'm going to see her resting place."

"Brave, to live out in the wild alone."

"She could take care of herself, believe me," said Aya.

In a copse of trees nestled in the elbow of two hills, something moved. At first, there was just a flitter in the darkness, then the leaves on a bush rustled, then all was still. Aya seemed unfazed, and the Pilgrim was of course unaware.

—Did you see that?—said Max.

Aya didn't even bother to answer, and Max's imagination began to run wild. There were all kinds of animals in these hills: mountain lions and brown bears, and yet more frightening creatures.

—You should offer to take him to Lixus, at least—said Max. —Show him you have a heart. He needs our help, for he cannot see, and it's not safe out here.

*His sufferings are self-imposed. He could take the bandage from his eyes. In any case, his concerns are not mine.*

—Is this always the final effect of the use of the prime language then? That you become nothing but selfish?

Aya was silent, and Max knew he had hit home. He caught a glimpse of an entire complex of Aya's memories and feelings: the increasing distance from life caused by the Art, the slow alienation of the Magi from one another, the resulting wars, the grief at the loss of their perfect world, and, most cruelly, Aya's increasing distance from Iria: their fragmented conversations, their cross-purposes.

*You're not much fun, you know,* said Aya.

This time Max didn't respond. He preferred to let his words settle into Aya, and the mage retreated into himself, processing Max's accusations slowly. Max sensed Aya was conflicted about his attitude toward the world, like someone who had lost something important that they barely recall.

Finally Aya said, "Pilgrim, won't you ride behind me? We'll reach Lixus together a little quicker."

—So you have a heart after all—said Max.

A moment later the Pilgrim tilted his head up toward Aya, as if looking at him. Dried blood ran like thick tear trails down his cheeks. Beneath the bandages, the blood was brighter, still glistening softly.

"Pilgrim, your eyes." Aya stared in shock.

"Burned out, but somehow they were not properly cauterized. They are infected, I fear."

"That's barbaric, to deprive someone of their sight," said Aya.

"No, you misunderstand. I did it to myself. One must show one holds to one's ideas with certainty and commitment."

The horse and the Pilgrim both halted once more, as if some understanding had passed between them. After staring a little more, Aya stepped down to the dusty ground and helped the Pilgrim into the saddle. "Let me ride behind you. That would be best."

When the horse began to walk again, Max thought he saw movement in another copse of trees. Something was watching them.

# TWELVE

Evening was falling, casting long rays of gold over the rugged hills. Shadows deepened between the copses of trees. Stringy trees curled up over the road, like ancient twisted men reaching for the sky. Thick bushes clumped together on the slopes around them, blocking much of their view. But Max knew something was out there. He'd seen it several times from the corner of his eye, first in the scrub to the left of them, then flitting through trees to their right. They were just glimpses, for Aya still controlled his head and eyes. Max was uncertain of what to do. He needed to launch an assault on Aya, to take back control of his body, and the creature in the woods might provide an opportunity. But it would be no use if the thing tore his body to shreds.

—There's something out there—said Max.—Did you see it in those bushes on the hill?

Aya glanced to his right. *You're a worrier. Did you know that?*

The Pilgrim halted suddenly, and Aya brought the horse to a standstill.

"Did you hear something?" the Pilgrim said.

Aya pulled on the horse's reins, looked over his shoulder. "No."

Then it came again, echoing between the hills, a rumbling report. It might have been thunder, or it might have been a rockfall. That was it: the sound drifting on the wind that Max had heard earlier. It seemed closer now.

"I think it was an explosion. There, to the north." The Pilgrim gestured past the ridges and hills, toward the Etolian range, which rose up, snow still capping its highest peaks.

At that moment a creature burst into view, its powerful legs driving toward them, one of its three horrid dog's heads raising up, fixing them with a stare from the corner of one mad eye. The central head jutted forward, baring its yellow teeth, drool dripping as it ran. Meanwhile, the third head was lowered to the ground, as if following a scent. For an instant Max took in the horror of the beast in stunned silence, for there was an otherworldliness to it, as if it had been summoned from the gates of the underworld itself. Each head possessed not two but four eyes, the second two above and behind the first. It seemed like a bear-sized dog, but no dog Max had ever seen: its fangs were too long and cruel. There was something of a lizard to it; its fur gave way to gray scales as its powerful tail tapered off.

—Gods!—cried Max. —It's a Cerberus. Ride! Ride!

The horse reared up, and the Pilgrim slid back against Aya, who crashed to the ground behind it. Pain drove up Aya's back. The Pilgrim came down on top of them as the horse galloped off, its hooves throwing dust into the air.

By the time the Pilgrim and Aya dragged themselves to their feet, the thing was almost on them, its body a ball of terrifying muscle.

The Pilgrim held his staff out in front of him, but it would be no match for the savage creature. The knife in Aya's hand felt tiny and ineffectual.

With mesmerizing power, the Cerberus leaped into the air. In an instant the monster would crash onto them, rend them with its terrible claws, tear at them with its slavering teeth.

Then there was a burst of sounds, somewhere between the *ffft* of an arrow and the striking of wood on wood. In rapid fire, one after another, bolts plunged into the side of the Cerberus, even as it slammed down on Aya. One of the heads howled in pain, twisted around to look at the five figures rushing out of the bushes behind it. A second head lunged down at Aya, who dropped his knife and grasped the powerful neck, holding the head only inches away. The third head, growling fearfully, twisted and snapped at the blows from the Pilgrim's staff.

Then Max was aware of nothing but the yellow fangs, the red gums, the terrible smell of death coming from the creature's gaping mouth. Reverberations from thudding bolts ran through the

Cerberus's body and into Aya's arms. He looked up into the four eyes of the dog's head. The front two stared straight into his. The others—above and behind the first pair—fixed his from an angle, giving the thing a monstrously insane air.

Aya struggled for equations, but he couldn't grasp them; they were driven away by terror.

The Cerberus's head gave a final thrust, spittle striking Aya's face. The jaws snapped out. Hot breath warmed his face. Inch by inch the creature came closer, then a milkiness clouded the four eyes. The back two lost focus, rotated up and away from Aya. More thudding reverberations, a sudden warmth on his legs, and the Cerberus collapsed onto him, its strength drained.

Aya's breath was crushed from his body. He tried to pull himself out from beneath the beast, but the thing was too large, too heavy. Pain shot up his leg as one foot was twisted against the ground. He tried to draw a breath, struggled to take in the air.

"Get it off me. I can't breathe." Aya's voice sounded panicky, disturbed, not just by the creature but at his inability to fight it. He was a great mage, wasn't he? And yet the equations had fled from him.

Max heard the coughing of an engine, and one of the figures approached. He hadn't noticed it before, but the figure was encased in a strange metallic exoskeleton, a metal birdlike thing powered by engines strapped to his back. Steam and smoke coughed up into the air behind him. The man rolled the creature off Aya, and he could breathe once more.

When he had gathered himself, Aya got to his knees and looked at the dead Cerberus. "I knew we should never have grown those things. Stupid idea."

Five New-Men looked down at him, one standing in an exoskeleton. Like all New-Men, they were slim and slight. They looked like bandits, hands on hips, bolt-throwers—chunky contraptions with short barrels—held across their bodies or down by their sides. Everything about them—the dirty clothes, the shaggy hair—suggested toughness, but this was offset by their diminutive size.

"Whatever are you talking about?" said one of the five. Max realized she was a woman, her shaggy hair and boyish looks belying the fact that she was clearly a leader.

"He says strange things. I wouldn't worry about it," said the Pilgrim. "By the rapidity of your speech, I'm guessing you're men from Tir-Aki."

The New-Men glanced at one another quickly. "Very good."

Their leader looked at the fading horizon, then back to the dead Cerberus. "We'd better set up camp. Maybe a bit down the road, though. This thing's going to stink before long."

"Oh, it stinks already, I assure you." Aya wiped the thing's spittle off his face.

Soon the fire was crackling, and the leader of the Tir-Akians, whose name was Kari, settled down to talk to Aya and the Pilgrim. She laid out a thin silk shift in front of her and began to dismantle her bolt-thrower to clean it. Max was fascinated to see the inner workings of the mechanism, comprised of a compression chamber, a cartridge containing thirty bolts, and internal pins and wheels. He'd seen new automatic bolt-throwers in Caeli-Amur, but this was more complex than those.

Elsewhere, another New-Man adjusted things on the exoskeleton. "Why do I always have to tune it?"

"Because you're the one who gets to wear it," said two others in unison.

The New-Men were renowned for their innovative technology. Max thought of Quadi, his New-Man friend who had helped him construct the air-cart Max used in his journey to the Sunken City. What had happened to Quadi? He'd been gone by the time Max returned from Caeli-Enas.

"We were tracking that beast for a week. Whenever we got close, it sensed us and slipped away. Until it started hunting you, and we could finally catch up with it."

"Why were you tracking it?" said the Pilgrim.

"The creature took seven of our men out in the mountains." Kari gestured into the darkness. "We were sent to kill it so the workers would be safe."

"Workers, out there in the mountains?" said the Pilgrim. "What are you doing?"

"Building a railroad, of course. Straight through the mountains, to Caeli-Amur."

No one said anything until Aya asked, "But why?"

"Progress." The little woman's face lit up with excitement. "The adventure of development. To build new wonders. To change the world."

"That sounds awful," said Aya.

Kari shrugged. "We *are* Tir-Akians, you know. Anyway, the Prince of Tir-Aki has thrown his weight behind the railroad. He wants to see it finished before long. Where are you headed?"

"To the Teeming Cities," said the Pilgrim. "I have spiritual work to do there."

Kari frowned, began to reassemble her bolt-thrower. "Such a strange idea, the spirit. Do you really think there is something other than the material?"

"It's a metaphor," said the Pilgrim. "But the material world won't help you when the next cataclysm comes. At that point, your railroad will be thrown into the air, torn apart. Your machines will fall to the earth. Their gears will grind until they no longer work."

Kari gave a bemused frown.

"Don't worry," said Aya. "He's always like this. Probably would have been better if you'd let the Cerberus tear him to shreds."

"You would have missed me," said the Pilgrim.

Aya and Kari both laughed. It seemed the Pilgrim had a sense of humor after all.

In the morning they watched as the Tir-Akians left the road for the journey north into the mountains, where the railway was being built. Aya and the Pilgrim continued. Low foothills ran to their right, along the southeastern side of the Etolian range. Behind them the mountains rose up high, their peaks always capped with white. As they journeyed on, the Pilgrim spoke much of Caeli-Amur and its fate. Aya listened eagerly, grasping at the details, attempting to reconstruct the city's and world's histories. The Pilgrim indulged him for some time, then said, "Did you never receive any education, stranger?"

Aya said, "I come from a foreign country where they do things differently. Everything seems new and strange here."

"I sense a deep purpose to you."

"How can you be sure you will reach these Teeming Cities?" said Aya. "We barely survived one attack. Without the New-Men, we would both be dead. The wilderness is a dangerous place."

"Not as dangerous as Caeli-Amur," said the Pilgrim. "Out here, the threats are clear and obvious. Back there, everything is hidden. It always has been. When the Houses were overthrown, the seditionists claimed they would build a fairer new world. One of the seditionist leaders, Georges, made me lead him through the Arbor Palace and evaluate each of the objects there. In the north wing of the palace, hanging over the lake, he has a treasury he set up, filled with goods he clearly planned to steal. He was already buying town houses in the city, accumulating a private fortune. Not once did I see evidence of this new world they were promising."

Again these truths rattled against Max's beliefs. The mention of Georges sparked the memory of that strange empty pleasure palace beneath the mountain, where he had seen him with a second figure. Both were headed toward the Elo-Talern. *Who was Georges accompanying and what was he doing?* Max wondered.

Aya nodded. "Power corrupts. I have seen it myself. I myself have felt the lure and pull of that fool's gold. Alerion felt it too, and he capitulated."

"Alerion? The god?" The Pilgrim was confused.

"He wasn't always a shit, you know," said Aya.

—You were friends!—said Max. —You and Iria and Alerion together. You were close!

"Well, I wouldn't go that far. Iria liked him more than I did," said Aya aloud.

"What?" said the Pilgrim, now thoroughly puzzled.

—No wonder the war was so bitter—said Max. —No wonder you're so cold-blooded. There's nothing worse than the betrayal of someone close to you.

"There's nothing worse than listening to you and your amateur speculations," said Aya.

"Who are you talking to?" said the Pilgrim.

"Oh, just another little shit," said Aya. "Kind of like a memory you can't get rid of. But all memories fade in the end. Then they're forgotten."

# THIRTEEN

The garrulous Thom had vanished into the ether, and despite
scouring the Quaedian for several days, Kata and Rikard had found
no traces of him. Kata pictured him squirrelled away in his garret,
afraid of his enemies, afraid of what he knew, waiting for the Insurgent Assembly.

She pieced together what she knew: the Technis official Armand
had escaped to Varenis with the Prism of Alerion, said to contain
the dying spirit of the god. Aceline and Thom must have discovered the letter in the Technis Complex. Thom was supposed to
meet her at the Opera, but he had missed the rendezvous. Terrified of whatever else he'd discovered, he sent Kata with the letter
to the baths. There Aceline was meant to show it to the thaumaturgists as evidence that there was a conspiracy afoot. Meanwhile,
the thaumaturgists knew someone had been stealing funds from the
Marin coffers and smuggling them through the canals beneath
the city. To whom? And what was the dark truth Thom would reveal
at the Assembly?

Kata could ask Henri to find Thom, but she wanted the boy to
have a better life than the one she had grown up in. She remembered the brutality of her days on the streets. So instead she asked
another urchin, a young girl called Rikki, to find him. The whole
time Kata had felt the guilt of it: to protect one child and not another, was that what it was to be a parent in the world? Something
had changed within her. No longer could she treat lives in the same
cold and calculating fashion she'd been used to. When Rikki returned, she said there was a boy in the Quaedian who Thom had
sometimes used—a boy called Pol—but Pol had disappeared. Kata

told Rikki to stop searching. She couldn't bear the thought of her disappearing too.

As she mulled it over in her apartment, Henri said, "I know Pol. I could find him."

"If Rikki couldn't, then neither could you." Kata tried to convince herself.

"I could, you know. I know where he hides. I know everything." Henri broke into his unstoppable cough, which Kata decided she finally had to act on.

She led him through the factory district and toward the apothecary on Boulevarde Karlotte. Morning fog hung over the city and showed no sign of lifting. They climbed up the cold alleyways and stairs, past half-empty and barely functioning factories. Varenis now refused to trade with anyone who traded with Caeli-Amur. This had immediately closed off all imports and exports to the Dyrian coast, Numeria, the Northerners. Now bedraggled workers lurked around their former workplaces by habit, as if they might find their machines miraculously repaired. Others lay empty, ghostly remnants of industry in the hovering gloom.

Henri grumbled, "Don't need no apothecary."

Kata threw her arm around the boy's shoulders and pulled him toward her. "Years on the street. We need to have that cough checked out."

Henri pushed her away. "Don't. Anyway, it's you who should see the apothecary, what with you having fits."

"That's something I've had for years," said Kata. "You know I drink a preparation for that."

A group of urchins darted toward them from a side alley. They moved like a flock of birds, sensing one another's positions and adjusting their scurrying as they went. Several of them broke away from the main body, rejoined. Kata tensed briefly at the sight of them, for she knew their sly smiles were just as likely to hide deadly intent.

"Henri," said a girl of about twelve years old, evidently the leader of the group. Her shoulder-length hair was lank and almost a gray color. "Aceline's been murdered by the Houses. People are all worked up. There's a big mob marching on the Arantine. Going to be good pickings up there."

Henri took a little step away from Kata; she sensed his embarrassment at being caught with a mother figure.

The girl turned to one of the other urchins, a boy of about six with a dirty face and red hair who was pissing against the wall. She snarled in disapproval, revealing a crooked line of teeth in her pretty but severe face. The boy backed away, still pissing, as the girl turned back to Henri. "Who's this?"

"My friend Kata," Henri said.

"You want to come?" said the girl.

Henri took a few steps toward the group but was halted by Kata's quickly grabbing his arm.

"We've got somewhere to go, Henri," Kata said.

The girl shrugged and kicked the little redheaded boy's dirty shorts. "Jacques! No pissing in public. Come on, let's go."

The group scurried across the street, up another alleyway toward Via Persine.

Kata did a quick calculation: Ejan had released the information about Aceline's death. The Assembly was scheduled for that night. Using the citizens' anger would give his proposals greater force against their enemies.

They reached the apothecary's clinic, a tall shop with a line of advertisements running down its side: ILLNESSES. TOOTHACHES. LIMB SETTING. AGUES AND FEVERS. LUMBAGO. CURES FOR ALL AILMENTS." Inside sat three old women, a worker with burns on his arm wrapped in damp cloth, and a pregnant woman. They waited as the apothecary, a tall middle-aged man with silvery hair and a stern demeanor, called each into his room. He finally gestured to Henri. As Kata began to follow, he waved her away.

The apothecary closed the door, and Kata returned to thinking about Ejan's plans. Would Olivier and the other moderate leaders be able to resist them? In recent days Olivier had tried to put together a force of moderate guards, but they were loosely organized and confused. Olivier was better suited to being the editor of the *Dawn* than leading men.

The apothecary threw open the door. "The little rodent is gone.

I turned my back for a moment, and he took my poppy-paste and a bottle of laudanum."

At the rear of the apothecary's examining room, Kata saw an open door. Kata tried to repress the smile, but it burst onto her face regardless. "The rascal. I'll pay for your troubles."

The apothecary shook his head. "Yes, you will."

After tossing the man several florens, Kata headed for the Arantine, where she would no doubt find Henri, and where she expected the mob of protestors to be hard at work.

The fog had lifted, but now plumes of smoke rose over the Arantine, merged with one another into gray-black clouds, and drifted slowly south on the gentle breeze. At the outskirts of the grand suburb, a ragged couple carried a large statue of a Siren toward Via Gracchia. After them came more looters. Some had dug up furnace trees from the side of the boulevard; others heaved linen and chests. The smell of ash burned in Kata's nostrils.

Farther into the quarter, town houses close to the road were being raided. Many of the grand mansions were hidden behind walls covered with *Toxicodendron didion*—deadly vines that waved in the air, searching for their prey. Former House officials were no doubt cowering inside.

The looters seemed to be the most downtrodden people in Caeli-Amur, the most hardened by life—those from the slums around the Arena and the Lavere Quarter. They possessed no sentimentality, no concern for fairness. Life for them had never been fair, so why should they be fair to others? She knew these people, for she came from them herself. Luck had offered her a path out of these lowest levels of society.

Then she was in the thick of it. To her right, flames engulfed a building, the heat and smoke keeping Kata to the other side of the road. A group had set another house alight nearby. Already flames were licking up the walls. A red-painted wooden door burst open, and a family staggered out. A House official—a man of about forty, still slim but with a weathered and worn cast to his face—struck at the looters with a parasol while his wife and children scrambled away in a crouch. A servant ran for her life. The group got the better of the man as one of them struck him with a metal rod, and he went down. The official raised his parasol to defend himself, but two looters fell onto his arms, held them back. A third leaped onto his kicking legs. A moment later the rod came down again on his head with an awful crack, like wood striking wood. The House agent's family screamed as they watched; horror and hurt burning in their eyes. Blood spurted from the official's head like a fountain, but he retained consciousness. Again the rod came down. This time his eyes lost focus. A third time the rod struck, leaving a clear depression across the side of his head: his skull had given way; one eye was blackened and closed over.

The family fled, and the group returned to their task of burning the house to the ground.

Farther on, a group of women stood around a burning corpse lying by an open gate. The smell of burning flesh made Kata gag. She thought immediately of the thaumaturgists and Aceline. There was too much death. There was always too much death, but Kata couldn't find herself blaming the looters—she'd be just like them under different circumstances. Her mentor, Sarrat, had taken her in, trained her as a philosopher-assassin. She had earned an apartment, and even an empty villa to the south, but hadn't she done questionable things for them? She had left that life behind now, but did she have a right to condemn those who still lived it? Their actions repelled her, and there was no excuse for them, but there was at least an explanation.

Kata listened in on the women's conversation. The body was that of one Madame Eline, wife of an Arbor officiate. A baker woman had set her on fire. Madame Eline had died screaming, apparently. One of the women laughed. "Isn't that dress radiant?"

Another replied, "It really lights up the courtyard."

At that point, vigilant guards arrived. "All right, that's enough. Out you get." The women were ushered back onto the cobblestone street. In any case, Kata had seen too much. Out on the street, the vigilants were repossessing the stolen merchandise, arresting the most violent looters. There was no chance of finding Henri among the tumult, so Kata headed for the Opera. Before long, preparations for the Assembly would begin. She would wait there for Thom.

Citizens crammed into the Opera in a great steamy mass: delegates from factory committees, members of the philosopher-assassin factions, vigilants and moderates, all bumping and pushing their way toward the Grand Theater, where the Insurgent Assembly would sit. Above the entry hall, the animate lights flittered and danced excitedly.

As Kata made her way through the crowds, she felt someone seize her arm and pull her to one side. Olivier backed up against one of the walls, his gentle face stricken. The muscles on one side of his face tightened. "Kata, thank the gods, you're here. Ejan's going to make his move tonight. The vigilants will entrench themselves as the city's defenders, and without Aceline, the Moderate Committee is split about whether to support him or not."

"Thom will arrive," said Kata. "We have to wait and see what information he has. He will know what to do."

So they watched as the crowd passed, many of the citizens waving at them or greeting them with cheers. Olivier and Kata searched for the garrulous Thom, with his great beard, his pendulous stomach. Slowly, the crowds thinned and the air lightened. The entry-hall lights retreated up to the roof or floated through to the theater itself.

"He's not coming," said Olivier in a panic.

Kata pressed her lips together. "You'll have to speak for the moderates."

"Why don't you take Thom's place?" said Olivier. "The other moderates would support you. You're proficient in rhetoric. I remember you facing up to Ejan back before the overthrow of the Houses."

Kata found herself clenching her fists, the day's events leaking through her skin. "Find someone else. I'm just a foot soldier. That's all I *want* to be."

She could not speak for the moderates. One day her files from Technis might surface, and if they did, she would be unveiled as a former spy, her group discredited.

Olivier's face seemed to collapse. "All right, yes. Right. We'll see what Ejan proposes. I can do this. I will show them. Who knows? Maybe Thom will arrive."

A few stragglers drifted through the hall, leaving only guards lounging around, bored looks on their faces.

People leaned in from the corridors outside the Grand Theater; others sat on the steps between the seats. The entire place was a massive heaving throng of humanity. By the time Kata pushed in and propped herself up against a wall—a blue-suited and grubby worker on one side of her, a maid on the other—the Insurgent Authority had already sat itself in one of the seating boxes, which disconnected from the walls of the vast hall and floated above the crowd like some physical manifestation of the relationship between the parties.

On the Authority sat three vigilants—Ejan, Rikard, and a man called Georges, who had an air of exhaustion yet was said to be filled with unusual drive. He was in charge of cataloging the assets of the former Arbor Palace.

Olivier represented the moderates. Aceline's place had been taken by a second moderate, Elise, but Thom's position remained empty.

Representing the thaumaturgists, Prefect Alfadi leaned calmly against the back of the box. What position would the white-eyed thaumaturgist take?

The final representative was Dumas from Collegium Caelian, the representative of the three Collegia. Dumas's head seemed too large for his body, as it sat low so that his neck was obscured. Deep lines were etched between the flaps of skin on his face.

Shouts and calls already echoed around the amphitheater, and this raucousness would continue throughout the meeting. The place was a heaving mass of opinion, a steamy compact body with its own urges, its own moods. In the first weeks, the liberated air was breathtaking, as silenced subjects found their voices. Each meeting seemed a revelation, each debate vital and alive, each decision a wonder of democracy. Like the marches, things were now attaining a darker, more desperate air.

Kata had seen Ejan's gift for oratory before, but when the

Northerner opened the meeting, she was again surprised by his skill and certainty. The man was born to be a leader—born to a chief in the ice-halls to the north. He spoke with a simplicity that summoned surety in the audience. Ejan's cold certainty quelled all doubts in their minds. But this time his aim was different: now he roused them into a fury over Aceline's death.

"Today a mob ran through the Arantine, looting and killing, without any discipline, without any leadership, without any mandate. They only serve to discredit us in the eyes of our allies. And yet, they had cause, for our leader Aceline is dead. Our hero Aceline has been murdered, struck down by an assassin's blow. Struck down by our enemies!"

As Ejan spoke, the speaker's box floated over the theater, dropping close to the voting delegates in the stalls at the front, drifting from side to side as he concentrated his focus, turning his head to address each section. The box then rose up to the back galleries, which were filled with the nonvoting citizens, languorous philosopher-assassins and seedy Collegia men. Kata looked on anxiously from their midst.

Ejan argued that there was little doubt the murder was part of the Houses' strategy to crush the movement and reinstall House rule.

"Strike back!" voices called. "Crush them!"

Ejan explained that the Houses had been blockading the city, and had now moved on to assassinating their leaders. It was time to halt the sabotage. As he finished talking, he demanded the passing of three resolutions: that a Criminal Tribunal be set up, led by the vigilant Georges, to try the enemies of the insurgency; that the Authority be given the right to command the thaumaturgists; and that the seditionist guards and thaumaturgists be instructed to break the blockade of the villas to the south and requisition the grain.

The crowd called out, "Death to the Houses! Death to our enemies!"

The voices against were weaker, less sure of themselves. Even to Kata, they sounded halfhearted and unconvincing. "Negotiate!"

Kata had known these motions were coming, and there was a

logic to them she couldn't fault. But the logic didn't warm her heart, for Ejan was appropriating power from the full Assembly and concentrating it in the nine-person Authority that even now floated above the gathering. This was the beginning of the militarization of the city. The vigilants stood on the brink of victory.

By the time Olivier stepped forward, the crowd was full of frenzied passion. He began to speak, cleared his throat, and began again, his voice wavering. He clutched the side of the box as if he might fall.

Olivier urged that there be no violence yet, that the thaumaturgists should be allowed to choose whom they served, just like any citizen. What use was freedom from the Houses if it was so rapidly denied? There should be no reprisals against the enemies of the Assembly, for such a process was open to abuse: to false reports of sabotage, to personal vendettas being played out. To resort to Ejan's resolutions was a sign of the defeat of the seditionists' ideals.

With each word, Kata felt herself crumble. Her fists were clenched, a lightness clouded her vision. *Olivier,* she thought, *you must win the people with your conviction as well as your arguments.* His logic was sound, but it gained no purchase on the crowd. *Were the moderates on the wrong side of history? Surely not,* she thought. Yet fewer voices cried out in support. Was it that a call for rational debate was, by its very nature, less likely to inspire violent passions in its supporters, for violent passions were exactly what they were arguing against?

And where was Thom? Why hadn't he come? Perhaps he would be able to sway people with his passion, with his desire for a better world, with his insistence that they start to build that world now, with his certainty that you could not reach the goal of a just and peaceful society by means of violence. But he was nowhere to be seen. Had he abandoned them?

When Olivier was finished, the floor was thrown open to the delegates. Again and again, men from the factories, men with rough voices and weathered faces, the poor maids with reedy tones, and fiery-eyed students spoke for Ejan's resolutions. By the time Alfadi rose to speak in support of Ejan, Kata sensed that the debate was long lost. Ejan's strategy had worked. He had released news of

Aceline's death just in time to sway the citizens. She saw a flash of impending death and was sickened.

The lightness swirled in front of Kata's vision. She became instantly aware of the pressure building within her. *Oh no,* she thought. She staggered toward the door, reached for her flask, and gulped the preparation as she bumped through the crowd and into the corridor. The passageway bent before her eyes. She fell against the wall, slipped down as a veil of whiteness came over her. The fit pulled her away on its white tide. Her body rattled and shook. She bit her tongue, tried not to breathe in the blood. Someone grasped her, but she couldn't see through the veil. She was sucked away by the tide.

Then she was aware of Rikard above her. He pressed a belt between her teeth. Her body was filled with a deep ache. He brushed her hair back gently with his hand. "You're okay. You're okay, Kata."

When she came to her senses—her tongue swollen, her body filled with dull pain—she found herself lying on a four-poster bed, complete with its own rod and curtains. She was in a bedroom, decorated with deep solar hues popular in the east: burgundy, cerise, vermillion. A crimson sheet with tiny mirrors embroidered into its surface billowed from the roof. Stained-glass lanterns hung in opposite corners. A barred window afforded a view of the city.

"I was worried," said Rikard.

Kata felt an appalling vulnerability. She pushed him away, staggered to her feet.

"Kata," he said. "You're not well. You've had convulsions."

She reached a corridor and staggered on, her body aching. She found her way back into a group of milling citizens, barely aware of their protests, unsure if the Assembly continued or not. She burst out from the Opera and into the cool night air. The stars above shone with unusual brilliance, their light cold in the autumn.

Kata found herself walking alone along Via Persine, Caeli-Amur's greatest thoroughfare, where the seditionists had faced the House Technis forces and where the philosopher-assassins had unexpectedly joined them, spinning and rolling out of the alleyways and shops and falling on the Technis guards' flanks.

How long ago that seemed! It had been a time of such promise, where anything felt possible. How quickly that time had closed off. The world of justice and freedom seemed to her like a mirage in the desert, forever receding as they approached. Now desperation clutched her, for she knew what she was about to do was wrong, but what other choice did she have? She needed to find Thom.

She returned to her apartment to find Henri and Dexion playing a game of Pierre's Blindness, Henri laughing as Dexion—blindfolded—failed to act out the moves. Instead the minotaur tripped, fell to his knees, and cried, "Ahhh!" as Henri gave him the customary kick on the backside.

Kata could not smile, for her chest was constricted by anxiety. When Henri turned to her, his eager eyes bright, she said, "Talk to your friend Pol. Find out where Thom's garret is. We need him."

The boy nodded, kicked Dexion (who was still struggling to his feet) in the backside again, and ran to the door.

"Hey, not fair!" said Dexion, pulling off the blindfold. But the boy had slipped off into the night.

Despite the pain in her body and the lightheadedness from her fit, Kata could not sleep that night, for she was racked with guilt. What had she done? She had dragged Henri into the affairs of the city. Who knew what dangers she had exposed him to. She wanted to rush out of the apartment, find him, stop him. But it was too late. He would be long gone. Instead she lay in bed, tossing and turning, waiting for him. When the sun rose to the east, he still had not returned.

# FOURTEEN

Dexion had fried up slivers of spiced meat for breakfast, but Kata couldn't eat. He quietly looked at her. In these moments she became aware of his magnificence, of the shining alien blackness of his eyes. He shook his head, and the dozens of tiny colored beads braided into his mane danced in the air. The scent of cloves and ginger drifted over from his hide.

She saw a glimpse of his future maturity, all his bursting passions transformed into a deep intensity. Minotaurs never lost the force of their feelings, but as they aged, their infectious joy gave way to more profound emotions. Now she felt the energy of Dexion's emerging gravitas, and it silenced her, too.

Dexion buckled on a belt and a serrated short-sword and strapped on battered bronze armor. He was readying himself for the Arena, where he intended to participate in the Autumn Games, a season of spectaculars leading up to the Twilight Observance.

Dexion went down on one knee and buckled on a dented thigh guard. "You should see the preparations. The Collegia have really thrown their weight behind the games. There's talk that they might flood the Arena and have gladiators battle giant squid, or create a Numerian jungle complete with crocodiles and monkeys. They're recruiting and training cohorts of fighters."

"The games have always been nothing but ways of controlling the population, of creating something false for them to care about, while the true heroes are elsewhere," said Kata.

Dexion tossed his head; his beads danced in the air. "You should see the beauty of it though. There's something glorious about the movements of the gladiators, about the spectacle of the fights."

"There's something barbaric about it," Kata snapped. "I don't want you to go."

Dexion shrugged as he opened the door to depart for the Arena. "Look, don't worry so much. You're so filled with anxiety, Kata. Has anyone ever told you that? No, I don't suppose they have. So here it is: Henri will be back, okay? He knows the streets."

After he left, Kata waited for Henri, but he did not return. Eventually she left to meet Rikard at the Opera. For a while the daylight had chased away her worst fears, but as she strode down Via Persine, they closed in on her again.

Broadsheet sellers stood before the Opera building in Market Square, calling out the names of their papers, the slogans of the day. Kata moved from one to the other, buying copies of them all.

The *Dawn* contained several sophisticated pieces arguing against the Assembly's resolutions. The appropriation of powers by the nine-person Authority was a reflection of the city's weakness, not its strength. It was reported that Georges's Criminal Tribunal was already drawing up lists of "opponents" and increasing surveillance of them—it was preparing for repressive measures.

Yet others put forward their own more marginal views. The ultraradical papers emerging from the university claimed the Assembly's resolutions did not go far enough. They were calling for a seditionist war against Varenis to spread the revolt. The entire city, they claimed, should be militarized.

Rikard sat on the steps, drinking a bowl of soup. He gave her a hard, distant, touch-me-not smile. Seeing her scanning the broadsheets, he said, "There'll be war with Varenis soon enough anyway."

Kata sat on the stairs next to the young man, embarrassed by last night's events.

"We've no chance against their legions." Kata looked up briefly into the sun, which hung low over the ocean.

Rikard shrugged. "First we eliminate the enemies here, then we face them as a united force. Anyway, we fight, after all, for an ideal. You can't underestimate the hold ideas have on soldiers. People will die for what they believe in. Without an ideal, they flee like rabbits."

Kata snapped at him. "How could you support last night's

resolutions, Rikard? You're smart enough to see the consequences. To repress opposition will just drive it underground, the way the Houses did to us. It will still exist, slowly building in the dark. Better to have it out in the air, where you can argue against it."

Rikard's cold smile now said: *You're from the streets. You should know better about the world's cruel ironies.* "The Criminal Tribunal is building a killing machine up on the Standing Stones as we speak. The Bolt, they call it. It's quick, painless. We don't take pleasure in the liquidation of our enemies, but they force it on us."

The name of the new machine brought terrible visions to Kata's mind. "What if one day *you* oppose Ejan? Will *you* then become an enemy? Perhaps all of us will face the Bolt one day."

Rikard wiped his empty bowl out with a rag, placed it back into his bag, and squinted up into the sun. Its warmth reminded her of the hot summer that had just passed.

"I'm sorry about last night," said Kata. "You were kind to look after me."

"We're on the same side, you know, Kata. We all have weaknesses. You have an illness, but it's nothing to be ashamed of."

Kata rubbed her face with her hands. She hadn't the strength to lie. "I'm learning to leave the shame behind, finally. I think. What are your weaknesses, then?"

Rikard stretched his arms up over his head. "You're the expert on that."

Kata closed her eyes, felt the sun's rays on her cheeks, saw the red glow of her lids, and opened them again. At that moment Henri came skittering across the square, and Kata felt a surge of relief. She held back the urge to run toward him like some panicky mother.

Henri glanced suspiciously at Rikard, then leaned in and whispered in her ear. "Pol's scared, hiding. Says someone is after him. Anyway, he told me where Thom's crib is."

Kata put her hand on his shoulder. "Thank you."

"That'll be three florens," Henri demanded.

Kata pushed him away and shook her head at the little brat.

Henri broke into a devilish smile and protested. "I needed to spend three florens for the information. It wasn't easy, you know."

Kata shook her head. "We'll talk about it later."

Kata looked down at Rikard, weighing her words carefully. A chasm had opened between their views. She wrestled with her conscience before saying quietly. "Henri can lead us to Thom's workshop."

In the deepest recesses of the Quaedian, the alleyways became so narrow, the damp walls practically brushed their shoulders. Kata found herself following Henri, stepping carefully to avoid the rivulets of water that ran along their center. The tenements and apartment blocks rose high above the alleys, and the whole place was thrown into shadow, except for those rare moments when the sun angled through the buildings. They pressed themselves against the walls to allow other passersby to squeeze past. The narrowness of the cramped area was oppressive, and Kata felt an ever greater feeling of apprehension. So much would be revealed once they talked to Thom. But with each step, her unease grew.

Eventually Henri pointed toward a nondescript opening where a set of stairs led up into the gloom. "Room 601."

Kata placed her hand on Henri's shoulder. "I want you to go straight home now. Lock the door and only let me or Dexion in. All right?"

Henri smiled as if she had made a terrible joke, but her seriousness chased it quickly away. "I suppose, if that's what you want." A moment later he dashed down the alleyway, turned at the first intersection, and then was out of sight. Kata thought she caught a glimpse of a figure stepping gently back into the shadows even farther down the alleyway. Had she imagined it? She squinted and tried to see, but there was nothing there.

Rikard pulled her by the arm. "Come on."

They climbed the stairs up to the top level, gloomy light penetrating through little slits cut into the stairwell. On each floor, a dank corridor ran through the middle of the building, apartments to either side. At their far ends, another slit in the wall allowed dim light and a breath of air.

By the time they came to the sixth floor, fear had clasped Kata's mind. It was as if she had become an Augurer and had had some dark premonition.

The number 601 was painted on the nearest door. It was a corner room, not a garret at all. She exchanged anxious glances with Rikard before knocking on the door and calling for Thom. There was no answer. She knocked again, using insistent, rapid blows, and Rikard called out.

Finally a door nearby opened. A women with mousy hair and deep-set eyes that made her look older than she probably was craned her neck around the doorway. She squinted at them through the gloom. "Oh, it's you again."

Kata stood stock-still. Then, in a flash, she leaped away from Rikard, her stilettos in her hands.

Rikard backed away from her, confusion in his eyes. "What?"

The woman looked on, seemingly engrossed by whatever drama was playing out.

"You've been here before. You liar." Kata screamed inwardly at herself: *How could I have trusted him?*

"I swear to you." Rikard's face was tight with alarm. "I have never been here."

"No—you, young woman. *You*," said the woman. *"You're the one who has been here before."*

A shiver of fear rushed over Kata. "No," she said quietly. "No, I haven't."

"You came to see the fat man about a week ago," insisted the woman. Then she seemed to decide that Kata must be lying, and the rest came out slowly, without conviction. "He wouldn't let you in. But you . . . but you finally convinced him."

Kata's arms dropped to her sides, rapid thoughts chasing one another through her mind. "That's the secret. Thom arrived at the baths, yet was also at the Opera. I was here and yet was not here. Could it be a shapeshifter or illusionist?"

Rikard nodded. "I think you're right."

Kata rushed back to apartment 601 and pushed on the door. It wasn't locked, and swung ominously open. Blazing light cut through an open window. Canvases and paints, sketching paper and books, and strange sculptures were strewn across the floors, crammed into the corners. The place was messy, cramped, cluttered. But it was the artist himself, bent backward unnaturally over a chaise longue in the center of the room, who caught their attention. Flies buzzed around Thom's corpse, landing on his blistered and burned face, disappearing into his open mouth and nose. The smell of death saturated the room, seemed to have sunk into everything.

"Oh, oh, oh." The neighbor, who had followed them to the doorway, fled back down the hallway from the terrible scene.

Clamping a handkerchief to her nose, Kata stepped gently inside. Rikard closed the door softly behind them.

Thom's face was blackened with horrific burns. On the floor near his body were the same signs of incinerated bloodstone. A small table had been turned over, and the couch had been pushed across the floor and now sat at an angle. Behind it, a pile of canvases had been knocked over and now lay flat on the floorboards.

Kata felt the strength leave her legs, but she held herself up by force of will. Aceline, Thom—one by one the leaders of the moderates were being killed. Flashes of the artist's death flared into her mind unbidden: he lets the killer in, thinking it's her, but something about her tips him off. They fight, and the shapeshifter's body reveals itself. Bloodstone burns on Thom's face, and the murderer forces him down over the chaise longue. It's not a fast execution, but a long death.

Kata rifled through the canvases, but the images had been cut away, leaving only holes. What had been painted on them?

Kata walked away from the body and into the separate sunroom, where Thom's lithographic press sat: a grand metallic structure, like some multilayered table, wheels in its center.

She stood there, looking through the open window and onto the building facing her, and over the rooftop gardens, vermillion tiles, and small bronze domes. A white bird landed on the roof opposite, waddled along its peak toward her, stopped.

"There's no sign of the book Olivier mentioned. Others. Some by Andrenikis. Piles of broadsheets," said Rikard.

The bird pecked at something on the roof, turned, and took to the air. The world was unaffected, untouched by all their hopes and dreams. How could that be so? How could life go on?

Kata could hear the sound of Rikard sifting through the apartment. She looked back over the lithographic press to Rikard. "The killer would have taken the—"

Kata stopped, then stared at the press's limestone slab, where she could see an image etched. Her mind moved rapidly, and strength shot back into her. She walked to the slab, cocked her head, and tried to make the image out. The machine was almost ready to print. She took a poster-sized sheet of cardboard from a roll nearby and placed it onto the limestone slab.

"What are you doing?" Rikard sounded annoyed.

"Setting up the press. Thom's paintings were destroyed. Why? Because he had painted something they didn't want us to see. But the killer didn't think of the lithograph. You wouldn't, unless you were an artist and knew how it worked."

She knew how to operate the press, having drifted among some of the aestheticist philosopher-assassins years earlier. For the aestheticists, everything—life, death, murder—needed to be beautiful, a work of art. When not carrying out their killings, or debating the meaning of elegance, they were often artists themselves. She'd drifted quickly away from them, for she was a child of the streets, and abstract beauty seemed too much of an indulgence for her.

Now she swung the press into action, clamped the poster, waited a moment, unveiled it. The image was surprisingly realist for an artist who had shown himself predisposed to Vorticist imagery, complete with its avant-garde obsession with angles and shapes, with the machinery of life. This image, however, showed Thom himself, peering over a book. Books covered every wall of the ancient room in which he sat. Great mechanical arms held small platforms loaded with shelves high above the floor. Behind Thom, stained-glass windows arched up in brilliant reds and blues. Between them stood windows opening onto the Quaedian and Caeli-Amur.

"The Technis Library?" asked Rikard.

"Look at the scene through the windows," said Kata. "It's up on the Southern Headland. I'd say it's a room in the university library."

Kata lifted the poster from where it lay. It caught the light, and she saw another figure in the background, a dark shadow looking on. The figure held an eight-sided shape in its hand that gleamed with sickly arcane power.

"Look there. That must be the Prism of Alerion," said Kata. "This is Thom's final message to us."

"If so, why didn't he tell us in person?"

"He was afraid," speculated Kata. "Something tipped him off, I think. He saw something he wasn't meant to. I don't know—maybe he actually saw his double. So he hid away, for he knew he could trust no one. Remember, Olivier said he looked terrified just before Aceline died. And this dark figure in the lithograph suggests he knew he was being watched."

"So he planned to return to the Assembly to unveil his dark truth. But when a replica of you arrived, he let his guard down," finished Rikard.

Kata thought of Maximilian. "I knew an illusionist once. He told me it was difficult to keep the illusion for any period of time. That at some point, part of your real self would shine through. So when Thom recognized it wasn't me, there was a fight. The shapeshifter killed him using the same conjuration he used on Ivarn and Uendis."

Rikard nodded. "It's all about the Prism of Alerion. So the shapeshifter insinuated himself—"

"Or herself," interrupted Kata.

"Into the room with the baths. They all thought that the shapeshifter was Thom, to begin with, at least. The shapeshifter moved quickly, killed Ivarn and Uendis using this cruel burning conjuration. But why didn't Aceline fight?"

"Maybe she was afraid. She was small, and gentle. From the location of the bodies, we could presume the deaths occurred closer to the door. She backed away, hoped Ivarn and Uendis would be victorious, but they weren't. Then the killer went to work on her."

"Thaumaturgists have all kinds of powers. Isn't it possible she was held unnaturally in place, paralyzed by a charm?" said Rikard.

The thought terrified Kata. She imagined Aceline fixed by some terrible equation, unable to move as the killer loosed the mites on her, as they plunged into her nose and up into her brain.

"Once the killer had taken Aceline's memories, he or she strangled her. There would be no rush, no need to use thaumaturgy," said Rikard.

"It's possible," said Kata. "It's possible. What, then, did Aceline know?"

Kata looked out over the roofs again. Birds wheeled in the sky far away.

"She knew about the prism and Armand's allies. Perhaps not their identities, but she certainly knew of their existence." Rikard stood next to her, looked outward with her. "We've two directions we can go. Into the canals, to try to trace the money passing from Marin to . . . to who? It must be the Houses—the remnants of Arbor or Marin or Technis. The money is going south, to the villas perhaps. Or we can go to the library in the university."

"Let's talk to the neighbor." Kata stepped quickly into the corridor, knocked on the neighbor's door, hardened herself. The woman did not respond. Kata knocked more insistently. "I know you're there."

Still, the woman refused to respond. Kata looked at Rikard and back to the door, which looked rickety. She turned the handle, but it seemed to be held by a bolt. She counted down from three, nodding as she did so, and the two of them slammed against the door. There was a crack of splintering wood, a cry from the room beyond. Again she counted, and again they crashed against the door. This time it burst open.

The woman cried, backed against a far wall, but Kata was already on her, one of her knives pressed against the woman's throat. The skin broke slightly beneath it. "If you think that woman was me, then you know I'm a killer. So tell me about the conversation you heard, and you'll live."

The woman started to tremble. Kata had to hold her up against the wall to prevent her from slipping down.

The woman's voice came out broken and hoarse. "He wouldn't let you in, and you said, 'I know, Thom, that you're afraid, which is why we must tell everyone about this. You already know Aceline's dead, don't you?' And he says, 'What?' and you say, 'Yep, they killed her. So you're the moderate leader now, and we have to talk about what to do.'"

"Was there anything else you noticed about the woman?"

"She had these kind of . . . kind of frightening eyes that looked right through you, kind of unreal-looking. And then she says, 'Thom, Aceline met those two thaumaturgists from the Brotherhood of the Hand, and they were killed too.' Then she says something about the canals near Operaio Bridge, Thom mumbles something, and she talks about the Assembly and resolutions and how they had a case against Ejan. And she says, 'Let me in.' And so he does."

Kata pressed the woman harder against the wall. "And that's all?"

Fear made the woman dribble, so Kata figured she was telling the truth. She let the woman crumple into a corner of the dirty room, whimpering.

As Kata stormed away, she caught Rikard's amused glance that said: *See, you're tough after all.*

He followed her into the corridor. "You realize that if we're dealing with a shapeshifter, well, it could take the form of any of us." Kata looked at Rikard and felt a flash of fear. She saw the same thought in his head.

"We need a secret word, then," Kata said. "Something only we would know. To ensure that the other is really themselves."

They eventually settled on *Aya's Day.*

While Rikard roved through the room once more, Kata found a local urchin to take a message to Ejan. When she returned to the apartment, Rikard looked up at her from where he stood over the body. He pointed toward Thom's hands. "Skin and blood under the fingertips. Thom fought the shapeshifter."

*Good,* thought Kata. She hoped the artist had done at least some damage.

They found nothing else in the room, and soon enough Ejan

and his bodyguard, Oskar, arrived. Behind them, the two old embalmers carried bags of equipment.

"Oh, he's just like the thaumaturgists," said one.

"Yep," said the second embalmer. "Oh well, another baby born,
another one dies. That's the cycle, isn't it?"

"That it is," said the first.

Chills sunk into Kata, and she turned rapidly to Rikard. "I have
to go."

The walk home was nightmarish. Everyone seemed a threat.
Each person, a shapeshifter ready to strike. All eyes seemed filled
with menace. Even as she tread warily, her mind was awhirl. Thom
was dead: What did it mean for the city? What did it mean for
the moderates? What did it mean for her? It was all too fresh to
comprehend.

When she returned to her apartment, her mind still reeling from
the horror, she found Dexion lounging half asleep and alone in the
parlor. His armor was piled in a corner, dirty and even more battered. He stirred a little on his bedding, rumbled deeply.

"Where's Henri?" asked Kata.

Dexion's long lashes opened, revealing his inky black eyes.
"Henri isn't home yet."

He did not return that night, or the following morning. This
time Kata knew he was really gone.

# PART II

❧❧❧

# NIGHTS

Iria was always the most solitary of the gods. If Panadus was the ruler, Aya the joker, then Iria was the artist. She was not so much beautiful as full of grace and style. Responsible for many of the world's wonders, Iria designed the city of Lixus, with its glorious walkways and wondrous curves. Indeed, the curve—the circle, the ellipse—was her signature form. Effortlessly, she graced the walkways of Lixus, overlooking magnificent white-and-silver-sailed ships. Her dresses were intricately designed: held out by internal hoops of different sizes, themselves sewn in at various angles. She moved in perfumed clouds of jasmine and orange. She basked in the golden sun and the silver moon as if she owned both of them.

An artist needs time away from society, the better to digest it and regurgitate it transformed and reconfigured. She built herself a tower—the Sentinel Tower, she called it—from which she would watch the world from afar.

A strange couple she and Aya made, for as she was solitary, he was social. Can a joke exist if there is no one to hear it? And yet they seemed to work perfectly. A rebel joker and an artist, arm in arm at the ceremonies, loved by all.

All except Alerion, who adored Iria but whose hateful eyes fell always on Aya.

—Theram of Lixus, *Portraits of Iria*

# FIFTEEN

Armand drifted in and out of a nightmarish reverie. After his ab-
duction in Varenis, he had been put on a train, which now rattled
through the night. In a semisleeping state, half conscious of the
burst of steam from the chugging engine and the heat of the thirty
or so bodies around him, he confronted Valentin.

"You betrayed me when we could have achieved so much! Why?"

Each time the visions repeated themselves, Valentin responded
differently. Sometimes he simply smiled and stared. Another time
he looked at his feet and wrung his hands, stricken with guilt. In
one dream, he explained, "It's all the play of power, Armand. It's
all part of the game. You must learn to be *realistic*."

A shudder of the train awoke Armand. After what seemed an
eternal night, light filtered through the cracks between the wooden
boards of the train walls. The smell of sweat and illness was over-
powering, and yet Armand knew he had already grown accustomed to it. Periodically, someone would shuffle over to the hole
cut into the floor to relieve themselves. Children clutched their
parents. Lone prisoners averted their eyes in shame or fear. Armand's mouth was parched, yet there was no water.

*So this is what has become of us,* thought Armand. *We have been
reduced to animals.* Armand's eyes roved over his desolate companions. Each knew their fate, but none spoke of it. It was too horrible to mention.

Near the doorway of the carriage, a man looked calmly at the
other prisoners. His hood covered his bearded face, but his eyes
still shone with a soft intelligence as if he were considering his
predicament. When he locked eyes with Armand, he nodded equa-
bly. It was the first acknowledgment Armand had received, and

something about it comforted him. For the first time on that dreadful trip, he felt as though he existed.

Armand crawled across the floorboards and leaned against the sliding door, which most of the prisoners avoided. That door represented their future, something none of them wanted to get closer to.

"Which direction are we headed, do you think?" said Armand.

The man nodded again, this time toward the shards of light that cut through the gaps in the walls. "There are slave camps all over Varenis territory, but I'd say southwest, around the mountains."

"The mines," said Armand.

The man gave no response, which seemed to indicate agreement.

They sat in silence for a long time. In the far corner, an injured man moaned. At the beginning of the trip, he had staggered into the carriage, ashen-faced, clasping his stomach. He wasn't bleeding, but there had been something wrong. "I resisted. I fought," was all he said. There was a tinge of blue to his skin, and periodically he clenched his jaw so that the muscles and tendons rose to the surface. Now he drifted in and out of consciousness. His voice was a croaking thing. "Water. Water."

An older woman placed her hand on his brow, rested it on his shoulder. She looked hopelessly at a young woman nearby who shared her plain flat-faced features.

The children seemed to accept their lot, though they, too, occasionally asked for water. Armand supposed they were more flexible than the adults, able to face their existence without grown-up denial or resentful judgment. A squarish young man, as wide as he was tall, started to cry. But no one paid him any attention. Everyone was caught in their own private torment.

With a spurt of desperation, Armand leaped to his feet and, as the others watched dully, tried to pull open the sliding door. It held fast. Just as quickly, he sat back down and leaned against it.

Eventually he asked the hooded man, "Why did they send you?"

"Oppositionist," he said calmly. A little while later the man added, "I always thought they would eventually catch me, send me to the camps. There's no space for oppositionists in Varenis. It's not like Caeli-Amur."

Armand remained silent. Here he sat, next to the embodiment

of everything he loathed. "If you were in Caeli-Amur, you'd be called a seditionist."

"I often thought of traveling to Caeli-Amur, but my home is Varenis. What can you do?"

"You seem to accept your fate," said Armand.

"We're but little particles on the river of history. We don't choose what happens to us, only how we respond. Why should I rage or cry against history? No—we must take her as she is."

"On the contrary, we have to *make* history. We'll have to escape the mines quickly. I don't think anyone lives for long." Already Armand was envisioning a plan. When he returned to Varenis, he would find Rainer, ally himself with the belligerents, and wreak revenge on Valentin. Yes—Valentin would learn that loyalty was a principle worth cultivating after all. Armand did not believe a word of Valentin's story about his grandfather. Valentin was a liar, and he would pay for that. All Armand needed was some leverage to make up for the missing prism.

The man pursed his lips and spoke happily. "And after escape, we'll have a nice coffee at a place I know in the Kinarian Pocket. They do a fine lemon tart there too."

Armand smiled at the incongruous thought. "What's your name?"

"Irik," the man said. He didn't ask Armand's name.

"I'm Armand."

For seemingly no reason, the train would occasionally grind to a halt. Hours later it would shudder back into motion. Outside it began to rain, and the prisoners tried to push their tongues through the cracks in the walls to absorb some of the moisture. But it was thankless work.

Eventually the light softened and night descended. The rain fell heavier here on the western side of the Etolian range.

Armand's mouth felt as though it was filled with dust, and he found himself looking around, as if water might be hidden in the carriage somewhere. He, too, pushed his tongue though the spaces between carriage walls, but he found that all he could taste was the earthy wood, which seemed to dry his tongue out even more. When he sat down, his stomach ached. He had never felt such a thirst before, and his inability to quench it became a private hell. His cold eyes roved over the other prisoners with cold indifference. They began to resemble nothing but bundles of rags.

The cold settled, and the prisoners huddled together like animals. There was no conversation in the dark; there was nothing to be said. Armand pressed himself into one side of the group. He felt warm and rancid breath on his cheek, heat emanating from the pile of bodies. On the other side, the cold fell on him like icy dew.

Only the injured man lay alone, sprawled now on the floor. His moans grew weaker and weaker until they stopped altogether. His silence passed unnoticed as the black night wore on interminably. Bodies shifted and moved. There were groans and sighs. In the morning, the injured man's corpse lay stinking and cold. No one dared touch it, and they all stayed as far away from it as possible.

Armand's bitterness fell away from him in that terrible train, and he laughed at his plan to return to Varenis. In that darkness, he felt stripped of all hopes, all dreams, all ambitions. From now on, his only goal would be to survive.

Around midday of the second day, Armand spied a rough town through the cracks of the carriage. Dirty and dispossessed barbarians begged on the streets, piles of logs lay stacked by the side of the train, the streets were thick with mud. They swept through the place quickly. Later that day Armand became vaguely aware of the light in the carriage shifting, as the train slowly turned in a new direction. The air became cool and moist as they climbed into the forested mountains.

Finally the train shuddered to a halt. Armand dragged himself to his feet and peered through the cracks. Guards dressed in black leather loitered aimlessly between this prison train and a second one on a track nearby. Some leaned on long pikes, muttering a few inaudible words to one another; others stared dully into the distance, unimpressed by the new arrivals.

One guard dressed in a long leather coat looked strangely like a schoolmaster, a stubby nose hidden in his soft round face. He pointed toward the front of the train and called out to someone, "As usual. As usual." As the guard gestured, Armand pressed his exhausted eyes together, opened them again, but the sight remained: the man's left eye was red, as if a blood vessel had burst and now filled it with blood. Bright spidery veins ran away from the edge of his eye. As he turned and marched away, a shot of fear ran through Armand.

Other prisoners pressed against the carriage walls, feeling a mixture of fear and desperation. They could hear the doors of the carriage in front of them sliding open. Before long the guards directed disoriented prisoners forward. An old woman stumbled and fell, struggled to her feet again without help, and continued with the rest of them. A child of about six had lost his parents and stood crying as the streams of prisoners moved around him.

"The grinding wheels of history, eh?" Irik peered through the cracks beside Armand.

"Where are they all from?" said Armand.

"Same as in this carriage: criminals, economic prisoners, rebels from the colonies—and one oppositionist." Irik's eyes lit up with irony. "Maybe it's that skinny one over there, the one looking for his spectacles in the mud."

A large metal latch clunked, and their door rolled open with a boom.

"Out." One of the guards pointed toward the front of the train, but they didn't need encouragement now. Desperate need to escape the corpse forced them out; hope of water drove them on.

A misty rain drifted down onto them. As he stumbled along with the others, Armand looked up at the craggy ranges that rose up around them. Here and there clumps of gray and green bushes and vines clung to the steep slopes. Elsewhere, carpets of lichen looked soft and inviting. In some places the earth had been sheered away from flat faces of rock, leaving only the bones of the mountains. The peaks were hidden by low clouds that reached down with long watery tendrils toward them. He had been right: they had been brought to the mines on the western side of the Etolian range. Somewhere ahead of them lay the mountaintop retreats of the Augurers. Even farther, as the mountains slowly became foothills on the far side of the range, was Caeli-Amur.

"Water, water," begged some of the prisoners.

The guards simply pushed them along. "Down to the end of the line."

Some of the prisoners fell to their knees, greedily lapping at a large puddle lying by the train.

Armand rushed forward, but a strong arm grasped him. Irik spoke with certainty. "Those pools are stagnant. There will be water later."

A group of guards kicked the drinking prisoners. "Get up!"

Several staggered to their feet and wandered on, but others remained crouched over the pools. One of the guards plunged the tip of his pike into the side of a kneeling woman. She groaned horribly, dropped a hand into the pool. The others scuttled away, leaving her crying and holding her side.

"Get up," the guard kicked her.

The woman moaned as she tried to get to her feet. The guard kicked at her again, and she splashed onto her side into the pool. A moment later the pike plunged into her stomach. "Get up!" Her head thrown back, she held on to its blade.

Irik pushed Armand along with the rest of the prisoners, leaving the woman to die alone. The image was seared into Armand's mind. The prisoners came to a wide and empty space at the front of the trains. Surrounded by guards, they milled around uncertainly. The tracks led off to one side, curling their way along the valley, past a walled camp, and toward what appeared to be a distant factory. On the far side of the field were three large buildings, like storage sheds with vast open doorways. A fast-flowing river cut through the center of the valley, where copses of pine and silver birch grew. Fed by water from the mountains, the river apparently flowed down to the great forests and plains to the north and west, where barbarian tribes still thrived. That would be the way to escape.

A high voice startled Armand. On a platform to one side of the field stood the round-faced guard with the bloodred eye and the long black coat. He had now placed small pince-nez on his nose, even though he looked over them to address the prisoners. His high and reedy voice rang shrilly over the field as his eyes roved over the pathetic crowd. There seemed to be a faint and luminous redness around him, an unnatural halo.

"Welcome to Camp X, the pride of Varenis's work camps. I am Commander Raken. Here I will be your leader, your teacher. Together we will mine bloodstone for the Empire's thaumaturgists. You will learn to embrace the freedom offered to you by work. All those fears and worries your old life brought will be eradicated. You will come to enjoy life here, stripped of all the useless concerns that once cluttered it. You will discover a new meaning in serving the greater good. So, prepare yourself for your new life, and you may find peace in this place. Resist, and you will surely be broken. Women to the shed on the right. All the men into the shed on the left. No exceptions for children." As he pointed, Armand noticed red spidery veins running along his arm.

Armand followed Irik to join the men, ignoring the wailing of women who struggled to hold on to their boys, the cries of men holding on to daughters.

In the great shed they began a process that stripped them of their identities. Ahead of Armand, prisoners surrendered all their possessions to gray-overalled men, prisoners themselves. Some resisted and were beaten; most acquiesced silently. Instinctively, Armand took his grandfather's ring from his finger and slipped it into his dry mouth. He tried desperately to salivate as he watched those ahead open their mouths for inspection. With a frenzied effort, he gagged, got the thing down. A moment later he was stripped, his mouth checked for hidden treasures, and then he was clothed in the same gray overalls and functional boots as the others.

"Your number is printed on the front of your overalls. This is how you will be known," the supervisor said as he pointed toward his own number—7624—sewn onto his overalls, over his heart. He grinned, revealing black and rotten teeth. The top left section of his forehead had a long indentation, as if years before he had been struck by a pole, caving in his skull. The veins on 7624's forehead glowed an uncanny red; the light they threw out seemed to contain its own shadow within itself. Chills ran through Armand, for he knew the sign of thaumaturgical sickness.

Several others showed the same odd changes: spidery red veins climbing over their limbs, up their necks, or over their faces. One of the new prisoners, an old man with a shock of white hair, stepped toward number 7624 and spoke politely: "Please, we're all terribly thirsty. Would it be possible for us to have something to drink?"

Number 7624 smiled ironically. "Oh, they'll be water enough. Soon you'll wish there was no water at all."

Armand sat on a bench, waiting for other overall-wearing prisoners who were shaving the new prisoners' heads with shears. Armand kept still as his hair came off, then staggered forward toward the end of the shed, its door open to a cold wind.

"You look like a bird, number 2591." Irik stopped beside Armand. "Looks like you're on your way to happiness."

With a grim smile, Armand glanced at Irik. The laughing eyes, the sculpted high cheekbones, the finely shaped forehead—the man was quite handsome.

They followed the line of prisoners, led now by guards, along a winding road. As they walked, they passed strange melted red statues that threw off the same weird light. Bodies were barely discernible beneath the melted forms: arms and legs; tilted heads; mouths open in wonder or terror, or perhaps both; eyes staring wide.

"We must escape this place," Armand said.

Irik laughed softly. "You think so?"

Constructed from wooden uprights and wire mesh, the high walls of a camp rose up before them. Guards stood on high towers behind huge bowless, pressure-powered ballistae fixed to rotating stands. Past the camp, a factory pumped out smoke from some furnace. There, prisoners loaded a train with metal barrels containing bloodstone.

The newcomers shuffled underneath the camp's sturdy gate, where they broke into a run toward a row of water pumps lining one wall. Armand found himself struggling against the rushing bodies, pushing them aside. As one prisoner pumped the water, others cupped their hands, drinking frantically. Someone jostled Armand. He shoved back and saw an old man with his shock of white hair fall down. But Armand didn't care: he needed water. He held his hands beneath the pump. The water tasted cool and sweet, better than any drink he had ever tasted. He could not drink enough of it.

Again and again he cupped his hands until he was bloated and thought he might vomit.

Finally he stepped back to see Irik looking on calmly. The man's self-control was enviable. Perhaps it had been steeled through long years of deprivation as an oppositionist in Varenis. When Irik was finally able to approach the water pumps, he did so without rushing. This was the man who Armand needed to ally himself with if he were to survive.

Eventually one of the black-clad guards stood before them and pointed to a row of low-lying buildings across a central square. "Your bunks are numbered. Today you rest—you are lucky. Tomorrow you will begin work. Then you'll know the meaning of life in Camp X, and you will curse the day you betrayed Varenis."

When the bell rang in the evening, Armand dragged himself from his tiny cot and stepped out into the drab yard. He surveyed the camp, which was composed of primitive wooden buildings circling the central square: four long sleeping halls, a row of outhouses, an infirmary and mess hall (which were the largest and best constructed of the buildings), a small carpentry shop and mechanics shop. There was no beauty here, just brutal functionality. Cracks gaped between the buildings' timber beams, which the weather had stripped of most of their paint.

Apparently, the guards lived off site somewhere, but there were always several of them standing by the ballistae on the wall, ready to strike down escapees or troublemakers.

Darkness loomed over the valley; the evening air was cool, intimating the winter to come. Through the wood and wire walls, Armand could just see a second camp across the valley in the distance. That was where the women were taken, he presumed.

Along the road from the factory, prisoners trudged toward him. When they entered the camp, Armand followed them into the mess hall. He collected a plate of food from prisoners who worked in the kitchen, and spotted Irik seated at one of the tables nearby. The oppositionist was seated between two other grim-faced prisoners.

Armand made his way to the table. "Excuse me," he said to one of the prisoners as he tried to sit between him and Irik.

Irik looked up, amused, then back to his plate.

The prisoner bared his blackened teeth and pushed Armand back.

"Can you just let me—" Armand tried once more.

The prisoner growled like an animal. Then he was standing, the number 2267 sewn on his muscled chest, which was now directly before Armand's face. Armand looked up, past the scar that ran across the man's neck—perhaps someone had slashed him with a knife—and into the lurking brutality of his expression. He was all rippling muscle, like one of those fighting dogs that people dragged around the Lavere in Caeli-Amur.

Prisoner's 2267's shove was rapid and forceful. Armand stepped back, lost his balance, regained it briefly, then his plate crashed to the floor, upside down.

The man faced Armand, his eyes unmoved, his massive hands clenched, ready to smash into something. The hall now fell silent. Hundreds of eyes were on Armand. Only the group of barbarians—who apparently were allowed to retain the beads wound into their beards and feathers in their long hair—continued eating as if nothing had happened.

The sound of a chair scraping the floor broke the silence. A man stood from his place at the head of a central table close to the kitchen. His pale moonlike face looked coldly on; his eyes, equally circular, were blank and devoid of warmth. There was something imperious about that look, which was offset by the man's babyish face. This incongruous combination made him seem all the more terrible, as if he were an ancient boy-king looking over the scattered bodies of his enemies on a desolate battlefield. There was something familiar about him too, and Armand tried to place him.

"Bendik. Enough," said the moonfaced man.

Prisoner 2267—whose name was Bendik, apparently—sat back down and resumed eating.

As the moonfaced man sat quietly, the prisoners turned back to their food, leaving Armand to pick up his plate. Sadly, his pasty food was now spread over the floor.

Armand returned to the kitchen, but they refused to give him more food. The elderly kitchen hand crossed his arms. "What have you got to offer *me*, then, boy?"

By the time Armand returned to rescue his pasty meal from the floor, it had already been scooped up by others.

Desolate, he found a half-empty table populated by those most afflicted by the bloodstone disease. About half of them picked perfunctorily at the plates before them. The others stared into space, their focus turned inward on whatever terrible process was running wild inside them. One of them ran his hand over his arm, its veins crystallizing a deep crimson. "It's starting. I can feel my thoughts changing, like there's a low hum in the background. A distant hum beneath the surface of things." He looked up at Armand. "It's not so bad, you know. You enjoy it after a while." He started to cry softly.

Another prisoner with scarlet eyes looked at Armand. One side of his face seemed frozen, so that when he spoke, only half of his mouth moved. "The bones move, but we're not aware of it. The hum of things. Humans—we live in such a state of hurry, always trying to get here or there. Always straining, cutting things down, building them up, cutting them down again. Restlessness. But the stones know there are slower rhythms, longer cycles. They can move, though. Soon we will hear their thunder."

The number 3329 was sewn onto the prisoner's overalls. He took a shallow breath from the side of his mouth. Inside it, his teeth were as red as his tongue. Shades of crimson played across his skin. The bloodstone disease was moving through him in different concentrations. His eyes flicked open suddenly and he leaned forward, coughing at first, then a flow of red liquid spewed from him onto the table. Armand leaped back as the liquid instantly crystallized into bloodstone, though Armand knew this would contain none of the mineral's thaumaturgical properties—those would be retained inside the body.

With horror, Armand walked away from the table. Many of the

other tables were now empty. He shuffled, ravenous, toward the door, when an arm pulled him to a bench.

Irik pushed his plate toward the now-empty space opposite him and nodded toward it: he'd saved half his meal for Armand.

Armand fell upon the paste, scooping it into his mouth with abandon. Each terrible tasting mouthful was like a gift from the gods, and his body awoke from its long-suffering dormancy.

Irik grabbed his arm again. "Slowly. You'll make yourself sick."

Armand spooned the paste into his mouth with greater care. The food was gone too quickly, but at least it was something.

"I will repay you," said Armand.

Irik ran his hand over his chin. "That seems unlikely."

Armand's bunk was hard, and though he was exhausted, he couldn't sleep. Heavy rain rattled against the roof. Though other prisoners snored and moaned around him, the room echoed with the ravings of Prisoner 3329. "Into lines of greatness, forever we fall. Let me lie down and rest. There is no time for this. There's never any time."

Somewhere a child was crying. They would die fast, Armand realized. Not even a father could save them.

Armand thought of Irik's kindness. How strange that the oppositionist should be so generous. But Armand had come to realize that one's political opinions were of little relevance to personal kindness. An oppositionist might be caring, just as a traditionalist like Valentin might be selfish.

Prisoner 3329 called out, "Tomorrow. Yesterday!" Then he said, as if to someone in the room, "Humanity is finished. A thought doesn't need to be short. No, it can stretch like time itself. Can you feel it? I don't feel right. Something's not right. I don't feel like I'm the same. Am I the same? I can feel it, running inside me. Oh dear, oh gods."

# SIXTEEN

A deep and ominous bell rang in the morning. Armand lay in his cot, his body refusing to move, his eyelids impossibly heavy. Around him, prisoners were shifting slowly, each in their own hell. Eventually Armand dragged himself from his bed, his limbs heavy, bereft of energy.

In the dining hall, he sat silently next to Irik as they ate thin porridge. Around him, the prisoners looked on with gaunt and broken faces. Many seemed skeletal, as if the men had already died and their skin had shrunk around their bones. Misery hung in the air.

When they shuffled into the muddy square in the middle of the buildings, cold misty rain was already sweeping across it. The prisoners lined up, as one would in an army barracks. Immediately the cold seeped into Armand's bones, and he started to shiver.

To his right, he noticed a smaller group of prisoners lined up at a right angle to the main group. At its head stood the moonfaced leader, who Armand felt certain he had met somewhere.

"Who is that?" he whispered to Irik.

"His name's Tiedmann."

"Oh," said Armand, the name rattling around in his mind.

Next to Tiedmann stood Prisoner 7624, who had supervised their arrival the day before. He ran his fingers along the indentation in his forehead as he examined the prisoners. This smaller group stood straighter; their uniforms were cleaner, their boots newer.

Commander Raken paraded across the square, examining the prisoners, poking at the first line with his black baton. He lifted a barbarian's long braided hair, examined its beads and feathers closely. "We're going to have to shave you after all. Special dispensation so you would behave! We were kind to you, and for what? So you can infest us with lice?"

The barbarian trembled slightly, in fear or rage.

Then Raken turned on his heel. "To work!"

The children were left behind to clean and carry out odd jobs, while the men, surrounded by guards, were marched out of the camp's gates toward the factory. Near the factory wall the train waited. Through its open doorways, Armand could see the carriages were already filled with metal barrels, marked with BLOOD-STONE in shadowy white letters.

Behind them, he noticed Tiedmann leading his team to the mechanics shop. Meanwhile, some of the Northerners headed for the carpentry shop. *That was where you had to work if you wanted to survive,* thought Armand.

"Eyes forward." A guard slapped Armand with the flat of his pike.

Helpless, Armand followed the rest of the prisoners through the gates, past a grim cemetery. Copses of birch, leaves yellow with the onset of autumn, dotted the landscape. Farther on were clusters of pines. The slate-gray sky seemed like a huge roof suspended between the mountaintops.

Prisoner 7624 stepped in front of the factory building. A number of prisoners congregated in front of him: *The factory workers,* Armand reasoned.

The remaining prisoners broke rank and pressed toward him. "Me. Me."

"Back." He sneered at them, his black teeth like crumbling tombstones jutting from the rotten ground.

Two of the accompanying guards stepped beside him, their pikes lowered frighteningly.

Prisoner 7624 picked out prisoners, who stood to one side. "You. You. You."

He pointed to Irik. "You at the back. The rest of you—on."

Armand followed the sorry remaining prisoners to a towering granite cliff. A dark opening was cut into its base, like the maw of some beast, calling them in and down to their deaths.

On nearby rails rested wooden carts, like smaller replicas of train carriages. The prisoners broke into teams of eight, and a second supervisor assigned the new ones to the smaller groups. Armand didn't want to think of the missing members, or what had happened to them. "Remember the quota of a cart for the day. You all know the penalty for failure."

A soft-spoken western barbarian—his hair tied behind his head and braided with wooden beads—directed Armand's team to a cart. In unison, Armand's team leaned against it. At first the cart barely moved, but once in motion, it whined and groaned its way into the cavernous opening of the mine.

In the darkness of the tunnel, the cold bit at Armand's ankles and hands, clamped down on his face. Someone lit a lamp, hung it from a hook on the side of the carriage, and they continued down to where the cold deepened into an icy clasping hand. The cart's wheels whined as they turned, the sound echoing weirdly against the stone walls. Armand sensed the great weight of the mountain above him. To Armand it seemed as if they were eight little ants crawling along a tiny passage, only a little bubble of light in the darkness. From the roof above, drops of water periodically fell on Armand, running down his now sweat-soaked uniform.

They plunged down a second tunnel. The roof closed in on them, and Armand had to watch that he did not bump his head. The ground was wetter and wetter beneath his feet, and he periodically slipped and almost fell. Anxiety gripped him, for he imagined that the timbering that held up the roof might give way at any moment and crush them all. At times he imagined he could hear the beams groaning. While the air above had been icy-cold, as they marched onward, it became leaden and hot. Armand felt his slick uniform grip his body.

Eventually they reached the end of the underground passage. Their leader held up his lamp, illuminating the vein of bloodstone that ran like a jagged red scar in the black rock.

"You're on hewing, to begin with." The Westerner unhooked a short-handled pickaxe and handed it to Armand. Five others joined him, and they began to strike at the rock face. The rock was hard, and the pick rang painfully in Armand's arms when he struck it.

"Don't break that pick," one of the others said.

Armand gradually realized that the trick was to plunge the tool into a soft section of the rock, found at the edges of the bloodstone seam, and lever it away. Meanwhile, the remaining two workers sorted the bloodstone from the rest of the debris and scooped it into the cart.

If he struck the bloodstone, it would occasionally shatter into little clouds. These he stepped away from, for inhaling the dust would infect him with the cancer. After he did this several times, the barbarian leaned toward him. "If we fail to meet the quota, you don't want to be the one blamed."

Soon Armand was breathing in the bloodstone clouds as if they were the freshest air.

Water dripped relentlessly down, and Armand's feet were constantly soaked. Yet the temperature was feverishly unbearable. Before long, his back was in agony. To prevent it from seizing up, Armand changed his swing, reversing the positions of his hands on the pick's handle. But soon enough he felt as if a hot spike had been driven through his spine. He stopped, rested for a moment, began again. So it went on interminably, until Armand thought he might scream from the pain. He worked more and more slowly, aware that those beside him kept on relentlessly. Despair took him then, and he could feel his will breaking.

Finally the Westerner poked him. "You're on shoveling now. Make sure it's the bloodstone, right?"

The Westerner swapped the shovel for Armand's pick. Armand began to scoop through the rubble, separating as much of the bloodstone as possible from the rest of the rock and scooping it into the cart. Some of the red crystal was still joined to some stone, but he did not worry about this—there was already plenty of similar material in the cart. It would be separated in the factory. Scooping was significantly easier than hewing, but after a while the prisoners rotated once more, and Armand again had the pick in his hand, the savage pain shooting down his back. When the Westerner called out, "Break," Armand collapsed onto the ground, sweat-covered and in agony. As he lay, his back seized up in spasms.

Armand pulled his knees up with the intention of rolling over so he could talk to the Westerner, but the idea of moving again was too much. Soon they would begin work again, and the agony would return. He breathed deeply, his face pressed against the cold wet stone, and waited with dread.

Finally the barbarian called out again, and the prisoners took to their feet. Armand struggled up, took up a pick. Moments later he was again in torment. So the hours wore on, Armand stuck in some hellish trance. The heat, the wetness, the exhaustion, the suffering—he could not conceive of a more terrible combination. Mechanically, he continued, his mind dulled, the stone wall magnifying and distorting eerily.

A deep rumble filled the tunnel, as if the mountain were breathing out. The timberwork above groaned, and dust fell from the roof. The other prisoners pressed themselves against the rock walls. The rumbling passed and the mountain rested once more, leaving Armand blinking in the whirling dust.

Without a word, the prisoners began to work once more. So the hours wore on interminably. Finally the Westerner checked the cart and called something indistinguishable to the others, who hooked their tools onto the side of the cart. Together they began to push the cart back up along the tunnel.

In places, the tunnel was flat and they were able to build up momentum; in others, the tunnel took on an incline and the cart slowed to a crawl. Finally the carriage rolled out of the tunnel mouth, reached the crest of the slope, and rattled with ease toward the wide factory entrance. Armand no longer put any strength into pushing it, but the others didn't seem to notice.

Inside the factory was a burst of warmth and action. The bloodstone was tipped into huge furnaces. Chemicals were added, and a number of prisoners were employed in skimming impurities from the boiling surface of the liquid. From there the liquid was poured onto huge sheets, where it cooled into a crystalline precipitate at the far end of the factory. Finally it was shoveled into barrels and loaded onto the train carriages.

Watching the details of this process, Armand could see why working in the factory was coveted. The factory was kept warm by the furnaces, but there was enough air from outside to breathe.

Meanwhile, there were only a small number of tiny motes of blood-stone in the air. Here one would be less vulnerable to the cancer.

His gang stood beside their cart, which was not quite filled to the top. There they waited as, over the next half hour, the other gangs pushed their own carts into the factory.

Prisoner 7624 inspected each of the carts with an eagle eye, occasionally poking the stone, before he decided they had each made their quota and the prisoners were marched back to the camp. As they came near, Armand noticed a small body being lowered into a grave in the cemetery. One of the children had died.

Once inside, he shuffled to the outhouses and, with disgust, retrieved his grandfather's ring. Once cleaned, he slipped it through a piece of twine he pulled from the frayed bottom of his pants. He hung it from his neck and it fell beneath his jacket. There it would stay, hidden, the last remnant of his past life.

A little later Armand collapsed onto a seat in the mess hall and stared at the plate of paste before him, so tired, he could barely eat. Eventually he forced the stuff into his mouth.

"If we're to survive, we have to ally ourselves with one of the factions," said Irik.

Armand lifted his eyes. The oppositionist had been sitting beside him, unnoticed. Irik stretched his arms above him as if he weren't tired at all. He nodded at the moonfaced man. "There are the collaborators led by Tiedmann, who help the guards to enforce the camp's rules. I think there's little chance of allying with them. As far as I can tell, they practically run the place. Captain Raken spends all his time conducting experiments off camp somewhere. Then there are the barbarians, who are a little caste unto themselves. They are experts in carpentry and are sometimes allowed to work in the forest. Then there are the rest of the men here. These masses die fast, or contract the bloodstone disease and are transformed."

Armand looked across the hall at the throng of stinking humanity, wretched and dissolute, staring into the air as if they were already dead. In the far corner, the barbarians sat, whispering in their strange harsh dialect, filled with hard consonants and lilting vowels.

In the center, Tiedmann sat imperiously at the head of his table, his pale face frightening to look upon.

"Or we could build our own faction," said Armand.

"We'll have to be gone before the winter sets in," said Irik. "That gives us, what, two weeks?"

Armand could barely control a despairing chuckle. "Impossible. We'll barely know the routines of the camp by then."

Irik glanced up at Armand from under his eyebrows. "Did you think it possible you would be here two weeks ago?"

Armand remained silent. Eventually he drew a breath. "If we could get onto the barbarians' forest gang, we might make a break for it."

Irik shrugged, unimpressed by the idea. "That seems the only way. But *how* to work in the forest or the carpentry workshop?"

Armand looked at the quiet barbarians with their beards and long hair and wild eyes. They were opposite of the civilization he stood for. There were hundreds of tribes, some in small groups in the mountains, others in hordes that swept across the plains, still more in the forests. Each spoke their own language, had their own primitive and cruel customs. What did he have in common with them?

The following day Armand returned to the mine. At times the pain running along his twisted back was unbearable, and he found himself moaning loudly. When they broke for a rest, he collapsed to the tunnel floor and lay on his back, spasms running up and down his body, seizing him.

He cared for nothing, but the slow truth of his predicament began to impress itself. He needed to act. And so against the cries of his body, the second and third waves of spasm that rolled down his back, he dragged himself to where the Westerner rested against the wall.

"I'm Armand."

The barbarian looked at him with disdain. Even his eyebrows were wild and bushy, and his face was covered with pockmarks from a childhood pox. "Ohan."

"Where are you from?" said Armand.

Ohan turned away from Armand, answered disinterestedly. "The plains tribes to the west. We were the first to resist Varenis. The others in the north—the people of the ice-halls—still trade with them. But soon they'll know what the name Varenis means."

Armand needed to capture the man's attention. "I'm from Caeli-Amur."

The man's voice picked up with interest; he turned to Armand. "The free state? Independence is something to be savored."

"Yes, but you need order to accompany it. How long have you been here?"

"Since spring. Six months. Back home, the temperatures are dropping on the plains. The rivers are running wild. The long struggle of winter is about to begin."

"Caeli-Amur's winters are mild," said Armand. "I think we won't have as good a time of it here."

Ohan said, "Few survive more than half a year here. If the cold does not take you, the bloodstone will."

"I hear there are forest gangs who cut trees. Perhaps there's a way of escaping," said Armand.

The Westerner twisted the beads in his beard and said obscurely, "That is not the way." His eyes caught Armand's with a thoughtful look. A moment later he stood up. "Back to work!"

That evening Armand led Irik to the long table where the Westerners sat whispering to one another. Armand put on an easy, gentle manner. "Ohan, this is my friend Irik. He is an expert wood-carver. Perhaps there might be a place for him in the carpentry shop?"

Ohan and the other Westerners turned coldly away from them. Armand looked at Irik, who gave a merry little laugh and looked down at his paste. "Guess they don't want any distractions from *this*."

As Armand lay in his bed that night, he listened to the ravings of 3329. The man's voice had gained a deeper resonance, now with grumbling bass notes. The words themselves were disembodied, ruined, ragged things, descending into incoherent burbling and nonsense. Some unseen change had leaped through 3329. He had reached some new stage of his transformation.

In the morning the man was gone, his cot empty. When Armand trudged from the mess hall after breakfast, he noticed 3329 standing alone near the gate. As 3329 coughed out his incoherent ramblings, bursts of crimson liquid and scarlet dust came with them, though he seemed unaware. When the gates were opened, the prisoners marched toward the mines. But the bloodstone-affected man was allowed to wander across the land outside. Prisoner 3329 now radiated an uncanny red, as if he were lit from the inside. His body was unnervingly plastic: it lost its structure, recomposed itself.

Armand watched over his shoulder as 3329 shuffled out alone, a man caught in some feverish nightmare. When he found a place away from the path, he collapsed in on himself, as if sucking all his energy in. His body hardened, as melted wax congeals as it cools, resting in a twisted stance: widened at its base, narrower as it spiraled upward, his frozen face turned to the sky as if he could see nightmare creatures flying overhead. There he would live with the other statues in that strange bloodstone world, each thinking their metallic thoughts, dreaming their crystalline dreams.

When Armand emerged from the mine in the afternoon, the mist had turned into the season's first snowfall, which melted as it touched the ground. Before long the place would be blanketed with white. Shortly after, the snow would be knee deep, then waist deep. This would spell the end of any hopes of escape.

# SEVENTEEN

Aya pulled the horse to a stop as they looked over the edge of an escarpment. To the south, marshy swampland gave way to a vast sandy plain, flat and featureless, stretching off into the distance. And there it was: Lixus, a parody of Aya's memories of the city. The towers and minarets stood broken, as if some giant had smashed them with an immense war hammer. Unknown fires had licked up their walls and blackened them. The walkways that had once curled so gracefully had collapsed, their remnants jutting up into the sky. The sea, which had long since been drained away by the cataclysm, had left the ships half sunken in the sandy remains of the harbor, where they lay like the bones of huge whales. More lay farther out, dotting the sandy desert off into the distance.

—They call it the Ruined City—said Max, from his powerless place in the depths of his mind.

The Pilgrim's uncanny sense told him they had arrived. "Soon all cities will fall into this state. You look now upon the future."

"Is there nothing that hasn't been destroyed?" Aya's devastation seemed complete. A memory welled up and enveloped Max, and he found himself in a strange ancient world, looking out over Lixus's harbor.

*Still naked, Aya leans against the railing, feels the air against his face. He closes his eyes, listens to Iria dressing herself inside. When he opens them again, he gazes at the white-sailed ships cutting through the deep-blue ocean. How magnificent they are, riding on their whitecaps.*

*Iria raises her voice so he can hear her from inside. "You have to beware, Aya. There's going to be war."*

*"Alerion is such a bore, isn't he?" says Aya.*

*She comes to the door half dressed, leans against the jamb. "You underestimate him. While you're darting across the sea, exploring the jungles, he's preparing to move against you. You're so trusting, Aya. Or careless. I can't tell which."*

*He examines her, for her tone is strange, but now she's dropping a dress over her head and her face is hidden.*

*"You worry too much," he says. "Drusa has organized everything for me at Caeli-Amur, anyway. She's prepared the carapaces."*

*Iria steps out onto the balcony, and though she's fully clothed, the smell of sex drifts around her.*

*"Drusa is simply an Aedile," she says. "She holds no power. She doesn't care for you the way I do." Iria wraps her arms around Aya from behind, perches her chin on his shoulder. "We should never have studied the Art. That's what it comes down to. Look at us: we were all friends once. Now we've drifted away from one another like motes on the wind."*

*"You and I are still together," says Aya.*

*Beneath them, students wander along a beautiful grassy walkway. Lixus was designed for efficiency and simplicity. Mosses grow in strips up the tower walls, to help with insulation. The gardens dotted around the city possess only a few exquisite flora. Technology was hidden behind the walls, beneath the buildings. Lixus embodied everything they had meant to build.*

*"You're my real love," she says obscurely.*

*Another couple stands on a balcony on one of the nearby towers. Aya feels he's watching himself. Are they fighting over there too? "I'm leaving tomorrow."*

*"Please stay," she says. "Come with me to Sentinel Tower. We can live there until all this trouble passes over."*

*"That's your place," he says.*

*"That's our place. I built it for us."*

*Her face is warm against his cheek. "You know, there are abandoned pyramids in the jungles, decorated with bas-reliefs about the original inhabitants' history. They had an entire civilization before us. Tragic, really. I want to document them, if I can."*

*"You'll get bored."*

*"Probably, but for the moment it's fascinating."*

*Iria holds on to him, presses herself to him.* "Watch out for Alerion. He'll start a war, Aya."

Nearly a thousand years later Aya looked down at the ruined city, but he was staring into the past. Sensing this, Max surged up, grappling for the controls of his body, feeling for the tiny nerves, grasping here for those that controlled his musculature, reaching here for his respiratory system.

Aya was taken momentarily off-balance. He slipped, lost a grip on things. Max sensed his body contort, his face twitching into a grimace as the implacable struggle occurred within. Max broke through the surface of the deep sea. He took a breath, and his body did also. He felt the cool air on his skin; he moved an arm.

A powerful force knocked Max aside. All sense of his body slipped away, and pressure pushed him down. Again he was drowning in the deep, beneath the water, a remorseless hand on his head.

"I can feel your struggle, stranger," said the Pilgrim. "You hoped for something else, but I don't know what."

Aya shook himself, regained a sense of the body. *You are courageous, Maximilian. But I am the stronger of us.*

As they followed the road toward Lixus, the vegetation thickened. Wiry trees curled up to the sky. Vines and creepers hung between their branches, a thick wall of green. Springs dotted the eastern side of the Etolian Mountains, feeding the little towns and cities like Caeli-Amur. Around Lixus they were many, feeding the thick vegetation. The city itself had been known for its hot springs and baths, greater even than Caeli-Amur's, and mostly in the open air.

Before long, they began to pass overgrown tombs of Lixii, inscriptions on their sides naming them: LUCRECIA OF EVADNE TOWER, PERFUMER; MARIUS OF WATCHER'S TOWER, CALLIGRAPHER; TERTIUS OF ISOPA TOWER, GLASSMAKER. Lixus was said to have been a city divided politically according to its many towers. The tower you inhabited defined your identity.

Lixus was once considered the most beautiful of ancient cities, but now it was said that outcasts from across the world—rag people, madmen, and visionaries—made it their home. Max's imagination had set to work, conjuring all kinds of dangers. The Arbor outpost would make it more dangerous, for who knows what dictatorial structure the Arbor officiate Karol had built here, or how he'd responded to the overthrow of the Houses.

—Let's not go through the city—said Max. —We should pick up the road on its northwest side.

*That would require passing over those rugged ridges,* said Aya. *No, the quickest way is through the city.*

The tombstones eventually gave way to wildly overgrown spaces that might once have been carefully tended gardens. Occasionally, crumbling espaliers could be seen behind swathes of vines and strange fluttering creepers with purple flowers. Elsewhere, steam rose from hidden springs and wafted across the sky.

Far away, Max heard the crying of tear-flowers. He worried that Aya would not understand the significance, but he felt the mage tense at the sound. Aya knew instinctively that these high wails came from a deadly creature.

Again the Pilgrim sensed Aya's agitation. "They've been crying for some time now."

The bloodred afternoon sun was setting to the west. Over the sandy desert, the bones of the ruined ships seemed aflame with crimson light. Golden rays caught the giant ruined stones of the once-great towers, painted them in amber.

The city was like a ruined necropolis, each building a tomb long since raided by grave robbers. The towers loomed over them, their black walls warmed slightly by the dying afternoon light, green creepers and mosses climbing up their heights. They kept to the surface level, avoiding the curving walkways that rose up before breaking in midair, vines falling from them like green waterfalls.

"Do you see them?" asked the Pilgrim.

"Who?" Aya looked around.

"The people watching us. Arbor guards, perhaps."

Aya looked again into the shadows of the towers, through gaping doorways, past broken walls. In the darkness lurked even darker shadows: gaunt figures dressed in shredded robes like the ragged feathers of dying crows. Aya would catch a glimpse of them; then they were gone, fading back into the deep.

"I think you may have trouble converting the population of Lixus, Pilgrim," said Aya. "They don't look the type to listen. Your friend Karol seems to have failed, unless he's found some hideout."

"The last I heard, Karol's outpost was surviving well. He sent letters describing his progress. They were rebuilding. They had planted orchards."

The line of sunlight slowly rose up the towers, leaving dark folds of shade below. Around them, walkways curled up gracefully, but many of them had partially collapsed, leaving a chasm before they began their downward turn.

They rode through empty squares, their patterned marble pavement cracked, weeds standing tall like little sentries. Elsewhere, iron walls that once fenced off gardens were now thick with a morass of green leaves, decorated with wondrous golden, white, and purple flowers. Every so often, wafts of steam rose from shrouded hot springs.

Shadows moved menacingly in the dark doorways or broken gaps in the walls of the towers. Others scuttled between the towers themselves, as if an army of them were following Aya and the Pilgrim at a distance.

"You there! Come and speak with us. Where is Karol?" called the Pilgrim.

No one answered. In distant windows, high in the towers, the firelight began to flicker.

—This is not safe. We need to get out of the city—said Max.

Aya kicked the horse into a trot. Behind them, the shadow-people now took to the street, a shuffling, rambling little army. They began to hum a deep and eerie drone that echoed between the buildings. The frightened horse shook its head, neighed, and broke into a gallop.

"Let me speak to them!" the Pilgrim cried.

"I think this is perhaps not the best time to prophesize, Pilgrim." Aya let the horse have his head.

The shadows now emitted wild guttural cries, fluttering and waving their rag-covered arms as the horse rode past them. On and on the horse rode, deeper into the city, the crowlike figures running behind them.

"We're nearly at Oppua Plaza. The northwest road leads from there," said Aya.

—That's what they want—said Max with sudden fear. —They're herding us to the plaza.

But it was too late. A golden glow appeared ahead as Oppua Plaza lit up with light. The horse reared up, came down, and circled wildly. With a flash, the sun's rays disappeared, and the plaza opened up before them. Shaped like a long teardrop, the bricks of its marble pavement were patterned red and white, in forms resembling a school of slender fish.

On a central stage stood a ragged man wearing a crown made from the head of a blood-orchid. His square face was savage and wild-eyed, and his demeanor was both tragic and fierce as he raised his arms in the air, a gesture of triumph.

Silence fell over the plaza, and the hushed scarecrow figures gathered in a wide semicircle, blocking off any escape. Then, in unison, they waved their arms and once again hummed their frightful leaden dirge.

On the far side of the plaza, in the front of a shattered amphitheater, stood a row of tear-flowers, six feet tall with heads like bloodied plates. A couple of them sang their mournful song, just audible above the mob's hum. At their base lay half-dead bodies, slowly being absorbed into the flowers. Max knew that little by little they would start thinking flower-thoughts, until they no longer knew if they were the person beneath or the flower above.

The high call of these magnificent flowers was gently enticing. Max sensed Aya's urge to lie down next to them, to feel their sweet nectar drop onto him as it began to dissolve him and bind him to the flower's aerial roots. But Aya resisted.

The man on the stage swung his arm around, and a dozen or so men quickly approached the horse. They wore the uniforms of House Arbor, but they were so dirty that the green could barely be discerned beneath the muck and filth.

Aya looked up at the man on the stage. "I think we've found your friend Karol."

# EIGHTEEN

The Tower rose high into the air, one of the few that stood intact, a graceful curved structure. Once it would have been beautifully patterned with grasses and mosses, but now the walls were overgrown with intermixing flora: orange and green swirling mosses, dangling vines with purple flowers.

Aya and the Pilgrim were herded inside. It took a moment for Max's eyes to acclimatize. Everything inside the massive hall was built from ruined machinery. Massive cogs had been converted into tables. Tree-trunk-sized chains laid out the border of a pathway; the innards of machines dotted the space as carriage-sized sculptures.

On a dais at one end, a giant throne had been built from a complex fusion of latticework, bolts and screws, pistons and gears, and old odd-shaped pieces. Growing over its armrests, sprouting from its back, delicate candle-flowers lit up in the darkness. It was at once menacing and magnificent: lost technology fused so bewitchingly with Arbor's flora.

Furnace trees emitted slight warmth; it was not yet winter, when they would burn hot, like little stoves. On one wall of the tower, *Toxicodendron didion* grew like a vast curtain. Its thick leaves wrapped around a number of rotting bodies, which the vine was slowly devouring. The stench of death mingled with the sickly sweet scents of jasmine and snap-rose.

Two plots of blood-orchid, like columns marking the bounds of a central forum, trembled at their approach. As large as a human, their flowery heads had an unearthly, alien beauty. The pink veins in their otherwise snow-white leaves indicated that they had fed recently. Their vicious mouths, developed out of the staminode in the center of their flower, were hard to see among the other two stamen, themselves like fist-sized purple sponges. Unlike their noncarnivorous cousins, the blood-orchids had developed a long petiole, which they held against their body but could strike out with like a whip and entangle their prey, dragging it into their beautiful and dangerous flowery heads.

Karol led them safely between the rows, to the dais, where he collapsed into the throne as if overcome by lethargy. "Bring them chairs."

Rickety wooden chairs were dragged onto the dais, and the crow-people gathered around, their faces filled with sinister intent. They had resumed their unnerving drone, an accompaniment fit for the end of the world. Karol's guards stood even closer; some still held pikes traditionally used by House Arbor.

"Karol—you remember me," said the Pilgrim.

Karol looked on dumbly, his face drained of energy, a certain flabbiness where Max imagined it once might have been square and harsh. His voice came out, a mumbling, rambling thing. "You? Who are you? Is it you, René? Is it really you? Have you been sent to us from Arbor? Has help finally arrived? But no, we don't want help, René."

*Could this man really have been a star, rising through the ranks of Arbor, a favorite of Director Lefebvre?* Max wondered.

The Pilgrim said, "I was once called René, but I no longer answer to the name. Call me Pilgrim. For it is time we recognize our impotence in the face of the catastrophes that have happened, that are to come. We are helpless in the face of the dialectic of nature. I think you understand that now, don't you?"

The words did not seem to have any impact on Karol, who stared out blankly over the waiting throng. He seemed to be talking to himself, rather than to Aya and the Pilgrim. "We were abandoned. Go to Lixus, they said. Colonize. Build an Arbor empire. Bring everything and everyone into the House's fold. Find out what secrets lie in Lixus. But everyone knew there were no secrets here. No technologies ready to be used. Only an empire of madmen and sinners. We begged to return. We begged to be relieved. . . ."

"Yes, Karol, look where you are: surrounded by ruins."

Karol looked defeated. "Ruins. But who's to say that the Houses were better than this? When I came out here, I had such high hopes, you know. I would rebuild this place and return to Arbor a hero. But the ruins—you don't know what they do to your mind. They start to enter you. Rubble everywhere, cluttering you up."

Karol's voice trailed off into a whisper.

"A colony will not withstand the coming trials," said the Pilgrim. "Nothing does. A language lasts, what, a thousand years? A civilization, five hundred? All the time the workings of matter come to crush us. There is no human act that can withstand them."

"You're right," said Karol. "Humanity is finished." He sat upright, as if stuck with a knife. "And we have built our own civilization! We serve new gods now. Look now at my empire! I am king of the blood-orchids. You should see them move. If you speak to them, they respond."

The Pilgrim sat back, apparently shocked that the conversation had jumped off track. "But they are only plants. They are semisentient. They're not gods. There are no gods. There's just the coming chaos."

"No, no, René. You don't understand. They are *evolving*; they are the firstborn on this world, and they will outlast us. You understand that, don't you, Pilgrim?"

"There is a higher order—the universe!" countered the Pilgrim. "And I will take any who will come to the Teeming Cities, where we will spread the word, tell the world of the coming apocalypse. Come with me, Karol—bring your people."

Karol had now worked himself into a feverish state. "Ah. You don't understand, but you will. Oh yes, you will, René. They are the inheritors. They have needs and wants. And blood-orchids want to eat!"

At this, the mob flapped their arms and hummed their strange dirge louder than before. A wildness came to their eyes and they called out, "They want to eat!"

Max didn't like the sound of that. He felt suddenly vulnerable, trapped in his own mind as these two madmen carried on their disturbing conversation.

Karol collapsed once more into his chair, as if his bones had given way. He looked wearily at Aya and the Pilgrim. He seemed to be snapping between two personalities, a wild, energetic one and a drained, broken one. "I can't do this anymore. It's . . . I wanted to be, someone, you know. To do something. I could have been. I should have been—something."

Still the crowd hummed and waved their rags in the air. The blood-orchids joined them, singing in a deep thrumming tone, its rhythmic bass so like the hums of the worshippers.

"You don't have to," said the Pilgrim. "Come with me and alleviate your suffering."

A jubilant savagery was fixed on Karol's face. He leaped to his feet, raised his hands in the air. "Feed them!"

A group of crow-people leaped up, grasped the struggling Aya and the Pilgrim, and dragged them from the stage. The crowd parted, leaving a space between the two rows of blood-orchids, which quivered as they sang.

Aya and the Pilgrim were thrown onto the ground between the two rows. As they scrambled from the dirt, the crow-people backed away, forming lines at each end of the strange forum to keep their prisoners trapped between the flowers.

—Blood-orchids can't move, so we should be out of range of their petioles for the moment—said Max.

Aya seized the Pilgrim's arm, and they began to back away toward the Tower's door, where the line of flapping crow-people waited for them, humming in some feverish fury. Several ran toward them, then backed away again.

Aya and the Pilgrim froze, for the orchids wrenched themselves from the ground, their tuberous roots acting like two clubbed feet. One after the other they came, breaking from their beds and shuffling toward Aya and the Pilgrim, their stamens quivering at the scent of flesh.

—Oh no—he's right. They've evolved somehow—said Max.

The Pilgrim fell to his knees, shaking now. He could sense the impending attack. Soon the orchids would drag them close, envelop them in their petals. The orchids had desires. They would suck on blood and bone.

Aya scrambled around in his memories, searched for the prime language, the base equations for organic matter. But he could not find them.

—Do something—Max said, panicking.

*Shut up. I'm trying to concentrate.* Again Aya riffled through his memories. Where were the equations? What were the words and grammar? Where was anything?

In that moment Max gained a sharp view of Aya's fragmented mind. The missing years, the missing knowledge, the missing parts of the prime language—segments of him had been lost in the transfer to Max's body. Perhaps other parts had been lost even before that, in the Library of Caeli-Enas. There was no denying it: the greatest of Magi, the jester god Aya, was a fractured relic of his former self.

—You don't have them. You don't know the prime language.

A petiole whipped past Aya's neck. The flowers continued toward them, step by ungainly step, goaded by the maddening drone of the crow-people.

*Give me a moment.* Aya dredged from his mind other grammatical structures, words that applied not to flora but to animals. He conjugated them differently. The syntax was all jumbled, but he covered the silences with yet more equations. As he cobbled together this crippled version of the Art, the world lit up as the deep structures of things revealed themselves.

Max had experienced this immanence before, but this time it had a different quality. Behind the world of life lay the world of darkness, the Other Side. Superimposed on this one, he saw the rise of a hill, a set of stairs cut into it, running off at a subtle and oblique angle. This ancient Art was the language of the deep structures of the world of life and the world of death combined. For a moment he existed in both.

Aya felt the orchids' dumb sentience. Through him, Max experienced their plant thoughts, felt the movements of the air on their leaves and whiplike petioles, sensed their surroundings as they did: through touch. They saw their latest meal in front of them. They yearned for it, trembled and quivered for it, sang for it.

Aya reached into their minds, rearranged their thoughts. It was a clumsy process. He was forced to throw equations around like a juggler. But, somehow, draining his strength with each hurried invocation, he reached the orchids.

One after another, the carnivorous flowers halted. One started to shake uncontrollably, its mind unable to process its contradictory desires. Another wilted rapidly, as if a month had passed without feeding. The others stood stock-still, frozen.

Their songs died.

At that moment Max realized he could take back control of his mind and body. He could strike at Aya while the mage was in his trance, engulfed in the Art. Max readied himself, saw Aya's concentration elsewhere, his tenuous grip on his inner functions. But Max held back, afraid of the consequences.

Holding the orchids in place, his hands held out as if to physically stop them, Aya turned to the aghast crowd, whose faces stared at this man who could control the orchids. "You are a false king, Karol. These orchids are nothing but plants. The Pilgrim here is right: there is a universe beneath us all, a force that connects us, which *is* to be worshipped, if anything is to be worshipped at all. If you seek some kind of salvation, follow the Pilgrim."

At this, Karol cried out. The bulk of his lieutenants hummed frantically, but the orchids did not respond.

Aya reached into their minds and put them to sleep, as if they faced a long cold winter. They shrank into themselves, the petals closing over their stamens, their heads drooping to the ground like chastised children. They would not wake.

The immanence faded, along with the perception of the Other Side. Aya was finished with the Art for the moment, but Max knew the Art was not yet finished with him.

Some of the crow-people now fell to their knees in supplication. Others ran from the hall, their faith in tatters, or perhaps they were unable to assimilate these new events. Yet others gathered around Karol and his remaining lieutenants, who backed away.

Karol staggered from the stage toward Aya and the Pilgrim. There was no energy in his body; each step seemed to take something out of him. His roving eyes were filled with desolation, shifting at times into resignation, then back to sadness. He passed close to Aya and stared at the mage. The skin around his bloodshot eyes sagged, revealing a line of red flesh beneath. He gazed balefully at Aya for a second, then continued through the door.

A short while later only a few of the crow-people remained. Aya stepped across to the stage and leaned against it, exhausted from his use of the Art. This was one of the highest costs of thaumaturgy, but it was Aya's clear separation from events that shocked Max. Aya looked at the people around him from an Olympian distance, some faraway place where Karol and the crow-people's concerns were but tiny specs in the vast seas of infinity. This was the cost of the prime language. Max built a wall against it.

*The distance will pass eventually, but you never quite return to the place where you began. It will stay with you, like a scar. That's the cost,* said Aya.

The Pilgrim came to sit on the stage beside Aya. "Perhaps *you* are the prophet. You have halted entropy here; perhaps *you're* meant to lead the movement against the coming apocalypse. Perhaps *you* are the one we've been waiting for."

Aya elbowed the Pilgrim's ribs. "Or perhaps I'm a joker sent to test you."

The Pilgrim's head fell forward, a mirror image of the blood-orchids. "I am beset with doubts." He placed his hands over the bandages covering his eyes. "I wish I could still see. This was all a mistake."

Aya looked at the man impassively. "Perhaps, but what is there to do but to go on?"

Some part of the Pilgrim broke. He stood up. "I will march to the Teeming Cities, and there I will spread the word of the coming apocalypse. There I will tell the world that we must change our ways, and prepare for it. For we must survive it, I see now. Somehow, we must survive it. Who would come with me?"

A hundred or so flapped their rags and hummed in agreement.

That night the Pilgrim sat up with his new followers, and they

discussed the apocalyptic philosophy. Aya drifted in and out of
sleep on a pile of rags nearby.

In the morning Aya put his hands on the Pilgrim's shoulders.
"I hope you reach the Teeming Cities and fulfill your mission,
whatever that is."

"And I hope you reach your own destination. But remember,
we rarely find what we search for," said the Pilgrim.

—You like him—said Max.

*He has the strength of his convictions. How could you not admire
that?*

Aya left the Pilgrim with his people, and led his horse from the
plaza toward the northwest road. To his right, a single tear-flower
cried mournfully, like a lost child. Again, the urge to lie down beside it gripped Aya. He fought it off as he approached the body,
lying beneath a now silent tear-flower. Already, nectar covered the
man, and several of the aerial roots had implanted themselves into
it, reaching into the flesh beneath.

Aya squatted beside Karol, looked into the dreamy eyes that
stared into a faraway world.

"It's not so bad, you know," said Karol. "It hurts at first, but then
you start to feel the wind on your petals; you understand things
you didn't previously. You come to know that the world isn't simply constructed for humans, that there are other rhythms, other
perceptions. It's a great release, you know. A relief, that distance."

"I know that distance," said Aya.

Karol closed his eyes, opened them again. "I am not sorry for
what I've done. I am sorry for the rest of you though."

Karol closed his eyes but did not open them again.

Aya led his horse along the northwest boulevard and through
the ruins of Lixus. Before long, he knew, he would be out of the city
and into the hills. There he would find Iria's Tower. The thought
pierced him like a spike. What would he find there? Would the
Sentinel Tower be in ruins? Would Iria herself lie there, or perhaps
her bony remains?

*Iria,* Aya thought. *How I loved you.*

Hidden inside his own mind, Max felt a quick surge of optimism.

He knew now that Aya was not only a mage, not only a joker, but that he was human. He'd saved the Pilgrim. In fact, he liked the apocalyptic. And he had loved Iria. There was good in him, after all, and if there was good in him, there was hope for the both of them.

# NINETEEN
ᖇᗝᗢᖆ

No matter how many florens Kata and Dexion showered on people in the Quaedian, no one could tell them of Henri's fate. Kata had to restrain the minotaur, whose anger and grief threatened to spill over into violence. "I'll break them with my bare hands," Dexion repeated again and again. In these moments he seemed to grow to twice his size, violent energy threatening to burst through him. At other times, Kata might have been afraid of this explosive passion. It only took one glance for passersby in the street to back away from his fierce mien.

*How incendiary his emotions are,* she thought. Something had shifted in her own feelings as well. Where once she would have felt only despair, now it was mixed with anger, too. Vengeance—that was what she sought. She wasn't the only one. As they searched for Henri, she had been vaguely aware that news of Thom's death had led to more marches and more riots.

Three days after they found Thom's body, they decided Henri was gone for good. That night Kata curled up with the minotaur for comfort, wrapped her arms around his massive torso, and listened to his breathing. In the morning Kata's eyes felt as though they were filled with sand. The urchin had been her chance at redemption. In her mind, he had come to stand in for her own childhood, as if somehow by keeping him safe she were keeping that little lost girl safe too.

She rolled over on her bed, stared through the window at the blue sky. She was being drawn back, she knew, to her childhood and youth. She was being drawn back to her mentor, Sarrat.

She left Dexion asleep and dragged herself up and into the threatening streets, expecting at any moment to be attacked or killed. She willed her enemies on. She wanted to face them, even if they were shapeshifters who burned faces with their thaumaturgy. This morning, even the rangy cats scuttling along the alleyways looked meaner than before, ready for a scrap.

Not far from Via Gracchia, a small apartment nestled away from the bustling city. The small white houses in the area pressed up against one another, and against the cobblestone streets. But this house stood alone, with an exquisite pebbled garden and rugged desert plants circling three of its sides. She remembered the first time the Technis official had brought her here. How frightened and excited she had been: a philosopher-assassin was about to adopt her. No longer would she sleep on the streets. Now she could *really* live. She remembered that trembling little girl with pity. That child hadn't yet learned that though she might be able to escape the streets, she couldn't escape herself.

Kata took a deep breath and strode toward the sliding door, where she stopped, slipped off her boots, and knocked three times.

"Come in, Kata," a voice called out from within. It annoyed her that he still recognized her footsteps.

Kata stepped into the sparse central room and, without speaking, crossed to where Sarrat sat cross-legged. She sat opposite him, cursing to herself as she did so. She wasn't here to comply with his practices, and yet she behaved much as she did when she was his apprentice.

Sarrat's head was shaved, austere like his house and gardens. The man's olive skin was smooth, and he had an ageless quality. He might have been anywhere between thirty or fifty, with only a broken nose disfiguring his unwrinkled perfection.

For a long time they sat facing each other without speaking. Kata felt the rush of shame and discomfort wash over her, as if all her sins were there for him to see.

"I was wondering when you'd return," said Sarrat.

Kata didn't respond immediately, but when Sarrat simply looked at her, she spoke to break the discomfort. "I've done contentious things. I'm not sure who I am, exactly."

"Have you ever known who you are?"

Kata shook her head. "As a child, all I could do was survive. No one knows who they are when all they can think of is how to reach the next day."

"No," said Sarrat. "There you are wrong. If all you think about is making it to the following day—*that is who you are.*"

"I've killed innocents," said Kata. "I've allowed innocents to die."

Sarrat nodded. "So has everyone. What is it you want?"

"I want . . . I want . . ." She wanted understanding. She wanted him to say it would be all right. She wanted sympathy. She wanted all the things he had never given her, not in all the years he had been her mentor. Eventually she said, "I have sided with the seditionists."

"Isn't that just a philosophy that tries to control things, to bend things to its will?" said Sarrat.

"I'm not here to talk philosophy with you." Kata shifted uneasily on the cold floor.

"Isn't that what we are?" said Sarrat. "Philosopher-assassins?"

Kata spoke through clenched teeth. "We're just assassins. We simply add the philosophy to give us an air of gravitas."

"I suppose you think I'm being patronizing, don't you? You always do. But I see you're still restless, always searching for something new, someone new."

Kata drew a ragged breath. He always knew how to antagonize her. She decided to shock him. "I killed a minotaur. I killed a child."

Sarrat looked at her calmly. "All things die in the end, Kata."

The next thing she knew, she was on her feet, kicking out at Sarrat, but he was no longer there. Standing several steps back, he caught her foot and swept her standing leg away with a quick trip. She spun in the air, planted her hands as her body fell, twisted her trapped foot free. With a catlike twist, she cartwheeled through the air, landed on both feet.

Now the anger engulfed her. She shot forward, struck out three times rapidly with a closed fist: low at Sarrat's stomach, at his head, low again. But he parried each blow with swift, delicate, open-handed blocks. Each failure fueled her wrath. She dived at him, determined to take him to the floor, but Sarrat had danced away. He was still in his fighting stance, and she was left belly down and prostrate.

"You always fight in anger or fear." He shook his head sadly. "That's how I know you have not reached peace with yourself. That's how I know you can't be trusted: because you don't trust yourself."

Kata stood up, anger coursing through her. "It was a mistake to come here. You're self-satisfied; you sit here as if the world doesn't touch you."

"That's not so," said Sarrat.

"I despise you," said Kata. "For your distance from the world. You can't feel. You don't feel. I am your failure."

"You are," said Sarrat sadly.

She spat at him—a way to dirty his clean apartment—and stormed away, leaving her former mentor to clean it up. When she was back in the alley behind Via Gracchia, she collapsed, distraught, broken, hoping he would come to her, like the father she hoped he would be, and comfort her. But he never came.

In recent days Rikard had been away on vigilant business. Apparently, he had been helping to organize a force of guards destined for the villas. But he had left a message at the Opera to meet him at the Standing Stones on the tip of the Southern Headland. It was time to return to the trail of Thom's killer.

He was seated on the small semicircular amphitheater that curved around a cluster of twenty-foot obsidian monoliths, black and glassy and alien. Some said the stones predated even the Gods; their origins lay in some even more ancient species or deities. In the center of the cluster, vigilants were building a wooden machine: the Bolt. They nailed and hammered and drilled, and the machine rose up, a complex construction, a little like a war scorpion surrounded by a wooden cage.

The head of the Criminal Tribunal, Georges, watched over the process with deep-set eyes. He gazed at the mechanism impassively, squatting down to examine it before rising up and circling it with interest.

Beside him, Dumas, the head of the Collegia, was remarking on the workmanship. "It's the best way, really. I mean, when you behead someone, it can all go terribly wrong. A slight angle, and the blade ends up in the skull, and the poor soul kicks out and writhes around, and then you have to pull the damned thing from the bone and, well . . ." Dumas's flabby bulldog cheeks hitched up for a moment in a black grin. "It has a certain drama to it, I suppose."

Neither Kata nor Rikard said anything when she sat next to him, though the vigilant occasionally turned his head, looking over the city to their left. Eventually he broke the silence. "Are you going to the Moderate Committee tonight? I hear there will be a debate about your attitude toward the vigilants. How do you think it will go?"

"Do you expect us to support this?" She gestured toward Georges, who was running his hand over the solid wooden beam at the center of the Bolt.

Dumas leaned against one the Bolt's uprights, gestured to the killing beam. "Straight through the bones and organs. Instant, you know. There's something nice about using a machine, isn't there? No one actually has to swing the blade. Executioners end up with awful problems, you know: nightmares, regrets. You have to find new ones all the time."

Rikard turned his head, this time looking south, down toward the water-parks, then back north again. "If the majority see the need, we expect the moderates to support it. It's democracy, Kata. That's what it means."

Kata followed Rikard's gaze. "What are you looking for?"

"We're being followed, I think. I'm not sure. I haven't really seen them. I've just felt them. A sort of tickle on my neck." Rikard rubbed his neck at the thought of it.

Kata surveyed the drifters who had made their way up on the Thousand Stairs or from the Lavere below, men and women of the Collegia. Children dressed in fine clothes and shoes had drifted down from the Arantine. Their eyes were wide, for they sensed the Bolt was not an implement of their class, that their officiate parents might spend their nights fearing the knock on the door.

"Good. I want the killers to follow me," said Kata. "I want them to turn a corner to where I'll be waiting for them. I want them to cry when they see me."

Rikard threw his arm around her affectionately and rubbed her shoulder. "Look, we'll find Henri. He's a smart boy. He will be all right."

How strange of the vigilant to comfort her like this, as if they were old friends. It was almost as if he actually cared for her.

She nodded without conviction. "The university library room depicted in Thom's lithograph—I still think that was Thom's message to us. They may have a record of the book Thom was reading."

The steam-trams had finally all broken down or run out of fuel, so they took a carriage pulled by a skeletal horse across town, through the barren streets, past beggars holding signs which read: PLEASE HELP and I'M A SEDITIONIST WHO IS HOMELESS and, simply, BREAD. No one was giving them anything, though. The city had run dry.

An hour later they passed through the university's long passageways, caught glimpses of the scenes depicted in its famous windows, scenes from the past captured and replayed decades or centuries later: a band of youths chasing goats along an ancient alleyway, a line of figures holding candles and chanting in a dark field that was no longer there. Then, as they turned a corner, vistas of the serene city, its wide spaces and classical buildings, the brilliant blue sky overhead, free of pollution. A wild fancy took her: if she waited long enough, she might see Henri—and whoever had captured him—in the alleyways.

A change came over Rikard as they entered the library. His head swiveled around in wonderment. Long walkways passing overhead like spiders' webs, staircases climbing up and up into the gloom above, and books! Books everywhere, lining the walls, stacked in piles where they had overflown the shelves.

Tall windows opened out to the sky on the entire southern wall. Windows like those pictured in Thom's lithograph—and yet, this wasn't the room. Skinny students worked at long tables lined up in a central hall. Even the overthrow of the Houses had not ended their study, though they seemed more emaciated than usual. Behind a semicircular desk against one wall stood several librarians, checking out books for students or helping them in their research.

Kata kept moving closer and closer to the side of the library until she came to the western wall, the one closest to the cliffs. A huge dark bookcase filled with large dusty books blocked her way.

"It's through here, somewhere." Kata looked up and down for a door. "There must be another entrance."

She felt a tap on her shoulder, turned to see a middle-aged librarian staring distrustfully at her. The librarian smiled without conviction. "The reading room. It's for House officials and professors."

Rikard pulled from his bag a document bearing the stamp of the Authority. "The House officials are no longer in charge. We are."

The librarian's air changed instantly. She smiled, and her voice took on a light maternal quality. "Yes, of course. It's exciting to meet such important representatives. I voted for you, you know."

"For whom?" said Kata.

"The moderates, of course."

Kata smiled teasingly at Rikard, who shrugged in response. There was no baiting the young man, it seemed.

"I knew Aceline's sister, before she moved up to the Dyrian coast. Lovely girl she was." The librarian led them along the wall, shifted several books aside, and unlocked a hidden door. "Through here."

A passage led to a beautiful semicircular reading room, the windows showing views of the nearby cliffs and, far up the mountain, the Artists' Square. Down to one side, the narrow streets of the Quaedian lay beneath them: alleyways, walkways, plazas, and roofs of all sizes and shapes. The walls were covered with books; a slight musty smell drifted in the air. In the center of the room, great mechanical arms held little platforms in the air; they rose up like spindly towers, their book-filled shelves held safely aloft.

A chill ran over Kata's skin. "Thom the artist was here. Do you know him? Do you know what he was studying?"

"Yes, of course. He came here several times and studied one of our precious books. I'll fetch it, if you like." The librarian approached a large mahogany cabinet with a hundred or so drawers. She opened one of these catalog drawers, pulled out a card, carried it with her to an angled bench. She slid open a panel, pulled a lever, and one of the platforms shuddered down toward the ground, its arm bending and retracting into the floor.

"The most valuable of books are stored up in the air. Unless you know how to operate the arms, they would be impossible to reach," said the librarian.

The librarian opened a door in the waist-high balustrade and, with a finger raised to the books, began her search. Kata was not at all surprised when she turned. "It's gone. I don't understand how it could be, but it's gone. I suppose it could have been misfiled. . . ."

"You won't find it," said Kata. "May I see the reference card, though?"

"Yes, of course." The librarian passed the old yellow card to Kata.

*The Alerium Calix: Construction, Structure, and Command*
By the Aediles Philan and Drusa
Note: Beware the thaumaturgical properties of the book. Unknown ideograms engraved on cover of skin. Those who studied it have reported illness.
Contents: A recording of the description of the construction of Alerion's prism by two of the Aediles involved in the process. Included are a summary of Alerion's last days and his travel to Caeli-Amur, the extraction of his spirit into the prism, and the thaumaturgical laws according to which the mythical prism can be controlled.

Kata's mind began to whir: the prism again. Thom had sought this book, which described the prism and its workings. Was that simply to discover its nature? It was possible, she supposed, that Armand didn't know how to use the thing. It was an ancient artifact, after all, its powers lost to antiquity. Or was the book of value in itself? Whatever the case, this book was the key. Thom and Aceline had died for it. But there were still unanswered questions:

Who had killed them and why was money being smuggled through waterways beneath the city? Kata's thoughts returned to the letter. *Our best plan should be realized by the Twilight Observance,* it had read. The Twilight Observance was a month away, but what plan would they realize?

That evening, Kata found a rear seat in the automaton factory where the Moderate Committee met. She preferred to remain far from the center of the hall, where the speakers would stand. As moderates streamed in, she glanced once more around the giant subterranean space, where huge machines were used to build yet more machines. It was an experimental factory, and one of the first to break down under the blockade, so now the masses of pistons and pylons, the giant pincered arms reaching into the darkness, were silent.

Soon the members of the Moderate Committee faced one another while workers watched from among the machines, where they perched on giant arms, leaned against pylons in the shadows, or sat uneasily on iron girders.

Olivier wore a worried expression as he addressed the group. "I returned with Ejan and the delegation from the villas. They will not stop their blockade, unless we provide them with machines, with boots and coats, with mechanical ploughs, with all the goods from the city. They spat at our feet as we left."

The audience began to hoot in disapproval.

Olivier continued, "Ejan has made his plans clear. He aims to crush the opposition. Georges runs the new Criminal Tribunal with savage efficiency. They hold court in the old Arbor Palace, where hundreds are already imprisoned. Each day they deliberate on cases brought by the guards. Most are condemned to death by this new machine, the Bolt. Any moment it will start its deadly work."

Before he could finish, calls came from among the machines: "So it should!" and "We're starving here!"

Olivier's line of argument would not win the population, not when the city was so desperate. He hesitated, stuttered out his words. "Ev . . . even . . . even if they are guilty, death should not be the punishment for anything in the new world. But we have few allies in this. Elise is our representative on the Criminal Tribunal. Elise?"

Elise rose to her feet. She was olive-skinned and lean. There was something fragile about her, as if she was a spare part that might break at any moment. But her voice was clear and fresh. "The thing is, without some repressive measures, how can we discourage those who would undermine us, who would sabotage our efforts? The villas are still blockading us, and we *have* to feed the city. To argue against the tribunal is to undermine our own support, for the populace itself knows we must defend ourselves, that we must eat."

"We have to act! We have to fight!" came the calls from the machine-gallery.

Kata found herself on her feet. "You don't understand!" she yelled. A moment later all eyes were on her. She had not wanted to play a part in the moderates' leadership, and yet here she was, standing and arguing. Her words came out smoother and calmer than she'd imagined they could. "The point is not merely to respond to the vigilants' positions but to elucidate our own. We should start from first principles. How should we treat our opponents? How do we deal with those who do not agree with us? Remember, the workers in the villas are participating in the boycott too. Haven't we failed to convince them? Isn't the greater responsibility on us to show them we're on their side? Imprisonment should be enough of a deterrent, especially for those who, in other circumstances, would be our people. The moment the death penalty becomes necessary is the moment we have already lost."

This time Kata was subjected to boos.

"The time for such a position has passed."

"Loose the Bolt, I say!"

But others cheered: "I have a brother working at the villas! He's poor, just like us!"

Kata pushed ahead. "To acquiesce is to allow Ejan to consolidate his position and erode ours. And as his policies become increasingly dictatorial, they reconcile the citizenry to their own passivity, and the new order's base will crumble. No, if we don't fight now, everyone loses."

"If we fight now, Ejan will come for us next!" said Olivier.

So the debate raged on. Kata sat down and decided she would not speak again, and yet she'd felt good stating her mind, standing up for what she believed in. So it was with a heavy heart that she watched the decision to support Ejan prevail. Many among them hoped that the crisis would pass once the grain had been appropriated. Meanwhile, the moderate guards—fully four hundred of them—would join in any assault on the villas. *It's democracy*, thought Kata. *Like Rikard said, that's what it meant.*

As she left the room, Kata knew in her heart that the moderates would pose no threat to Ejan now. The problem was, without Aceline and Thom to make cogent arguments, to use their influence to convince their followers, the moderates would just follow Ejan's policies.

As Kata strode from the factory, an urchin came running toward her. For a moment she thought it was Henri, but the little boy's hair was too light. He passed her a letter and scurried off.

The message had no signature, just a sketch of two hands joining—the mysterious symbol tattooed onto the bodies of the thaumaturgists—so she presumed it must have come from the thaumaturgist Detis who had rowed her and Rikard through the Marin Palace. The note contained only one line: *The transactions in the canals have begun again.*

# TWENTY

After long nights of searching the canals, Kata began to think they would never find the smugglers. As the darkness deepened and the temperature dropped, she wrapped her jacket around herself. Their gondola, directed by a boatman named Pierre, drifted slowly beneath one of the tiny bridges. Starlight illuminated the canal water, making it look like a river of silver in the night. Kata knew it was only an illusion. Daylight would show the canals to be dirty and full of refuse. Even now occasional gusts of stench drifted around them, for summer had passed and the early autumn rains had not yet flushed the canals.

They had chosen the area near Operaio Bridge, which Thom's neighbor had mentioned. In the days before the uprising, the canals would have been filled with gondolas, lovers taking romantic rides beneath the picturesque bridges, alongside the gothic walls with detailed bas-reliefs carved into them. Or groups of drunken students would have piled into flat-bottomed boats, singing and pushing one another into the waters. But these days they were mostly empty, for hunger had stripped the city of much of its previous vitality. Now the waterways took on a ghostly air, fog hovering over the water. The bridges began to loom out of the wavy darkness, the opening to the underground canals like openings to the underworld.

They had taken to whispering, for any sound seemed to carry.

"Let's leave," said Rikard. "There's no point."

"This will be the last night," said Kata.

They passed through one of the narrowest canals, the gondola bumping against the walls as it drifted along, the lamp hanging in front of their vessel casting a soft sphere of light before them.

Creatures scuttled along the walls here, rats and perhaps other things too.

The canal flowed through a dark tunnel, and before long, the sound of crashing water filled their ears. A little farther ahead, a waterfall from a second canal cascaded into the first. The roof of this second canal was too low for any boat to pass along, and it would be impossible to hitch their boat up in any case, so they continued for a moment.

"Wait," said Kata. "Go back."

Pierre stopped the boat, stepped across to the front, and began to paddle them backward. He stopped them before the rushing waterfall. They all took deep breaths. Hidden behind the waterfall, a third canal led away into the darkness.

"We'll get wet," said Pierre.

Rikard shrugged. "Do you know this route?"

"No," said Pierre.

"Let's get wet," said Kata.

By the time they'd entered the new waterway, their clothes clung to their skin and their feet stood in inches of water.

A whole new system opened farther inland. It was mostly underground, with occasional small openings in the roof giving them brief visions of the sky above. Their lamp cast eerie shadows against the wall.

As they passed a larger waterway, the voices of several men carried over. Rikard extinguished the lamp, and they inched forward in darkness. The sound of their boat bumping against the wall seemed to echo loudly. Once again, they came to a T-intersection. A hundred feet or so down the new canal, two boats were moored at a small landing. Lamps threw yellow light onto the congregation; spectral forms huddled in the darkness. Kata squinted: yes, she could just make out a group of black-suited thaumaturgists speaking with the people on the other boat.

She strained to hear what they were saying. Fragments drifted down to her: "The rest can wait—"

"—as though there hasn't been enough anyway."

"—followed. Should be ready by the Twilight Observance, but we're supposed to wait for Varenis."

"—wait for what?"

"For them to march on the city. The seditionists will send out their forces and then . . ."

Cynical laughter echoed toward them. Without needing any encouragement, Pierre gently rowed their gondola backward. He found a small niche and maneuvered into it; there they hid and waited.

Before long, the sound of men talking became louder and louder, until it seemed as if they were right beside Kata. One of the boats was approaching quickly, while the other had presumably left in the opposite direction.

"—middle of the night. I'm sick of it."

"If they gave it to us all at once, then we wouldn't have to come back."

"They don't trust us."

For an instant she was certain that the men would look to their side as they passed and see the three of them hiding. Silently, she pulled her knives from their sheaths beneath her shirt and waited. Her heartbeat thumped in her ears. The water next to them lit up with an eerie warm glow. The second boat drifted into view, not ten feet from them. It was impossible that they would not be seen. Kata prepared to strike. She saw the rough faces of the men before her; one passed a bottle to the other, who took a swig.

Darkness engulfed them again, and Kata breathed out.

They followed the boat as quietly as possible along the canal, which continued far underground. Streams joined it periodically, for much of Caeli-Amur's water came from underground springs that ran off the mountain or the hills to the west. Most were natural, but some were underground aqueducts built by the ancients, their sources lost long ago.

Intersecting canals became rare, a sign that they had headed to the south of the main network. Kata figured they were beneath the Quaedian somewhere. The boatmen ahead took little care to disguise their passing. They were drinking and relaxed, perhaps from making the journey often. Their voices echoed along the underground waterways, the light from their boats swinging and bobbing as they went.

Finally the boat ahead stopped, and the gang disembarked. Pierre allowed the gondola to drift toward the landing as their lamplight disappeared from sight.

Pierre hitched to the landing beside the other boat, while Kata and Rikard climbed a set of damp rocky steps. Above them, the first gleam of dawn brushed the eastern sky. When they stepped into the open, the stench of refuse drifted around them.

Kata turned to Rikard. "We're in the Lav—"

Glimpsing movement at the corner of her eye, Kata dove to her right, close to the wall, but it was too late. Something struck her in the side, and she went down. Glancing back, she saw one of their attackers land a single blow to Rikard's head, which felled him. He was unconscious before he hit the ground.

Kata dived and rolled, pain roaring through her side. Two attackers rushed toward her, but she already had her knives in her hands.

She threw one knife, striking the first man in the eye. The knife jutted from his head like a broken branch from a tree. The man crumpled as if his legs had been cut from beneath him.

The second knife flew past the shoulder of the second attacker, who swung a brutal-looking club down at her head. But she had already rolled past him, turned and leaped on his back. She snapped one arm across his neck and locked her hand into the elbow of her other arm.

The man tried to cry out, but not even a gurgle escaped his lips. Rather than try to pry Kata's hands loose, he swung at her with his club—a fatal error. The bludgeon glanced off the side of her cheek, a bruising but insignificant strike.

Her pressure crushed the man's esophagus and closed off the blood to his head. The club fell from his hands, rattled on the ground. He tried to unhook Kata's legs from where they were wrapped around his waist. He staggered, and a second later collapsed to his knees and crashed to the ground. Kata held on until well after she felt him go limp.

She recovered her knives, stepped lightly across to where Rikard was slowly regaining consciousness, his eyes blinking and staring. "Where am I?"

Kata looked past the slums to the massive building ahead of them, built from metal. She knew this place. Everyone who had visited the Lavere knew it. "We're at the Collegian Caelian." Kata knew now for sure whom the money was going to: the flabby-faced Dumas, the D who had written the letter to Armand, the D who employed slaves, the D who had constructed the Bolt.

"Come on. We've got to get away," she said.

They staggered down the stairs once more and struggled onto the boat. Pierre rowed them rapidly away as Rikard lay dazed. He brought his hand up to his head, groaning.

"We were attacked. You beat them?" Rikard was confused.

"It's all right now," said Kata.

They paid Pierre to drop them near the Opera, where Kata took Rikard's shoulder. "We have to get you home. I'll call a carriage."

The carriage rattled up into the roughest area of the factory quarter. The weak early morning light was pale and almost colorless. Kata stared at the passersby: lone drifters still up from the night before, a few workers heading to work, others wandering around at a loss now that the industries were closing down. Mean-looking youth loitered on one corner, but Kata was unafraid. If anything, they should be afraid of her.

A squat little worker's cottage lay nested between two apartment buildings. Rikard opened the door and led her into a parlor, where he crumpled onto a couch. "I've got a terrible headache. Gods, I've got a lump the size of a pumpkin."

A wide-hipped, broad-faced woman in a nightgown ambled in after them. She had the look of someone who took no prisoners. "Good, that will serve you right. Drinking or drugs?"

"Mother, this is Kata. Kata, this is Corette," said Rikard.

"Would you like some coffee?" Corette's voice was as rough as the streets outside.

"Please," said Kata.

"Me too," said Rikard.

"I'm not sure you should." Kata looked from Rikard to Corette. "He suffered a blow to his head. He shouldn't sleep, but I'm not sure coffee is a wise idea either."

"Oh, don't mother me, Kata. I've already got one mother. Believe me, she's tough enough."

"Tough enough? I let you traipse around the city and return home at all manner of the day or night. You need discipline." Corette laughed. "A good dose of it."

This time Rikard smiled sweetly. "Coffee, please."

Corette put one hand on her hip. "I'd offer you food, Kata, but we're all out, and the factory's closed, so there's no money coming in. Who knows what we'll do now."

"Coffee is fine," said Kata. "Thanks."

Corette sauntered back out of the parlor, and Kata turned to Rikard. "Your mother?"

He nodded, sat up a little more, and fixed Kata with a stare. His voice filled with leaden seriousness. "I know what you are, Kata. You're a philosopher-assassin."

Kata stared at him, speechless, panicked. He had guessed from the fight with the smugglers, and now this was it: her secret was out. She would be disgraced. She might even find herself in the Arbor dungeons with the rest of the seditionists' enemies.

"Look at you," said Rikard. "Trained, athletic. I was knocked out with a single blow, and yet you defeated two armed men in a matter of seconds. You've been keeping it a secret, though. Since before the overthrow. Why would that be?"

Kata didn't have the strength to lie, but she didn't have the strength to tell the truth, either. If she didn't say anything, perhaps she could believe the conversation wasn't happening.

"Were you spying on us for one of the Houses?" said Rikard. "I remember there were suspicions, back before the overthrow. Everyone thought we had been infiltrated, and then one night—wham, the Technis guards were on us."

Kata tried to conjure up a defense, but nothing came. There was no defense. "I'll hand myself over."

Rikard examined her. Then his voice warmed. "But you've changed, haven't you? I know you and trust you."

"You shouldn't," said Kata.

"But, you see, it's just that attitude that proves yourself to me. Anyway, who among us has no sins?"

"Will you tell Ejan?"

Rikard shrugged. "He has enough on his mind, don't you think? The next Authority meeting will order the assault on the villas to break the blockade. We, on the other hand, must capture Aceline's killer." When Kata said nothing, he added, "You see, Kata, you've changed me, too. A little, at least." She startled, and he added, "Don't get too excited. I'm still a vigilant."

After that, Corette brought in tray with a little pot of coffee cooked over a stove and three small cups. "It's the best I could do, I'm afraid. Blow to the head, huh? I should give you a blow to the head, young man."

"You should," said Kata. "Beat some sense into him."

"I knew it was a mistake to introduce you two," said Rikard.

# TWENTY-ONE

Armand swung his feet over the edge of his cot and placed them on the cold wooden floor. Outside, the morning bell rang. He rested there, looked down at his thin legs. His body had changed. His features were beginning to resemble the gaunt and skeletal faces of those surrounding him. The prisoners arrived as individuals, but the camp was ironing out the differences between them. Like tributaries flowing into a river, the prisoners were becoming one—a great flood of humanity, gray and uniform, headed for death.

Irik and Armand had started to accept their fate. Armand had seen it happening to those around them: men broken down, giving up on life. The autumn cold had set in, striking the weakest with illness, sending them prostrate to the infirmary, where they quickly died. Perhaps they were the lucky ones. Others who had been taken by the bloodstone disease raved incomprehensibly as the spidery redness crawled through their bodies. In the last week, another man had shuffled out of the camp and planted himself on the ground beyond the gates. It took about six months, Armand understood, from first infection until final transformation. *But none of them would last that long with winter coming,* he thought.

Armand ran his hand over his mattress. Beneath the canvas cover, he felt the pouch of bloodstone he'd hidden in the straw underneath. If he were a thaumaturgist, he would be able to use the bloodstone to invoke some force to break down the walls of the camp, or to make himself invisible, or fly into the sky, or something. But of course, Varenis's thaumaturgists were scattered across the Empire, waiting for the stone the prisoners were mining. Armand dreamed of returning to the city to wreak his revenge or to rise

204 * RJURIK DAVIDSON

back to his rightful position. Of course, the bloodstone would not be enough of a weapon to influence anyone in the Directorate. He needed something more. Still, it was something.

When they finished their watery porridge, the prisoners began the slow shuffle to the mines. As Armand's gang descended into the darkness, he felt a rumble from afar. The vibrations hummed up his legs. Like the others, he instinctively squatted down and pressed himself against the cart. In the last week, the mountain had shifted on its haunches several times, leaving the ground shaking and rattling, sending huge slabs of rock sliding down faraway mountain faces. As before, the rumbling passed and all was again silent.

The gang reached the dark end of the tunnel, and Armand began to strike at the rock face with his pick. His body had become hardened to the rigors of the labor; no longer did his back cramp and spasm. Instead it ached like a hot coal, and he entered a death-like stupor where the long hours seemed as one. Carelessly, he breathed in the bloodstone particles drifting around in the air.

A second deep and ominous rumbling broke Armand's trance. Dust and debris fell from the roof, and the timberwork began to groan. Armand heard a crack, and, in an instant, the crew dropped their tools and squeezed themselves against the sides of the tunnel. One of the beams gave way, and several large rocks fell onto the tracks. Then all was silent. Only after the rumbling had passed did Armand's heart begin to race. Like the others, his eyes roved over the walls and roof, expecting them to give way.

Ohan pointed to Armand. "Lift those rocks into the cart."

Armand took two steps toward them, when, in the far distance, he heard a soft whisper that slowly turned into a hum. In an instant he recognized that the earth was moving, but this time it came from far away. It grew in strength with each second like a terrible tidal wave rushing toward them.

Armand dropped his pick and raced through the dark with the rest of them, bouncing off one another in their panic, striking the stony tunnel walls, fleeing for the surface. Someone behind him held a lamp, and it scattered jittery light. One moment Armand could see the tracks and the tunnel, the next nothing but darkness, then once more the road was lit up.

Armand lost his feet, smashed his hands against the rough ground, scrambled up again. The roar of the mountain filled his ears, magnifying in the tunnel. Still the sound rose, until it was a deafening roar. Everything shook, dust poured from the roof, and the quake struck. Beams exploded above him. The air was filled with particles and debris. Armand lurched to one side, his arms struck hard rock, something smashed down onto his foot, and sharp pain drove up his leg. Rocks peppered him from above. Everything was momentarily black. Then all was still.

Armand pulled himself to his feet as the dust around him settled. The roof behind him had given way completely. A still-lit lamp was lodged in the rockfall beside a protruding hand. Two others had escaped with Armand, but the other five of their gang were smashed beneath the rockfall or trapped behind it.

One of the prisoners pulled the lamp from where it was stuck. "Let's get out of here."

"Anyone there?" called Armand.

"They're dead. Or they soon will be." One of the prisoners started to move away.

Armand thought he could hear something from behind the rockfall, but he couldn't be sure.

"Come back. I think I heard something," said Armand.

But he was left in the steadily enclosing darkness. The other two were already around a corner. Only one side of the wall was illuminated, and soon he would be immersed in complete darkness.

Armand raced after them. By the time they reached the outside, other gangs had emerged, covered in dirt. Yet others remained beneath, dead or dying in the darkness of the mountain. Lost souls without hope.

Tiedmann's man—the collaborator 7624—lined the prisoners up and counted them. That was what they were: only numbers. But Armand began to put together a plan. He saw now how he might gain the trust of the barbarians, if Ohan were alive behind the fall.

Armand approached Prisoner 7624. "There are survivors below. We have to get them out."

The collaborator sneered. "They'll be dead soon enough. You should thank the gods you escaped."

Armand thought of those below in the darkness, black desolation filling them. It might have been him. His fists clenched, and he pictured himself striking 7624 down for his callousness. Armand took two steps toward 7624 and dropped to his knees. "Please, let me lead a team to save them. They're our brothers."

Prisoner 7624 frowned. First he seemed confused, then he seemed to give up as if it was too much bother. He waved his bloodstone-infected arm. "Go on then, with anyone who wants to go with you. You have until the usual time."

Armand looked around desperately. He needed help, but no prisoner stepped forward. In desperation, Armand grasped the two men from his own crew by the arms. "Come with me."

To his surprise, they followed him passively. Perhaps they had grown accustomed to obeying orders. He didn't know their names, and with their gaunt, skeletal faces, they had the look of the prison's many gray men eking out their last days.

Together they pushed a cart down into the deadly tunnel, down into the blackness. *This is my chance,* thought Armand as he strained and heaved. He didn't want to become like the men who walked beside him. It all rested on the hope that Ohan was still alive, and that rescuing him would bring Armand the favor of his tribesmen.

When he reached the rockfall, Armand listened, but there was no sound beyond the dripping of water from the roof.

"We have no idea how much rock has fallen," one of the gray men said. "By the end of the shift, we'll never have moved enough."

"The others will be sent back to work mining bloodstone," said Armand. "At least we have a higher purpose."

They began to shovel away the rock, pulling out boulders and piling them into the cart or tossing them against the side of the tunnel, finding more rocks and shattered fragments of timberwork behind them. Occasionally they listened but heard no signs of life. So the hours went, deep into the afternoon. The shift came to an end, the tunnel still blocked by a wall of rubble.

Armand felt crushing disappointment, but there was little else he could do, so the three of them placed their hands against the cart's cold side, ready to drive it up to the open air.

"Ready?" said one of the men.

Armand stood back, held his hands in the air. "Wait."

The three of them stood in the shadowy hellhole, listening. Yes, there it was, a soft tapping from behind the rock: *tock, tock, tock.*

"Do you hear that?" Armand cocked his head to listen. There it was, a definite sound. Someone was alive behind the rockfall.

Armand unhooked a pick from the cart, but one of the other prisoners grabbed his arm. "We have to go. The shift is over."

Armand grimaced, looked back at the rockfall. They might work all night and not break through. He sighed, felt defeat rush in on him. "We'll come back tomorrow."

He hooked the pick back onto the cart, and the three of them strained and heaved and sweated and cursed until they finally burst out into the cold twilight of the surface, where streaks of amber smudged the chilly sky.

In the icy twilight air, Prisoner 7624 directed the factory workers back to the camp. At the factory entrance, warm gusts of air coursed from the furnaces and kissed Armand's frigid hands and face. He thought of the dark tunnel and the brutal task facing them tomorrow. He steeled his voice and approached 7624. "There are men alive below. Tomorrow I'll need some men to dig them out."

Prisoner 7624 stared balefully at Armand, raised his gleaming red hand to the depression in his forehead. "That vein of bloodstone is lost. Tomorrow you'll work with another gang at another seam."

"We can't leave them down there."

"Just be happy it's not you, prisoner. What, are you going to stay up all night, thinking about the poor critters shivering down there in the cold and the dark? No, you're not. You're going to forget about them and focus on yourself. That's what everyone's going to do. Now get out of here." Prisoner 7624 bared his blackened teeth, like an attack dog ready to growl.

As Armand shuffled back to the camp, he realized the terrible toll the day had taken on him. His arms and legs trembled from exhaustion; his emotional reserves were gone. He felt like crying but didn't seem to have any tears.

In the evening Armand sat beside Irik, the barbarians beside them grim-faced at losing Ohan. Armand only had a few more bursts of energy before he would be reduced to one of the gray-faced men, incapable of action, who haunted the camp, who took even his orders . . . ghosts who were not yet dead.

The Westerner chieftain, whose name was Ijahan, pulled at his white beard and leaned toward Armand. Worry had carved lines on his face, and Armand could only imagine the years he'd spent trying to save his tribe from Varenis before he ended up here. He was lean as a reed, and there was a ropy toughness to him. Without the feathers in his hair he might have been mistaken for a weathered ship's captain who had seen too much sun and salty spray.

"Ohan is perhaps alive?" Ijahan said. "You tried to rescue some of the men today, they say."

Armand nodded toward the Tiedmann's table. "Our supervisor, 7624, won't allow us to continue tomorrow."

Ijahan drew a deep breath and looked at Tiedmann and his collaborators, sitting at the front of the hall like lords. One of Ijahan's men said something to him in their strange western dialect. He nodded. Together they stood and approached Tiedmann, pleaded with him, but the moonfaced man shook his head and waved them away.

Seeing this, Armand racked his brain: How might he buy Tiedmann's favor? He was still wondering this as he forced himself to his feet and approached the table, where he slipped onto the bench beside Tiedmann. He would improvise.

"We've met before, you know," Armand said.

The man turned his baleful round eyes to Armand. From up close he appeared paler still, as if no blood moved beneath that skin. Tiedmann's stare frightened Armand, who sensed the man couldn't see anyone else as a person, wasn't aware of their hopes or emotions. There was no empathy there.

"Ha!" said Tiedmann.

Armand sensed 7624 standing behind them, ready to pounce and drag him across the room. Armand pictured the man kicking him viciously into unconsciousness as everyone else watched.

Armand refocused on Tiedmann. "*Met* is not exactly the right term. We've seen each other. When you were the Director in Varenis. This is a camp for political prisoners. Of course they sent you here. There's quite a struggle going on since you were removed. Valentin, Rainer—they're all fighting like dogs over a bone."

Tiedmann's face tightened at the mention of his previous office. Armand tensed, expecting the chief collaborator to call for 7624.

Some crisis point had been reached. Before the man acted, Armand rushed on: "You spoke occasionally to Director Autec of Technis. I was his assistant, you see."

It was then that Armand's path seemed to open up before him. He hated the next words that fell from his mouth. "In any case, I have come to offer you a trade."

Filled with guilt, he reached beneath his uniform, hesitated for a second, then brought forth his grandfather's ring, which he placed on the table before them. He then reached forward and slipped it over his finger. In an instant, the ideograms rose from its surface, hovered above it, a hologram of the engravings below. He slid it off onto the table again, and the symbols settled back into the metal. "Thaumaturgy."

Tiedmann reached for the ring with stubby sausagelike fingers, but Armand's hand closed over it. "You must allow me a full team to rescue the men buried by the rockfall."

Tiedmann's avaricious eyes settled on Armand. He grasped Armand's hand with his own. "Give me the ring."

Armand felt the corners of the metal jutting into the skin of his palm. He held tight.

"You can have your team," said Tiedmann. "Three days. You can have three days."

Armand opened his hand. A moment later the ring was gone, hidden in one of the folds of Tiedmann's uniform. The former Director smiled cynically.

As he settled back into his seat, Armand's gaze roved across the hall. As he stared out at the gray mass, Armand realized with a jolt that all the children were gone. He closed his eyes and tried not to think of their fates.

Two of the team reconstructed the scaffolding above. The rest of crew dug through the rocks and rubble. Periodically they listened for sounds from behind the rockfall. In the morning they heard a faint tapping, but by the afternoon it had fallen silent. Still, they made good progress, but there was no telling how much of the tunnel had collapsed. When the shift ended in the late afternoon, they still faced a wall of rock blocking the tunnel. Armand hoped the survivors would last another night. They would have water, at least, but would they survive the cold?

The following day they returned, but there was no sound of tapping. Desperation gripped Armand. He felt hope slipping away, but they kept digging. Armand's back entered a new stage of pain, which seemed to shoot down his right leg. He felt numbness and tingling in his toes. But he wouldn't give up.

Halfway through the afternoon, one of the prisoners cried out. "Look, look!"

Excitement buzzed in the darkness. The man had pulled a rock away, but it only revealed a cold and dirty hand jutting out through the rocks. The body they uncovered was crushed and broken, a man-sized rag doll whose legs and arms flopped in unnatural ways.

By the time the shift was over, they still hadn't broken through.

That night Armand lay awake on his hard bunk, staring into the night. White spots drifted across his eyes. There was no hope now, he realized. He had given away his ring for nothing. He would not rescue Ohan, or anyone else. He would not escape. Soon he would die.

On the final morning before his gang would be sent back to the bloodstone veins, Armand approached the rockfall with the same ambivalence as the others. The morning was half gone when one of the prisoners said, "There's that tapping again."

Armand's heart leaped. This time he didn't have to strain to hear it. It came loud and clear, like someone knocking on a door. He redoubled his efforts, but morning gave way to afternoon and there seemed no end to the slog.

Eventually one of the crew said, "That's it. Time to go."

"No!" commanded Armand. "We're staying. It's not long now."

The men leaned against the cart, ready to push, but Armand grabbed one of them, shoved him back to the rockfall.

"Just a little while longer," commanded Armand.

They began again. Armand almost expected someone to strike him from behind. But on and on they worked, and the others did not abandon him. Until, finally, Armand pulled away a rock that opened up a black and empty space.

A Westerner's voice came through the breach. "What took you so long?"

Armand felt like crying. "Are you hurt?"

"We're alive," said a second voice. "There are two of us. The rest, dead somewhere. But we're alive."

They loaded Ohan and Prisoner 8891, whose arm had given in to the bloodstone disease, onto the cart. They were dehydrated, emaciated, injured. Ohan seemed to have cracked a leg, while 8891's chest had been crushed by a rock. He coughed up blood as they laid him down. When they rolled them out into the cold air, the guards were waiting.

Prisoner 7624 sneered. "Get these two to the infirmary."

About half of the infirmary's cold beds were occupied. Some of the patients lay staring silently, like gaunt cadavers watching for death himself to enter through the door. Others moaned and called out, fevers gripping their bodies and minds.

An exhausted doctor—himself a prisoner—gestured for them to lay the two men on cots at the end of the room. As the others rushed off to the mess hall, Armand fetched water for the survivors. When he returned, the Westerner chief Ijahan was squatting by Ohan, talking in the hushed guttural dialect.

"He says you insisted we be rescued," said Ohan.

Armand shrugged. "What if it had been me locked in that deep darkness? We must help one another if we're to survive and escape this hell."

Ohan looked on quietly. "Well, perhaps one day we can return the favor."

"Let's hope neither of us is trapped beneath the mountain again," said Armand.

Ohan nodded seriously, but his voice was light and ironic. "What, you have somewhere else to be?"

Armand remained silent, let the joke wash over him. There were so few pleasures in the camp, so little hope, it felt like a moment in a warm bath.

"Perhaps we can help." Ohan smiled slightly.

When Armand reached the mess hall, the food was gone, but a barbarian was waiting for him with a plate of paste. He gestured to it and nodded. Armand fell on it ravenously. As he lay in his bed that night, Armand felt happy for the first time. He ran Ohan's words through his mind again. *What, you have somewhere else to be?* the man said. *Perhaps we can help.*

# TWENTY-TWO

After the collapse of the tunnel, Armand replaced Ohan as the leader of the mining crew. He kept the time, directed the prisoners, worked hard himself. He watched as those around him lost all initiative and drive and accepted his orders like cattle. His own strength eked away by the day; his muscles wasted into thin and wiry things; his mind lost its agility. His back seared with pain, needles stabbed down his leg and foot. He could only think of the most basic tasks: filling the cart with bloodstone, falling asleep as quickly as he could on his wooden cot each night, scraping every ounce of the morning porridge and nightly paste from his plate into his mouth. The breakdown of a man happened quickly.

Ohan had been transferred into the carpentry shop, which the barbarians ran. He was the last of the Westerners to escape the mining gangs. Now all of them were constructing a new barrack in preparation for a coming influx of prisoners. Safe and warm, they seemed to have forgotten Armand, whose thoughts of escape were now nothing but a child's faraway dream. He had given away his grandfather's ring for nothing.

The prison had been growing for some time, it seemed. The Empire's conquered provinces were resisting, internal dissent had increased, and Varenis had responded with greater violence.

Armand had once thought that for an authority to rule, it must stick to the principles of civilization, respect, honesty. But after Varenis, he saw that power was a vicious game in which such principles often played little part. He should have known that, considering the fate of his grandfather, but he had been brought up on principles and couldn't let them go. He still believed in loyalty, but Valentin had shown him there was little place for it in the world.

*No,* thought Armand. *I will not allow them to turn me into them—people for whom there is no good or bad in the world, people for whom there is no meaning but survival, conquest, the lust for power and personal gain.* That was everything he opposed.

It was a surprise when someone whistled to Armand and Irik as they crossed between buildings toward the mess hall. Ohan leaned against one of the barracks, crutches propped under his armpits.

Armand stared at the barbarian blankly, his exhausted mind unable to comprehend what Ohan had said.

"I'm Irik," said the former oppositionist.

Ohan nodded and turned back to Armand. "Perhaps you'd like to visit the carpentry shop this evening. A little while after eating."

Armand sensed something was happening. "Irik also."

Ohan pressed his lips together and shook his head. "Only you."

Armand glanced at his friend. The oppositionist raised his eyebrows and closed his eyes, resigned to his exclusion. He reached out, held Armand's hand briefly with his own warm one, squeezed, and let go.

Ohan hopped away on his crutches toward the mess hall. Armand watched until the Westerner passed through the open doors and into the sparse building.

He and Irik found their own table to eat at, away from the tribesmen. They didn't speak. Armand couldn't admit that the barbarians might be taking him under their arm but leaving Irik out in the wild. When they left the hall, he, too, squeezed Irik's warm hand, then let it drop away.

Back in the barracks, Armand lay on his cot for a while, resting his aching muscles. For the first time in days he felt something other than exhaustion and resignation.

The carpentry building was a medium-sized wooden hall with just a few strips of paint left on wooden beams. When Armand was halfway there, he saw 7624 staring at him from the square. A shock of fear struck him, but he walked on, feeling the malevolent eyes on his back the entire way. *There's something wrong in that man's head,* thought Armand. Something had broken, and the two parts couldn't be rejoined. Alarmingly, 7624 seemed to be taking quite a dislike to him. Through the open window of the carpentry shop, a Westerner said something to the others inside. Everyone, it seemed, was watching Armand.

Armand stood before the door at a loss, confused by the memories of long-gone etiquette. Eventually he turned the creaking handle and stepped inside. In the center of the carpentry shop sat many of the barbarians, including Ohan and Ijahan. Together they were quite a sight, for they were the only prisoners allowed to retain long hair, strung with red and orange beads, green and yellow feathers. The Commander had never carried through on his threat to shave them, and even in their grubby state, the colors were glorious in the grayness of the camp.

"My barbarian friends," said Armand.

The chieftain Ijahan smiled, an expression that seemed to shift the great lines across his face. "We don't think of ourselves as barbarians, Armand. The rulers of Varenis are the barbarians."

Armand saw the logic to the man's argument. The barbarians had their own culture, their own practices. He had little doubt that there was a nobility to it, even if they didn't have the trappings of higher civilization. Indeed, they possessed the same principles he adhered to—loyalty and honor—while Varenis was a cutthroat world of maneuvers and betrayal.

No sooner had he found a seat than three little knocks came from the direction of the far wall. Two of the barbarians quickly pulled the table back from the wall. Another pulled away a mat and lifted a handle hidden in the dirt. A square section of the floor rose, then a hand appeared, holding up burlap bags filled with material. The Westerners rapidly hid these behind a pile of planks. Then a Westerner's head poked through the trapdoor.

Ohan gestured to Armand. "If you want to escape, you must dig. Ten more body lengths and we should be beyond the fence. Then we dig ourselves up and out. When we are ready, we will escape at night. The guards won't notice we are gone until morning. They may expect us to head west toward the plains and away from the mountains. Instead we will journey south along the mountain range. There are still tribes there who live beyond the province of Varenis's empire. They will help us and we will join them. After the winter we will return for the women."

Armand's skin crawled with an unnerving energy. This chance to escape would only come once, he knew.

Armand descended into the passage and crawled along, a flickering little oil lamp in one hand, two empty burlap bags in the other. He ached terribly. Soon he would be nothing but a bag of bones.

The tunnel came to a rough end. He seized a sawn-off pick that lay on the ground and began to dig away at the rocky earth, periodically filling the bags. Exhausted from the day's work, this task seemed a special kind of agony. His shoulder muscles blazed with pain. He felt his neck spasm. His back was aflame. Yet he forced himself on.

When he returned, he knocked on the trapdoor above him three times. A second later he was out into the carpentry shop. Another Westerner took his place below.

Armand braced himself for his demand. "My friend Irik must escape with us. He's loyal, hardworking, honest—all the things that are too rare in this world."

The chieftain took a deep breath. "Only you. No one else. You must promise this."

Armand looked down at his rough and worn boots. It suddenly struck him that they had been worn by someone before him—a dead man. That they might be worn by another, if he didn't escape. Irik wore similar boots.

"I beg you," Armand said. "Please."

Ijahan shook his head, pulled his white beard. His responsibilities seemed to have drained him.

That night Armand couldn't sleep as he considered how to help Irik. He could escape with the Westerners and come back for Irik when they returned for the women. Yes, that was what he would do. But in his heart, he knew Irik would never make it through the winter—none of the prisoners would—and there was no way he could help Irik now. He tossed and turned, unable to make himself comfortable. The pain was too great.

# TWENTY-THREE

Max felt that with each step, Aya was taking him back in time, back, back into an ancient and lost world. The ruined road wound its way slowly into the rugged hill. Its broken cobblestones were uneven, either sunken into or jutting from the ground. The land had shifted over the centuries, lifting sections up on angles, twisting others out of alignment. Birch and pine forests covered the hill in copses, at places thick and ominous. *No one has passed this way for a millennium,* he thought.

—You'll never find the tower—said Max. —The landscape has changed too much.

*I'll feel my way there. I can almost feel Iria calling me.*

—She's dead. She's been dead a thousand years.

*You think death is forever? You think I can't summon her from the ground?*

—I know you can't. You're not a god, after all. You're just a man, like me. But tell me this: When you built this mythic world, this pleasure park, what did you think would happen?

*Most people lived simple lives at first. When there's not great history, people don't feel the need for fame or for heroic deeds. They lead small lives, and are happy. But some of us had other callings. The Aediles were in charge of administration—public service took their fancy. And us— those you call the gods—we learned the Art. It was the Art that was our downfall. We wanted to create, you see, but the Art pulls you away from the human world. It changed us: Iria, me, Alerion, all of us. We should have turned our back on its powers, but its powers devoured us. Is that really what you want, Maximilian?*

Max hesitated. His dreams of heroism had scattered, his hopes of leading the seditionists nothing but hot air, his ambitions nothing but childhood fancies—so much had changed for him. What would he give for knowledge of the prime language? He wasn't sure.

—If I could learn the Art, I could play a part in making the world better—he said. —I could help the seditionists, help everybody.

*That's what we all thought. You start hoping to build things. You end with war machines dancing and burning in the Keos Pass. You end up hiding in the Sentinel Tower.*

Aya became silent and brooding, and Max didn't trouble him again. He felt pity for the mage, even though Aya planned to return to Caeli-Amur with the Core of Sentinel Tower and eject Max from his own body. But still Max saw Aya as a lost soul, thrown into the future where everything he'd loved was gone, where the world he'd built was ruined. It was impossible not to feel for the ancient mage, who had lost everything.

Occasionally the road sunk under the ground. They would ride carefully forward until it reemerged later, like a swimmer resurfacing after a dive. Toward the end of the day, the road became more intact, though the landscape was becoming increasingly mountainous. Dark clouds engulfed the Etolian range to their north, snow-capped the highest peaks.

The road crossed desolate bridges, which spanned frightening steep gorges. At times these bridges were broken, their midsections having collapsed into the ravines long before. Here, Aya led his horse down dangerous animal paths, across fast-running streams of clear water, and up the steep slope on the other side.

By the third day the road clung to the sheer sides of higher ranges. It seemed impossible that they would be able to continue indefinitely—sooner or later they would come to an impassable gorge. As they got closer, the great vertical faces of the Etolian Mountains rose up impressively.

—Before long we'll have to turn back—said Max. —There's a reason this place was undiscovered.

At that moment they passed around a face of the sharp incline, and the view silenced him. A vast valley opened to their right, reaching deep into the mountains. Along both sides of the valley, far into the distance, stood colossal statues of the ancient gods and heroes. Not only Aya and Alerion but Panadus and Iria and the other gods. Imperious, they stared over the vast space, their countenances cold and commanding. Farther into the distance, a massive minotaur's stone muscles bulged as it struggled with a sea serpent. Farther still, a Siren cried out to the empty space, its alien jaw distended. On the opposite side of the canyon, a Gorgon faced them, its head a mass of writhing snakes; and at a greater distance a winged horse leaped into the air.

*The Valley of Icons,* said Aya. *The Mountain Giants built it. You see, there are places in the world you do not know about. There are things only I can show you.*

The road curled to the edge of the canyon, the valley floor terrifyingly far below. Aya dismounted, led the horse toward the cliff's edge. Every now and then he glanced across the valley, until he finally hunched down, threw a handful of sandy earth out into the air. The grains bounced against something solid but invisible.

Aya took the horse's reins, then stepped out into the void and onto what seemed to be an invisible bridge, spanning the abyss.

—This is how Iria kept herself hidden—said Max, conquering his fear.

*There's a way of making the bridge materialize, but I've forgotten the formulas.*

So Aya led the horse across the invisible span. Max felt the mage's trepidation. Whether it was from the terrifying drop beneath them or what lay ahead, he couldn't be sure. At the far side of the canyon, a hidden road curled around the arm of the mountain, and the Valley of Icons passed from sight.

They came to a smooth dark tunnel that led straight through the mountain. Aya halted, feeling the cold air drifting from the darkness.

*He's afraid of what he might find,* thought Max.

Aya pulled on the reins, and they were engulfed by darkness. The distant opening on the other side of the tunnel was a sheet of brilliance growing slowly as they approached. First a bridge appeared in the sheet of light, like something emerging from beneath water. Then a tower came into view: it jutted from the rock far below and reached up to the sky like a needle. Great cracks ran through the melancholy tower's curved stones. Elsewhere, vines gripped stubbornly, a shawl of bronze and gold, already shedding their leaves in preparation for the winter. To either side of them stood the colossal statues of the Valley of Icons, massive and stirring.

Aya tied the horse to one of a series of iron rings that ran along the bridge wall. Without warning, he collapsed onto the cold stones of the bridge and stared up at the empty windows above.

Max felt a flood of grief wash through him. He caught Aya's uncertainty, his desire to turn back and leave whatever ghosts still lived in the tower to themselves.

—We can't simply sit here like banished children—said Max.

*There's something heartless about you.* Aya pulled himself to his feet, hesitated for a moment, and then forced himself to walk toward the tower door.

# TWENTY-FOUR

Stairs led both upward and downward, following the curve of Sentinel Tower's outer wall and leaving a vast empty space in the tower's center. Up, up Aya climbed, passing wide empty windows, their panes broken long ago. A cold wind blew across the valley and whined desolately through the apertures.

Finally the stairs came to huge metal double doors, which hung dented and out of shape on their hinges.

*Something is not right here. These doors have been forced open.*

Aya stepped into the open room. A window, this one still filled with glass, ran around the entire wall, affording a panoramic view of the valley. Here, each of the statues could be seen in their full wonder: the vast stony muscles; the expressions on their faces alternately savage, desperate, melancholy, imperious. At the north end of the valley rose the awesome peaks of the Etolian range. There were places where they were impregnable even in summer. In winter, most of the passes were deadly.

In the center of the room, a smaller spiral staircase led farther upward. Elsewhere, furniture was strewn around the place as if it had been ransacked: one chair thrown on its side, a vase broken on a table, cushions strewn on the floor.

—Robbers.

*No.* Aya walked heavily across to a panel on one side of the room. Fingers tracing over its ideograms quickly, he spoke a word in the prime language and turned to face the room.

A moment later a pinpoint of light appeared in the center of the room. Slowly, it inflated until it filled the space, an image-sphere projecting a second almost identical room on top of the first. But this one showed the tower in its prime: the chaise longues in their place, their cushions bright and clean. The delicately carved table stood between them, exotic mountain flowers rising from a thin flutelike vase. In places, the image momentarily shimmered and broke into numbers and logograms that seemed to fall from the sky like snow. A moment later the image recomposed itself.

Across this ghostly room walked a tall elegant woman. She wore a wide asymmetric gown that hid her figure. Her hair, drawn back sharply behind her head, swung gently as she walked, as if mirroring her calm demeanor.

The woman's expression was both tranquil and severe. Her arched eyebrows gave her an imperious look appropriate to a god, even if she was only one in myth. Her skin was preternaturally smooth, her lips thin, slightly offsetting her beauty. Max could see her resemblance to the statue in the Valley of the Icons, but this Iria was gaunter and more commanding.

She sat on one of the chairs, leaned toward the table, and took from it a small round fruit. She took a bite and looked out over the valley, then closed her eyes a moment, as if thinking.

*Isn't she the most beautiful creature you've ever seen?*

—She has that aura of power and of loss.

An image of Kata came to Max's mind, and with it a flash of his own grief. Whatever romance had passed between them, he'd cut off before it began. Was he so different from these ancients?

*Iria was one of the great Magi herself. She could have ruled a world like yours as a god.*

—Then she, too, suffered from the Art. I can see now why she chose such a remote place to retire to. Far away from the world.

*You know nothing of her. She rarely used the Art. She felt more than any of us. She felt too keenly.*

Aya watched the ancient images sadly for some time as Iria moved about her room, then stared over the vast valley with its magnificent statues. At one point she took a circular ball sitting on a stand in a cabinet and looked into it.

*I gave her that memory ball. See, she's looking at the two of us, traveling the world together. She loved me, see!*

Seemingly bored by the images, Iria placed it back on its stand.

She yawned, revealing delicate little teeth, and closed her eyes, let her head fall back.

Aya spoke a word, and the image of the room froze momentarily, then sped up. He turned, put his hand on the panel, and closed his eyes. Images rushed through the room at a frightening speed. They watched long days of Iria, alone, passing through her life: descending the stairs in the mornings, staring at the valley for hours, reading, ascending the stairs now and then, and finally disappearing above at night.

Aya, staring at the panel, stopped the breathtaking scenes with Iria standing bolt upright, only a foot from him. Her face was frozen in alarm. She looked up, and it seemed that she was looking into Aya's eyes; but it was only an illusion, for their intensity was directed elsewhere. Something new was happening.

Iria turned around, took two steps toward the center of the room, and faced the entry doors, which stood firm, their corporeal counterparts hanging beneath them, warped and bent.

Aya rushed through the doorway. For a moment the light of the ancient doors blinded him. A second later he leaned over the landing's balustrade and looked down the center of the tower. The recording superimposed itself all the way down.

For a second nothing happened. But a moment later a figure winged its way up at pace, an arm flapping beneath a length of a purple cloak. Max could feel Aya's tension as he watched.

—Who is it?—Max asked.

*You know who it is.* Aya's voice had a shocked tone.

—Why is he here?

The figure came into view. He strode up the staircase, two steps at a time, a purple cloak flapping behind him, dark hair falling about a handsome but cruel face. His eyes stared forward, almost aflame with intensity. Strange armor, marked with symbols and logograms sliding over its bulging surfaces, encased his body.

Alerion reached the landing and stepped through Aya with a flash of brilliance. Using either the Art or the armor's thaumaturgical powers, he kicked at the door with impossible strength. The door burst open, bent by the force. It flapped for a moment and slowly superimposed itself onto its warped material sibling.

Alerion strode forward, planted his feet wide, a boastful and angry pose.

In the center of the room, Iria faced him. Her chin held high, her eyes challenging—her full beauty on display.

Aya circled the room to see their faces, and Max could feel his terrible tension. The ancient mage had not expected this. Fear and uncertainty were breaking down the mage's defenses, and Max sensed an opportunity.

"You must come back to Varenis," said Alerion. "You must explain yourself to the city."

"Explain myself to *you*, you mean. In front of everyone, so that I might be shamed."

"Panadus agrees. So does everyone." Alerion relaxed his pose: he clearly thought he had the upper hand.

"It'll be a show trial. Like you'll have for Aya." Iria didn't take a step back.

Alerion slouched onto one of the immaterial chaise longues and arrogantly swung his heels up onto the table, knocking the vase to its side, breaking it. "Aya is no more."

Iria shuddered, then froze in position as if she were in pain. She breathed rapidly, yet restricted by a contraction of chest or stomach muscles. Her body leaned a little forward, as if she might sit down at any instant.

"Don't pretend to be surprised," said Alerion.

"You shouldn't have locked him up." Her voice was broken now. "He wasn't meant to be locked up. You know that. He was always too much of a free spirit."

"You can complain now," said Alerion. "You were the one who betrayed him."

Aya backed away from the scene, held one hand out as if the images might strike him.

"I didn't want him dead!" Iria screamed.

Alerion stood up rapidly, throwing the chaise longue back. Its cushion flew across the room as it rolled and settled onto its material duplicate. "You knew what it meant. Don't deny it. You came to me, suckered up to me with your honeyed tone: 'Let me retire to my tower. Let me live in peace, and I'll give you Aya's movements. You will know his army's plans. His strategy.' You even put your hands on me. You remember that!"

Iria turned away from him, closed her eyes. "You said you would treat him with respect. Stop the war. That's what I wanted."

Alerion's laugh was cruel. "You tell yourself these lies so you can live with yourself. But we both know what you are. You've used the Art too often, and now you have no feelings. Now you care only for yourself." Alerion's tone softened. "Look at yourself, Iria. You're locked up here alone in the mountains. You were always special. Why waste it?"

Iria turned around, stared at him, her eyes narrow and full of hate. "I won't go back."

At this, Alerion rushed at her, knocked another of the chaise longues aside. It spun and superimposed itself onto a dusty thing in one corner. His hand grasped her face. He leaned in, his lips running over her ears in a circular, leering touch.

"I'll give you until the morning," he whispered. "Look outside, Iria. I have brought my bodyguards. They will carry you back if necessary. You will return to Varenis to show that we are again united."

Iria shoved him off, her voice full of soft anger. "You've ruined this world, Alerion. It was meant to be our paradise, but poison now flows on the battlefields. You've even altered its geological movements. Heat is flowing chaotically beneath the surface. There is no future here, you know. Not now."

At this, Alerion walked away, his face suddenly stricken with guilt. He wasn't so sure of himself, it seemed. "We'll repair it. We can do anything—you know that."

"Hubris—that's what swallows you up, Alerion. You do know what that is?"

Alerion paced to the doorway, turned back. "Until tomorrow, Iria. You and I can rule together. We can forget the rest of them. The Aediles will follow us if we unite. We can rebuild. You and I."

"Aya is my lover," said Iria. "He always has been. He's the only one I loved."

Alerion sneered, shook his head. "We both know he only ever cared for himself. Don't make us drag you back."

With a sweep of his purple cloak, he was gone, through the doors and down the stairs.

Iria stood silently for what seemed an eternity. She was so still that she seemed to have become almost a statue. Abruptly, she looked at one of the overturned chaise longues, as if it might hold the meaning of events. Some part of her kicked into action, and she walked serenely across to the wall, slid her hand across it, revealing a cabinet hidden behind. From within she took two separate jars of semidried leaves and dropped their contents into a glass, into which she poured a honeyed liquid.

—What is it?

*Etolian hemlock, I'd say, mixed perhaps with vanilla leaves and honey mead.* Aya's tone had a distant quality to it. Some part of him had retreated.

Iria stirred the preparation with a calm matter-of-factness. She held it up, catching its green and gold swirling colors in the light, then stirred it again. Without a moment's hesitation she brought it to her lips, swallowed it in a single gulp. She placed the glass back into the cabinet, which slid closed of its own accord.

Iria rolled her shoulders, walked gracefully to the spiral staircase, and stepped lightly upward.

Aya followed mechanically behind. Max could sense his dissociation, a dull whiteness behind the eyes: everything appeared as if from down a long tunnel, Iria doubly spectral, a recording seen from a distance. And yet Iria seemed to be right before them, her slim figure elegantly stepping, her delicate musculature visible beneath the back of her dress.

The palatial bedroom also offered a panoramic window, this one with doors opening out onto a balcony. But it was to the bed that Iria walked, toward a dry and shriveled cadaver that lay there, the remains of an asymmetrical dress clinging to it. The cadaver lay in repose, quiet and calm, but its sunken eyes filled the room with desolation.

Iria sat on the bed, kicked her legs out, and fell into the cadaver. At times during the following minutes, she shuddered, convulsed. Her image shook itself free of the corpse, settled back onto it, until finally the shuddering stopped and she was still, a ghost settling back into its body and there finding rest.

Aya retreated even more into himself, so that only a fragment remained conscious of events outside. His grief was far away, deep down.

*Now,* thought Maximilian. *Now is the time.* He struck, rushing forward like a tidal wave flooding over all the structures of his mind, engulfing them. He scrabbled for the controls of his body—felt them: the muscles of his arms; the skin; the legs holding him up; his back, so long. His neck gave way, and he hauled it back up with sudden focus. The bodily sense—the feeling of corporeality—was strange and alien.

Aya did not fight. Instead he was swept away and he fell down, back to his dark basement of the mind.

—Where's the Core? Show me.

But Aya did not respond. Perhaps he was gone, dead, dissolved into nothingness. *Perhaps that was for the best,* thought Max. Even if he were to lose the knowledge of the prime language, he would be himself again.

For half an hour, he called to Aya. —Where's the Core, Aya?

Eventually Aya responded. *It's a terrible thing, seeing the past. And yet the thing is, I didn't feel it enough. I saw Iria and Alerion, but a distance lay between us. It's an awful thing to be one of the Magi, to lose connection to what you love, to look on from faraway and distant heights. I wish I were like you, that I could truly feel. That I was really human again.*

Max made a sudden raid into Aya's mind, riffled through his memories of the Tower. They came to him like fragments of broken glass: he saw the wonder for the first time, needlelike and magnificent; felt Iria's embrace in the bedroom above; listened to snatches of the lovers' conversation. Aya did not resist.

The Core was in the base of the Tower, Max discovered.

He left the body of Iria, the recording still superimposed over it, and followed the stairs, past the doorway to the bridge, and into the darkness below. He lit a lantern, its flickering flame illuminating the stone walls until he steadied it. The staircase turned away from the Tower wall, descended another fifteen steps, and led into what at first appeared to be a narrow passageway, then revealed itself as the walls of two machines. Their irregular sides were covered with protuberances comprised of what might have been complexes of pistons and gearboxes, latticework fanlike components, wheels and cogs and cam followers, all of varying sizes.

Max passed along this space and realized that the basement was a single open room, its many passageways formed by the sides of machines. He continued, making several turns, until he reached the center, where a single wide pillar stood. A wheel was fixed into its flat surface.

Max hung his lantern from a hook on the low roof. The wheel spun easily, and the outline of a door appeared in what had previously been a smooth wall. The door swung outward, revealing a lever, which he shifted up. The previously imperceptible humming slowly stopped; the machines surrounding them seemed to sigh and become silent.

Max pulled the cylinder, which was about two feet long and the width of a birch trunk, from its casing. The object was unnervingly light, and Max sensed it was charged with thaumaturgy. He examined the intricate patterns on its sides. He could see that though it appeared to be a perfect cylinder, it was forged from many parts—delicate toothed wheels and gears, ratchets and clamps—that could emerge to interact with other components from its encasing mechanisms.

Max carried it up and out of the Tower. Once he had slipped it into the long saddlebag used to carry large items, Max looked back up at the Tower. Aya was still hidden down in the depths of Max's mind, defeated by what he had seen.

Now that he had taken the Tower's Core, Max sensed that its protective mechanisms would no longer function. It, too, would begin its slow decline into dilapidation. The winds would beat it, the snows force their way into its cracks, turning to water in spring and melting farther in. Its stones would wear and disintegrate. All that time, Iria's remains would lie on the bed, a symbol for everything that was ancient. One day the panoramic windows would break, opening up the Tower's insides. Then she, too, would be swept away by the unceasing actions of the elements, until finally the rocks would reclaim their own, leaving nothing behind.

Max pulled himself up into the saddle, the Core in the bag beside him. It would provide the power the Elo-Talern needed, the power that would allow one personality to be retracted from Max's body. *All things come toward their end,* he thought. He needed to free himself from Aya. Then he might rejoin history, rejoin the seditionists, finally do something of use. Everything else he had done had been a failure. Yet he knew to free himself from Aya meant abandoning the prime language. An uneasiness filled Max's body, for though he knew this was the solution, deep down he rebelled against the idea.

# PART III

## MIDNIGHTS

When we look upon the Bolt—that terrible construction—then the Bolt looks back into us. When we kill, murder pierces our souls. For this reason, the Bolt is the tragic symbol of our age, an impossible instrument ushering in an impossible world. It is the heart of our contradiction, the contradiction in our heart.

Any revolution is a desire for freedom, a liberation from bonds that hold the citizens too tightly. A new world is invented, where each person is given scope to develop their own talents. Yet from the very beginning, freedoms must be clamped down: there can be no freedom to return to the old state of affairs, no freedom to undermine the freedoms of others. For as long as the old elites are marginal, they can be tolerated, but the moment their actions clog up the levers of liberation, they must be subdued.

On this contradiction we now flounder. When I think of that construction up at the Standing Stones, I feel a shiver run through me, I feel the cold wind blow over my skin, I feel the sun setting over the mountain that overlooks our great city. I feel the shadows lengthening, I feel the darkness falling slowly but certainly, threatening to snuff out the light of everything we've built.

—Olivier Hubert, the *Dawn*

# TWENTY-FIVE

For a moment, as Kata descended the stairs, she thought she saw Henri behind her: a glimpse of his ruffled hair, his pale face, but when she turned, he wasn't there.

Dexion was already putting on his armor, strapping his massive war hammer to his belt. He was scheduled to appear in the finale of the Autumn Games during the Twilight Observance, and his natural charisma and exoticism meant he would be a key player.

Kata moved gingerly past him and pulled up her shirt to examine a great black bruise darkening her side. Seeing this, Dexion grabbed her wrist, held it up in the air, and poked her playfully in the sensitive spot.

"Ow," said Kata.

"Oh, that's a good one," Dexion said cheerily. "I don't think they're broken, but they might be bruised right here."

"Ow! Hey!" Kata wrenched her arm away.

"Don't whine. It's nothing. Look at this." Dexion raised his own shirt. A jagged scar ran down the curves of his ribs and across his sculpted abdominals. "That's where a Numerian pirate sliced me with his cutlass. We were sailing from Aya to Numeria, but the pirates had been raiding the coast for some time. They snuck up on us in the night, burst out of the low-lying fog. By the time I made my way on deck, they were crawling all over our cutter like spiders. I took two out, but a third hit me from the side. I cracked his head against the mast, though. And here . . ." Dexion began to catalog his scars and injuries: this one, from another minotaur on the island of Aya; that one, from a lover he'd had on the Dyrian coast.

For the first time in days he seemed like the more youthful minotaur she'd first met. But she knew he was changing. In spurts and starts, his joyous humor was being transformed into a kind of grandeur. He seemed somehow bigger than when she'd first met him. His sheer physicality had always dominated the space around him; in the street, citizens' eyes were drawn to him, quickly averted, then allowed to wander back shortly after. But he'd always had a frivolous joy to accompany his fearsome mien. Now a new gravitas radiated from him.

Seeing her making mental notes, he stopped. "What?"

She smiled. "Oh, nothing."

It was midmorning by the time she met Rikard at the Opera. They agreed it was time to report to Ejan what they knew: someone had been passing money from the Marin Palace to Dumas at the Collegium Caelian. But Ejan was absent, and no one knew where he was. Eventually, a captain informed them that Ejan was entangled in an emergency meeting of the nine-person Insurgent Authority. Then Rikard himself was called away to help prepare the vigilant guards. The Authority was debating an assault on the villas at just that moment.

Kata took the time to visit the busy offices of the *Dawn*, where scruffy militants debated the paper's editing, proofreading, and typesetting. Kata joined in, enjoying the minutia of the work, rearranging paragraphs, checking each word, seeing the final polished copy. It distracted her from the loss of Henri, from the debate, from her own troubles.

It was late afternoon when the meeting of the Authority finally ended. Olivier entered the offices, his face grim. "The assault on the villas has been organized."

Kata looked up from the manuscript before her. "You went along with it? Are you afraid we lose support every time we oppose the vigilants?"

The militants gathered around, leaned in to hear the to-and-fro of the debate.

"Look, I don't like it either, but the city *is* starving, and the villas *are starving us*," Olivier said uncomfortably.

"I suppose you support the Bolt, too?" Kata placed her hands on her hips, leaned forward. "We may as well liquidate ourselves into the vigilants! They're in charge anyway."

Olivier raised two palms into the air. "I've written a piece warning of its dangers, but what else are we to *do*?"

So the usual debate went around and around until Kata was tired of it, tired of feeling that they had only impossible choices to make.

As she left the Opera, Kata observed the dark mood of the city. A defiant rally had taken over the Market Square. Slogans read: STRIKE AGAINST THE VILLAS! and EXPROPRIATE THE GRAIN! Ultraradical agitators passed out broadsheets calling for a war of liberation against Varenis. The evening light turned the hazy sky a luminous overheated gold, common autumn weather in Caeli-Amur, as cool and hot air mixed where the ocean met the land.

Kata hurried home, hoping to see Dexion's calming presence. On her way, the ominous sky darkened—sunset fell earlier now— and a fog dropped over the city. She left Via Persine, littered with raggedy beggars holding out empty wooden bowls, and passed into the factory quarter, where her footfalls echoed eerily along the streets, and figures loomed suddenly from the murk.

She came through the eerie haze to find a small boy in front of her apartment. He was standing on his tiptoes for some reason, knocking on her door. She thought she knew his name, but still said, "Are you looking for me?"

He turned, nodded solemnly. "I'm Pol. Henri sent me. He's hiding. Come on." Then he dashed down the stairs and scurried up the alleyway. "Come on."

Pol had been Thom's little urchin, and he might know all kinds of information, but the first thoughts on Kata's mind were of Henri. She hurried after Pol, desperate hope driving her on, into the depths of the roughest zones of the factory quarter. Here the alleyways were abandoned, and dilapidated factories stood alone, their windows broken, doors hanging loosely. Most of these had been empty even before the blockade started, though gas lamps cast dim light from the street corners.

"Henri must have been frightened," said Kata. "He's hiding here, isn't he?"

The boy ducked into one of the factories without answering, and Kata slipped in after him. Lamplight shining through the broken windows illuminated the haze that hung in the factory, embracing rows of dark machines.

"Hey, not so quick." She wondered why he didn't answer. "You worked for Thom, didn't you?"

The boy led her along several pathways between the machines, toward the center of the vast hall. The hazy light caught one side of his face, leaving the rest in shadow. "Yes, I worked for Thom. Come over here. Henri's here."

Something strange echoed in his voice, as if there were a second, deeper voice echoing behind the first. Kata froze. She felt like a thousand ants were crawling over her.

"How do you know Henri?" Her voice seemed weak in the other-worldly atmosphere.

"We grew up on the streets." The boy seemed small, but he seemed to be large, too, in a way she couldn't comprehend. It was as if there were two of him, the little child and a hulking creature superimposed on top.

"Of course." Ice ran up her spine. "Why is he hiding here?"

"It's the safest," said the boy. Now she heard it definitely: the voice, rich and deep echoing within the voice of the child.

*Oh no,* thought Kata, backing away: the shapeshifter.

"Where are you going?" Pol came toward her, was lost for a moment in the shadow of a machine. He emerged again into the light, a lithe woman with a stern face and shoulder-length dark hair. Frosty fear ran along Kata's arms. The second Kata smiled cruelly. There was something wrong about her dark eyes.

Kata turned and ran as her double sprang after her.

"Where are you going?" The double's voice was cold, probably male.

Machines whipped past her. Where was the door? She circled the machines several times, guessing at its direction. Pain ran up her damaged ribs and she knew this would hamper her in a fight. Escape was the best option.

Along one dim passageway she spied the exit, a black slab against the general gloom. She hurried toward it. If she could make it onto the streets, she would escape the trap.

Her double stepped out into the pathway before her. Now the

shapeshifting Kata's hand glowed an impossible red. Kata slid to a stop. The killer strode toward her, each step more menacing because it was made by some dark replica of her.

Kata spun and ran deeper into the factory, turning randomly along the rows. She came to a stop, slid down between two machines, and listened.

The sound of footfalls sent panic through her. The worst of it was that she couldn't tell how far away the killer was. At times the sounds seemed distant; at other times, almost on top of her.

She slipped a knife into her hand. Fighting her fear, she waited. The footfalls stopped too, and silence reigned in the factory. It seemed like Kata sat there for an age, straining to hear the slightest sound, the softest steps. Eventually she slid from her position between the machines. As quietly as she could, inch by inch, she moved through the shadows back toward the exit.

A black figure came at her in the dark, its hand aglow like searing embers packed together. Kata snapped into action. She ducked beneath the reaching hand, catching again a glimpse of two figures—one lithe, the other hulking—superimposed in the dark. She brought her knee up into the chest of her assailant. There was a crushing groan, and she knew she'd struck true. With a backward whipping motion, her elbow cracked into the killer's head, and the lithe figure evaporated, leaving only a hulking shape stumbling in the darkness.

She threw a knife, but it spun past the assassin's ear and rang against a metal machine.

Kata hoped she might make out the killer's identity, but all she could see was the beastly shape turning in the dark, its blazing hand ready to strike. She fled, down, down the rows until she reached the door. Plunging into foggy night air, she raced along alleyways until they widened into streets. Figures passed the other way, but she didn't stop running until she reached her apartment. Dashing up the steps, she threw open the door to the sight of Dexion frying meats over her stove.

"Ah, I was wondering where you were. Are you hungry?" he said.

Kata slammed the door and locked it. She leaned against it,

breathing hard. The light, the warmth, Dexion's protective bulk—
the factory seemed nothing but a surreal dream.

"Are you all right?" the minotaur said.

"I'm not sure," said Kata. Pain ran up her ribs like flames licking up a dry wall.

The killer knew where Kata lived. It was a terrifying idea, that anyone could be a shapeshifting murderer: a washerwoman on the
street, a close associate, Dexion himself. How could she trust anyone? She would have to rely on her instinct and the fact that she
had been able to see through the shapeshifter's disguise before.
One's true self, it seemed, was hard to hide after all.

In the morning Dexion insisted on accompanying her to the
Opera. Even more beggars held out wooden bowls on Via Persine.
The city had begun to starve. The poorest had become desperate.
Soon the rest of them would be too.

"Don't mother me, minotaur," she said.

"You're not used to it, are you?" He waved her good-bye and
continued to the Arena.

Rikard rushed toward her across the entry hall, pushing others
out of his way. "I've been waiting for you," he said breathlessly.
"Ejan's up at the Bolt. Prefect Alfadi caught the thieves who were
stealing from Marin's treasury. Apparently, they faced the Criminal Tribunal yesterday and they're already on their way to the
Standing Stones."

"No!" Kata frowned.

"Come on." Rikard was already heading for the square.

They raced through the Lavere on foot, up the Thousand Stairs,
across the tiny plazas, and past the gorgeous little boutiques and
tiny eateries, many of which were now boarded up.

Everything was happening too fast for Kata's liking. The smugglers caught, tried before the tribunal, and now headed to their
deaths, all so quickly? She sensed some vague connection between
these events and her fight in the factory the night before. Something was wrong.

A crowd surrounded the Standing Stones. It seemed to Kata
that most of them had come up from the Lavere and the slums, a

collection of low-on-their-luck ruffians, some missing teeth, their clothes little more than black rags. They leaned over the palisade that protected the pathway to the Stones, grinning and calling to one another. Hundreds more gathered on the amphitheater steps.

The Bolt stood on a wooden platform in the center of the Stones. Black-suited guards were positioned on each of the platform's corners, pikes in hand. More guards roved officiously through the space that curled around the area, protecting it. To the side of the platform, two more of the killing machines stood half finished.

At the top of the steps, Kata spied Ejan and Alfadi looking on together. Alfadi pointed toward the monoliths and explained something to the vigilant leader.

Kata and Rikard forced their way toward him, through the masses of pressing bodies, sweaty and stinking and hot. About halfway there, Kata made out Dumas's bloodhound face, surrounded by Numerian guards, fine dark-skinned men who had noble bearing despite their subjugation. She noted Dumas's baggy clothes, one size too large, as if he were hiding something. Before the overthrow of the Houses, he was said to have spent much of his time across the sea. Kata wondered what else he had acquired there besides slaves. Like most of the Collegia, he swam beneath the surface of things, a silent invisible creature. He was unmarried, she knew that much for sure, preferring—or so the rumours went—the louche attraction of the prostitutes of the Lavere, many of whom he probably owned. *What kind of man was happy to own others?* she wondered. A man didn't succeed under the regime of the Houses, as he had, without all sorts of transgressions.

As she passed by, Dumas waved, and smiled malevolently. Did he know she and Rikard suspected him?

Ejan caught sight of them as they approached. "I'm so glad you've arrived."

At that moment a cheer went up among the crowd. A prison cart rattled along the street, ratty-looking prisoners gripping the bars and staring balefully over the crowd. A woman in a pretty but stained dress reached out to the throng, but no one responded.

Among the dozen prisoners sat three thaumaturgists, bound and gagged on the floor. One of them was Detis, the thaumaturgist who had rowed Kata and Rikard through the Marin Complex on their first visit. The greenish tinge of his skin seemed darker now, and his haggard look seemed desperate. His suit was torn near the neck, revealing a glimpse of the tattoo of two hands clasping—the sign, she figured, of the mysterious organization called the Brotherhood of the Hand.

Kata's mind raced: Could Detis have been the one who wrote the letter to Armand? It was possible, certainly. As a thaumaturgist, he might have known Armand at Technis. Yet why had Aceline decided to meet up with two of the Brotherhood at the Baths? Kata desperately wanted to slow events down. Instead, they were rushing past like a thousand deadly arrows.

Since she had last seen Alfadi at the Marin Palace, he had allowed his hair to grow around the sides of his formerly shaved head. White as his pupils, the hair gave him a venerable air that muted his radiating power. He was changing, too. This city had a way of wearing everyone down.

Alfadi touched her on the arm. "We caught them returning to Marin in a gondola. There was barely a need for a trial."

"Then you know they were passing money to the Collegia and Dumas," said Kata.

"We're keeping an eye on Dumas right now," said Ejan. "At the moment it looks like it's simple corruption. You know the Collegia—always after financial gain. What do you expect from merchants and petty tradesmen?"

The guards dragged the first man—head bowed, hair lank and greasy—to the killing machine.

A black-suited guard gestured dramatically to the man. "Sub-officiate Lakartis, you have been caught conspiring against the citizenry, committing sabotage, and resisting the new order. Before you face the ultimate judgment of the people, what have you to say?"

The man looked up, his grief-stricken face taking on a vicious aspect. He spat at the masses, who hooted and catcalled back at him, waving fists in the air.

The guards pulled the man back into the contraption, locked

him into the exoskeleton. The structure held him tight, a deadly wooden embrace.

"I want to speak with Detis and the other thaumaturgists," said Kata. "Before they're put to death."

"The trial was yesterday," said Ejan. "They've confessed."

That fact apparently closed the door on the affair. Dumas was under surveillance, and the Collegia would have to prostrate itself before the Insurgent Assembly. Yet something still felt wrong to Kata. She looked around for support. "Rikard?"

Rikard shrugged, pressed his lips together. "Justice must be served. We're too late for the interrogation."

"But we weren't even told they were caught!" Kata hated the pleading tone of her voice.

"It's not all about us, Kata," said Rikard. "Everyone's doing the best they can."

Alfadi touched her arm again. When he spoke, his voice was powerful, resonant, and cultured. She noticed a slight accent of the Teeming Cities for the first time. "That was my fault. I'm sorry. They confessed so quickly once we caught them, I didn't think it important to involve you. Then they went off to the Criminal Tribunal, where Georges made quick work of them. I thought it was case closed, clear enough. Don't blame Ejan—if anyone, blame me."

But she did blame Ejan, because this turn of affairs suited him perfectly. He was getting everything he wanted, while the moderates were irrelevant, useless.

Below, the guard stepped closer to the crowd and looked up at the onlookers on the theater stairs. "Subofficiate Lakartis, I hereby pronounce your unworthy life at its end."

In one horrible instant the cylindrical beam burst through the man's chest. Blood and shattered remnants of organs and bone sprayed out over the ground in front of the platform. The subofficiate's eyes rolled around in his head, as if he were trying to make sense of events. Then, as he lost strength, his head reeled to one side. Several men lifted up their children so they could see better.

Kata closed her eyes for a moment. The cheers and cries of the crowd washed over her. She turned to Ejan. "This is wrong. If anyone should be up there, Dumas should."

"Do you have actual evidence against Dumas? The thaumaturgists weren't handing the money to the Collegia's leadership, but to others lower down. It was simple theft, from what we know. Anyway, the Collegia follow whoever is strongest. And we're about to crush the final resistance. They'll be on our side when we move on the southern villas shortly."

"More meat for your Bolt?" said Kata.

The body of Lakartis was dragged from the platform and thrown into a second cart, already filled with broken bodies. Then they dragged Detis toward the platform, still gagged so he couldn't invoke any conjurations. He struggled and moaned, but on they carried him. As they fastened him into the machine, he looked up at Kata. His eyes widened, and she sensed he was trying to say something: Was he hoping for her to save him, or was it something else? A dark patch of discoloration pulsed beneath one cheek, as if the effects of thaumaturgy were intensifying in his dire situation.

The guard spoke again. "Thaumaturgist Detis Adirno, you have been condemned for stealing from the Marin treasury. House assets now belong to the citizens. Let all who watch know this: we will not tolerate saboteurs or parasites. Your sentence?"

"Death!" called the crowd.

"Death!" said the guard.

The Bolt fired. An explosion of blood and guts. Kata watched as the man's eyes, still fixed on her, lost their light. His strength gave way, and his head fell to one side.

Unable to watch, Kata pushed through the leering crowd. Again Dumas smiled at her from his place on the steps. There he stood, happy and free. What kind of justice was this? She couldn't help the thought it prompted: Ejan and Dumas must be working together. She was surrounded by men in power. There was a cover-up happening here and there was nothing she could do.

Something snapped in Kata. She was a woman of action who had held herself back. *Enough is enough*, she thought.

Rikard took her by the arm. "Kata, come on."

"Your leader must be stopped," Kata said.

"It's the will of the people. The Authority was elected. They're simply representing what the citizens want. What they *need*."

Kata turned to Rikard. "The will of the people is something shaped by people like you."

"And by you, also." Signs of strain were visible on Rikard's youthful face.

Kata crossed her arms, glared at him. "Yes, and by me, also."

Rikard frowned; he seemed to sense some change in Kata. "What do you mean, Kata?"

"We're not going to work together anymore, Rikard. I won't work with any vigilant."

Rikard looked stunned, as if she had shoved him physically away. "But the search for Aceline's killer?"

"We'll never find them because of you vigilants. You've forced me to choose between that search and continuing Aceline's work. You disgust me, Rikard."

"We're friends."

"We weren't ever friends." Kata pushed through the crowd. She had spent enough time in the shadows. It was time for her to take a stand, whatever the personal consequences. Would Rikard tell Ejan about her past? Would it destroy her, or bring the moderates into disrepute? She would have to take the risk.

When she strode into the Opera, Kata's eyes were fixed forward. She found Olivier and a group of moderate militants working in the *Dawn*'s editorial offices.

Olivier looked up. "Kata, we're almost finished typeset— What is it?"

Kata examined the little group for a moment as they stared, wide-eyed, at her. "We must call a meeting for tomorrow and gather as many supporters as we can. If we don't act soon, the city will be in Ejan's hands. We must also reorganize our guards. We need a professional force to defend us."

"What do you mean, defend us?" said Olivier.

Kata widened her stance, as if she were ready for any kind of conflict. "We have to be prepared for the moment the vigilants declare us to be enemies. Soon they'll make no distinction between those who oppose them and those who oppose seditionism."

"If we build up our own guard force, that will risk civil war," said Olivier. "You know Ejan. He will see us as a threat."

"No, this is what will *prevent* a civil war," said Kata. "Ejan only understands force."

"Who will train these guards?" said Olivier.

"I will," said Kata, but she knew she couldn't do it alone. She needed the help of an expert. She needed her mentor Sarrat.

# TWENTY-SIX

Once again Kata found herself standing in the alleyway near Via Gracchia and looking at the delicate stone garden, its hardy desert flowers unconcerned about the world. Kata stared at the apartment and calmed herself. She strode forward and slid open the door. Sarrat was not in the room, but she heard a voice call out, "Who's that?"

Kata walked to the center of the room, sat down, and waited. This time she would be calm when he entered.

Kata was pleased to see the mild surprise on Sarrat's face. "I thought you were never coming back."

"I never said that," said Kata.

"No, but I know you," said Sarrat. "Explosive emotions all bottled up. When they blow—"

"Not anymore," said Kata.

Sarrat sat down in front of her. Not a muscle moved on his smooth face. He breathed calmly through his crooked nose. His heavy-lidded eyes drooped so that he looked like he was half asleep.

"I have found my philosophy." Kata hesitated, decided to leave it at that.

A slight smile rose on Sarrat's mouth, and Kata quieted the touch of anger that rose in her.

"I am developing it, I guess," she added, then cursed herself for explaining. "That's why I need your help. I need you to help me train an army."

"An army?"

"Your tendency to answer in questions is as annoying as ever."

"Is it?"

"History is being made," said Kata. "It's not clear who—or

which ideas—will triumph. It's time we attached ourselves to these ideas, bring them into being."

"I only train specialists. You know that." Sarrat was a typical Cajiun philosopher: trained in the desert monasteries of Caji, deep in Numeria. Ascetics and elitists, the Cajiun philosophers believed only a select few could learn their practices and their style of fighting. Kata had done the latter well but had failed at the former.

"I have come to convince you to change your mind," she said. "Philosophy is not only for the elite. That is the truth of seditionism."

"That is not Cajiunism. Patience, simplicity—we are aloof from the material world, where most live their lives. Look at this room." Sarrat made a circular gesture with his hand at their surroundings.

"Compassion: that's the beginning of Cajiun philosophy, but you divorce it from society," said Kata. "You think compassion is an individual thing, one person to another, but what about the fact that some people stand on mountains and others are on the plain? Some are born into the Lavere, others in the Arantine. Shouldn't your compassion distinguish between those who ruin others and those who try to stop that ruination?"

"You have left Cajiunism behind, then?" Sarrat sounded disappointingly calm.

"This brings Cajiunism down from the air and back to the ground. I stand for something now. What do you stand for, separation from real life?"

Sarrat's eyes closed ever so slowly, until he seemed to be asleep. Then, in an instant, he dove at her, his fingers aimed at her eyes. The move took her by surprise, but she fell back in time, rolled to her right along the floor, and leaped to her feet.

Sarrat stood in fighting stance before her. He meant to test her, to see if she still fought without anger or fear. The realization drove fear into her, for she doubted her ability to control her emotions.

"Is this a form of penance, for the innocents you killed?" Sarrat circled calmly.

He spun his leg at her head in a graceful, deadly curve. She raised her arm to block it, but a second later Sarrat had deftly changed its course and it crashed into her already damaged ribs.

Kata staggered back, the pain searing through her. She collapsed to one knee, drew a ragged breath. "In a way."

"So you are aligned to these seditionists out of guilt." Sarrat lunged forward, but Kata was already up. She raised her foot and pushed him back with it. He danced to one side, spun backward, his straight leg moving in a second delicate and deadly crescent, aimed again at her head.

Kata ducked underneath it, and her low kick swept Sarrat's leg from beneath him. She knew she could not defeat him: she'd never been able to. But she leaped at him anyway, hoping to hold him down, trap him in a lock or a choke. He pushed her off, rose to his feet, backed up a few steps, and regained his balance.

"I seek to give and not to take. That is the difference between how I feel and how you think I feel," said Kata. "A guilty person wants acceptance, penance, something that will absolve them of their sins. I seek no such absolution. I regret many of my actions. But that is not what drives me. This is no personal thing. This is for others, not for me."

Kata skipped forward, throwing straight punches one after the other, which Sarrat dodged with a series of rapid side-to-side movements.

With blinding speed, he threw his fist in a vicious overhand punch at her cheek. As Kata ducked, she felt it glance off the top of her head. Still, she lunged forward and took Sarrat crashing to the ground. For a second she was on top of him, but then he swept her beneath him, spun around so that he lay in the opposite direction as her, caught her leg between his, and clasped her foot in a cruel footlock. The pain was immediate. He would tear her tendons.

Kata looked down at her leg, and at Sarrat. "You've beaten me again."

Sarrat nodded and twisted her foot in an even more unnatural angle.

Kata grimaced, but she had fought without anger or fear. "That's why I need you. I need you to help me train my guards."

Sarrat let go, stood up. For the first time since she met him, he broke into a broad smile. He was missing some teeth toward the back of his mouth that she'd never noticed. The smile creased his face. For a moment he seemed both older and younger than he did before.

"I thought I'd failed with you," said Sarrat, "But it seems I was wrong."

The Arena in the Technis Complex was small and dusty. Kata had been there once before, when the Technis officiates had put on a grubby spectacle for their agents, pitting defeated strikers against wild animals. With a shudder, she recalled the sad death of an elephant, stabbed with the surviving workers' spears.

Now lines of moderates wandered in. Once assembled, they were a motley group of about four hundred, some of whom had been guards for a while. Only confirmed moderates could sign up at the registration table at the Arena entry. Kata did not want the social climbers and crawlers who would try to slip their way in.

"Not much to look at," said Sarrat.

"I've ordered new uniforms that will make them look less scruffy."

"What color?"

"Silver," said Kata. "The color of Cajiun priests."

She made four veteran seditionists from before the overthrow of the Houses—Terris and Ilena, Alani and Frederic—into captains, each with a hundred guards under their command.

"Why are they the captains?" A man shuffled forward from the general throng. His thick legs gave him a look of preternatural balance, as if his slight torso was the thin sailless mast of a boat, anchored to the bulk beneath. As the legs moved, so the carriage above swayed in tune. "We should elect our captains. By the gods, we should elect everyone."

"I don't know you, friend." Kata felt sands shifting inside her. He was right: they should elect their captains. They should not reproduce the top-down structure of the vigilants. But the logic of conventional practice was relentless, she saw, and she found herself sliding toward it ineluctably. Many of them didn't know one another, and there was no telling who might be elected. What was more, Kata knew she needed to forge her army quickly.

"I'm Luc." The man planted his two feet as if he were planting a tree, and eyed Kata.

"There is no time for such delicate niceties. I am appointed by the Moderate Committee, who *were* elected."

"Sounds like a vigilant argument to me," said Luc. "People on top appoint. The elective principle—that's how the new world should operate."

"All armed forces need discipline. All need direction." Kata raised her voice and spoke loudly to the rest of the group. "Those who don't wish to submit to the authority given to me by the Moderate Committee are welcome to leave now."

Heads turned, looked to one another for a response.

"If people are appointing themselves leaders, then I shall appoint myself one." Luc stepped out from the congregation and faced them. "First off, the captains shall not be these four, but rather—"

As the man spoke, Kata walked up beside him and, in an instant, seized the pressure point in his neck. He folded up under her grip and fell down, unconscious, in a cloud of dust. Kata thought, *Your sturdy legs didn't hold you that time, did they?* She couldn't tell if she was angry with him or with herself.

She turned to her captains. "Take him out and make sure he doesn't come back in."

As she stepped back to let Sarrat begin his instruction, Kata caught a glimpse of a dark-haired young man seated in the Arena's seats. She made her way beneath the Arena and climbed up the stands to sit next to Rikard.

Seeing her expression, he raised his hands. "I was just about to leave anyway. Our guards are marching on the villas in a few days. Don't forget that you'll soon be eating because of us." He looked over the guards in training below, then back at Kata. "Not much of an armed force."

"It's sad, you know," said Kata.

"What?"

"Us. We're enemies again. How did that happen?"

Rikard shrugged and pressed his lips together: it had become a regular expression of his. He was upset about it too, it seemed.

The next morning the textile workers delivered the uniforms to the Arena. They were not silver. They were gray.

Kata worked hard organizing her new center in the Technis Palace, which had been half abandoned since the overthrow. Only seditionists had passed through, carrying off files and books and anything else that might be of use. Now it was occupied by moderates, some overawed by the place, others curious at what they might find. Many decided to live there, and carried all kinds of goods in with them: bedding and food and clothes and lanterns and assorted knickknacks. Kata couldn't help feeling ambivalent about moving into the Palace. It felt like slipping into the clothes of your oppressor: they were finely made and comfortable but stained by their history.

In the evening she strode through the Palace's strange rooms and grottos, up and down stairs in its ramshackle construction. The southwest wing had ground to a halt: the rooms, which had once circled around one another, were now stationary, locked in a single configuration. Technis's great library had been plundered, but she hoped one day to restore it. Many of the books had ended up with Alfadi and the other thaumaturgists in House Marin, and she figured it would take some prying to return those.

In the Palace's upper levels, she saw Dexion striding toward her. *How easy his life was,* she thought. He was not engaged in these events. Instead he pursued his own interests and had no responsibilities to anyone.

The minotaur bent down rapidly and threw her over his shoulder.

"Now, where are the dungeons?" he boomed.

Kata struck him on his back. "Dexion! No! I'm meant to be a leader. You're undermining my gravitas."

He strode on. "What gravitas?"

She stopped striking him, knowing that would only seem more undignified.

He put her down just as quickly. "I came to tell you that my first fight is organized. You are going to be amazed at the Arena,

Kata, when you see what's planned! And those who survive are to be promoted to gladiator captains!"

Nearby, a pair of grand doors hung askew from their hinges. Kata had been here before: the room had been Director Autec's former office. The last time she'd been here, Director Autec's disturbing body had been sprawled on the ground, a ragged gash cutting deep into his neck. Autec's body was gone: into the lime pits on the far side of the mountain with the rest of the dead. She thought of the Siren she had embraced on the balcony so long ago. The Siren had escaped, perhaps even back to her island in the Taritian archipelago.

Inside the office, spidery cracks ran along the walls, as if they had been subjected to intense pressure. Mounted on a pillar in one corner of the room stood a glassy head-sized sphere, its metallic latticework insides clearly visible. This she knew to be a communication device, linked with a second sphere somewhere else. At the far end of the room stood the Director's large desk, its drawers open, papers scattered on the floor. Behind it stood a strange egg-like machine, black with uncanny silver ideograms inscribed into it: ancient technology whose potential unnerved her.

Dexion ran his hand over the sphere on the pillar. "Where does this scrying ball connect?"

"Probably to one of the other Houses, or to Varenis."

Kata watched fearfully as Dexion grabbed a lever at the base of the sphere, pulled it down. For a moment nothing happened.

"Perhaps the ball on the other side isn't functioning," said Dexion.

A moment later a pinpoint of light appeared in the center of the ball. Slowly, it grew, engulfing the ball, and a second room was projected into the offices, a shadowy world superimposed on their own.

Behind a ghostly desk stood a man, his wiry gray hair and genial face undercut by an air of tension and fatigue. A deep red birthmark disfigured one side of his face. "It's about time you reached me. Oh, a minotaur—you've returned to the old ways, I see."

"There is no return to the old ways," said Dexion.

"Caeli-Amur always had a nostalgia for the ancients. Surely, that's why you're the delegates from this Authority of yours I hear about. You are the delegates, right? Shall we talk?"

Kata was transfixed for a moment, made a guess. "It's a relief that the Directorate of Varenis wants to talk, after so hastily imposing its embargo on us."

The man brushed his wiry hair back, seemed to calm himself. "You seem like reasonable people and I'm a new Director, not responsible for the old policies. My name's Valentin."

Kata took another, wilder guess. "Armand surely explained to you that we will not stand for those who seek to reassert the old order. You understand that, right?"

Valentin laughed bitterly. "Armand! Dead in the mountains, I'm afraid, having left me with, well, nothing much at all. Just useless things. The truth is, I need your help, and I'm the only chance you have. We have the same enemies, you see. There's a faction here who wants to crush you, string you up on dark machines. And to do so, they have to replace me. Even now they're circling like carrion birds. If you were to release the House officials that have been imprisoned and send a request for Varenis's aid, indicating you're prepared to become an autonomous Department of Varenis—paying the appropriate taxes, of course, but having complete self-governance—well, then we can avoid any bloodshed. Allow us to invest in Caeli-Amur. We can get your factories working again. We'll send you emergency funds to restart your economy—at the appropriate interest, of course."

Possibilities opened up in front of Kata like a hundred tracks crisscrossing across a hill. She saw that if she could accept this proposal, she might offer a way out of the never-ending conflict Caeli-Amur seemed to be plunged into. She could take it to a meeting of the Assembly and offer a different policy from Ejan's. The desperate people would surely accept it. Thus she would defeat Ejan and rise to the key leader in the city. She saw that the insurgency itself might actually survive and be stable—yes, a province of Varenis, but an autonomous one.

Kata made some more quick calculations. If this Armand had made it to Varenis, then this Director was his contact, the man who possessed the prism. That stood to reason. Her mind jumped tracks. She decided to test the water.

"What about this book?" Kata left the question vague. She kept her eyes fixed on the Director's every expression, on the way his nonplussed look filled quickly with anxiety. Yes: she had outwitted him, though she didn't know quite how. Before he could speak, she added, "*The Alerium Calix*. What should we do with that?"

The Director brought both his hands down onto the table and half stood. "That's what I need! The infernal prism has complex thaumaturgical locks that even the Sortileges cannot lift. And now I'm paying for this fact. Me! I had nothing to do with it! Yes, we can do a deal. Certainly. What can we work out together?"

Here, then, was her chance. Here was a way to outflank Ejan. But Kata stopped herself. She had learned enough about power to understand the traps of politics, the labyrinths in which one became lost. At first she would think herself victorious, but soon Varenis would use their influence to tear all the wealth from Caeli-Amur, to strip it of its art, its energy, its creativity. Did she trust the Director of Varenis? Of course not. In any case, she didn't possess *The Alerium Calix*, and she had no idea where it was.

"Lift the embargo first. Let merchants return to Caeli-Amur," she said.

"Send me the book, and I think I can negotiate that. Do you have it there? Show it to me so I can believe you."

"It's in the hands of the Authority," said Kata a little too quickly.

His spectral eyes pierced her; this was a man used to the bluff and double bluff. "You don't have it either, do you? Oh gods. You're a clever liar. So we're back where we started. I can lift the embargo if you first accept my proposals. Release the prisoners and become a Department of Varenis."

"I won't help you," said Kata. "I can't."

"I won the Directorate with a policy of appeasement and negotiation! To refuse me is suicide! Do you want to go to war?"

Kata turned the screw once more. "Our Authority would never allow it. We're not even the Authority's proper representatives. We're just here by accident."

"You're not? What good are you to me then? Nothing, it's all come to nothing." The man collapsed back into his chair and stared out his window, a grayness setting on his craggy and handsome features. He seemed to have died a little death.

A few days later, Kata leaned against one of the statues under the Opera's portico and watched black-suited vigilant guards march in a long line toward Cable Car Tower. There guards crammed into cars and were carried up over the city to Via Gracchia, from where they would march south, toward the villas. When they arrived, no negotiation would occur, for the time of pleasantries was over. The blockade would be broken, resistance suppressed, the grain stores sacked. A flood of prisoners would be carted back to House Arbor's dungeons.

Ejan's icy face appeared beside Kata. He'd grown a sharp blond beard, which Kata had to admit suited him. He'd added a white cravat to his usual suit and she was surprised to find him hand-some. "Organizing your own guards, I hear."

Kata rested her face against the cold marble of the statue. "The city needs as many defenders as it can get."

"You're right." Ejan scratched his face; perhaps the beard was itching. "The stronger we are, the better placed we are to instill order."

Kata could never read the Northerner. Everything he said seemed so emotionally detached. Once, she had found it disquieting, but she had grown used to it. She chose a direct approach. "This is the path to dictatorship. Is that how you see things ending up, with yourself up there on the mountain, looking down at the rest of us scurrying in the streets? With you deciding who lives and dies?"

Ejan's head bobbed backward in surprise. His eyes focused and he was with her then, in the moment. "What? No, I just want us to stick together. Before I left Njagar ice-hall, I watched a Consul from Varenis sail into our harbor. It was summer and there was barely a scattering of ice on the ground. The Consul ventured into the hall and wondered at our sleeping pillars, at the silhouettes that moved inside the ice-walls. But what he desired most was to recruit giants for Varenis's legions. In return, he offered technology from Varenis. Like all the kings of the ice-halls, my father agreed. We hunted giants for the Consul, he provided mechanical tools and luxuries. One day, another king's son came to our home. His companion was a giant. The man had one black eye, filled with blood like that of an Augurer—impossible, I know, for all Augurers are women, but true nonetheless. He warned us that Varenis would soon march north and enslave us all. My father sneered at the man and his giant friend, warned them that on another day he would have driven the man into the mountains and sold the giant to Varenis. Such is the way of the Northerners. Centuries of war between them have made for a belligerent and independent culture. Not much longer after that, we heard that Varenis had enslaved the barbarians of the plains and foothills to the west. Still, the Consul said Varenis would respect our boundaries. I knew that as long as the Northerners were separated from each other, they would never be able to defend themselves against the Empire. Unity is strength. You see, we can't be divided, not when Varenis might send troops south at any moment."

"I've also got stories to tell," said Kata. "Those men who died by the Bolt, the ones caught at House Marin: they weren't guilty. You're part of a cover up because it suits you. Dumas is at the center of it. You think you're using him, but he is using you. You're working for our enemies, even if you don't know it, and by doing so, you're digging our grave, Ejan."

Ejan's eyes seemed to intensify into a surprising pale blue. "You're clever, Kata. Don't let anyone ever tell you differently. But you can't sow your moderate doubts in my mind. A good try, though."

The lines of guards marched on, packing themselves into Cable Car Tower, peering through the swinging carriages' windows as they swung up to the cliffs. Some laughed, but others looked grim and unhappy.

"So how many are you sending to the villas?" asked Kata.

"A thousand," said Ejan.

*So many,* thought Kata. "Is that all you have?"

Ejan smiled a little at her insult. "I worry that one day you will oppose seditionism as a whole. That would be terrible, not just for the city, but for me personally. Now that you're organizing your own guards, so much rides on you."

"It does?" said Kata. "Yes, I suppose it does."

# TWENTY-SEVEN

Each night, Armand helped dig the escape tunnel. Each day, he directed his crew in the mines. His body and mind were weary. Shafts of pain drove down his legs to the ever-growing numbness in his feet. His lower back seized up, and he often found himself moaning. At other times he stared mindlessly at the bloodstone seam until with a jolt he perceived the resentful stares of his crew. Soon they might depose him as leader, he realized, or a sudden blow to his head would fell him and he would be no more. The stories of those who failed to fill their carts were whispered in the nights: experiments off camp somewhere, where a liquid form of the stone was injected into your arms, legs, eyes, or funneled into your orifices under varying conditions. Experiments that led nowhere, but—so the whispers went—to horrid mutations and deformities, corpses with bloody bulging eyes and strange crimson liquids that still ran beneath the skin, even after death.

Each evening, as Armand approached the barbarians' workshop, he felt the eyes of other prisoners on him. It was only a matter of time before the escape plan was uncovered. Someone would talk, or the guards would notice the empty cots in the night. That would mean death—if they were lucky—or perhaps those terrible experiments.

The Westerners had measured out the length of the tunnel until they could be sure they had passed the ground beneath the camp's perimeter fence. Three more days, they decided. The first would take them to the perimeter fence. The second would take them beyond that hateful boundary, where they would stop digging, just before they reached the surface. On the third they would break through to the icy air of freedom and make their escape.

Armand's plan was to drag Irik behind him at the appointed time and present the barbarians with a fait accompli. It would be risky, perhaps fatal, but the alternative was to leave the oppositionist to waste away in the camp, or to be killed by cold or bloodstone disease.

With two nights to go, Armand staggered back from the carpentry shop. A yellow light marked the cold dawn sky. High above, thin streaks of cloud stretched across the sky. The air was frigid, clasping him to its frozen bosom.

Prisoner 7624 eyed Armand malevolently from his place by the barracks, the light catching the indentation on his forehead. "I see you . . . you barbarian lover. What do you think you're up to, huh?"

Armand ignored him, but 7624 stepped across and clutched Armand's arm, twisted him back. "What do you do there? Touch one another?"

Armand stared blankly, trying to think. This was it—the game was up. "What of it if we do?"

Prisoner 7624 sneered at him, pushed him away. "You disgust me, 2591. You're not men. You're not real men."

Armand stumbled on, turned back, and spat out, "My name's Armand!"

Irik's barracks were the same as his own: an impossibly cramped long hall with bunks lining the walls. Armand slipped sideways between the bunks. Prisoners snored. Another man raved, the bloodstone fever taking him. "Oh gods. Oh gods. The red river is running in me. You should feel it. Oh gods."

Armand squatted by Irik's cot, brought his face close to the oppositionist's, and whispered, "You must prepare to depart. In two days we head west with the barbarians."

"West? There is another, better way, if we do indeed escape. But alas, in two days I'm on an all-night shift, loading the train."

Armand hesitated. "We have to get you off that shift, then. Best that you become ill."

"Ill? How can I make myself ill?" Irik's breath rose hot and stale near Armand's ear.

"Fake it, if you must. Or make yourself sick in some way. We must have you in the infirmary by tomorrow."

The following evening Armand staggered into the yard after a long day in the mine. Hearing a commotion behind him, he turned to see Irik shuffling forward, supported by two prisoners. When they reached Armand, they let Irik collapse to the ground.

"He's your friend," said one of the prisoners. "Only has himself to blame. Drank stagnant water by the train lines, the damned fool. Right before the all-night shift. The damned train arrives tomorrow."

Irik vomited black bile onto the ground. Armand picked the oppositionist up, threw Irik's arm over his own shoulders, and helped him toward the infirmary. Lying on his bed, surrounded by the dying, Irik smiled, his face wan and strained. "Mission accomplished."

Armand shook his head. "You'd better recover quickly."

Irik shrugged, rolled over, and retched, but nothing came out. He had emptied himself. As he settled back, he smiled weakly. "Of course."

Armand slipped from his bed in the cold and dark. He passed through the narrow path between the bunks and out into the night. The sky was clear, the stars brilliant and icy like the air around him. The clearest nights were the coldest, as if the indifference of the stars were shining down on them all.

As Armand reached the carpentry shop's door, he caught a glimpse of 7624 leering suspiciously from the mess hall. In his gleaming red hand, the man held a spear horizontally by his side, like a soldier in the Lyrian phalanxes. As he opened the door, Armand heard three knocks from inside the shop. Westerners began to move the table, while Ohan and the chieftain Ijahan greeted Armand with brisk waves.

"Wait," said Armand, sensing that 7624 intended more than surveillance. But the table was already away from the trapdoor, and an arm was holding up bags of dirt.

Armand closed the door quickly and peered through the window frame in time to see 7624 running toward the carpentry shop, spear in hand.

"7624 is coming," Armand said.

The Westerner emerging from the tunnel scrambled up and out. The other two, assuming he would duck back into the tunnel, had pushed the table over the manhole. For a moment they stumbled around one another. Ohan tried to stand on his injured legs, but he fell back onto his chair instead. The manhole remained uncovered.

The door burst open beside Armand, who backed away. Prisoner 7624 strode into the room and narrowed his eyes at the manhole. Turning his back to Armand, the collaborator lowered his spear toward the Westerners, who stared at him stock-still, their guilt heavy on their faces.

Without thinking, Armand leaped ineptly onto 7624 and wrapped his arms and legs around the collaborator, who staggered under the weight of them both.

Already, Ijahan had a hammer in hand. With a deft flick of his wrist, he turned 7624's spear away from his body and stepped close. There was a soft crack as the hammer came down, right into the depression that ran along 7624's forehead. Prisoner 7624 cried out, loud enough for the prison guards to hear. Again the chieftain raised the hammer. It hovered momentarily above 7624's head, and Armand—still clasping the collaborator from behind—noticed blood and a tuft of hair stuck to its dark metal. Then the hammer came down again. Blood spattered over Armand's face as the chieftain yanked the hammer out and brought it down again and again. The collaborator's legs gave way, and Armand found himself inadvertently holding the man up. Finally Ijahan stepped back, and Armand let 7624 crumple to the floor.

Armand wiped his face. His hand came away covered with blood and hard little bits of something. He retched.

Two barbarians quickly dragged 7624 toward the tunnel. "We'll put him in the tunnel after Armand descends."

Armand looked again through the window, expecting to see guards rushing toward the workshop. Anxiety rose like a white fog over his eyes, but to his disbelief, the space was empty. He breathed out. The fog passed.

Quickly, Armand grabbed a lamp and dropped through the opening in the floor. As he crawled on his hands and knees into the blackness, he heard the corpse forced into the tunnel behind him.

He set to work, another long brutal shift that seared his body with pain. He moaned softly as he worked, tried to tell himself it wasn't so bad. But that was folly. It was an infernal hell, and he started to cry as he dug. He cried from the pain, from the indignity of his position, from the betrayals of Valentin, from the harshness of the world. He cried for Irik and he cried for himself. He cried and dug, dug and cried, until there were no more tears.

When he was finished, he twisted himself around and crawled back carefully. As he held the little lamp before him, he kept expecting the corpse to loom toward him, as if it were still alive. Finally he made out the broken and crumpled form and realized he couldn't reach the trapdoor without crawling over it. Placing the lamp behind him, he pushed himself over the now cold body, the roof of the tunnel pressing him down onto the cadaver. His hand touched something wet, and he pulled it away quickly. Already there was a smell, which would only intensify. He started to breathe shallowly, as if the air might somehow infect him. Reaching out, he knocked on the trapdoor. To his relief, it swung open quickly, freeing him from his grisly situation.

"We should be able to dig up now. The last, final shift!" Ohan hobbled toward the trapdoor. Despite his cracked leg, Ohan took his turn like the others. Everyone needed to pull their weight. Armand had come to respect these people. They lived by simple, sometimes hard principles. Soft-spoken and plain thinking, they possessed a nobility that far surpassed the corruptions of a Valentin or Tiedmann. Ohan in particular had become a sort of silent friend; he and Armand could communicate with tiny gestures. They understood each other.

Armand left the chieftain sitting by a table, looking out the window into blackness. The other two Westerners slept on the floor. One raised his head wearily as Armand opened the door, then lowered it back to a pillow of rags and wooden remnants.

Armand could not sleep for the few hours remaining that night. How long would it be before the disappearance of 7624 was noticed? The next day they might escape. But if they were discovered, that would be the end. By the time the eerie morning light filtered into his barracks, his eyes burned with exhaustion. He dragged himself up, and when he stepped outside, the ground was again covered with a light dusting of snow. This time, it did not melt as it touched the ground.

The following day was a brutal, horrid affair for Armand. His back went into seizures, and he continuously found himself lying down as the other miners glared. He was thankful to make it to the day's end, and for the quota to be reached. He had been lucky, he knew. He would not last much longer if he had to stay in the camp.

The evening light was slowly fading as Armand staggered back from the mine. Light patches of snow still clung to the ground. As he rounded the factory, Armand stopped dead. A train had rolled in during the day, its great black engine sitting on the tracks, magnificent and silent. Behind a row of carriages were empty trays, ready to be loaded with bloodstone. New prisoners emerged from the sheds next to the clearing, dressed in their gray uniforms. To Armand they seemed chubby and filled with life. Looking at his gaunt and exhausted crew, he thought, *Is this what I've become so quickly?*

Commander Raken, wearing a pince-nez, and a group of accompanying guards, strode beside the train. Among them marched Tiedmann himself. But it was the sight of the creatures lumbering behind them that shocked Armand. Their trunklike legs rippled beneath their greaves. They were ten feet tall, massive bronze corsets covering their bodies. But it was the coldness that shone from the single glassy eyes fixed in the center of their heads that sent a churning into Armand's stomach. The Cyclopses carried tridents that jutted ominously into the sky. Armand remembered seeing the squad at the Palian wall. How long ago that seemed.

Cyclopses were used as auxiliaries in the Varenis legions, complementing forces in border camps or in other difficult duties, such as guarding slave mines. Armand knew these massive and powerful cousins of the stone and ice giants to the north would easily be able to hunt down any escapees.

He hurried to the carpentry shop, where the smell of death

drifted up from below. Even before he spoke a word, Ohan said, "We must continue anyway. Everyone must go to eat now. We have no time to lose. As soon as the last light drifts from the sky, we begin the escape."

The Cyclops squad set up their army tents in the square and built a fire. The succulent smells of their roasting meat and spiced vegetables drifted toward Armand, tormenting him as he raced to his barracks and stuffed his pouch of bloodstone into the side of his boot.

As he was returning to the mess hall, Armand stopped and watched the Cyclopses as they pressed closer to the fire. The creatures usually lived on rocky islands out in the ocean. Like the island of Aya, which spawned the minotaurs, or the Taritian archipelago where the Sirens lived, the Cyclopean islands were craggy and warm.

One of them grunted. In a strange clipped accent, he said, "Always the mountains. Always in winter."

Another pulled a spit of roasting meat from the fire. "At least we're not up in the northern ice-halls. That was cold *and* dangerous. When that ice giant hit Akius with that rock and his entire chest caved in . . . I still dream of it. The way his eye kept moving, even though his body was flattened like a pancake."

"The way we nearly froze on that glacier," said another. "I still can't feel the tips of my fingers."

The Cyclops closest to Armand fixed him with his single large cold eye. He rubbed his hands together close to the flames as he stared ominously.

Armand hurried on, thinking of the paste waiting for him in the hall. When he arrived, Tiedmann was sending his lieutenants from table to table, asking for 7624. Where was he? He hadn't been seen for the entire day. He wasn't in his cot or in the infirmary. Someone had to know.

As Armand shook his head to indicate ignorance, he noticed Tiedmann's eyes lingering on him. It was hard to imagine him without the intensity of those stony eyes, set in the wide planes of his face. The man had barely changed since Armand's arrival. The same air of hostility hung around him and Armand could sense the man's urge to dominate. Everything about him screamed that he would survive, no matter what. Armand thought of his grandfather's ring, which he had traded to Tiedmann. What else might the former Director take from him? Armand lowered his eyes to the rough table in front of him and hoped Tiedmann would look away.

As he left the mess hall, Armand looked up at the sky. In the west, the sun was long gone. To the east, the sky was a dark purple, shading into black. As he walked toward the carpentry shop, Armand looked back to see Tiedmann standing in the doorway of the mess hall, his vast head dark against the light room. There was nothing for Armand to do but to continue on as if everything were normal.

When he stepped into the carpentry shop, the smell of death hit Armand again. In other times, he would have gagged, for it was foul and impossible to ignore. Now, however, things had become too desperate. The barbarians moved around, busy with preparations: packing equipment and the little food that had been scavenged.

Armand turned from them and craned his head through the window to see Tiedmann, and two lieutenants carrying long black truncheons, walking toward the shop. Behind them, the fire threw light onto the massive faces of the Cyclopses not far away.

Armand clasped his head in his hands. "Tiedmann's coming with two men."

The chieftain grasped a hammer, Ohan a chisel. They sat quickly on stools, and the rest of the Westerners squatted around a pair of dice they often played with. Armand saw a rough piece of wood nearby that would serve as a club if he needed it, but he was painfully conscious that he was standing, awkward and out of place.

"Tihan is digging through to open air. But we're waiting for the others who are still at the mess hall, or in the barracks," said Ijahan.

*And Irik,* Armand thought to himself.

The door swung open, and Tiedmann stepped into the room, his two lieutenants pressing close behind, their truncheons swinging ominously in their hands.

From where they lounged, the barbarians' expressions were

brooding, unwelcoming. For a moment, a mad notion leaped into Armand's mind: thin and wasted, with colourful feathers and beads still in their hair, they looked like wild pugnatious birds, ready to defend their nest.

Ohan smiled grimly. "Tiedmann, the new barracks will be finished in the next week." He gestured to the frames of the new cots, which were now close to assembled.

"That's not why I'm here. We seem to have misplaced my lieutenant, 7624. He hasn't been seen in a day. Yet he can't have left the camp." Tiedmann sniffed a moment, grimaced a little. His eyes darted for a moment to one side, to a Hessian bag full of equipment for the breakout, but he didn't appear to register it.

"Are you sure he hasn't escaped?" asked Ohan. "He didn't seem like he belonged here."

Tiedmann's bodyguards gripped their truncheons more firmly, ready to strike at the merest encouragement. They didn't seem to like Ohan's joke.

But it distracted Tiedmann for a moment. He smiled thinly, then contemplated the new beds once more. "What a good job you've done on these cots. You'll transfer them to my lieutenants' barracks when they're done. The ones there can be moved to the new barrack."

Ijahan nodded in agreement as he spun one of the beads in his white beard between his fingers. "Of course. We can make you some new mattresses with sawdust, if you like."

Tiedmann scrunched up his button nose again, his eyes roving around the room. "Can you smell something?"

The lieutenants spoke, one after the other.

"A stench, sir."

"An odor."

"No doubt about it, sir."

"Rats," said Armand. "They hide among the wood and die there."

Tiedmann looked at Armand. When their eyes met, Armand saw Tiedmann register the lie. He cursed himself: he was never any good at duplicity.

Tiedmann took a few steps toward the far wall, where the

trapdoor was hidden. He sniffed once more and his head recoiled. "It seems to be from over there."

Armand prepared to strike one of the collaborators, but this time he knew their cries would rouse the Cyclopses. The escapees might rush into the tunnel together, but he would never make it to the infirmary to save Irik. In any case, it would not be long before all of them were captured. Their plan had always relied on surprise.

Tiedmann wheeled around. "Yes, the smell seems . . ." But his voice trailed off as, from this new angle, he caught sight of the hammer that the chieftain wielded, the staves of wood and chisels lying close to the barbarians squatting around their dice. He glanced at the door, then added slowly, "Yes, the smell is a rat, I'd say. Well, if you see 7624, send him to me immediately."

Everyone understood the situation. As Tiedmann backed away, several barbarians stood up, their makeshift weapons now in their hands, and pressed in on the three collaborators. When Ijahan nodded, they followed them through the door and across the ground toward the square, ensuring that Tiedmann and his men did not call out.

"A rat. Terrible things. Definitely a rat," said Tiedmann unconvincingly.

Armand rushed behind the strange little group, the remaining barbarians trying to appear casual as they scampered from the mess hall toward the carpentry workshop. There was no time. At any moment the barbarians following Tiedmann would turn back. Then the collaborators would call for help, and the guards and the Cyclopses would descend on the carpentry shop, murdering or capturing any remaining escapees.

Armand broke into a run. When he reached the infirmary, he glanced back. The two groups of barbarians had now met and were headed back to the shop, leaving Tiedmann and his bodyguards to walk on. At any moment the cry would go up.

Armand dashed into the infirmary, where Irik sat on his cot, already dressed. Beside him, his dinner paste was left half eaten.

Irik smiled weakly. "I'm ready."

"Now. Run."

Armand hurried back into the cold air just as the call went up:

"Alarm! Alarm! The barbarians!" Someone rang the bell. Armand raced up the slight incline toward the carpentry shop, got halfway there, then turned to see Irik struggling weakly after him.

From the square, Tiedmann was directing spear-wielding guards toward them. Farther behind, the Cyclopses grabbed their massive tridents. A moment later they would begin their terrifying charge.

*We'll never make it,* Armand realized. The Westerners would be scrambling along the tunnel, but there were too many of them: Armand, Irik, and several more would be trapped in the workshop. If they weren't impaled there and then, they would be made a ghastly example of later, or perhaps sent to the laboratory for bloodstone experiments.

Armand threw the door open, Irik close behind him. Five Westerners milled around the trapdoor. Ohan stood by the open window, his wooden cast still clasping his leg. With natural grace, he nocked an arrow to a longbow. By his side stood a leather quiver with twenty or so more, made from slivers of wood, but with iron tips.

Armand's heart leaped with hope. The other Westerners had thrown bows of their own over their backs. Wooden sword-length spikes, also tipped with iron, swung from their belts.

Ohan nodded to the floor near the trapdoor, where a small bag, a bow, and a spike lay. "Yours are there."

The barbarian then turned, drew the bow expertly, and loosed an arrow through the window. From the outside, Armand heard a scream. Ohan nocked another arrow, his movements flowing gracefully. The arrow flew through the window. Armand watched it glide through the air and strike a guard in the stomach. The guard clutched at it, looking down, his face trembling as if he might cry.

The guards hesitated, but behind them came the Cyclopses. Huge boots seemed to shake the ground. Massive thighs and arms rippled as the creatures moved.

The last of the Westerners plunged into the tunnel. Irik threw the bow over his shoulder and grasped the wooden spike, but Armand seized the bag before the oppositionist could take ahold of it.

"You first," said Armand.

Irik dived into the tunnel opening. His feet protruded for a moment, but then he dragged himself along the tunnel floor and was gone.

"Ohan!" said Armand.

Ohan looked back a moment, even as he reached for another arrow. "Armand, I was never going to escape."

"You can. We'll carry you if we have to. The others are waiting."

Ohan shook his head, loosed another arrow, turned back quickly. "Look at me, Armand. Look at my leg. I'll hold them off. Go now."

Armand hesitated. He couldn't leave the barbarian here, not after everything.

"Now!" yelled Ohan, then turned and loosed another arrow.

The last thing Armand saw was Ohan drawing the bow once more, his face a study of calm concentration.

Armand plunged through the trapdoor. Halfway along the tunnel, he heard the door bursting open far behind. Screams echoed around him as he scrabbled along on his hands and knees.

Irik helped Armand scramble up into the cold night air. Already the first group of Westerners was gathered in a copse of pine trees that ran up against the steep mountainside.

The two friends ran toward them, aware that at any moment the Cyclopses and guards might charge at them from the front gate. Armand's breath was heavy in his ears. The cold wind brushed his face. Irik fell, stumbled, and made it to his feet again before they joined the Westerners in the copse, a group of looming shadows in the frigid darkness.

They had run east, farther along the rising valley into the mountain range, the opposite direction to the one they needed to take.

"We must cross the river and double back," said the chieftain. "We'll find a pass that will lead us south."

"Guards," one of the barbarians said. With the same grace shown by Ohan, he loosed an arrow out into the darkness.

"We will go our own way," said Irik. "You should come with us. The Cyclopses will expect you to go west and south. They'll catch you."

"We won't go any other way. That is the way home for us, and there is safety in numbers," said Ijahan.

Armand was surprised. What was Irik planning? "Perhaps he's right. They have hunting skills and knowledge of how to survive out here."

"Even so," said Irik. "We have our own path to walk. We are not heading west, but farther east, into the mountains."

"When the heavy snows come, those routes will be impassable," said Ijahan. "You'll die in the cold."

"Still, we must head east, Armand and I. Don't you agree, Armand?" There was a certainty to Irik's voice. "It will help both of us escape, too. They will now have two groups to track."

Armand looked at the shadow of the oppositionist crouching beneath the pines. He now remembered Irik's words only days before: *There is another way.* Irik had trusted him. Now it was time for him to trust Irik. "I'll travel with Irik. We began this journey together. We may as well end it thus."

Three of the barbarians were keeping a steady stream of arrows flying through the air into the darkness. "We must go!" one of them hissed.

The chieftain drew a deep breath and lifted his bag from his shoulders. "You'll need this."

"So will you," said Irik.

Ijahan slung it over Irik's shoulder. "Not as much as you. Go now, and remember our people. I think it unlikely we will resist the Empire long."

Armand and Irik headed deeper into the pine trees, where it was even darker than the open air.

# TWENTY-EIGHT

Armand and Irik hurried through the night, moving over the rocky ground, past huge granite boulders that lay scattered across the landscape. They raced from one copse of trees to another, passing beneath mountain pines where they found them, hoping their tracks would be lost in the fallen needles. Clouds parted and a half-moon lit their way. The mountains loomed to either side of them.

Neither of them spoke. They were fueled by excitement and fear. Their first goal was to put as much distance between themselves and the camp as possible. So they marched on through the freezing cold, their faces rapidly becoming numb, the flesh and bones beneath their skin aching. Only Armand's left inner arm held some kind of heat. He didn't want to think about why, but he did press his other hand against it, and it helped to warm him.

They stopped in a clearing and rustled through the bag that Ohan had given them. Inside, they found soundly made hats and mittens, sewn from Hessian bags and filled with some unknown fabric. Rough blankets had been torn into strips to make scarves, which they wrapped around their faces.

Onward they marched, climbing ever higher until the wan light of dawn claimed the eastern sky. Armand was happy that the pains in his back and legs had much improved. The walking apparently helped settle them down. The snow was still patchy here, but ahead, Armand spied the pass that led farther into the mountains. There it might lay thicker, though he hoped the weather would warm once more and melt it away. It was strange that something so clean and beautiful could invoke such dread.

He had been in the Etolian range several times as a child. His father had taken him to visit the ruins of the ancient villas, destroyed during the war between Aya and Alerion. Armand's father had been an amateur archaeologist, and they had scoured the remnants, sifting through the debris between shattered and crumbling walls, occasionally uncovering fragments of ancient machinery, tiny and complex latticework from mechanical apparatuses whose function had long ago been lost. Those days seemed so far away now, from another life.

To the north lay the Site, the wastelands in the Keos Pass. To the east and south the Etolian range gave way to the foothills surrounding Caeli-Amur. Directly east, somewhere in the rocky crags, stood the Needles, spikes of rock jutting from the earth, some close together, others standing like lone sentries. Perched on their tops were the Eyries of the Augurers.

Armand considered this for a moment, and an exciting new possibility flashed before him. House officiates had sometimes made the pilgrimage to the Eyries, where they would enter the Augurers' Embrace and see the future. They saw flashes of coming events. They glimpsed the birth of children and deaths of parents. They discovered conspiracies set into motion by best friends and sudden acts of generosity by enemies. They perceived horrific assassination attempts and secret and torrid affairs. They foresaw the answers to questions that had not yet been asked. They saw themselves grown old and wise or bent and broken. When they returned, the officiates could set that knowledge to work in their favor. Yet stories abounded about the darker consequences of the embrace. Some were driven mad by the knowledge. Others felt their ambitions leach from them.

If Armand could reach the Augurers, he would be able to experience the Embrace himself. His visions of the future might prove a decisive weapon when he returned to Varenis. All it required was to buy the Augurers' favor.

But the thought of the vast and craggy peaks ahead drove fear into his heart—it was a mad plan that could lead to their deaths. Where, then, were they headed?

Armand glanced at Irik and stopped. The man's face was a sickly green, his eyes a noxious yellow. He had been in the infirmary for a reason.

272 * RJURIK DAVIDSON

"It's time to rest," said Armand.

"When we reach the pass." Irik looked up at the gap between the mountains.

Armand nodded. "If you need to stop, you must tell me. We can't have you collapsing."

Irik didn't reply. Perhaps he hadn't the strength.

When they entered the pass, Irik crumpled to the ground. They rested a moment, and Armand searched through their bags again. The barbarians had packed dried dinner paste in little packets. He passed one of the pouches to Irik. "Eat."

Irik shook his head.

"Eat, or I'll make you eat the way an adult does a child. You're an oppositionist, after all," said Armand.

Irik grinned weakly and took the pouch, forced a few mouthfuls down. Armand scooped the paste out and ate ravenously. The sun's rays struck them, and though it didn't give them much heat, it cheered them up a little. Then Armand stood up and looked back toward the valley. In the distance, the camp was visible, a series of tiny dots near to the horizon.

"How did you get here, Irik?" said Armand, as much to himself as to the other man.

Irik took a deep breath. His voice was contemplative and quiet. "My father worked in the Directorate—a petty bureaucrat, never likely to rise too high. It's a burden, you know, living a life of middling privilege while all around you are injustices. My early life was one of ease. I attended the best gymnasium, an entire building near the Plaza of the Sun. The elite of Varenis, they worship wealth. For them, greed is good. It is an ideology that colors their entire worldview. They literally don't see the poor, don't see injustice. For them, everyone is responsible for their position in life. They talk of investment and return. I saw that above me, and I couldn't live that life. It repelled me—the hypocrisy, the self-centeredness."

Armand realized now why Irik was cultured and kind, not like one of the rough worker-seditionists of Caeli-Amur. "So, you had better tell me why we're heading east, don't you think?"

Irik crossed his arms against the cold. "As a child, I dreamed of the ancient lands. Regularly I ran to the Directorate's library

and spent hours poring over the classical maps. I loved to see the
blank spaces surrounding Teeming Cities, and wondered what
might exist there. But also I loved to imagine visiting the Augurers in their rocky spires. Several of the maps showed ancient roads
cutting through these mountains to the Needles in the west. They
must pass somewhere around here. We simply have to find the
roads. It's the only way we can escape. The barbarians will be
caught, you realize."

"Yes, I know." Armand looked out at the spectacular mountains surrounding them, their peaks of ice and rock, the wisps of
clouds that moved quickly above them. This plan to cross the mountains relied on one essential thing: that the snows hold off. Should
a strong winter storm fall upon them, they would surely be lost.
Armand's eyes roved down to the forested slopes and the valley
below. Armand took a sharp breath. Farther down the valley, four
figures marched toward them. Too big to be humans, tridents held
in one hand, the figures moved with rapid certainty.

He looked down at the ill man, then back at the figures. For a
moment he thought he saw a fifth, smaller figure, moving in front
of a copse of gold-leafed trees.

"How far behind are they?" Irik asked.

"We should get moving," said Armand. He felt stiff and cold
when he stood. He pressed his inner arm against his stomach and
held it there like a bottle of hot water. He couldn't bear to tell Irik
about it.

Later in the afternoon, Armand and Irik crossed the ice-cold and
fast-flowing river in the hope that it would throw off their pursuers. At other times, they doubled back along their trail and took
another path. Perhaps these tactics helped, for they did not see the
Cyclopses again. But as evening came, they again reached a pass
that afforded a survey of the valley behind. Between the now-sparse
copses of trees, Armand spied the Cyclopses. The creatures were
closer still. He despaired, for if the brutes caught up, they would
have no chance against them.

They camped that night among the pine trees. So far they had
been blessed. It had not snowed again, though the night was

dreadfully cold. The two of them huddled together in the warmth. Armand wrapped his arms around the other man, felt his hot and shallow breath on his skin. This man should rightly be his enemy, yet here they were, the two of them, each other's only support. The thought of Irik's death filled Armand with a deep-felt grief that settled in his stomach like a stone.

The next day they kept a lookout for the mountain goats that wandered along the mountain tracks. Armand managed to bring one down with an arrow. He killed the struggling thing with the wooden spike, but the affair was messy and distressing. Irik helped as much as he could, but he seemed sicker and weaker than before. He found it difficult to hold his food down, though he continued uncomplainingly. They cut meat from the goat and placed it in the empty pouches that had held the scavenged paste. When they continued, Armand wondered if they'd live to regret leaving the bulk of the goat behind.

The pass narrowed, and they followed a mountain goat track. Patches of snow lay in the shaded areas. Armand briefly looked back from a craggy lookout to the base of the track. The Cyclopses were closer still, but now there were only three instead of four. Anxiety rushed through Armand. Was the fourth somewhere close? He looked across at Irik's wan and sickly face. The oppositionist would not last much longer at this pace.

Later in the day they spied a snow leopard perched on a rock face of one of the mountains. Its wonderfully long and thick tail hung like a rope from the ledge. Its gray-blue stripes would camouflage it when the snow set in. The majestic creature looked down at them with intelligent sky-blue eyes.

"When we find the roads, we'll continue on to the Needles," Armand said. "I mean to go to the Augurers, to foresee the future."

"They say foreseeing is the most elusive of things," said Irik. "No one knows the truth of it. It's a cipher no one can unravel. What could you seek to learn?"

"I must return to Varenis. There are things that must be done." Armand weighed his next words carefully. "You should come with me. It will be a difficult road that leads through the wastelands of the Keos Pass, but I will protect you."

"No one can protect anyone in Varenis," said Irik. "It's not that kind of city. I will go to Caeli-Amur to join the seditionists."

Armand held Irik closer, felt the man's warmth. "You know the seditionists have no future."

"We don't fight only for a future," said Irik. "We fight also for the present, because one must. If you see injustice in the world and you don't act, what are you? You're already dead."

"But stability, principles, honor, and respect—these are the things that bring peace and happiness," said Armand. "Everyone should know their place."

"Did these principles bring you peace and happiness?" Irik challenged Armand.

"You can be quite a brat, you know." Armand clenched his teeth. The man was infuriating.

"And you're quite the pompous arse," Irik spat out.

For a moment there was silence. Irik elbowed Armand in the ribs, and in an instant the two of them broke out giggling. Armand wondered how long it had been since he'd laughed.

"This is the closest to happiness I've felt," said Armand.

"In the ice, under a rough blanket with a mortal enemy—*that's* the closest you've come to happiness?" said Irik. "I'll remember to stay away from you, then."

Again they laughed, and the laughter seemed to feed on itself until Armand said, "Stop it. My stomach hurts."

When they had calmed down, Irik said. "It must just be my fever, but your arm seems unusually warm."

"It's your imagination," lied Armand.

Soon afterward, Irik broke into a feverish shudder. His teeth chattered, yet he was sweaty and shaking. Armand wrapped his arms around the oppositionist until they both fell asleep under the silent trees.

The next day, the terrain became rough and rugged. High in the mountains, the fast-flowing streams cut through stony plains, and the going became tough. Snow capped the peaks around them, but the plain itself was like some strange desert, great round pebbles smoothed by some unknown process, as if they marched on an ancient riverbed.

Several times Irik fell; each time it took greater effort for him to get back on his feet. Sweat poured from the man; his face was gaunt, drained; his fever ravaged him.

At midday, when they stopped to rest, Irik lay on his back, his bag beside him. He looked up at Armand. "Go on without me."

"Never." Armand sat beside the man, put his hand on the other man's chest. "The Cyclopses will find you, and if they don't kill you, they'll return you to the camp."

"Armand, I thank you for your kindnesses. I never expected to live long, in any case. An oppositionist rarely does."

Armand threw his bag to the ground. "No!"

"Go. Go on."

Armand collapsed on his back beside Irik. Above them the sky was cobalt blue, vast. He felt he might cry. Sitting up, he picked up the bow and looked at it for a moment. It was primitive, but the barbarians had fashioned it well. He nocked an arrow. "I'll wait with you, then."

"Then you'll die too," said Irik. "There's no way you can fight one Cyclops, let alone four."

"Maybe I can cut them down with the bow."

"They have slingshots. They're trained. Are you?"

Armand looked back up at the sky. He spied a spear-bird circling far above. Even at its height, it was an ominous sight. *Oh no,* he thought. The spear-bird had seen them and would enter its death spiral before too long, the terrifying gyre he'd seen often in the hills around Caeli-Amur, as the birds picked off lone sheep or wild horses. The worst thing was to try to run, for then the spear-birds would break from their death spiral and glide at terrifying speed, leading with their razor-sharp beaks—deadly spikes on which to impale their prey.

Armand glanced at Irik, began to look up again, but then saw, perhaps a mile away, three Cyclops coming over the stony plane toward them. One had broken into a run and was now ahead of the others. They had seen Armand and Irik and would not let them escape now.

Irik smiled weakly at Armand. "I'm a bit better now. I'll be ready in a moment."

"It's too late for running." Armand gestured to the spear-bird above.

Irik looked up, stared at the bird impassively. "So it is."

At that moment the spear-bird entered its death spiral. Armand watched in wonder as the bird circled high above, making elongated, elliptical movements. But the bird was not in quite the right location. Its gyre was slightly askew.

"It's not us! It's not coming for us!" Armand yelled.

The spear-bird came down, winding faster and faster, a terrifying flight, its leathery wings like those of the gliders that hung over Caeli-Amur. In that instant the first Cyclops, who was far ahead of the others, stopped, looked up, and, realizing the danger he was in, pulled his slingshot from his belt.

"Now," said Armand. "Let's go!"

Irik staggered to his feet, lifted his bag, and, with surprising feverish energy, started running. Ahead stood a cliff, with dangerous-looking goat trails climbing frighteningly up it.

Armand practically danced across the stony ground, certain that any moment his ankle would roll and he would be left clutching it and moaning. Still faster he ran, leaving Irik in his wake.

He reached the cliff face and knew it was both necessary and impossible to climb the goat trails. They were too sheer and treacherous. The idea sent him into a panic. He remembered gripping the rope in Varenis as he escaped the Belligerent watchmen, sure he would fall to his death. He looked up at the cliff again: they would have to try. He would conquer his fear of heights, or die trying.

As Irik rushed to his side, he looked back to where the spearbird circled with impossible speed, a cyclone of wings and beak, a blur in the air. The first Cyclops crouched on the ground, one hand above his head like a builder beneath a falling stone. He was transfixed, terror of the bird paralyzing him—few could face a spearbird's gyre calmly.

Armand was vaguely aware that Irik had begun to climb, but he was mesmerized by the death flight before him.

"Up now, Armand!" called Irik. The oppositionist was still apparently seized by the burst of feverish energy—possibly his last—and he was already a third of the way up the cliff.

The second two Cyclopses flung slingshot stones at the spear-bird, but it was like flinging missiles into a hurricane. In an instant the lone Cyclops had disappeared into a fury of flapping wings.

Armand scrambled up one of the goat trails. In no time, the drop beneath him was precipitous and terrifying. Above him, Irik's foot slipped over a foothold, sending dirt over the precipice. The oppositionist's hands splayed out as he pressed himself to the cliff face. His bag went over the edge. Despairingly, he looked down past Armand to where it lay.

"Leave it. Keep going." Armand himself was gripped by terror. In his mind, he saw himself falling from the cliff again and again. His legs were shaking. He placed his hands on the rocky wall to calm himself.

In places the trail stopped, only to begin again three feet higher. Quivers of fear shot through Armand as he scrambled up. Half-way up the cliff, he came to a series of ledges that ran up like a sheer ladder. He froze and began to shake. The terror swept him away, like a snowflake on the breeze.

Irik called from the crest of the cliff. "Come on, Armand. Up."

"I can't." Armand was paralyzed. He grasped the ledge before him with desperation. Looking down at the rocky floor below, he knew a fall would kill him.

"Armand, come on!"

"I can't! I can't!"

He heard something from above but was too afraid to look up.

Irik's voice was closer now. Impossibly, despite his illness, the oppositionist had climbed back down to Armand. His soft voice lilted with sardonic humor. "Look at us two, Armand. A bratty oppositionist and a pompous traditionalist, scaling cliffs and running from Cyclopses. You wouldn't want to be anywhere else, would you?"

Armand pressed his face against the rock, felt its coldness against his cheek.

Irik spoke again. "It's a black joke, life. What do you think the Cyclopses are thinking? 'Why do we have to chase those two? Why can't we just go home? I didn't sign up to face spear-birds in the cold. The whole thing is just *so annoying*.'"

Armand smiled. "You think we're messing up their plans for the day?"

Irik spoke louder and more sardonically now. "I think we're messing up their plans for the *week*. I mean, they look quite peeved down there."

Armand chuckled, and the fear abated a little. He looked up and Irik reached down. "Come on."

Armand continued the nightmarish climb, calmer now, his hands steadier, his legs more assured. Finally, impossibly, he reached the top of the cliff, where he collapsed, heaving and sweating beside Irik. Armand looked across to his friend, who now stared into the sky blankly. His face was as green as lichen. How much courage it had taken for the oppositionist to come back for Armand.

On the plain below, the two Cyclopses were standing around their fallen comrade. The spear-bird had taken flight under the barrage of slingshot stones, it seemed. Armand watched as they left the crumpled figure and began to march to where the cliff tapered down to a sheer incline, far away. From there they would climb up to the plateau and continue their relentless chase.

"It's time to move again," said Armand.

Irik looked up from his resting place. His face was pale, his breath ragged. "Just a little longer."

When they began to move once more, it seemed to Armand that they might have reached the highest pass between the mountains. Ahead lay a crest, beyond which he could only see sky. He was filled with hope.

As he let the strange feeling wash through him, he felt something soft touch his face. He looked up to see the first flecks of snow spinning onto them. Black clouds rolled across the sky. His hope blew away on the gusts of icy wind.

"Perhaps the shadow will help us." Irik stared blankly as he walked. Sweat poured from his body as the sickness played out its patterns inside him.

"What shadow?" asked Armand.

"Surely, you've seen it. The shadow. The figure looking over us. Cloaked."

"It's just your fever speaking, Irik."

"What fever?" asked the oppositionist. "It's you who has the fever. I'm ice-cold. I'm as cold as the heart of Varenis itself."

Yet they continued, two tiny figures in a massive hostile landscape, until the dark sky cracked open and the snow fell in great swirling swathes.The storm closed in on them as twilight fell. Armand could only see thirty feet ahead, through dancing, swirling flakes of snow.

*There's something beautiful about the wild indifference of this world,* thought Armand. Beside him, Irik swayed on his feet.

"We have to find somewhere to shelter." Armand led them closer toward the sheer slopes of the nearby mountain. Here they found small overhangs, but Irik shook his head as if to say they were too small.

"We have to choose one of these," said Armand.

"No," said Irik. "There's a house up here."

Armand grasped the man. "There's no house."

"My mother's house is right here. Can't you see it? My mother—she's the figure who has been watching over us. The shadow."

"Is your mother dead?" asked Armand.

"Yes," said Irik, who began to cry.

"There is no house," said Armand. "Come, let's huddle beneath this outcrop."

He pushed Irik beneath the rocky ledge, turned to wedge himself in, and started at the great hulking form of a Cyclops, standing in the roiling snow, trident in hand, staring at them.

The Cyclops called out in a guttural language, filled with clicks and aspirations. His comrades were apparently nearby.

Armand grabbed the wooden spike. He would die here, he decided. They would have to carry his corpse back to the camp with Irik's. Never again would he work in those mines. Despair now filled him. He had endured so much. Now all was at an end, all his hopes and plans. He found himself moaning softly, as if he might be dying already.

The Cyclops called out again in his native tongue and began to march forward. Its single eye pierced Armand with animosity. The violence would be swift and brutal.

At first Armand thought it was a tiny bird darting from the ledge above. It made a soft sound—*phht*—like the wooshing of air. The Cyclops screamed, his hand over his eye.

Then there was a mechanical sound from above. Armand craned his neck to see, but the ledge obscured his vision. There was a click and then a second rushing sound. The blinded Cyclops grabbed at its neck and thrashed around.

A moment later a hooded figure leaped into the snow in front of Armand. Its cloak flapped dramatically around it, and a chunky modern bolt-thrower swung in its hand. With the grace of an athlete, the figure dashed across the snow toward the towering Cyclops. In a rapid motion, it placed the bolt-thrower beneath the Cyclops's chin. There was a clunk, and his great head was thrown back violently as something burst from the top of it. The massive creature stood motionless for a moment, then collapsed straight back into the snow.

The hooded figure strode purposely back toward the overhang. Armand pressed against Irik, gripping his spike grimly, determined to defend them both.

Recognition struck Armand with the force of a blow. The shadow, as Irik had called it, was the same red-bearded assassin who had tailed him from Caeli-Amur all that time ago.

The figure threw back its hood. There was no beard after all. Instead, a woman shook out her bright red ball of hair. "These new bolt-throwers—I *like* them!"

"Who are you?" said Armand in amazement.

"I'm your guardian god, Armand Lecroisier," the woman said.

"That is *definitely* not my mother," said Irik.

# TWENTY-NINE

Max's journey back from the Sentinel Tower to Lixus passed quickly, and before long, he stood on the hills overlooking the city. Lixus looked like a watercolor painting: solar hues brushed the ruined towers romantically. Max had no desire to enter the city at night, so he camped on the ridge and watched the towers slowly fade into inky silhouettes. He ate simply, enjoying the quiet in his head. Aya had sunk so deep that he was almost not there at all.

The following morning Max rode through the vast empty streets of Lixus and reached the plaza. The tear-flowers had been hacked down, their platelike heads shriveled on the ground under them. Karol's corpse lay beside them, still encrusted with a layer of hardened nectar. Since Max had left, the flowers' roots had plunged into Karol's body. Once they had sucked Karol's essence into the flower stems, but since they had been cut down, they had hardened and dried. Now Karol's head tilted back, his mouth half open, his eyes staring off into the land of death, tiny rootlets crisscrossing his cheeks, curling around his lips. The officiate's expression was caught between excruciation and euphoria, between entrapment and release.

The Towers were empty. Perhaps the crow-people had followed the Pilgrim south to the Teeming Cities. It would be a long march, and many of them would die, but perhaps they would find the meaning they were all searching for. Now an air of melancholy engulfed Lixus. Were the vacant, crumbling towers, the overgrown gardens, the deserted hot springs all glories destined for ruination? Max scavenged some abandoned provisions and continued.

---

It was afternoon when Max came to a crest and looked over at the rolling hills. When he passed this place some weeks ago, it had been a picture of bucolic prettiness: the villas perched on the hills or snuggled in the valleys, the fields and greenhouses and olive groves. Now he watched an ominous scene. Like ants on a dead body, columns of black guards marched along the roadways, descended on the villas and farms. Everywhere he looked, they clashed with defending forces. The dead lay strewn in gutters or propped against walls. Plumes of smoke twisted into the air from burning buildings.

Max continued into the maelstrom. Before long, people streamed past him. First came the remnants of House agents—officiates, subofficiates, and intendants—on horseback. They rode with fear in their eyes, saddlebags filled with whatever booty they had rescued, scarcely giving him a second look as they headed south. Then came those fleeing on foot. The bulk of these were simple rural folk who had worked the farms, the goods in their arms just rags and trinkets.

A hearty-looking old man halted beside Max's horse. "Turn back, traveler, turn back! The seditionists have come and they're razing everything."

Maximilian's heart lurched. "But why would the seditionists do that? No, it's impossible."

The old man looked back at the scene behind him. "You're right—impossible."

The man ran on without another word as a group of black-suited guards rode toward Max. As they raced past, they eyed him suspiciously. They were hard-looking men and women, their flat, angular faces and steely eyes filled with ruthless determination. Menacing short-swords dripped with blood.

In the middle of the road, an abandoned carriage lurched to one side, its axle broken from speeding over the potholed road. Its horses were gone, and clothes and knickknacks were strewn on the dirt around it.

A villa stood at the end of a short road to Max's right. Several seditionists were busy setting its walls alight with hay and firewood. Others were throwing stones at the villa's first story. From the upper windows a bolt-thrower appeared. One of the arsonists screamed, went down clutching his side.

Through the frosted glass walls of a greenhouse, Max saw figures engaged in a bitter skirmish. Several of the silhouettes went down in a rain of blows.

Max rode closer. Through the greenhouse's open doors, he caught sight of sapphire bushes, their blue petals waving desperately about. A black-suited guard hacked at banks of delicate herbs, candle-flowers, and scarlet livid-moss. Many of those beautiful plants had thaumaturgical properties. Beside the beds of flora lay corpses of gardeners, hoes and pitchforks clasped in their hands.

Max leaped from his horse and strode into the damp heat. Lush and sickly scents wafted over him.

Three more guards hacked away at the fire-trees. Elsewhere, shivering-moss lay hewn from its bed, its bright green color slowly fading, its motion smaller and smaller.

"Those are precious!" said Max.

One of the guards—a pear-shaped woman—turned, and in smooth liquid tones said, "Look, it's the owner."

"I'm not the owner, you imbecile," said Max. "You should know who I am."

"Ejan gave us the right to do whatever we like out here. 'You're off the leash!' he said. So bugger off." The woman sneered, turned back to the garden, slashed away.

Max grabbed the guard by the shoulder, turned her around. "You listen—"

The short, sharp blow hit his head from behind. The world slipped. An immense rug was pulled from beneath Max's feet. He was on his knees. Ringing sounded in his ears.

"No, you don't—" But he wasn't all there. He was far away, noticing strange little details. One of the sapphire flowers, torn from the ground, was shuddering where it lay. The guard's belt had been tightened; the belt's pin had widened one of the holes considerably.

The woman looked down at him. "What did you say?"

Max touched the back of his head. Blood covered his hand, warm and slick. "I'm Maximilian."

"And I'm Ursilia the Gorgon, from before the cataclysm." The woman looked up at her comrade, who apparently stood behind Max, and nodded.

The rug was violently pulled again. The world spun, or perhaps it was Maximilian who tumbled, until everything became a blur. Then the blur sped into a vast whiteness, and he was spun off into oblivion.

There were trees around him, thin tree trunks densely packed together. No: they weren't trees—they were legs. Things clarified. Eerie light glowed from soft lichen growing on the walls. In one corner of the stone room, red vines clutched a body that hung suspended in their leafy clutches. A species of *Toxicodendron didion*, perhaps designed to grow beneath ground. Had the man thrown himself into its lethal embrace out of despair, or had he been grasped by the deadly plant as he wandered around the cell? Max rolled to his knees, looked up at the group of people in the center of the stony chamber. Six men stood in a little circle, their gray clothes hanging limply. Against a far wall sat a group of better-heeled men—House agents, Max presumed.

"There's no escape." One of the men brushed his straggly, ratty beard as he talked to the circle. "Even if you got past these bars, the grounds are protected by tear-flowers, snow-orchids, and blood-orchids. You'd end up in one of their maws and be worse off than that fella there." He nodded toward the corpse hanging from the vines. With the mention of the deadly flora, Max knew he had to be in the dungeons beneath House Arbor.

He searched around for his bag, his possessions, the Core. None of it was there. For a moment he buried his face in his hands. He felt broken, ruined. A vicious headache split his skull.

Aya rose up for a moment, like a feverishly ill man raising his head. *This is a universe of disappointment, you see. There's only one escape, only one place of safety.*

Several of the men looked down at Max, then away again. The House agents didn't bother to glance at him at all. Now Max heard cries from beyond the iron bars at one side of the cell. Apparently, there were many such cells down here. Maximilian touched the back of his head gingerly. His hair was matted with blood.

"When I was at the tribunal," the second man said, "I begged that bastard Georges to show mercy. I admitted to being a privateer. But they were just things I'd stolen from the Opera, you know. I worked there before the bloody uprising. So I slipped in and made off with food cards and a bunch of forms. Made good money, too. Anyway, I admit to it all, beg forgiveness, and that bastard, he says mine is the worst crime of all. 'The Bolt for you, my man,' he says."

From beyond the cell, the groan of a door opening. Absolute silence now, as everyone waited tensely. Anxious eyes darted around the circle. A squad of guards marched past them and into the darkness, and the men breathed out. An iron door opened down the passageway. Someone read a list of names; there was a rattling of chains; then suddenly screaming of several voices at once.

"Please, no, there's been a mistake."

"Please, let me see the tribunal. Let me . . ."

"It's not right. It's not!"

The door clunked shut again. Out of respect, the cell remained silent until the group of ten prisoners was led past the cell and out of the dungeon, their chains rattling.

# THIRTY

Over the following days, Max watched one after another of the inmates hauled in front of the Criminal Tribunal. When each man returned, there was nothing to say. None of them were released. All of them were destined for the Bolt.

Max would be the exception. Despite Georges's corruption—his conspiracies with the Elo-Talern, his stolen goods in one wing of House Arbor—he would not risk condemning a former leader of seditionism, a veteran of the struggle before the overthrow of the Houses. Once Georges saw him, Max would be freed.

Until then, Max waited and watched, ever more frustrated, as each morning and evening another group was led along the corridors, begging for forgiveness. More prisoners were crushed into the cells: petty criminals, spies and saboteurs, outspoken supporters of the Houses. Max could never be sure how many of these dark brooding characters were guilty of these offenses.

To distract himself, Max hacked at his beard with the one communal razor they possessed, though he knew his curly hair had grown long and wild. There had been knots in it before; now there were long matted clumps he could not separate. These would have to be shaved off.

Finally the lank-haired guard called Max's name. Max was taken out, shackled, and led with a group along grim corridors lit by luminescent lichen. They climbed a staircase, and the lichen gave way to sad-looking candle-flowers that threw a gentle white light onto a luxurious walkway lined by alcoves decorated with broken statues and dying plants.

Max was pushed into a great semicircular theater, its walls formed by the same wiry vines. The theater seats were intricately sculpted from the aboveground roots of pillarlike trees. Vines draped from the trees and walls and intertwined with one another, resembling one great leafy organism. A dozen furnace trees stood like sentinels throughout, and Max could feel the warmth thrown out by the nearest one.

Several hundred people packed into the theater, and the Criminal Tribunal sat at a table carved from black wood. Of the three presiding members, Maximilian knew only Georges, who sat officiously in the middle of the table. Despite his intensity, Georges had always looked exhausted, and recent events had clearly not helped the matter. His square, lantern-jawed face drooped even more heavily, and his perpetually deep-set eyes practically disappeared into his face. Presiding over the tribunal was apparently difficult work, though Max could hardly see why, considering there seemed to be only one possible outcome.

As Max was being pushed into a small square enclosure, he called out, "Georges, enough of this—"

The guard struck Max in the stomach. He doubled over, the wind sucked from him. A low hiss carried through the theater and gave Maximilian hope. Perhaps the audience would be on his side. On one side of the theater sat a group of university students, young and with bohemian clothes and short beards. Scattered among the crowd were white-haired retirees who might have wandered down from their equally white houses near Via Gracchia. They were not the mob of the Lavere.

Behind the tribunal, a line of golden-plate helianthuses gleamed like little suns. As he peered down at Max, Georges seemed as if he had a halo. "Prisoner, you're charged with obstructing the action of the Caeli-Amur guards, sabotage of the new order. How do you plead?"

"Georges, it's me, Maximilian." Max looked to the other two tribunal members, two women who watched impassively. Did his matted curly hair and shaggy beard obscure his identity?

Georges closed his eyes slowly, as if Maximilian's words wearied him further. "Claiming to be one of the fallen heroes of the movement will not gain you leverage."

Hoping for help, Max looked up at the leafy galleries hanging above, packed with yet more spectators. He caught a glimpse of a figure—tall, standing stiffly—looking down at him. Was it Ejan? But the figure was just one of many, all of them obscured by shadows. Max turned back to face the tribunal.

"Well?" Georges sighed.

"I *am* the seditionist Maximilian. Georges, you *know* me." Maximilian raised his shackled hands to his face, felt the straggly beard that grew thickly. "Fetch any of the veterans, and they will vouch for me."

One of the two other tribunal members, this one a pretty and willowy woman, held up a few sheets of paper in her long fingers. "Prisoner, I have before me an account of one of the guards whom you assaulted in the region of the villas. The account claims that as the guards were undertaking the orders of the Insurgent Authority itself, you attempted to stop them. You struck one, and attempted to rescue the property of House Arbor. Do you deny the accusations?"

"They were destroying—"

She spat back zealously, "And what were you doing in the region, if you were not fighting on the side of the Houses?"

"I was returning from a journey to Lixus."

Georges crossed his arms with disdain. "Everyone knows Lixus is nothing but a deserted ruin. You had better invent something more plausible."

Max felt events slipping away from him. He was suddenly sure he would not escape this tribunal. He would end up like the rest of the prisoners, condemned to the Bolt even as they begged for clemency.

—Aya, help me—said Max, but he heard nothing in return. He could feel Aya's bulk within him, hidden away, but the god felt like a great marshy pit, sodden with depression.

Max scoured the audience once more. Several voices called out, "He's harmless! This is a farce!"

Max decided it best for the moment to refuse their game. He countered their charges with his own. "I returned with a power source, the Core—a long cylinder. Where is it?"

Until now the last member of the tribunal had looked on silently.

Now she leaned over the imposing table. Older than the others, she had a fragile build, short hair, and olive skin. She had the earnestness of a child, and Max sensed she might be an ally.

"What is the function of this cylinder? Why did you carry it?" she said.

Max thought of explaining the Core, but he hesitated. They would look on his story as nothing but a grandiose tale. He doubted the truth could save him. Desperation was now taking him. *There is a chance,* he thought, *that I can use thaumaturgy.* He could draw the ideograms in the air, though his hands were shackled, and incant the words quickly. Once invisible, he could sneak through in the resulting pandemonium. He glanced at the door, where mean faces leered in at him.

"Well? If you don't speak, we can't help you," she said.

Max tried to buy some time. "Where is it?"

"You see, Elise, he is willfully obstructionist," Georges said to the woman. "If you had done nothing wrong, you would have nothing to hide."

Seeing the tribunal's intransigence, Max quickly changed his strategy. He would try the truth after all, and hope it would lead somewhere more hopeful. "I ventured to the Sentinel Tower, Iria's tower, in search of its Core, which is an engine of sorts. I want to use the Core to . . . Well, when I was in the Library of Caeli-Enas, I—"

Georges interrupted. "Fairy tales."

Elise leaned over the tribunal's desk. "I'd like to hear what he has to say. Each has a right to answer the charges, Georges."

"Let him speak!" cried out some of the spectators.

Georges yawned angrily. "This is the third time you've demanded we give a prisoner more than their due time, Elise. To the first two I acquiesced, but no longer. Must I remind you we have another twelve prisoners to condemn today?"

"Judge," said Elise.

"Ah yes, judge. Nevertheless, to these mad stories, I put my foot down. I move that the man face the Bolt on the morn. All those in favor?" Georges raised his hand together with the willowy young woman.

Elise looked down at the table, her face a picture of resigned melancholy.

Max began his incantation, his hands drawing the ideograms as quickly as he could. As they did, they left little traces of power in the air behind them.

"He's a thaumaturgist! He casts a charm!" Georges screamed.

Max's words tumbled from his mouth. He completed the ideograms, and the world lit up with vitality. Now invisible, he turned quickly, just as something crashed onto his temple. Pain jagged into his skull, and the charm was destroyed. The world took back its mundane form, and he felt it slipping under him. As he lost consciousness, the last thing he heard was the baleful laughter of Aya.

All morning they waited. Apparently, things had slowed down at the Standing Stones—some part of the process had broken down. It was afternoon by the time guards came for Max and nine other prisoners. He was gagged so that he might not use the Art. The group was shoved into a horse-drawn carriage, enclosed by bars. As it rattled away from the Arbor Palace, Max looked out at the lawns and hedges, the carefully crafted gardens of House Arbor. The plants had started to grow wild, and weeds were sprouting around the lovely trees and statues. Brilliantly colored beds of flowers had been trampled. Only the aqueducts and walkways that crisscrossed through the air still seemed to be in good condition.

From the woods that encircled the grounds, Max heard the wailing of tear-flowers. They seemed to be crying out for the condemned men.

The carriage carried them past a huge circular statue depicting the gods at war. Aya, the rebel god, threw lightning bolts as the others chased him.

—Look, Aya. It's you—said Max.

*I look quite handsome, don't I? I hope they remember me like that.*

Max looked at the classical palace behind. Towers spiraled on one side; arches crossed to the opposite wing above a glassy lake. In places, vines, flowers, and mosses had somehow grown into the side of the Palace's walls. They appeared to be part of the structure now.

—You escaped once. Why not now? Help me, Aya. I know you can.

Max remembered Aya had given him matter-shifting equations when he had been caught in Technis's dungeons. He had broken his chains, shattered locks. But Max could not recall them clearly. His mind had been a jumble back then, fragmented pieces that didn't add up to a whole. And the prime language *was* a language. To learn the equations was not to learn the underlying grammar.

*Don't you understand, Maximilian? It would be better if I died,* said Aya.

—Perhaps better for you, but not for me.

Before long, the cart was clattering along the cobblestoned boulevard, through the Arantine. They passed grand, stately mansions set far from the road: the houses of officiates, mostly, or wealthy foreigners from Numeria, or the Teeming Cities, or Varenis, even. Some probably belonged to the leaders of the Collegia and the more powerful thaumaturgists.

—Aya, I beg you—said Max. —We can still take the power source to the Elo-Talern and be free of each other. Is there nothing to look forward to?

*You are the stronger personality anyway,* said Aya. *You feel it, don't you? This entity I am—this is not the whole of me. Parts have sloughed off, like dead skin.*

Max caught glimpses of the Quaedian, the Opera, whitecaps breaking on the ocean. A crowd lined the road at the head of the Thousand Stairs and chanted, "Bolt! Bolt! Bolt!" Bits of rotten fruit and muck flew through the air, struck the bars, splattering the condemned men.

For a moment Max caught a glimpse of Oewen, who had once been Max's follower and student. Before the overthrow of the Houses, Max had tried to teach Oewen the basics of thaumaturgy. The young man had shown talent but not determination. A ray of hope rushed into Max.

"Oewen! Oewen!" Max's voice struggled to cry out, but each time his voice was muffled by the material crammed in his mouth. "Oewen!"

Oewen turned and searched the surrounding crowd, but the cart passed him by before he located the sound. Max hung his head.

Multitudes filled the street ahead, having climbed up from the Arena, where they had attended a spectacular. The cart's passage was blocked. Guards toiled hard at separating the crowd, and the cart moved forward with excruciating slowness. A cold wind whipped up and rushed through the bars of the cage. Max crossed his arms, huddled close to the dirty prisoners for warmth.

A massive cheer rose as the carriage stopped in front of the Standing Stones. Three machines sat on a platform in the center of the stone circle. One of them was broken, its mechanism cracked and splintered, its wooden supports hanging loosely.

—Aya!—Max called.

A black-suited captain leaped from the stage and spoke to the crowd. "Citizens! Citizens!" The man strode around, raising his hand in the air. "Another group of saboteurs and House agents. They think they are better than us. They kept their privileges from us. They ate fine foods and wines while they starved us. They are the representatives of injustice and betrayal. But what do we have?" The man halted theatrically. "We have the great leveler!" He swiveled around theatrically and gestured to the machines on the platform behind him. "The Bolt!"

"The Bolt! The Bolt!"

The captain held up a scroll. "I have with me a list of the crimes of these enemies of the people. A list of crimes so degenerate, so sick and bloodthirsty, you would not believe their contents. They are crimes not fit for the ears of innocents, and so I will not read them to you." The man now took on a downcast air, as if he were suddenly sad. "What lows have our enemies fallen to? How it tries our patience, our sense of solidarity, our sense of goodness."

The crowd now began a slow hoot, a slow booing.

The captain stood upright again and cried out, "So we must do our duty, even if it is not to our taste. One does what is right! And we have the great leveler! The Bolt!"

"Do what's right!"

"Do what must be done!"

The man unrolled the scroll. "Martin Lerouge. Step forward!"

A rat-bearded man fell to his knees and began to wail. "All I took from the Opera were cards and forms. I confessed! No. No. No."

"Pass him through." One of the guards opened the carriage door.

None of the prisoners moved, so the guard, emitting a great grunt, stepped into the carriage, lifted Lerouge up, and dragged him back onto the muddy ground.

"Arturi Helitis." The executioner called out.

A House agent stepped from the carriage and walked, dignified, to the Bolt.

The two men were strapped into the wooden mechanisms. A deathly silence hung over the crowd now. Only Martin's sobs could be heard drifting around the Standing Stones. Meanwhile, the House agent stared out calmly at the crowd.

"And so justice shall be served!" said the executioner.

There was a sudden thunk. Dark red vital organs and yellowy-white intestines burst from their insides and flew several feet onto the muddy ground. Martin looked down at the remnants of himself with horror, while the House agent simply closed his eyes. A grayness seeped into their faces.

In a matter of moments, men had unstrapped the corpses and carried them to one side, where a pile of bodies lay wrapped in sheets. Yet others shoveled the insides into buckets and scurried away.

The executioner looked down at his scroll, "Karl Ginburs and the false Maximilian!"

Max and the other man stepped from the carriage. As he was being strapped into the machine, Max began to see things as if through a long tunnel. He thought, strangely, that the Bolt was quite comfortable. He felt quite snug strapped into the mechanism, even though much of it was coated in blood and other matter.

"And so . . . ," the executioner began.

—Aya, please, I beg you.

*Good luck on the Other Side, Maximilian. The Dark Sun is quite
beautiful, you know.*

"Justice will be served!"

Max closed his eyes and heard the thunk of the machine as the
Bolt was loosed. He was surprised that there was no pain.

# THIRTY-ONE

Dexion dragged Kata away from her responsibilities at the Technis Palace. Today was the opening of the Autumn Games, which would continue until their climax at the Twilight Observance, and the minotaur was going to fight.

Crowds streamed toward the Arena with a color and cheerfulness reserved for fun seekers. The Collegia's flags flapped in the wind: the black hammer of Caelian, the wheel of Litia, and the storehouse of Avaricum. The Arena itself rose up, five stories of arched walkways, graced with marble statues looking over the gathering crowd.

Spectators waved and called to Kata and Dexion. A middle-aged man, whose bulbous stomach made him look like he was carrying a sack, called out: "Dexion! I've bet on you today with that rascal Urgad the bookmaker. He said that despite your size, you've no experience. But I said, 'Never bet against a minotaur. Never!'"

Dexion waved an acknowledgment. "I'd put the rest of your savings on me."

The man shook his head. "I can't afford to lose everything."

"You won't. You'll win it all!"

The man joined a line at one of the mobile bakeries selling steaming hot spiced breads. A joke was circulating: after the assault on the villas, the city was back to normal; the shops were stocked with bread, the dungeons with prisoners.

Street performers surrounded the stadium: fire-eaters competed with mimes, clowns, sword swallowers, and storytellers. Kata and Dexion passed street vendors selling sizzling meats, bookmakers surrounded by throngs of gamblers, prostitutes hovering around the Arena's great arches, and halted before the gladiators' side entrance.

"You're going to get yourself killed doing this," said Kata.

Dexion shrugged. "Death is part of life."

"It's part of my life," said Kata, as much to herself as to him.

"Watch!" Dexion suddenly tensed himself. His muscles bulged, veins swelled up. His head jutted forward, and from his mouth came a terrible roar. He seemed to grow in bulk, his inky eyes blackening even more. Kata took several steps backward at the sight of the terrifying creature. Kata had heard a roar like that before, when she had killed the minotaur Cyriacus. It shook her bones and rattled her nerves. Around her, others screamed and darted away.

Dexion breathed out, rubbed his hands together. His eyes now twinkled with laughter. "See you afterward!"

Still shaken, Kata passed through one of the arcades and took an elevator up several levels. The amphitheater was already half full. Crowds streamed in to see the one grand battle planned for the day.

Kata gasped at the scenery on the Arena floor. A miniature replica of ancient Caeli-Amur covered one half of it: the buildings were shoulder height, the streets a maze that only allowed the space for two gladiators to face each other in combat. In some places, tiny walkways climbed over this labyrinthine construction, while the larger buildings—the Opera, the university, ancient palaces—afforded space for several warriors to stand on their roofs. Blood-orchids stood along the Forum's central avenue. None of the House complexes were represented, so Kata sensed this was a past version of Caeli-Amur. The mountain rose up to the level of the seating a story above the Arena floor, and then quickly descended to ensure none of the gladiators could climb out. To complete the picture, the city's headlands jutted into a pool representing the ocean that covered the remaining section of the Arena floor.

Waist-high barriers protected the rows of seats from gladiators' missiles. Kata found a place about a third of the way back. Around her, the crowd whispered and pointed excitedly. As the Arena filled, Kata felt more and more stressed.

Next to Kata, a man sat with his son, who was about eight years old. The father gestured to the replica. "Our money's on the Numerian king Saliras, boy. His forces are going to be represented by the Collegium Avaricum fighters. Little Fish told me that they brought animals from Numeria itself."

The boy looked up at Kata, an overwhelmed expression on his round face.

So they were about to witness a re-creation of the battle against Saliras, when the Numerian king had brought his army across the sea to take Caeli-Amur. After the cataclysm, Saliras's forces had planned to conquer the entire world. Caeli-Amur had been close to defeat, when the minotaurs had arrived across the fog-laden sea and driven the invader back into the water.

The Arena quickly filled to overflowing. The low hum of chatter echoed around the seats. Kata felt sick at the sight of all these people, here to worship death. For most philosopher-assassins, these fights were the lowest form of murder: murder without thought or reason, for entertainment, to appease the population and keep them drugged with false heroes and empty victories. But Kata didn't care for philosophical objections; she simply felt sick that Dexion would soon take the field, and that he could easily die. The memory of Henri's loss still ached. She did not want to be left alone again.

She was still thinking about this terrible possibility when about fifty men from Collegium Caelian emerged from the buildings of the miniature Caeli-Amur, like ants from their holes. They quickly took their places on the city's walls, behind the tiny battlements of the buildings. One stood behind a scaled-down catapult stationed in one of the plazas, another behind a scorpion ballista—a wicked-looking missile weapon—placed on the Southern Headland. Saliras had landed on the Northern Headland and at the docks, but the Avaricum troops would likely choose their own place of assault. There was no sign of the minotaur.

A hushed tension hovered over the Arena as everyone waited for the appearance of Saliras's troops from the three arched entryways to the Arena.

A sudden roar rose up. Three boats floated between the dark arches and toward the city. Bowmen on their decks loosed flights of arrows, which trembled as they flew through the air. Arrows rained on the boats in reply, and the air was filled with screams.

The scorpion on the headland shuddered. A moment later a long thick arrow burst through one of the bowmen's chests on the boat farthest from Kata. Again arrows flew in all directions, several loosed into the crowd. Kata heard a cry from the audience, but her eyes were fixed on the battle. A catapult stone smashed against the wall above one of the arches. A second row of boats emerged. Two headed for the Northern Headland, close to Kata. The third headed straight for the docks.

When they reached the shore, cages were opened on the boats. Wild lions and leopards raced up along the streets. The crowd rose to their feet, letting loose a howl of delight. Kata looked around her. The man had lifted his boy up, and the two of them were screaming, their faces filled with bloodlust. Kata felt faint, not at the sight of the deaths below, but at the howls of the audience, at their leering faces and drooling lips. The very sky above seemed to glow ember red as the sun lit up the clouds.

The cats dashed along the maze of streets. Defenders turned, screaming, only to be dragged down by giant claws, throats ripped by fangs, stomachs gutted by raking rear legs. One of the lions rushed into the Forum, where one of the blood-orchids, its face like a great plate, swiveled. The big cat craned its head forward and sniffed at the flower. The orchid's head spat a thick red nectar directly into the lion's face. An instant later the flower head whipped forward and closed over the cat's head and neck. The lion backed violently away, tearing the flower's head from its stalk, but the flower's head remained closed over the cat, which leaped madly around, crashing into the sides of buildings.

The forces of Saliras had landed: a hundred of them. The two armies clashed at the Northern Headland and in the labyrinthine alleyways of the Quaedian.

A tall woman, her blond hair cut short with ragged jags, squeezed onto the bench beside Kata. "Thank the gods. Rikard said you might be here."

Kata remembered the woman as Maximilian's university friend Odile, who had provided him with the binding formulae that had allowed him to build his water cart, with which he'd traveled fatefully to the Sunken City. Odile had changed, though. She was thinner and bonier, her face more lined.

"And you've been well, Odile?"

"Well, to be honest, not so great."

"That goes for everyone. What are you doing here?" said Kata.

"Looking for you, as it turns out."

Kata brushed back her hair. She was distracted for a moment by the two forces below, caught in deadly battle. It seemed inevitable that the forces of Saliras would win, for eventually their numbers would show. The cats had been slaughtered but had sown death and despair among many of the defenders, who were now scrabbling back under the weight of Saliras's forces. Several had grouped up in little clumps, defending the streets tenaciously, but already they were surrounded, beset on many sides. At any moment they would be wiped out.

At that moment a great figure burst from the miniature cliffs. Dexion stood on a ledge, great hammer in hand, and roared. His horns seemed to glint in the light, his mane was braided, and he wore a great bronze breastplate, itself with a red-horned head pressed into it. For a moment all seemed silent. Then, for the second time that day, Kata heard a tremendous roar.

The crowd erupted with cheers and cries. The man and his son beside her were in rapture. They took to their feet with the rest of them. "Minotaur! Minotaur!"

Kata put her face in her hands. She could barely look.

Odile grabbed her arm. "One of our group returned last night and told me a curious fact. He said a man calling himself Maximilian was captured out in the villas to the south."

A chill ran up Kata's back. Surely, that was impossible, unless Max had been imprisoned in one of the Technis villas down south all this time. "Was the man liberated from a dungeon?"

Odile shook her head. "Apparently, he fought with the vigilant guards, tried to stop them from destroying property."

"It can't be Maximilian. He died in the dungeons."

Dexion fell onto the rear of one of Saliras's columns. He crashed into them like a catapult stone; they were thrown in all directions by the force of his onslaught. This was the decisive moment. The tide was turned. Madness came upon Saliras's forces. They fled, screaming.

"Anyway, I have more than enough to worry about." Odile brushed herself off anxiously.

The comment piqued Kata's attention. "What?"

"You recall Detis, a liberation-thaumaturgist. He had met you once, not long ago, he said."

"I met him at Marin's water palace. He was condemned to death by the Bolt for smuggling."

"Yes, but it wasn't true. Detis was one of us. A fair man. He told us that should something happen to him, you would be the most trustworthy person in the seditionist movement. I thought that might be the case anyway, having met you before."

"Us. Who do you mean?" Kata's senses were alive now. "I thought you were an intellectual, unconcerned with seditionism."

"Max was right after all," said Odile. "I thought I could stand aside, assess from on high, but I was wrong. Before the overthrow, the Houses cracked down on seditionists. There were fights in the courtyards of the university. Spies and agent provocateurs infiltrated the ranks of the radicals. One day the House thaumaturgists, in their black suits and death masks, came for me when I was in the university library. You can't imagine the terror their appearance struck in me. They had discovered I'd passed the binding formulae to Max, and I was destined for the terror-spheres in their dungeons. They chased me through the courtyards. But a thaumaturgist named Detis saved me, and I'll forever be in his debt. He had formed a group of thaumaturgists fighting for seditionism called the Brotherhood of the Hand. I joined him, but we are underground, because it's not safe out in the open. Too many of us have died already. Anyway, I thought you should know about Maximilian. If it *is* Max, perhaps you can do something. I always liked that curly-haired dreamer."

Odile stood up to leave, but Kata grabbed her arm. "Wait, why is it so dangerous?"

Odile shook Kata off, glanced anxiously around the crowd. "There are enemies in the highest places. We're constantly being watched, all of us. I have to go."

Odile walked off, stopped several feet away, looked back for a moment as if she might say something more, and then was gone.

On the Arena floor below, the defenders' victory was complete. Men swam back toward the arches while Dexion climbed the miniature Opera building. He raised his hammer in the air to chants of "Minotaur! Minotaur!"

Kata's mind raced as she rushed out of the Arena. She needed to see if there was any truth about Maximilian. She could head straight for the dungeons at House Arbor, but there was no certainty that the vigilant guards would let her in. The only way to be certain would be to approach Ejan.

The cold wind whipped around the streets surrounding the Arena. Inside, the roar continued.

As she hurried toward the Opera, Kata tried again to piece together events. She tried to keep her mind from running away with itself. The Maximilian in the Arbor dungeons was probably an impostor. He had been caught resisting the vigilants, attempting to defend one of the House agent's properties. The prisoner had probably once known Max and was using his name to try to escape judgment.

And yet the flame of hope sprung up in her. Maximilian's body had never been found. He had simply disappeared. She felt the pull of her former love. Love, like a vast sea into which you've stepped gingerly, only to realize you're caught in deadly currents that drag you out into its vastness. She would not step into that ocean again. Not now, perhaps not ever. Yet perhaps she was not responsible for his death after all?

In the southern wing, Ejan stood behind his desk, a map before him. He had adorned one of the walls with even more weapons: pikes and rapiers, blue-and-red assassins' scarves, throwing stars, rope darts, and other paraphernalia of death. In the corner, a fire burned, warming the room against the outside cold.

"Ejan, I must—" She stopped herself. On one side of the room, looking out at the pedestrians on Via Attica, stood Dumas, the leader of Collegium Caelian.

Dumas turned around and stared at her, the pink insides of his lower lids dragged down by his heavy cheeks. Two points of red emerged on Ejan's face.

"Ejan, I've heard there's a man claiming to be Maximilian in the dungeons of Arbor," said Kata.

The spots of red disappeared from Ejan's cheeks, and he regained his icy complexion. "According to Georges, the man's an impostor, a criminal attempting to save himself."

"Ah, Maximilian, I remember him," said Dumas. "Young idealist, from what I remember. Hotheaded. Filled with ideas. Ideas—what attracts you so much about them? Life is a practical affair, don't you think?"

Ejan sat on a chair and kicked his feet up onto the desk, an unconvincing show that all was well. "Alas, we're on the opposite sides of things there. Ideas are all we have. All the rest are but base and material delusions. You won't take your goods when you go, Dumas."

"And you won't take your ideas, either." Dumas grinned.

"Kata here agrees with me, don't you?" said Ejan.

Kata was still trying to connect the disparate information in her mind. "Yes."

Ejan sat up again, rolled the map up on his table. "Delicate things, these maps. I like delicate things, you know: flowers, vulnerable people. There's something tragic about a flower, don't you think? The way it only lasts for a short time. Mortality. That's what gets to me the most."

"I was just at the Arena," said Kata. "You'd have trouble there, Ejan."

"Oh, I don't think he'd have trouble at all," said Dumas. "He'd celebrate the fights, if they were for the right idea."

"Can you organize them for the right idea, then?" said Ejan. "But that wouldn't bring in enough money, would it? You prefer to put on spectacles like—what was it today, Kata?"

"A reenactment of the battle against Saliras," Kata said. "Caelian is organizing the fight season?"

In the corner, the log collapsed on itself, and the fire died a little. Dumas wandered over to it and stared into the embers for a moment before turning his back to the fireplace. Various expressions crossed his face, coming in rapid succession. Kata could only read one, a kind of resentment.

"Yes, since the Houses are gone . . ." Dumas held both hands palms up, as if to say, *Who else will organize them?*

Pieces were coming together in Kata's mind. Dumas was organizing the fights at the Arena. *He was the one who had written to Armand,* she thought. The letter had claimed he would have something ready by the Twilight Observance, which would be the finale of the gladiator games. Snatches of a conversation with Dexion came back to her now. *The Collegia have really thrown their weight behind the games. . . . They're recruiting and training cohorts of fighters,* the minotaur had said. There was evidence Dumas had been involved in smuggling funds from the Marin treasury. A question bubbled up in her mind: Was this money being used to recruit a gladiator army? The Collegia had chosen a replica of the battle against Saliras as their first spectacular: a perfect training ground for city fighting. She remembered Dexion saying something else: *And those who survive are to be promoted to gladiator captains!* She sprang for a new conclusion: this was the meaning of the letter, in which the mysterious D had written, *Our best plan should be realized by the Twilight Observance.*

And here was Dumas, free as a spear-bird circling the sky, fraternizing with Ejan. Why hadn't Ejan moved against him? Ejan, who was usually so decisive, so rigid and unbending, not one to compromise? She looked around at the weapons on the wall, including the assassins' scarves: some red, others blue. Weighted blue scarves like those used by philosopher-assassins connected with the secretive Arcadi sect. Weighted blue scarves like the one that had been used to kill Aceline. Kata felt suddenly afraid: she was in the presence of enemies. Maybe Maximilian *was* alive. If so, she would need a force of her own to save him from the Arbor Dungeons.

She muttered some excuses to the two men and left as quickly as she could. All the time she felt their hostile eyes on her.

# THIRTY-TWO

Kata dashed along the corridors of the Technis Palace, skipping past other moderates carrying foodstuffs and weapons, avoiding those calling out messages to one another, and ducking past the little circles and congregations deep in discussion. Pneumatiques above had begun to whir through the air again, though others were broken and still hung like ruined lamps.

As she headed for the meeting room that had been set up as a center for the captains she had been training, an arm shot out from one side, grasped her. Twisting rapidly, she prepared to strike out. A familiar young man cowered before her. It took a moment to place him: it was Oewen, one of Max's old followers. Oewen had disappeared with his lover, Ariana, before the overthrow. That wasn't unusual. Militants came and went, Kata had learned. The revolution was a great devourer of people.

"Oewen? I thought you were gone from the movement," she said.

"I am, Kata. I am. But I'm here for Maximilian. Is there nothing that can be done?"

She felt the shock of certainty. Her voice quavered. "You've seen him in the Arbor dungeons?"

"Yes, I've seen him, but not in the dungeons, though. I saw him in a prison cart on the way to the Standing Stones. He's headed for the Bolt."

Kata grabbed the man by the shirt. "The Bolt?"

The man nodded desperately.

Kata burst into a run. Her mind leaped from conclusion to conclusion. Ejan was the key. He stood to benefit from the death of Aceline; he was allied with Dumas; and now, through his henchman, Georges, he was allowing his enemies to be wiped out one by one.

She burst through the door and to where her captains were sitting, overlooking a map of the city. They looked up in unison.

"I need a force of two hundred guards—now!" she said. "Into the carriages and to the Standing Stones."

If Ejan wanted a display of power, he was about to get one.

The carriages sped along Via Gracchia. Pedestrians dashed to the side to avoid the oncoming column. Sitting beside the driver of the first carriage, Kata felt the cold wind rushing across her face. They reached the Arantine and were caught behind a steam-tram. Kata cursed out loud. With each moment that passed, Maximilian would be closer to death.

The tram clattered as it turned a corner, and then they were past it, rushing along the Southern Headland. At the Thousand Stairs they careened to a halt, for the way was blocked by a crowd of spectators, newly arrived from the Arena and come to see more death.

Kata pointed ahead and shouted at the driver. "Straight through them!"

The driver pulled on the reins. "I can't."

Kata leaped from the carriage and waved at her captains. "Come on!"

They pushed their way through the screaming crowd. Someone shoved back, and Kata lashed out, struck something hard, plunged on.

She heard a great cheer from the Standing Stones, and her heart sank. A round of hooting followed. Her mind filled with awful images. Then she was through, and into the open path between the wooden palisades. Crowds packed the terraces of the ampitheater. Collegia flags flapped in the cold wind.

Several dirty, downtrodden men looked out morosely from the bars of the prison cart. Maximilian was not among them. Bodies wrapped in sheets were piled up to one side of the Standing Stones. Despair clutched at Kata. Her eyes were drawn to the three Bolts standing on the dais. One was broken and unoccupied. In the second, a man's shattered body was held upright by straps and restraints. Kata did not recognize his square face. Beside him stood the final Bolt.

A vigilant guard struggled with the second body, momentarily obscuring Kata's line of sight. As he dragged the corpse to one side, Kata glimpsed a mop of matted curly hair, then a dirty wiry beard, and between them, the large eyes of Maximilian looking out in shock. He was gagged but still very much alive.

"Mechanism's broken. Same as the other one." A vigilant inspected the Bolt housing Max. "Too much wear, I'd say. Third one will probably go soon."

Maximilian's eyes roved, locked on Kata, widened with hope.

Kata turned to the gray-suited force behind her. The crowd was hushed now. They watched the moderates, uncertain about the meaning of their arrival.

"We're going to free him," Kata said quietly to her captains.

She strode forward and became instantly aware of the black-suited vigilant guards surrounding the Standing Stones, pikes in hand. There were perhaps a hundred of them, many standing up from where they had watched the entertainment around the palisade. Her forces outnumbered the vigilants by almost two to one, but would they stand up in combat? There had been so little time to train them, even with Sarrat's expertise.

The vigilant captain marched toward Kata. She had seen him before, pronouncing judgments, stirring the crowd to a fever pitch. "I don't know who you are, but back away."

Kata heard the sound of rapiers sliding from scabbards behind her. The determination in her tone surprised even her. "That man is the seditionist leader Maximilian. He has been wrongly imprisoned. We're here to free him."

"The tribunal says he is to be put to death." The captain gestured dramatically at the crowd. "What do we think?"

"The Bolt! The Bolt!" the crowd howled. They didn't like the idea of their entertainment being canceled. Kata wondered if, in the event of a clash, they would be prepared to join on the side of the vigilants.

"I am Kata, one of the moderate leaders. And I say he is to be freed. Who are you to oppose me?"

The executioner captain gestured to the crowd. "And so the moderates' true views emerge. Like rats they are brought out into the light. They would have us abandon the Bolt, capitulate before our enemies without a fight." He turned back to Kata. "Gutless, I say you are. Weak and indecisive. Let us do the real work of the revolution."

Kata took two steps toward him. He looked at her curiously first, then blinked rapidly with realization as he reached up to the two knives Kata had plunged into his neck moments before. His eyes took on a somewhat plaintive look.

"Indecisive, you say?" whispered Kata into his ear as his legs gave way, leaving her gripping her two dripping daggers.

For a moment no one spoke or moved. Then the vigilants charged. The clash of steel rang out. Kata loosed one knife, which struck a vigilant between the ribs. He staggered back, a moderate guard already piercing him with a rapier. A pike arced waist height at Kata, and she leaped into the air, heard the sound as it wooshed beneath her. A second later her other knife drove up through the attacker's jaw, pierced his palate, and lodged into his brain.

On all sides, her guards engaged the vigilants. Some were felled by pikes. Elsewhere they ducked and danced and fought at close range. It was not pretty to watch: their skills were rudimentary, but they were tougher than anyone the vigilants had ever faced. Once at close range, the action was short and decisive. One moment the battle was on. A second later the vigilants had broken and fled in all directions.

Kata leaped onto the platform, halted before Maximilian. Neither of them spoke for a moment. She was taken aback by his matted hair and scruffy beard, but there was still life in his eyes.

Kata cut the gag from his mouth. "I suppose we had better get you out of this, then," said Kata.

Max took a breath. "If you insist."

It took a moment before she could work out the strappings. Once he was free, she helped him back to the carriage. The crowd watched, confused. None called out. Then, suddenly, a great cheer went up. It seemed they'd had their entertainment after all.

"Where are we going?" asked Max.

"To the Technis Palace," said Kata.

"I can't seem to get away from that place," said Max.

"None of us can," said Kata.

"Why there?"

"\We are preparing for civil war."

"Against who?" said Max.

"Ejan," said Kata.

Max nodded. "I see."

Moderate leaders and activists flooded into the Technis Palace, carrying whatever they could, fear in their eyes. Across the city, moderates had fought a series of rearguard battles as they retreated to the Technis Complex. The moderate-controlled factories immediately went on strike; the vigilant ones made calls for restraint by all. Most of the factory committees called for unity, though the basis for this was fuzzy. Should the Bolt still function? Whose guards should be considered the real representatives of the citizenry?

Once back at Technis Palace, Elise stood before Kata, angry. "Olivier's been taken hostage. So have most of the editors of the *Dawn*. They tried to escape the Opera, but Ejan moved too quickly. This is your fault, Kata."

Kata ignored the complaints and raced to the balcony of the Director's office, where she surveyed the city. Vigilant guards had begun to surround the Technis Complex, building barricades in nearby streets and squares. Their captains surveyed the scene: directions were given, defenses organized. The moderates were under siege.

Maximilian washed in one of the communal bathrooms and returned to the Director's suite. Kata followed him into the bedroom, watched him stare at the water-sphere that filled an adjoining room. Steps led up to its opening, which was like the lid of an immense circular bottle. Once inside, you could swim through superoxygenated liquid just as in the Marin water palaces. The sphere would present worlds of fantasy to the swimmer, but they were also used for torture in the dungeons below. They could reflect back your own inescapable nightmares too.

Max drifted past her, back into the offices, and looked coldly at the egg-shaped machine behind the desk. The sight of him, after all this time wondering about his fate, filled her with a kind of surreal relief. He was alive, and a great guilt was lifted from her. But he had changed. His single-minded focus, his belief that striving for humanity was the most important thing in life, was tempered by a kind of watchfulness. His suffering had eaten away at his ambition, rounded him like a stone beneath the water.

She had changed also. Her yearning for him was gone. She had grown up, it seemed, and now stood on her own two feet. She didn't need to cling to someone else's ambitions to provide meaning in her own life. In fact, she didn't need anyone. Now it was a matter of what she *wanted*, and she couldn't be sure of that. The image of Dexion had begun to haunt such thoughts, but she wasn't sure how she felt about the minotaur, either.

None of this mattered, anyway. She had other responsibilities, a siege to face. All personal concerns had to be swept aside. And in that moment she realized how much like Max and Rikard and Ejan she had become. That, it seemed, was the price of leadership.

"Memories," Max spoke, almost as if to himself. "Why do you want to remember everything? Alerion, the time before the overthrow of the Houses—when everything seemed so simple. It would be better if we could forget it all, don't you think? We wouldn't have to carry around the load of the past. Yet we hold on to our memories. We save them up and replay them."

"The load of the past makes us who we are," said Kata. "We replay memories to make sense of ourselves."

She followed him out onto the balcony. Some of the vigilants were preparing fires for the night.

"Look at us, trapped up here," he said.

*Yes*, thought Kata. She thought of the Technis Director, Boris Autec. He had once stood up here, besieged by a surrounding army. She now knew how he felt, looking out over an enemy city.

# THIRTY-THREE

Armand examined the roof of the tent. Droplets of moisture hung from the fine material. Blankets covered all three of them, though the tent was meant for only two people. He closed his eyes again, rested in the warmth of the two bodies. How long since he had felt warmth like this? He couldn't remember. It must have been back in Varenis, an epoch ago.

"Your friend seems better this morning." The woman called Giselle stretched her hands up over her head, let them lie flat on the ground. Armand's ally Dumas had employed the philosopher-assassin to follow him, report back on his activities, keep an eye on the prism, protect him as he rose through the upper echelons of Varenis—and perhaps kill him if necessary. She did not say this last part, but Armand imagined it was the case.

Irik lay sleeping on his side. His face had lost the slippery sheen of fever. In those first hours after their rescue, Irik had raved deliriously, reaching out and trying occasionally to sit up. The illness had hit a crisis point, and the oppositionist had begun to shudder relentlessly, like a broken engine. Then, suddenly, he stopped. Armand thought the man dead, and his heart sank, but Irik took a lurching breath, seemed to collapse in on himself, and fell into a deep deathlike sleep. For the rest of the night they had huddled there, safe in the warmth of the tent as the snowstorm whirled around them.

"It took me days to find where they had sent you," said Giselle.

Armand nodded. "You might have come quicker."

"You might have let me know you planned to escape," shot back Giselle.

Giselle shuffled to the tent's door flap, slid on her thick pants and her woolen coat, which lay at the foot of the tent, and stepped out into the air.

Armand glanced at the sleeping Irik and followed Giselle into the cold. The snow had taken on a crystalline blue color, and the sun twinkled on the icicles that hung from the trees. Nearby, a blanket of snow had covered the immense corpse of the Cyclops, so that he might almost have been a sculpture made by children. There was something tragic about the sight, that frightening and majestic creature so far from his warm and rocky home.

Giselle pulled a second coat from her long backpack and passed it to him. "I only have one coat. One other pair of gloves. I thought I'd only be rescuing you."

Armand glanced back at the tent. "You would not have found me alive if it hadn't been for him."

"Well, we'll have to head back west. We can't pass through the mountains, and I've left provisions a day's march from Camp X."

"We're heading east," said Armand. "There are ancient roads through the mountains."

Giselle laughed at the risky suggestion. "Do you always want to make things hard for yourself? Winter hasn't set in yet, but we won't survive its worst storms."

"Even so, we cannot pass by Camp X again." Armand spoke with a firm edge to his voice. "We'll all be caught. Anyway, we still have weeks before winter settles in."

Giselle shook her head. "I've made it this far. I can face any Cyclops, any guard."

A voice came from the tent. Irik had swung his legs out and was preparing to stand up. "You can leave us if that's your wish, but it seems a waste after having gone to such trouble."

Giselle rubbed her ball of red hair, which sprang back from her hands. "It will take far too long. Dumas sent a message just before I left. They're sending reinforcements to Varenis. By the time we return, there will be people waiting for us, Armand. *Our people.* I'm not sure why, but he said it was crucial that we meet up with them. The quickest way is back past Camp X."

Armand smiled. "That's good, but I have another plan to carry out. I'm going to visit the Augurers. When I enter the Embrace, I will see the future. Then we will have a *real* advantage. Think of how I can tailor my actions, once I know what history has in store."

Giselle began to dismantle the tent. A moment later she stopped. "Seeing the future is proof of nothing. Yes, you'll see what lies ahead, as it is at the very moment of seeing. But after that, the future changes with each of your actions, until nothing is certain anymore. You can only ever see a future that will not be. Why do you think so few visit the Augurers now?"

Armand pulled the blankets from the half-collapsed tent and began to pack them into the bags. "Because the trip is too long and difficult. And, even still, there *are* pilgrims. Officiates from Caeli-Amur often made the journey before the overthrow."

"Did they return the better for it? Visiting the Augurers is always a curse." Giselle slipped the tent pegs into a small bag.

"We must take the curses we are offered." Armand squatted beside the bags as Irik handed him the tent poles.

"You're a pompous fool," said Giselle.

Irik looked to Armand and turned his palm up, his lips twitching with humor as Giselle echoed his own words. Seeing Armand's dark face, he simply smiled and turned away.

The sun shone brilliantly on the snow. Armand was forced to keep his eyes half closed as they followed animal trails close to the side of the slope, avoiding any snowdrifts. Across the valley, goats perched impossibly on the sides of cliffs, eyed the travelers disinterestedly, hopping from perch to perch. When they spied more of the beasts on a slope nearby, Giselle brought one down with her bolt-thrower. They butchered it inexpertly and stashed away as much as they could.

The valley cut between two mammoth peaks that reached like ragged claws into the sky. Great eagles hovered on the drafts around the craggy tips. Their graceful flight so far above, right beside sheer and smooth rock faces, gave Armand vertigo.

In the afternoon they came through the pass and halted at a precipitous descent to a valley far below them: the copses of trees, their branches weighed down with snow, the racing river they would have to cross. They would need to climb down to the valley and find a path up over the vast mountain range facing them.

"This was a mistake," said Giselle.

The height of the summits struck fear into Armand. How could they climb those sheer faces with their snowy drifts, overhangs, and vertiginous peaks?

"Giselle is right. We should turn back," said Armand.

None of them spoke as they looked out over the bleak and beautiful landscape. Armand thought about the journey back, the possibility of again being caught, of suffering a slow death in Camp X. Despair took him.

Even now, the cold bit at Armand's hands, numbing them. Irik wore the gloves and Giselle's coat for the moment, though she might take them back at any time, for they rotated regularly. Irik's strength was slowly returning. Now the man's fever had gone, and he slept soundly and ate well. He had lost weight he would not regain until the journey was over, but Armand no longer feared for his friend's life.

Giselle turned. "Come. We'll retrace our steps."

"Wait!" Irik's fine face turned to the south; his neck craned forward as he squinted. "A road. I think I see a road."

"There are no roads," said Giselle.

"There is one, spanning the valley to the south. Come! See!"

Armand rushed back to where Irik stood. He peered into the distance.

Irik pointed away across the valley. "There, against the mountains. It's just a fine line, but see: there are supports holding it up, I think."

Armand tried to follow the man's hand, but he could see nothing but mountains and rock faces and patchy snow. Low-lying clouds drifted between the mountains, momentarily obscuring them. "I can't see anything."

Giselle joined in the search. "You're imagining it, Irik. There's nothing there."

Irik faltered, his confidence draining. "I saw a line, but it seems gone now. The light, you know, it changes."

Armand peered to the south, straining to see something. Eventually he said. "There's nothing there. Let's go."

Irik followed him. "I so wanted it to be true."

The two men were already back on the trail when Giselle's voice came to them. "Wait. Just for a moment I saw it. A line cutting in front of the mountain."

Filled with hope, they scrambled south along the edges of the crag, finding goat trails, then losing them again. At times they were forced to climb up over sheer rock faces. In these moments Armand was terrified he would slide and fall. Images rose in his mind of his tumbling body striking rock and snow. The valley seemed another world, so far below. By the time night drew near, they had only made slow progress. They were compelled to camp on a slope, only steps from a terrifying cliff. The goat meat sizzled over their small fire, which brought at least some comfort.

Through the night Armand listened to the wind flapping against the canvas. He was sure they would slide away and over the edge. The others were sound asleep, but his body was rigid with anxiety, and his mind raced through the long hours of darkness, from their precarious place on the mountain to his uncertain place in the world. He thought of Valentin's betrayals, of Boris Autec and his former spy, Kata, of Dumas in the Collegia—everything seemed treacherous and insecure, just like his place on the mountain. His arm burned like a log in the fire, but he pushed all thought of it away. He was good at repressing things. He always had been.

The next day a thick fog hung in the valley, like a gray sea beneath them. If there was indeed a bridge to the south, it was lost in the fog. As he stumbled after the other two, the goat trail widened. For a while it stayed that way, clinging to the side of the mountain precariously, so that they made better progress. At midday they sat on the cold ground, chewing dried fruit and nuts that Giselle had brought, and looked out over the hovering gray.

"It seems we might even walk across that spectral carpet ahead of us," said Irik.

"Right across to the facing mountain," said Giselle.

"Come on, then." Irik smiled at Armand. "It's the shortest route."

Armand looked toward the edge of the wide trail, noticing absentmindedly that little square markers ran along the edge of the precipice. He peered at them for a moment, then blurted out, "This isn't a trail. It's a road."

As they continued, the road's form, clinging impossibly to the mountainside, became obvious. It was ancient, and whole sections of it had crumbled down into the valley below.

They came to a spot where they had to press themselves to the cliff and shuffle sideways, palms against the rock face, the terrifying precipice behind them. Armand's legs felt like they might give way, but he forced himself on, reaching a wider section where the road had given way completely, leaving only empty air. Another section stood farther on, a pinnacle of rock jutting up alone in the fog. With a mixture of excitement and terror, Armand looked higher up above it, seeing the image of some child's fancy, where a straight and strong bridge hovered in the air. They had reached their destination.

Joy rushed through them; Irik's head fell back in relief, and Giselle smiled and ran her hands through her thick red hair. They stood for a while, staring up at the bridge, their path to freedom.

"We'll have to jump." Giselle's eyes flicked from the lone pillar standing in empty space to the bridge farther on and higher up. "We'll jump over the first gap, then I can use my grappling hook to get us up to the bridge."

She strode back along the road, turned, and raced toward the void. With a graceful leap she flew through the air like a dancer, taking two graceful steps on the small section of road as she landed, and looked back.

Armand stared at the vast abyss. "I can't."

Irik patted him on the shoulder. "Imagine there is no cliff. The road there, it's just a patch of grass surrounded by dirt. See how easy it is? See?"

Armand's legs would not stop shaking. He looked back in the direction from which they had come. Only ghostly clouds lay that way. They had to continue on, and yet he thought he might vomit with fear. He turned, ran toward the abyss without thinking. Rushes of panic ran through him as he came to the edge, leaped high and long, and crashed onto the surface of the lone column of road. He slid toward the far edge. Giselle's hand closed around his foot, and he came to a stop, shivering and trembling.

He didn't see Irik make the leap, but he felt the man's hand on his arm a moment later. "See, that wasn't too hard."

Giselle was already on to the next task. The grappling hook struck and held. "We must swing out and climb up."

Armand looked at his feet, the rough boots that had belonged to some dead man long ago. He had come to know their bends and dents, their patches of gray discoloring, the wiry shoelaces.

A little while later Giselle's voice came from above. "See, not hard at all."

Irik held his shoulder. "You first, Armand."

"I can't."

"Here. I'll tie the rope around your leg so you can't fall," said Irik calmly. "There, safe as can be. Giselle is bracing the hook up on the road. All right, let me help you up now. Hold high up here, and we'll sit you on the edge so you don't swing out too far. There, ready? All right, here we go."

Irik pushed, and Armand felt the earth disappear from underneath him. He seemed to have no feeling in his hands as he swung out over the abyss like a pendulum. He tried to climb, but his arms were weak. He pulled, wrapped his lower legs around the rope, but instead of climbing, he slipped down. He clung to the rope in desperation. Beneath him lay a vast expanse of nothingness, the valley far, far below lost in a sea of gray.

"I can't pull him up. I'm not strong enough," said Giselle.

They waited there for a moment, no one sure what to do.

"We can pull him up together," said Irik.

"And how do you plan to get up here? Float?" asked Giselle.

Irik eyed the rope, judging the distance.

"No!" yelled Armand. "No!"

But Irik had already taken several steps back. He launched

himself into the air. Armand felt the rope shudder. A whipping motion rolled down it. Irik slipped down toward Armand. One foot crushed Armand's hand, and a second struck Armand's shoulder.

Armand felt a terrible pressure on his hands and where the rope was tied around his ankle. Then the hold on his ankle was gone: the knot had come apart. Armand slid down. His palms burned terribly; his legs swung in midair. He grasped harder, and for a moment the two of them held still.

Irik began to climb. Armand could not tell how long it was before the rope shuddered again softly. Then again. He was being pulled up.

"Remember to keep your body pressed against the hook," he heard Giselle say. "Yes, like that."

Armand's fingers struck the edge of the bridge. He held tightly as they were scraped badly. An arm grabbed him, and he clutched the bridge's railing. With a heave, he lurched over the barrier and collapsed to the ground, where he shivered uncontrollably. Irik placed his hand on Armand's head, a soft touch.

A single rail ran along the center of the bridge, though in places it was half buried by snow. They began their march into the fog, a vast and spectral world that seemed never to end. Finally a vast rock face appeared, patches of dark-green moss and lichen clinging to it. The road plunged into a wide dark tunnel. Giselle lit a small torch, and they continued into it.

So the day continued, through tunnels and out into valleys, until they camped on the road, the tent unsecured to the ground. As he lay against Irik's warmth, Armand felt a hand reach out to him. He held it softly. The hand moved slowly up to his stomach, gently caressing, leaving trails of fire and energy.

Armand rolled toward Irik, his lips close to the other man's ears. "You are . . . I have never met anyone like you."

Irik reached over to Armand's arm, which burned now with unnatural heat. The oppositionist ran his hand over the arm, up and down, a soft caressing touch.

"Your arm is like fire," said Irik.

"It is." Armand's voice was matter-of-fact.

"You didn't want to tell me you have the bloodstone disease?"

"What is there to tell? We have to reach the Eyries."

Irik sighed. "And after the Augurers—then what?"

"I will return to Varenis, avenge myself. I have people waiting for me in Caeli-Amur, building their forces." He hesitated for a moment, but he trusted this man. "And I have maps of the passages beneath the city. With these, my army can slip in past the walls, where the seditionists will focus their forces. The city will be mine before they know it. Then I can reinstate order."

"This will drive us apart." Irik took Armand's hands and clenched them tightly, as if he might slip away. They lay like this, dozing, waking occasionally to reach out to the other in the night.

In the morning Irik pulled Armand's shirt sleeve away, baring his forearm. A gleaming hot spidery redness splayed out along his veins. Armand looked down at the bloodstone cancer. Soon enough it would take his shoulder, and then, once it hit his internal organs, the thing would run wild inside him.

Armand pulled the shirt sleeve down. "Ignore it. That's what I've been doing."

So the days passed on that long road, curling around cliffs, cutting across expanses, diving through tunnels. Each day was the same; there seemed no end to the vast mountains.

Over a week after their escape, the three travelers entered a black tunnel that opened out into gleaming sunlight. They stopped in amazement at where the road joined a wide valley. Rising high between the mountains were clusters of thin rocky pillars. Terrifying stairs climbed each one, all the way up to their sharp peaks. Into the pinnacles were chiseled doors and windows; dozens of little roofs angled off the many-leveled towers. They had reached the Needles: the Eyries of the Augurers.

Around the Needles circled flocks of birds. Other, larger creatures rose on the winds higher up.

"What are they?" Armand asked.

"I don't know," said Giselle.

"Griffins," said Irik. "They're the Augurers' griffins."

# THIRTY-FOUR

Afternoon came to a slow end as the three travelers reached the first cluster of pinnacles marking the Eyries. The low sunlight bathed the spires in gold and orange and threw shadows across the many high windows.

With slow deliberation, they climbed the nearest staircase. Another vertiginous fall lay to one side, but Armand's vertigo had been crushed out of him by the incident on the bridge. He had been through too much to be afraid.

They stopped periodically, catching their breaths. At these times Armand looked out over the magnificent landscape. The nearby spires—part of the same cluster as this one—were pictures of surreal beauty. The last of the sunlight turned the rocks yellow and red so they burned like fiery embers.

The pinnacles widened as they reached the apex, where the stone citadel was built. Here the staircase curled out and around into a small forecourt. In front of its three walls ran crumbling white pillars; between these stood purple-veined marble statues of the ancients. In each of these walls were ornate doors, carved with baroque inscriptions and painted in reds, blues, and ochers. A fount stood in the center of the peristyle, like a giant chalice made from inscribed stone.

While the others wandered toward the doors, Armand peered over the edge of the fountain at the water, which looked clear and fresh. A moment later it changed, becoming milky and thick. Intense eyes appeared in the liquid, and then the face of an old woman filled out the image, hair wild and matted, nose hooked and proud. One look at her eyes—one black, the other green—and Armand sensed her fierce and ancient power.

Legends said the Augurers had once been normal women, but they sacrificed their humanity for the ability to see the future. Alien powers were spliced into them, and they were forced to retreat from the world to these rocky sanctuaries. Some said they demanded visitors mate with them, to produce a new generation—always of women. They always required payment.

Armand was fixed to the spot, drawn into those eyes, sucked in closer and closer.

*What do you want?* the crone seemed to say, and yet she did not speak. *Ah yes, I see. You are changing already.* The eyes seemed to laugh.

Though Armand tried to lift his head, his face came closer and closer to the water. Panic gripped him. The Augurer became his whole world, her face giant and leering. Her eyes drifted toward each other as he lost focus, so that both somehow became black *and* green.

*The middle door. We'll be waiting.*

Armand's face broke the surface, the crone vanished, and he jolted back up.

Unaware of his vision, Irik and Giselle were now examining the doors. The one on the left was decorated with a painting of the Long March of the Mountain Giants in which they traveled along the Etolian range, away from the disasters after the cataclysm, when the insect men descended on them like vicious ants. The middle door showed the ancient hero Kae-Marka sitting hand in hand with an Augurer, seeing his future death in the space between them. The right-hand door pictured Rian and his dog, Torro, on the seas, reaching the island of Aya. In the background, minotaurs were being born from the rock.

"The middle one." Armand reached for the door, though it had no handle.

"How do you know?" asked Irik.

Armand touched the door, and it swung eerily open of its own accord. In front of them lay a wide atrium, again with crumbling pillars running around it. He could see no other exit. Natural light shone through a shaft running high above, though there were many more levels to the Augurer's Eyrie.

An atmosphere of moody and decaying grandeur overwhelmed the Eyrie, and after the vision at the fount, Armand was tense and jittery. Though the journey had been physically dangerous, he felt the Eyrie threatened some deeper part of him. Perhaps Irik and Giselle were right: it was a mistake to try to see the future. And yet he would brook no opposition. He would continue on to the end, facing these sinister Augurers and whatever other ordeals stood in his way.

A mosaic of thousands of silver and blue tiles depicted a fierce chimera in the center of the floor. Where it breathed fire, the tiles were golden and red. The image did little to settle Armand's nerves.

Something flittered behind one of the columns.

"Who's there?" Irik's voice echoed oddly.

Armand took several steps to one side, but there was nothing behind the pillar.

"When the birds fly, do they think of the wind?" whispered a voice.

Armand spun around to see an old woman emerge from behind another of the columns. Her wild and matted hair sprang from her head like a white bush. Her left eye seemed blue this time; a raggedy white dress hung loosely from her thin frame. Was this the same Augurer? Armand could not tell.

The woman gazed at them with a piteous, imperious stare. She seemed about to break into cruel laughter. "I see the three of you—a strange bunch, no doubt. Don't think you can hide from us. No, no, when the future is sought, it is always found."

"Only I seek to see into my fate," said Armand. "The others are simply my companions."

"Five come and three cry their lives away. You will see past and future and they will be as one," said the woman. "And what have you to offer, Armand Lecroisier?"

Involuntarily, Armand took a step backward after she said his name, though he had not introduced himself. Chills ran over his skin and under his hairline. Fumbling, he reached into his bag, pulled out his little pouch. "Bloodstone."

The woman came to him impossibly fast, though she didn't seem to run. She snatched the bag from his quivering hand, poured a tiny portion of the stone onto her palm. She pierced Armand with a stare and then, ever so slowly, licked her palm with her long tongue. Suddenly she broke into a grin, her teeth a deep, bloodstone red. She looked like she'd been drinking blood. She ran her tongue over her teeth and grinned again.

"There is no good time to step from the nest." She turned and rushed away. They hurried after her, to a narrow walkway behind the pillars. For the first time, Armand noticed several cleverly hidden openings in the walls. The tunnels leading away were curved and smooth, as if washed by a thousand years of water.

Up and around they went, for the Eyrie was like an anthill, the passages curving and twisting without obvious design. Occasional windows allowed them to glimpse the majestic landscape outside. At other times they passed through chambers decorated with glorious mosaics and delicate hangings. Sometimes the Augurer pulled aside a hanging to reveal a hidden tunnel. Sibilant sounds echoed through the corridors; sometimes Armand fancied they were voices, and at other times they sounded like the groaning of machines or dying creatures. Armand felt increasingly nervous, increasingly out of control of the situation.

The Augurer instructed Irik and Giselle to wait in a room filled with soft crimson cushions. Meats, berries, and drink were already laid out on small tables. Armand's companions fell on them without a word, stuffing their mouths.

The Augurer took Armand by the hand, and her skin felt leathery and alien. Up and up she led him, until the tiny staircase opened to a high room, perhaps the highest in the Eyrie. Windows opened out onto the vast panorama around: a wall of snowcapped mountains to one side, other lone peaks here and there, the valley a vast plain before the mountains rose again to the east. The sun was gone now, and twilight had softened the light outside. A great mosaic spiraled in toward the center of the room, like water plunging down a drain. Each spiral arm was composed of black and white tiles, like a zebra's stripes. As he looked at the great fractal shape, Armand felt he was falling toward the core of the pattern. He lost all sense of perspective and looked away.

The Augurer led him to the central point. "Sit."

The Augurer faced Armand and took his hands in her own. His heart danced madly, and he felt intense burning in his left arm as she stared into his eyes, like some witch from the Teeming Cities. He was overrun with a sense of her atavistic wild power and realized now the rashness of his course. He was about to make a terrible error, one which he would not be able to turn from, one that would haunt him for the rest of his life.

Already the floor had drawn him into some uncanny trance. The walls loomed in and stretched out. Between the pillars flittered a young girl, perhaps eight or nine years old. She moved like a shadow, and Armand sensed that her eyes were both blue. When she reached the cusp of adulthood, one eye would fill suddenly with black blood, as some blood vessel burst deep inside and engulfed the entire thing—then she would gain the Augurer's gift.

A moment later everything dropped away except the Augurer's two eyes. Armand lost focus, and the two eyes drifted toward each other, as if he were seeing them from too close.

Quickly, they were superimposed, black and green on top of each other. Armand lost a sense of himself, and he and the Augurer became one, staring not into each other, but through that bloody eye into the future, into the world as it would come to be.

An image appears, like something rising from a depth. Armand sees himself, alone in a vast dark space, a strange book in his hands. The book gleams with the unhealthy light of thaumaturgy. Three circular sections of the floor are blacker than the rest, and Armand realizes they are pools of water. One of the black circles shimmers. Then another of the pools shimmers, then the third. Things are moving beneath the black waters. A snake-covered head bursts forth, then another, until there are three Gorgons dancing around him.

The image fades, and Armand is floating in a sea of indeterminate shapes. Now Armand sees himself, but with white streaks through his hair. From a cold stone throne, he looks out onto strange faces. There is something ruined in his visage: his eyes droop, one arm shifts restlessly. Armand wonders who all these subjects are, facing his future self. Yet they respect him, they fear him. He is victorious, he senses: all his dreams fulfilled, his ancestors avenged, his place in the world assured. He is a king! A surge of triumph rushes through him, a sweet ecstatic joy. Yet all these strangers stand so far from him, and he looks so alone.

Many more images rise and fall. He is sleeping; he is eating; he is crying. He is old. He is young. The images drop away again into shapes and colors.

But now he is younger again. Lines have only begun to etch his face. He is striding down long corridors; through the open windows he sees great flames leaping into the air. Caeli-Amur is burning. He carries a body as one would carry a child. He cries, falling to his knees, for he cannot carry the man any longer. His knees strike the stone floor, and he throws his head back, lets out a wail filled with emptiness and despair. He lays the body gently on the ground, pulls his arms away—one just a stump cut at the elbow—and, using his only hand, covers his face in Irik's blood.

*I cannot,* he tries to say. *I cannot continue with this.*

His own voice comes back to him, though it is the voice of the crone, also.

*The process has begun; it must run its course.*

They have leaped again in time; backward or forward, he cannot tell. Crowds of dejected prisoners are rounded up in Market Square. Twenty or more are strapped into cruel machines: complex constructions of scaffolding and harnesses. They hang there like spiders in the center of webs. Engineers and mechanics wander around the machines, adjusting. Thaumaturgists in their sharp suits look on, their faces cold and cruel, like the sciences they control. Armand strides past these seditionists: the glacial Ejan, who stares from his entrapment with cold hatred; other faces filled with desolation. He passes a great minotaur. The legionaries have cut his horns off, stabbed him several times—fatally, it seems. Beside him hangs the assassin Kata, her black hair covered with blood. Armand points at her with his stump. "This one, free her." She is unstrapped from her machine, looks back at the others, collapses to the ground, her face in her hands. She is broken; she slinks away and is gone. Levers are turned; the machines hoist the seditionists high into the air, and thaumaturgists move their levers. Light from the Other Side engulfs the seditionists, who scream pitiably. They shimmer. Their limbs disappear into the uncanny light, reappear. It seems like their bodies are beneath water, wobbling unnaturally: their heads bulging out, their hips shrinking to almost nothing. Armand turns away, tears in his eyes, and watches as the majestic Caeli-Amur burns around him.

Armand feels hands grasping his, sees black and blue eyes, separating as they come into focus, craggy lines down the Augurer's face, her hair waving and wild. In the Augurer's eyes, Armand sees something else now.

*You will be a king,* they seem to say.

After the Embrace, the Augurer took Armand onto a platform at the very tip of the citadel. They looked out over the vast landscape. To one side, the mountains were shadowy forms. To the other, dawn was breaking, a cold yellow light, stratus clouds stretched high like watercolors on a canvas. The Embrace had taken the entire night.

"You have a great future," said the Augurer. "You also have a painful path."

"Things will be different to the visions. I can change the future now that I have foreseen it."

The Augurer smiled, brushed her matted hair back with one hand. "The more you change your path, the less likely those triumphs will be. The triumph and defeat rest upon each other."

"I'll make it all a triumph. I'll have everything I want. Help me, and I will reward you."

"We will help you return to Varenis, but if we do, we will call on your favor again," she said. "Choose carefully, Armand, for the favor will not be a light one."

Armand did not hesitate. "I must return in haste. When the time comes, ask for what you need."

And so the Augurer led Armand back to where Irik and Giselle sat on cushions. They had spent the night eating and sleeping, it seemed. Outside, dawn broke. Armand collapsed into the cushions.

"What did you see?" asked Giselle as Irik looked on thoughtfully.

"Nothing. Everything." Armand looked away, picturing himself holding the dead oppositionist. When he looked back at Irik, the oppositionist shook his head as if he knew.

The heavy silence was broken by the sound of a large beast scrabbling on rock and the flapping of huge wings.

"The Augurers are helping us return to Varenis," said Armand. "Those are our mounts."

Giselle was on her feet, ducking down the passageway toward the sound. "Armand, by the gods. Armand!"

Irik grasped Armand's hand. "I'm not returning. I'm going to Caeli-Amur."

"Please, come with me," said Armand. He struggled to think of words that would express his feelings. None seemed adequate. "Please."

"Armand, I ask you," said Irik. "Forget this obsession of yours and come with me to Caeli-Amur."

From the passageway, Giselle called out. "They are saddled, too. And furs! Impossible."

Armand clenched his hands, unclenched them. "And you? Would you reject your oppositionism? Are we to live outside of history in Caeli-Amur, a quiet life together?" When Irik didn't respond, Armand added, "I will come with you, if you say yes."

Irik shook his head and turned away. Then he turned back. "Not Caeli-Amur, then. The Dyrian coast. It's far from events."

Now Armand closed his eyes. "You aren't supposed to say yes. You're supposed to say no."

Irik drew a sharp breath. "So it is, then."

The images of the future sprang to Armand's mind, of the dead Irik in Armand's arms. "Irik, I beg you: don't return to Caeli-Amur."

Giselle rushed back along the corridor. "What did you do, Armand, for them to treat us like this?"

Irik walked past Armand, a final gesture of rejection. Armand followed the oppositionist to a large open landing platform on which three griffins stood restlessly. He wasn't prepared for the size of the things, the powerful wings, the heads that cocked from one side to the other as they examined them. The large beady eyes were watchful and intelligent. To one side of the platform stood the Augurer. In the morning light, her left eye seemed again to be green.

Giselle had already mounted her griffin. She sat upright, the reins in one hand like an expert rider. "You should feel the power of them, Armand."

Armand looked at Irik for guidance, but the oppositionist nodded at one of the beasts. "Up you go."

Something broke within Armand, the last straw that was holding up all the softness inside him. The world was harsh, and he would need to become cruel to survive it.

And so Armand turned from Irik and approached the beast warily, aware of its talons, large as his forearms. Grasping the saddle, he pulled himself up, felt the beast move beneath him. He looked briefly down at Irik, who pursed his lips, waved them off.

As the griffin backed away toward the edge of the platform, Armand became aware of a second Augurer, this one with a single blue eye, standing behind Irik.

The griffin's powerful spring into empty space forced Armand down into his seat. He closed his eyes, held the saddle for dear life, and felt the beast drop toward the ground, his stomach lurching as they fell. Then, with a beat of its massive wings, they rushed upward again.

Armand turned back to the Eyrie, where the oppositionist stood beside the beast that would fly him to Caeli-Amur. Armand felt a crush of despair inside him. Would this be the last time he saw the man? He thought of the images from his future. What choice was he making? A choice not for himself, but for everyone else—for order.

As he watched the Eyrie fall away from him, he noticed a third Augurer, this one at a higher window. Then he saw a fourth, this one but a child. Then he realized there were a dozen or more, each looking from a window or ledge—watching him as he flew toward his future.

# THIRTY-FIVE

A good-looking young man, his stride wide and confident, crossed the square below. As he swept back his dark shoulder-length hair, he looked a little like Kata for a moment, his dark eyes glittering with intelligence, his face smooth and unlined. Maximilian remembered him, vaguely, as one of Ejan's followers—Rikard. The young man had an air of certainty about him, as if the world were made for him.

Beside Max, Kata leaned against the gatehouse's palisade and called to the guards, "Let him in."

They descended to the ground and watched as Rikard marched through the gateway, sized up Max for a moment before turning to Kata. "Surrender, and everyone will be saved. You killed vigilant guards under no authority but your own, but you're a legitimate part of the movement. Ejan feels terrible about Maximilian, but, you know, mistakes get made."

Kata widened her stance, planted her feet against the solid ground. "Rikard, think it through. Ejan knew Max was in the Arbor dungeons. His friend Dumas wrote that letter to Armand. We thought they were plotting to fight us in the open, but we were wrong. They have corrupted the movement from within."

"Ejan said you'd claim these kinds of things. But, Kata, really."

Max wanted to speak, but he held himself back. The overthrow of the Houses had happened without him. It had unveiled all his follies. To think that a single individual could have an influence on history, just one water molecule in the surging sea. *It was a convenient delusion,* he thought. Delusions kept one going, as a seditionist. They all needed them back then, when there had seemed little hope of success. Now those delusions were scattered behind him like the ashes of old campfires.

No: it was not he, but Kata, who had become a seditionist leader. She had certainly shown, as she ran from crisis to crisis, that she had a strong enough will. Max found her all the more attractive now, and saw her as the partner she might have been. But they had both changed irrevocably, and he had Aya lodged in his head.

In recent days, Max had felt Aya recompose himself, his form becoming more solid. The ancient mage was finally coming to terms with Iria's betrayal, with the ruin of the world. Before the mage regained too much strength, Max needed to recover the Core of Sentinel Tower, return it to the Elo-Talern, and eject Aya from his body. Maybe Rikard would help in some way.

Kata led them toward the small Arena. The sound of guards training floated over the walls. Though philosopher Sarrat had returned to his home, his work done, a group of philosopher-assassins—gratificationists, matriarchists—had aligned themselves with the moderates and were now leading the practice sessions. Max smiled to himself: Kata was showing off her force to Rikard, certain the information would make it to Ejan.

"We could storm this complex if we wanted to," said Rikard.

"Hear that?" said Kata. "That's the sound of trained militia. Even if you did defeat us, you'd pay too high a price, both in death and loss of face. The citizens would turn against you. The textile factories, the machinists, the builders—they're all on our side."

"Who has the thaumaturgists?" countered Rikard.

"No one," said Kata. "The Authority is split. The thaumaturgists won't follow any faction. You won't be able to command them even if you tried."

Max was still struggling to gain a sense of the vast changes in the city. Those who controlled the thaumaturgists had always controlled Caeli-Amur. There were surely those who had become seditionists, but others would continue to be troops for hire, mercenaries—especially those used to the privileges accorded to them by the Houses. Much depended on which way they fell.

Rikard grasped Kata's hands tightly. "Kata. As your friend, I beg you."

"A friend wouldn't ask this of me," said Kata.

"You know politics, Kata. Sometimes you agree with people you don't like. Sometimes you care for those you disagree with." Rikard dropped Kata's hands and looked down at his feet. "You've changed me. You've made me see subtleties where there were none. Please."

"Sometimes there is no room for subtleties. Sometimes things are fundamental," said Kata. "Ejan sent you because he knew you would have a greater chance of changing my mind."

"He wanted to come himself," said Rikard. "I begged him to let me go in his stead."

That silenced Kata for a moment.

"The assault will be in the next few days." Rikard stood before them, his arms hanging hopelessly at his sides.

Kata nodded. "Tell Dexion not to come here for me. Tell him to stay at home."

Rikard looked around the trees in the complex, the outbuildings, the mechanical attempts to reproduce the beauty of the Arbor Palace. He then walked back toward the gate.

Leaving Kata behind, Max hurried beside him. "When I was captured, I was carrying an object—a cylinder. Have you heard anything about it or where it might be?"

Rikard shook his head. "Georges has a room of captured goods in the Arbor Palace. But you won't have any luck getting it from him—not unless Ejan orders it."

"I must see Ejan, then."

"Now, *that* I wouldn't recommend."

As Rikard walked on, Max called to him, "So that's your new order, then? A gathering of thieves?"

Rikard seemed bereft, perhaps hurt. He took two steps back toward Max. "The room is on the third floor of the wing of the Palace that hangs over the lake. If Georges does have your cylinder, that's where you'll find it."

Moderates packed into a theater in the northern wing of Technis Palace. Open on one side, it afforded a view of the city, and the cool night air swept in from the sea. Older moderates anxiously argued for surrender. Against them, the factory delegates—hard men and women who had lived their lives in smoke and soot—argued both against capitulation and against conflict with the vigilants. It was an impossible position, but one which seemed to be winning. The only option they were left with was to hole up in the complex and wait for events to develop.

Max loved these citizens, silent and under the sway of the Houses for so long. Now they had found their own voices: rough, unsophisticated, but honest. He swore he could dedicate himself to them, once he had rid himself of Aya.

Still, Max's new modesty eventually drove him from the theater and back to the Director's offices. He slumped into the seat behind the desk, examined the memory-catcher. He had known at first glance what the thing was, for a fragment of Aya's memories had integrated with his. The bolts were fixed in a belt circling the machine. Max glanced beneath the desk, and there found the little bolt-thrower, aimed to fire at someone standing before it: an indication that the machine still operated.

He began to think again of the Core, lying in Georges's storeroom in Arbor Palace. There was no getting around it. He would have to retrieve it himself, under cover of night and illusion. He was preparing himself for the journey when Kata entered the room.

"I'm going to the Arbor Palace to retrieve the Core," said Max.

Kata took a deep breath. "I know I shouldn't, but I'll come with you."

Max's surprise showed on his face. Already she had rescued him from the Bolt. Moved though he was, he couldn't let her take this chance. She was needed here. "Look, if this is about us . . . You don't owe me anything, you know. And you're not my keeper."

Kata shook her head. "I'm not, but I do owe you something. You were the first person to show me there was more to life than seeking personal advantage. You showed me there was meaning in working for others. You're my . . . you're my . . . friend."

The word *friend* smacked him hard: to hear himself defined that way hurt. Was there no future for them, after all? He was to blame in the first place and it would take time to win her back. Still he held out hope. The truth was, her offer was too good to refuse. As a former philosopher-assassin—a fact she'd admitted to him before the overthrow—she would be invaluable in facing the dangers of House Arbor.

"Yes, of course. I need your help," he said.

"We have to retrieve the Core safely, though," said Kata. "Neither of us is allowed to die."

"You might have noticed, but I'm not always the best at keeping promises," said Max.

Later that night Max dropped to the ground beside Kata, inside the gardens of the Arbor Palace. They scuttled away from the *Toxicodendron didion*, which was beginning to rouse itself from Max's sleeping conjuration. After the charm, Max felt the nausea rise within him; his legs weakened. The Other Side leaked into him, but he would have to continue on.

*Extraordinarily primitive,* Aya's voice was again strong. *You call that a science?*

—Show me how. Show me the prime language.

Aya did not respond, but Max felt the god's restlessness once more.

Tear-flowers started to wail their beautiful, mesmeric cry, and Max thoughtlessly started to walk toward them.

Kata pulled him away. "Come on."

They crept silently past lush jungle plants, smelled thick jungle smells. Above them curled beautiful walkways and aqueducts. If they could reach them, they would be safe from the dangerous flora. He gestured to Kata.

She shook her head. "Too open. Too vulnerable."

They slunk on through the undergrowth, passing a bed of blood-orchids, which stirred at the scent of them. Leaving the deadly flowers behind, they pushed through a thick exotic bush. Max found himself quickly scooting over a floor of bloodred mold, which moved unnervingly beneath his feet. Tendrils rose up to reach him, like little hands of a desperate lover.

A moment later they were beside a pond. Unseen things moved beneath its dark surface, breaking its stillness. Kata dashed along the water's edge. Max followed her straight into a bank of razor reeds, which shook savagely. Kata leaped back, blood flowing from

334 * RJURIK DAVIDSON

her right arm. She checked the long thin wounds with a disgusted eye. "Damn it."

They came through the thickest part of the garden, to where many beds of tear-flowers and exquisitely crafted trees had been hacked and destroyed. They froze for a moment, for a carriage raced along the entranceway, past the great fountain and toward the palace. A heavy figure, face obscured by a hood, stepped from the carriage and entered the palace, accompanied by a bodyguard.

"We're not the only late visitors, I see," said Kata.

The carriage might have belonged to an officiate once. Those who had escaped to the Dyrian coast were safe for the moment. Many had been dragged back from the villas to the dungeons beneath the palace. Yet others had met the Bolt, their last dark friend. Yet Max knew there were still a few free House agents in the city, hiding in their mansions.

Putting such thoughts aside, they dashed to the palace wall. Kata tossed up a hook, which promptly fell back to the ground beside them. Her second throw was powerful and accurate. The hook lodged in the iron balcony on the third floor.

"You first," she said.

Max grabbed the rope and hauled himself up, up, winding his legs around the rope to steady himself. His arms began to burn from the strain by the time he reached the first floor. By the time he dragged himself to the second, they were shaking. He looked down, realized how high up he was. A tumble would mean a shattered leg, capture, the dungeon, and the Bolt.

*Don't fall now.* Aya laughed.

—You still want me to die along with you? Max built a little shield within himself, in case Aya decided to strike at him.

Aya laughed again. *You think I hate you that much?*

—You intend to drain my mind from my body. But I'm warning you, once we're back with the Elo-Talern, you'll be the one deposited into some inanimate world, like the one in Caeli-Enis's Library, where I found you. I have the strength. I am the whole personality here. You are but a fragment.

*It's war, then. War to the end. And you might like to ask yourself quite how whole you are.*

Max struggled to pull himself past the second floor. A groan came unbidden from his lips. He clung to the rope silently for a moment.

A candle was lit in a nearby room, and Max wondered who he had awoken. A window opened and a guard looked out, right in time for a dagger to drive directly into his eye, thrown by Kata below. He had forgotten how much of a killer she was. The man leaned back, as if someone had slapped him, raised a hand to where the dagger emerged from his face, and collapsed back with a soft thud.

Max continued up, straining. *Just one last haul,* he thought. But his arms stopped moving and he held on desperately, unable to continue.

Kata waved frantically. She risked calling out: "Come on!"

Max thought of the trials he had undergone; he thought of the peace he now yearned for. He pulled one last time, reached up, grasped the iron railing, and dragged himself against the wall, scraping his knees. He threw a leg over the railing and fell over it onto the balcony.

A few ludicrously short seconds later Kata squatted down beside him. He closed his eyes. Was there anything she couldn't do?

Opening the glass doors quietly, Kata stepped into the deserted room, which seemed to be the office of some House official. Sweating and breathing heavily, Max followed her. Across the room, an open doorway gave access to a corridor. From far down the passageway, loud voices carried to them. Kata cocked her head, listened, and whispered. "There's a guard in the corridor just outside the doorway."

Max strained but heard nothing nearer than the chattering voices.

Kata produced a strange implement from her bag: a tube with a spherical container at one end. Light as a dancer, she skipped into the corridor, raised the implement to her lips, and blew. Max followed just in time to see a cloud of crimson dust billow from the tube's end just as someone said, "Hey—"

Kata caught a black-suited female guard before she crashed to the floor. She dragged the unconscious woman into the room and laid her by the desk. Holding up her implement proudly, she whispered, "Haven't used that in a while. Quieter than any other weapon."

Snatches of conversation drifted down from a doorway at the far end of the corridor, the wing that apparently held Georges's storeroom. "No, it's fantastic. The two factions will wear each other out, but your vigilants will prevail, believe me."

As they sneaked forward, Kata made no noise at all, but each step of Maximilian's seemed to find a creaky floorboard.

Closer now, the voices traveled to them more clearly. "They say he's always been cold. The thing they don't seem to realize is that he has a mansion up in the Arantine. It's not just officiates and sub-officiates, you know. He has allies everywhere: investors from Varenis, foreigners, half the bloody thaumaturgists in the city."

They crept nearer. Maximilian drew ideograms in the air, spoke the words he knew so well, interlaced the equations just so, and fell into the beautifully lit-up world.

Now invisible, he continued after Kata, who tiptoed forward, light as a cat.

"'Half' is an exaggeration," said a rough voice, which Max recognized as Georges's.

"Yes, of course. But, you know," said the second voice, which Max thought he knew as well.

Kata pressed herself against the wall a foot before the open doorway, on the right-hand side of the corridor, from where the voices carried. She pointed to another large open doorway at the very end of the corridor. Through the opening, Max could see piles of goods packed on shelves and strewn around the floor. A great lock hung open on the door's latch. The two men had been examining the loot, it seemed.

Kata nodded at Max to go ahead. Meanwhile, she pulled the second of her knives from a belt hidden beneath her shirt.

With each of Max's footsteps, the floorboards creaked faintly. He tried to soften them, but it made no difference. As he passed the doorway to his right, he glanced in.

At the head of a grand sculpted table sat Georges, looking as exhausted as he ever had. Lying before him on the desktop were

several piles of gold and jewelry, several odd-shaped ancient implements, and a bottle of wine, which he picked up and began to fill
two glasses with. "Look, the truth is, we have to accept that people
change, but the roles stay the same. Ejan thinks there's a new world
being built, but he doesn't realize he's just filling the place of a
House Director, really."

Max shook with disgust. Here was his opportunity for revenge, but it was an opportunity he couldn't take. The alarm would
be raised, guards would come running, and he and Kata would be
slaughtered.

Behind Georges stood a rough-looking man, a little shorter
than average, whose head jutted forward like the spout of a jug.
Hanging from his belt was a mean-looking studded mace. Georges
had hired himself a bodyguard, it seemed. From the look of him,
perhaps a brutalist, one of a group of philosopher-assassins who
claimed the world was violent and cruel, and that there was no
space for delicate sensibilities. The mace was an expression of this
belief: a weapon for crushing and smashing.

On the far side of the table sat Dumas, who was the figure they
had seen arriving in the carriage earlier. His great bulldog eyes
roved from Georges to the treasure on the table and back again.
"He still thinks Caeli-Amur works like the ice-halls—they're
damned simple places, you know. For him, there is summer and
winter, the ice and the thaw, black and white."

The floorboards creaked beneath Max's feet again. For a moment the guard frowned and looked directly through the door.
Cursing silently, Max continued to walk slowly on.

"It'll be a good thing when he crushes the moderates. Clear the
board of a few pieces," said Georges.

"They'll never amount to much anyway. Too much faith in
chitter-chatter. Don't understand that power is all about force,"
said Dumas. "At least we're prepared now."

Max halted in front of the storeroom door, turned around, and
stepped back to watch the conversation. The image of Georges and
Dumas ahead of him was too much. This was the way the power
hungry made their way in the world, swapping favors for favors, coin
for coin, rumor for rumor, until they rose up above everyone else,

a caste unto themselves, vicious and self-interested. Anger surged within Max. The equations vanished from his mind. He materialized in the doorway, staring at the two corrupt men.

*That's what I like to see,* said Aya.

Georges cried out at the sight of Max, leaped back in his chair. The stunned Dumas gaped, mouth open, but the philosopher-assassin guard snapped into action and pushed past Dumas, his mace instantly in hand.

Max stepped back against the corridor wall, raised his arm up to protect himself from the weapon.

"Should I smash him?" The assassin stood in the doorway, his mace above his head, ready to bring it down.

"Please," said Georges. "He's proving particularly annoying."

The guard's mace fell to his side loosely, the strength suddenly leached from his body.

"Well, go on," said Georges, not understanding that it was too late.

The assassin twisted back toward the room, though his legs had lost all strength. Kata held him like a puppet, her face poked over the guard's shoulder. She had stabbed him directly in the heart.

"Hello, friends," she said. "If you were to cry out, I think I might be able to kill you both before rescue came. So, what are we going to do?"

The two men backed away as the mace dropped to the ground. Kata eased the body down gently.

"Let's work something out, shall we?" said Dumas.

Max seized the mace and pushed quickly past Kata. This time Georges raised an arm to protect himself. Max jabbed the mace into Georges's stomach. The blow sucked the air from the man, whose arms came down to protect his vital organs.

Quickly, Max raised the mace into the air and just as quickly brought it down. There was a terrible crack. A massive depression appeared on the top of Georges's head as his skull gave way. His eyes roved for a moment, looking up and back toward the indentation, and then he collapsed to the ground.

*Ooh, good one,* said Aya. *Pity that assassin wasn't around to see it. Confirmation of his philosophy, I'd say.*

Dumas dived to one side as one of Kata's knives flew through the air, lodging itself into the table. "Alarm! Help! Intruders! Killers!"

A bell rang. Doors opened and closed. The sound of running echoed down the hall.

Kata pulled Max out of the room. Already guards charged toward them along the corridor, pikes in hand. There would be no escape that way.

They raced into the storeroom. Kata slammed the door shut, slid a bolt into its strike plate, and rapidly pulled a heavy chest against it. Footfalls sounded along the corridor.

"Find the Core. Quick," Kata said.

The room was vast, filled with goods of all sorts: rugs and decanters, open chests filled with jewelry—all the loot from a war. Windows overlooked the dark lake beneath and the gardens beyond.

Max padded along the aisles, up one, down another, horrified by the stolen wealth. His eyes roved madly: here a row of paintings, there a pile of precious books. Then he saw the Core, lying on a shelf beside its bag. There was still hope.

*I can't wait to see how this turns out,* said Aya. *Do you think you'll make it? I don't think so.*

"The window, quick." Kata braced her body against the door just as bodies smashed into the other side. The door shuddered violently as the bolt was torn from it; the chest was driven an inch back.

Max slipped the Core into the bag and slung it over his shoulder. He was almost at the window when Aya came at him, a tidal wave of force. Max dropped to his knees, lost control of his limbs. Once again he was in a deadly struggle. He shuddered and fought, was forced backward by Aya's onward rush. He lost control of his arms and legs, but he held on to the center of his being and his mind. He fell forward clumsily, felt the cold wood smash his face.

"What's wrong with you?" said Kata.

Max was paralyzed. His body trembled from the conflict. His limbs shuddered, wobbled.

—I am the stronger—he said.

*That's impossible.*

—I am the primary personality. The body knows me, knows my thoughts, my feelings, my emotions, my directions. It is *my* body, and you are but a fragment.

Kata leaped over Max. He lost sight of her, heard a window open. A moment later he felt himself being hauled up. He was balanced on a ledge. Outside the gardens were patches of darkness, the lake beneath him a great black circle.

Another smash. Wood splintered and cracked. The door burst open.

"You'd better wake up, or you'll drown," said Kata.

Max felt himself fall and hit the water. For a moment he wondered whether the lake was filled with deadly creatures, just like the gardens around them. He held his breath and struck out at Aya once more, but he knew in his heart he had lost.

# THIRTY-SIX

Lost once more in the subterranean regions of his mind, Max watched the world through Aya's eyes. He lay recovering in the rooms that had once belonged to Technis's Director. Max recalled the flight from the Arbor Palace as he would a dream. They had come up out of the lake, coughing and spluttering up water, still holding the bag with the Core. Aya had been in control of his body and had plunged into the gardens. A blood-orchid had wrapped its whiplike frond around his ankle, dragged him toward its drooling head. Aya had tried to compose a formula to send the flower to sleep, but his strength had been used up by the invisibility charm and the savage struggle with Max, who lay in a dark stupor. Without Kata, they would certainly have died there, but she had arrived in time, cut him free, and led him back to safety.

Aya dressed himself and wandered into the Director's grand office, where the bag with the Core lay on the great desk. Behind the desk stood the egg-shaped memory-catcher, that other reminder of those days when things were falling apart. By the time the ancients had built those things, their paradise had been long disintegrating. The cataclysm had been upon them, the war between Aya and Alerion at its height. All their plans were gone. People scrabbled for escape or distraction. Pastimes and leisure became their sole focus and goal. The real world was coming apart, so they fled to false worlds in the water-spheres or escaped to long-lost memories using machines like the memory-catcher.

Aya threw the Core over his shoulder, happily. *It's time now, Maximilian. Time to free you from my body. It won't be bad. I'm sure we can find a pleasant enough world for you to live in. Well, so long as the power holds out.*

By the time Aya reached the great doors that opened up the empire of the Elo-Talern, Max had regained much of his strength. The seditionist caught fragments of Aya's thoughts, knew the mage was worried about his own precarious purchase on the body. But Aya's anger at Alerion and Iria gave him life. Anger was an emotion that gave direction, and the ancient mage began to think again of the world. So Iria had betrayed him. But that had been nearly a thousand years ago, during the breaking of the world. Hadn't he outlasted Alerion and the rest of them? Wasn't that the greatest joke of them all for him, the trickster god? Yes, now he would enjoy himself and take what he needed, beginning with this body.

The great circular door that opened into the realm of the Elo-Talern was massive, dark, and silent. Aya moved his hand across the door in a complex configuration once again, but this time it did not light up or hum. No silver ideograms fell like snowflakes on its surface. Something inside had irrevocably broken.

With intense apprehension, Aya found the hatch, half hidden to the side of the door. With great effort he opened it, revealing a large spoked wheel above him. He grasped the wheel with both hands, but it held fast. So he clambered up, placed his feet on one of the spokes. The whole thing slowly began to rotate. For an instant Max imagined himself to be a giant mouse on a wheel.

The vast door slowly ground to one side.

Aya leaped to the floor and stepped through the opening, where he stood horrified for a moment. It was not the impossible perspectives, nor the staircases like spider's webs, that unnerved both him and Max. No: it was the mold.

The last time he had been here, one corner of the room had been buried beneath a sea of crimson mold. Now the sea had joined up with the great towers rising around the room. Some of the Elo-Talern still lay on their chaise longues, clasping their tankards, covered with luminous purples and greens of molds and lichens. Those on the floor were submerged, swallowed up, lone limbs breaking the surface here or there.

Elo-Drusa leaned against the pillar. Again she clambered to her feet like a grotesque newborn pony. Most of Drusa's body had been engulfed with the mold; only one arm and a spindly foot remained free. Her mouth and nose was completely overrun by orange. One eye was long gone; the second could still be seen through the thin layer that covered it. She fell to her knees, crawled toward him, clambered up once again. She completely disappeared for several seconds into the Other Side, then reappeared closer to him. Drusa made a gurgling sound; spores burst from her mouth and floated into the air like orange snowflakes. They drifted around Aya, rested on his face. He brushed them off.

Again she gurgled, and again the mold spewed forth. A third time the spume flew forward, and guttural words could be heard beneath the hideous sound. "Finally! I've been waiting. Finally! We have a chance!"

She led Aya away through the sea of colored mold, which their passing feet lifted into the air. They traveled along a strange passage that twisted and turned like a corkscrew, and came to a hexagonal room. In one corner, Elo-Talern lay in a heaped pile, like dead spiders swept to the side. Every now and then one moved a limp limb.

From another corner of the room, a frighteningly tall Elo-Talern rose from the ground. He staggered toward them, his red robes blackened with stains.

"The Core? You bring the Core?" he said.

"We have it, Kalas." Drusa coughed. "Let's save ourselves. Let's regain our power."

And so Kalas led them down labyrinthine tunnels that burrowed inside an immense and complex engine. With each step, Max felt the tension increase. He wanted the Core to function so that he might be free of Aya, but he feared he would he expelled from his body, lost to the world. He prepared himself for a final desperate assault.

A huge wall rose before them, covered with dials and wheels and levers. Kalas pulled the engine's deadened Core from its cylindrical housing. Delicately, he took the Sentinel Tower Core from its bag and slipped it into the casing. Grasping a handle, he looked at Drusa. All was silent. The decisive moment was at hand.

Kalas pulled the handle down, and a great hum filled the room. Energy surged through the system. Lights blinked on, and there was a burst of warmth. That nightmare world seemed once more alive and filled with promise. The Elo-Talern would save themselves and restore themselves to their former glory as overseers of Caeli-Amur. Not everything was entropy. There was life!

Drusa laughed, coughed out spores that drifted on the warm dark air.

"It works!" said Kalas. "We're saved!"

The two spindly creatures embraced, laughed and coughed and laughed some more. They staggered around, full of joy, and Aya laughed with them.

The hum subsided, the lights dwindled, the warm air dissipated, and everything died. All was silent once again.

"No. No!" Drusa let out a hideous wail, her thin legs giving way beneath her.

Kalas checked some gauges on the wall, stared blankly at the others. "It's too depleted. The Core hasn't enough energy left."

"There must be a way." Aya spoke forlornly. This spelled the end of his hopes too.

Kalas shook his head in defeat. "Not here, not anywhere. The Library of Caeli-Enas is drowned. Everything there lost. Look— there is nothing but mold."

Drusa was crying, huge, awful wracking sobs. She was a bundle of wiry bones on the floor, her spindly legs like broken reeds. She looked up, seemed to laugh, coughed, spewed forth more mold, then lay down completely.

Finally she pulled herself up to a sitting position. "Seal us in and let us lie here until eternity finally drains the last meager strength from our bodies. Let us die our slow eternal death. Let the mold eat us, just as it will eat you. It will engulf you all. Nothing lasts."

Aya looked at the pitiful creatures as Kalas slid down beside her. "You cannot die, Drusa. That's what you've done to yourself. When the cataclysm came, you made yourself immortal. The Ascended, they called you. But it was no rise."

"But we can die by violence," she said. "And it's violence we deserve. We were trying to save the last of the ancient world. But this is what we created." She seemed to collapse in on herself, began a shuddering cough. The spores from her mouth hovered in the still air before falling to the ground. She sobbed some more, flashed out of existence for a moment, became a rotting black picture of death, flickered back into existence, and cried some more.

Aya turned and staggered away from the scene, up and out of the engine and the corkscrew tunnel, out of the Underworld. He sealed the huge circular door. This time he held his hand against the mechanism, invoked the prime language, melted the door so it would never again open, and left the Elo-Talern to their eternal rest, to their eternal half sleep. He wondered if they would dream, but he knew in his heart it would instead be nightmares. He and Max would never escape this body. There was no point in fighting with each other.

Aya didn't struggle when Max ejected him from the strategic center of his mind. *What does it matter, anyway? You will control this body, then I will, and so it will go. There's no way out for us now, except death.*

# PART IV

❧

# TWILIGHTS

*Aya was dead, Iria lost in the mountains. Panadus and the others had left, never to return. Now Alerion's spirit was eking from his body, just as order was leaking from the land. He was dying.*

*Around us, the land rippled like blankets. The sea surged up over the coasts, fled away, leaving boundless plains of sand. Fire swept vast regions to the west, blackening the earth. Great columns of refugees marched across the land, but there was nowhere to hide. The cataclysm was upon us.*

*We were not Magi, but we harnessed as much of the Art as we could. We knew Alerion's strength would help us in the days ahead, and so we began the ritual described herein. We placed the prism in the center of a sphere of power. Alerion's body hung above it like a spider in a web. Night and day we invoked the forces of dark physics. At the moment of Alerion's death, we caught his life-force as it shook itself free of its body. That force—a soul, for want of a better word—we bound into the prism.*

*When we were finished, that occult object stood alone in the circle. Only it lived. Only it gave us hope. Only the prism promised us a future free from the destruction unfolding all around us.*

*The prism: how it thrilled and terrified us!*

—Aediles Philan and Drusa, preface to *The Alerium Calix: Construction, Structure, and Command*

# THIRTY-SEVEN
༄

A hundred thousand candles lit the evening of the Twilight Observance in Caeli-Amur. Perched in niches and crevices, burning safely on windowsills, candles lined the streets—one candle for each of the souls who had lost their lives out in the Keos Pass when Aya and Alerion had battled nearly a millennia ago. For three days—the duration of that ancient confrontation—the candles would be kept burning. The finale of the gladiator season traditionally occurred on the final night of the Observance, when Dexion was scheduled to fight once more.

Meanwhile, another battle was about to explode. Like an army of black ants, the vigilants crawled around the Technis Complex, ready to attack when the order came. Long ladders lay ready on the cobblestones; scorpion ballistae were placed on platforms, their heavy bolts piled in crates beside them; guards began to form huddled detachments, ready for the assault.

From Kata's place on the Director's balcony, many of the attackers' faces seemed cold and even cruel. Half of the grubby seekers of power and influence in the city had flocked to the vigilants, ingratiated themselves to them, started to scale their hierarchies—a thousand little Georges sniffing out opportunities.

Kata closed her eyes, felt the chill wind brushing against her skin. She heard the soft jingle of a guard's belt and scabbard below, the whine of the wind passing over the wall, her own breath in her nose. Then she heard other grumbling voices drifting over the wall. "This isn't right. Our brothers and sisters are up there."

Ejan ran the city now, as he had always planned to do. If Kata didn't die in the fighting, she imagined she would end up at the Standing Stones as the Bolt continued its gruesome work. Or perhaps they could all sneak away through the subterranean tunnels beneath Technis Palace. There were many secret routes down there, some only small tunnels reaching nearby squares, others plumbing deep into the earth and led far away. The moderates would be no more, but they would be alive.

In disgust, she returned to the Director's office, where Max sat at the desk, staring blankly into space. He had returned from his journey to the Elo-Talern. He refused to discuss it, but from what she could tell, it was a failure. To think it had come to this for both of them: total defeat. It would not be long before the vigilants began their assault.

Kata leaned against the egg-shaped machine, laid her head on its surface, felt its cool metal on her skin, and looked at him. "It will be better to die fighting than to surrender."

Max broke from his reverie. "Well, at least we'll have our memories. We could save them up the way the ancients did, leave them for some unlucky person to experience in the future."

"Save them?"

"With that machine. The memory-catcher. Imagine the poor beggar who ingests our memories, thinking they would see some glorious past, filled with exotic joy." There was a tinge of humor in his grim smile.

A chill ran along Kata's neck. Her mind jumped into gear: the memory-catcher, the thing she had searched for all those weeks ago. And here it was in the Director's office, waiting for her all this time. She still possessed the memory mites taken from Aceline's nose. *What secrets do they store?* she wondered. The pain of losing Aceline hit her again, but she knew she would have to ingest the mites. She might discover for certain who had killed Aceline. And yet she felt ambivalent about experiencing such a strange intimacy with her friend. She wanted this final memory, yet didn't Aceline deserve to keep her secrets hidden?

She would have to buy time before the assault. In this task, only Rikard could help her. She called out for one of her captains, told him to fetch the vigilant. "Tell him I've discovered the memory-catcher. He'll understand."

Rikard arrived soon afterward, striding into the room with a black-suited adjutant. A rapier hung from Rikard's belt. Like Kata's own guards, he had foregone the typical short-sword that the vigilants had begun to wear.

"I've bought some time, but precious little. We've got until the middle of the night. I'm sorry, Kata. It's all I could do." Rikard's face took on a rare look of inner turmoil. "I'll stay here with you for a while, maybe even as the assault happens. I want you to live."

How strange that Kata had become a friend of this young man, who she trusted and respected, yet who fought for the other side. She held up the vial. "You realize the mites will probably confirm my theory that Ejan is behind Aceline's murder. Then what will you do?"

"It won't confirm your theory," said Rikard.

Kata handed the vial to Max. "Make it work. I need to ingest these memories."

Max sat by the side of the machine. He examined it carefully, his eyes glazing over as he looked inward. When he refocused, he carefully scraped the mites into one of the bolts at the side of the machine. This he placed into a hole in the mechanism's side. A metal vise clasped it; something whirred, clicked; then came the sound of rushing liquid. A panel slid open, revealing a glass with a small amount of black fluid.

"There's not much here. You'll only get fragments." Max took the glass, handed it to Kata.

Without hesitating, she downed the liquid and retreated to the chaise longue. The others stood around, nervously shuffling their feet, none of them sure quite how to behave. Rikard and Maximilian stood apart, stealing awkward glances at each other.

Kata looked to Rikard, whose face was lighter than usual. But, no, that wasn't it. Rather, Kata's perception had changed. Things seemed lighter, clearer, and yet every movement of her eyes left shadowy images on her vision. Frightened, she pressed her lids together.

*She remembers her feelings toward Max, how she had never trusted him. Ambition was like a twisted rod around which no healthy plant could grow.*

*She remembers the first moment she saw him, his eyes wild with plans, his hair sticking out like a wiry bush. She shows him the press on which they print the broadsheet* A Call to Arms, *the predecessor of the* Dawn. *She introduces him to the members of her group. He greets them cordially, and begins to explain his mad dreams of reaching the Library of Caeli-Enas. His aspirations come spilling out of him like the insides of a child's toy. The memory breaks off; it is not complete.*

With a jolt, Kata realized these were Aceline's memories, not her own. She groaned and heard someone say something. A rushing sensation overwhelmed her, as if she were a fountain, water rushing through her.

*She grasps what fragments she can, none of them complete, each the torn-up pieces of a long-lost page. She is a child, watching boats from the Southern Headland. Her mother returns from the Thousand Stairs. "I've brought you something!" She's at the university—there is a boy with dark hair and a soft mouth. She turns away from him. "I can't. I have things to do." She is in the seditionist group; she doesn't like the others. They are ambitious, lacking in self-consciousness.* They haven't had enough defeat in life, *she thinks. Max is worse than Ejan. He is ambitious; he covets his place in history. Ejan simply doesn't think about it at all; he is a cold machine running smoothly in the night. She watches them as she eats a simple soup in the large Communal Cavern. She looks down at her thin mattress. One of its sides has split, and straw is bursting from the opening.*

The memories were overwhelming, a drug rushing though Kata's body. Afraid, she grabbed the chaise longue beneath her with both hands, felt its solidity with her fingers, slipped back into the vertigo of someone else's memories. The drug swept her away again, and she discovered she could find the memories she wanted, though it was like picking up torn pages from a disintegrated book.

She shuffled forward, past the last days of the seditionist hideout, through the torture of the terror-spheres with their nightmare visions of burning alive, past the thrilling uprising on Aya's Day, until it's—

*After the overthrow of the Houses, and she is sitting beside Kata in the Opera, watching the others pass. She has come to rely on this dark-haired woman, though she has the opposite flaw as Max or Ejan. Kata is afraid of her power; she keeps herself small, like a little animal in the night. She has come to love her, for she sees in her the one thing a seditionist leader should have: no ambition at all. She wants to rest her head on Kata's lap, but she dare not.*

Back on the chaise longue, Kata let out a little cry of grief for her lost and lovely friend, but she kept moving, until—

*She's with Thom on the way to the baths. Flashes of his face: his beard and blue scarf obscuring the tightness of his skin; his eyes strikingly pale in the light. He assures her the meeting place will be safe. He has arranged a room in the Great Steam Baths, but it's not the same one where they met the two thaumaturgists the first time. She hesitates for a moment. "Come on," says Thom. Then she's in the room; the thaumaturgists are behind her. Magnificent colored mosaics cover the walls. A tiled Augurer stares at them through a window high in the Eyries.*

*"The Brotherhood of the Hand are organizing, but we daren't do it in the open," said Ivarn. "Not even the leaders know."*

*"Are there many of you?" Thom turns back from the mosaics he had been examining.*

*"Enough," said Uendis. "When the time is right, we will come out and support seditionism openly, but it's too dangerous now. Everyone is paranoid. There are rumors the Prism of Alerion has been found. Whoever uses it can stop the thaumaturgical sickness. All the thaumaturgists who seek personal gain will follow whoever controls the prism."*

*"The prism has been found," said Aceline.*

*Suddenly the four of them are standing in new positions. Time has jumped. The memory is fragmented.*

*Aceline leans against the wall. "Show them the letter, Thom."*

*Thom shakes his head. "I thought it best to keep it safe at the Opera."*

*Aceline looks at Thom. Something is wrong. The tightness on Thom's face, the deathly look in his pale eyes. A chill drives through her body, and she glances at the door. It is on the other side of the room. Thom is between her and the thaumaturgists. All are between her and the door. The two thaumaturgists are looking at Thom, uncertain. Fear crosses Ivarn's face, a fleeting shadow. Uendis takes on a shock of recognition. He raises his hand, begins to chant quickly.*

*"You . . ." Ivarn steps back, but Thom had already covered his hand*

*with a bloodred power. The fiery hand clamps Ivarn's face. The thau-*
*maturgist grasps his wrist, but a gurgling sound comes from his mouth,*
*and the air is filled with the smell of burning.*

*Thom's form begins to shimmer; a hulking shape appears beneath it.*
*Aceline backs into the corner, watching the desperate fight. Fear*
*courses through her. Again the memory skips. Aceline hears a knock on*
*the door and Rikard's voice, calling to her from beyond the chamber.*
*"Aceline?" She wants to get up, but her limbs have lost all strength. She*
*can't tell if it is fear, or if some charm has robbed her of all will.*

*Uendis's body comes down with a thunk, and the smell of burning*
*flesh is thick and sickly in the air. Both Brothers of the Hand are*
*dead.*

*Aceline cowers in the corner, raises her hands up against the sight of*
*Thom coming at her. His face is now bulging in odd places, and she knows*
*it is not Thom. The eyes are pale and filled with an icy coldness.*

*Thom cracks open a translucent circular syringe, and a thousand*
*specks crawl over her chest, up, up, over her face, like insects looking for*
*their prey. She reaches for them, but she can't move her hands. They*
*plunge into her nose and she tries to scream, but the whiteness takes her.*

*When she regains consciousness, Thom is holding up the dart, and*
*she can see the thousands of specks moving inside. He places it back into*
*his bag, smiles evilly.*

*She hears a woman's voice now—"Aceline! It's Kata!"—followed by*
*more knocking on the door.* Kata, *she screams in her head.* Please, Kata,
save me. Please.

*"It will only hurt for a little while," Thom whispers as he unwraps*
*the scarf from his throat. "Quiet now."*

*The scarf is now around her neck. She tries to take a deep breath,*
*but nothing comes. She tries again but cannot even manage a gurgle.*
*The room is filled with a cold mist. The whiteness takes her again. This*
*time she does not come back.*

Somewhere in the memory Kata thought to herself, *There must*
*have been another entryway into that room.* It made sense: the shapeshifter had organized the meeting in that particular room in
order to escape without coming through the door. Perhaps they
could retrace the assassin's escape route. If she could prove to
Rikard that Ejan was behind the murder, the vigilant leader might

be deposed. She could stop the vigilant attack on the Technis Palace and save the moderates. She could put the vigilants back in their place and disband the tribunal. She could stop the Bolt. She could do all this for Aceline.

Kata sat up on the chaise longue.

"What did you see?" said Max.

After darkness had fallen, Kata, Rikard, and Max passed along a dark and wet tunnel beneath the Technis Complex, up a narrow staircase, out through a nondescript door concealed beneath a bridge, and onto the streets. Their hooded cloaks wrapped around them, protection from the driving rain.

Kata had replaced her knives from the diminishing store at the Palace, but she still felt unsafe. They took side roads through the factory district, past where Kata's apartment lay. She wondered briefly about Dexion. As far as she knew, the vigilants hadn't arrested him, and of course he wasn't mixed up with Dumas. Most likely he was at the Arena, happily preparing for the spectacular on the final day of the Twilight Observance. Still, she worried she would lead him to his doom, as she had with her little urchin, Henri. She worried Dexion might decide to join her in her battles out of loyalty. She couldn't add the weight of his death to the others she was responsible for.

Crowds spilled from the baths, drunk and laughing, and staggered arm in arm off into the night. Kata watched them and yearned to live their lives for a moment. Through the steam-filled halls they passed, figures looming out of the semidarkness, towels hanging loosely from their waists, arms around one another.

The door to the private room was closed, and the sight of it ran memories—hers and Aceline's—through Kata once more. Kata felt terribly cold, as if she had spent a winter's night without shelter. They lit one of the lamps and examined the room again.

With Max holding the lamp in the air, they checked the corners of the room and the bath, inspected the floor, and searched for signs of another entryway, but found none.

Kata turned her focus to the mosaics. As the main doorway was set into the center of the image of Caeli-Amur, she took the lamp and quickly crossed to the other side, which depicted the Eyries of the Augurers. Kata remembered this unnerving image, surprisingly lifelike for a mosaic. She ran her hands across the rocky pinnacle, then back to the many windows at its bulging peak. She came to the Augurer, who sat in the center of the highest room, her wild hair waving in the air.

She peered closer and ran her hand across the wall until she reached the Augurer's right eye, black and piercing. The eye felt a little raised, and she pressed it gently. Nothing happened. She pressed it harder, with her thumb. There was a click, and a gust of cool air brushed her face as a cleverly hidden doorway opened up.

The three of them glanced at one another, uncertain and fearful. Cool subterranean air embraced them, and the lamp threw eerie and shifting shadows as they entered the dark tunnel. The steps continued deep underground, and Kata felt their vulnerability keenly. She expected a deadly blow to strike out of the blackness at any moment.

They continued as quietly as they could, as the stairs slowly evened out into a passageway. After a short while, the corridor opened on a small cavern. Moored on the slow-moving black water of an underground canal were two gondolas. The tunnel was larger to the right, whereas to the left it plunged into a tight, narrow hole that practically forbade entry.

Max stepped into one of the boats and attached the lamp to a hook on the curling prow. He pulled the long oar from where it lay inside of the gondola as the others clambered in. Once unmoored, the boat drifted gently toward the narrow left-hand tunnel, but Rikard used the oar against the current, steering them toward the ominously black opening to the right.

The roof above them was dark and damp, dripping water in places. The only sounds were the oar dipping in and out of the water and its creaking against the oarlock. The waterway led them ever into darkness, their lamp throwing a little circle of light over the black water.

Finally they came to a landing with dark and slippery stairs. Another gondola floated in the gloom, and they moored theirs beside it. Up the slippery stairs they climbed, careful not to slide on the little rivulets of water coursing over them.

The tunnel turned and twisted until they came to a cul-de-sac. A door handle had been built into the end. Kata grasped the cold metal and turned.

A burst of laughter came from the room beyond, loud and cold. "Yes, come in. You've done it now, haven't you? How troublesome. Do come in, though."

# THIRTY-EIGHT

Kata stepped carefully into the vast room, which was filled with the sound of water coursing through nearby channels. Lamps threw light onto these waterways, reflecting ever-moving waves onto the walls. They were in the Director's offices in the Marin Water Palace. How long had it been since the thaumaturgist Detis had first brought her here? Kata had failed Detis. He had died on the Bolt, condemned by the man who now sat behind the huge desk: the thaumaturgist Alfadi. A fearsome and frozen power lurked behind the man's white eyes.

Beside the desk sat Henri, playing with two mechanical gladiators. The toys had been charged with uncanny energy. As he set them against each other, the first swiped at the second with a sharp little sword. The second dropped down, throwing off sparks as the sword glanced off his helmet, to the delight of Henri, who looked on excitedly at the combat.

Kata's mouth went dry. She tried to swallow and failed. Confused emotions rushed through her: relief and sadness and disappointment. Henri was alive, but he seemed to be here of his own accord. He had meant so much to her, her chance to save a street child, to save some version of herself. She had been stupid to think those feelings were reciprocated.

Seeing her eyes fall on the urchin, Alfadi said, "Ah yes, little Henri here. He's quite handy to have around. He's a fine messenger, you know. Terrific at errands around the Palace. Can row a gondola all by himself, can't you, Henri?"

The boy looked up, grinned, turned back to the gladiators. The second gladiator was now clubbing the first with his small mace, snapping his head back with each blow.

"You can't blame him, Kata. He's from the street, you know, just like you."

"You don't know anything about me," said Kata.

"Well, what are we going to do with you now?" Alfadi's eyes roved over the three of them. "Kata and Rikard I know, but you—"

Alfadi's head dropped a little, and he looked at Max curiously. "You have the gift, I see. You're not one of these troublesome Brotherhood of the Hand people, are you? I'll bet you are. Undermining me at every step with your seditionism. Like a cancer, burrowing your way into everything. Secret groups. I mean, *really*." Alfadi raised his eyebrows. "Uendis and Ivarn—always sticking their noses where they didn't belong. But you, there's something strange about you."

Max didn't say anything for a moment. When he did speak, he did so with a striking certainty. "You're from the Teeming Cities. Did you know that those white eyes of yours were initially developed as a punishment for sociopaths, so that others might recognize them on sight? Somehow it became hereditary. Well, in your case, the sociopathy, too."

"How do you know that?" For a moment Alfadi looked disconcerted.

As they spoke, the truth worked its way through Kata, and her voice was tense with anger. "You killed Aceline."

"Persistent little mouse, wasn't she?" Alfadi spoke with the familiarity of an old friend. "Uncovering our plan to buy a force of thaumaturgists with the prism—you'd be surprised at how many of them leaped to my side at the first mention of it. Allying herself with the Brotherhood of the Hand. Discovering we were stealing money from the Marin coffers to raise Dumas's little gladiator army—what a *persistent little mouse*. And persistent mice must be trapped."

Kata walked over the stone floor and about halfway to the desk, the other two following right beside her. She knew they should turn and run, if they could, but neither Max nor Rikard were the running kind, and she still hoped to save Henri, even despite himself. A thought flickered across her mind: something was wrong.

She had forgotten something about the room. *It has changed since our first visit, but how?*

Putting the thought aside, Kata lashed out at Alfadi, hoping to hurt him. "But you failed in the end, didn't you? I mean, here we are. We discovered you. We've outsmarted you. You, who thinks he's so clever."

Alfadi's face darkened, and he gestured angrily for them to come closer. "Oh, I knew all about you seditionists. When I took Aceline's memories, I found out all about you, Kata. You were friends, weren't you, before I killed her? But you didn't know the depth of her friendship, did you? Yes, I can see it in the way your face changes. You were friends with Thom, too. You know the best part of it? Thom led me straight to the book. We wouldn't have known about it without him and his clumsy researches. And now it's all the way in Varenis, safely in the hands of our allies. At least Thom struggled in his last moments, though he didn't pose much of a problem. But you're right, Kata. No one did as well as you. Outfoxing me in the factory. You really are something."

Kata remembered the look around the shapeshifter's eyes in the factory. Yes, there had been something strange about them: they had seemed dark somehow. Overcompensation for Alfadi's white eyes, or consequence of thaumaturgy? "You won't succeed, you know. Not in the long run."

Alfadi beamed. "Well, we'll start with the short term, then, shall we? We can't wait for Armand to return. I mean, who knows what you've told people. My associates and I will have to act now. In which case, shall we make a deal? You can stay here as my guests until after the Twilight Observance. Our vigilant friend Ejan will crush the moderates, and wear out his own forces in the process. Then we'll arrange a new power, and all you seditionists will be back in prison where you belong. Except the three of you, of course. You will be free to go."

The best thing to do would be to run. Kata readied herself to burst into motion when the memory struck her like a blow. She took a step back, still looking at the ground beneath her feet. The last time they had been in this room, the floor was not made of stone; it had been translucent, a creature floating beneath it—a leviathan with a thousand eyes. She knew instantly that the stone was simply a thaumaturgical illusion.

She took another step back and said the first thing that came to mind. "Max, Rikard, come back over here. Let us discuss for a moment."

Alfadi smiled, and his hand moved imperceptibly. The stone flashed out of existence. Once more it was translucent. A chasm opened beneath the two men as an entire section of floor disappeared. Kata grabbed Rikard by the arm just as he went into the water. There was no hope for Max, though. He crashed into the center of the pool.

Kata herself teetered on the edge of the tank as Rikard thrashed in the water. Still grasping her arm, he scrambled up.

From the depths below something massive rose: a creature like a giant jellyfish, with a hundred tentacles propelling it. A dense multitude of eyes roved and swirled with alien intelligence. Max had no chance of reaching the edge before the creature was on him. But he made a couple of quick gestures, and a second later he simply disappeared. Where once he splashed and kicked toward the side, now he was gone, leaving behind only swirling water. Kata hoped the illusion would save him.

Kata and Rikard scrambled away from the edge of the pool, but already Alfadi was upon them, blocking off their retreat. The thaumaturgist's glowing hand clamped onto Rikard's face, and the young man screamed. A stench of burning flesh filled the air.

Behind them, the leviathan burst from the water, its two longest tentacles whipping out, their flat stingers reaching for meat. Maximilian was somewhere beneath it, hiding himself, invisible. Kata had to help him, so she twisted, spun one of her knives toward the creature's evil and intelligent eyes. The dagger plunged deep, just as the leviathan fixed a hundred more eyes onto her. The monster thrashed in rage.

Kata heard a thump and a crack as Rikard went down. Instinctively, she spun to the side, but Alfadi was already on her. He reached for her throat with a glowing hand. His eyes shone with an impossible darkness, a thaumaturgical fire.

She took a step diagonally backward and deflected the arm. Again the thaumaturgist lunged at her, and again she took a step back and to the side. This time she struck out with her open hand and caught the man in the ribs. She knew if she caused him enough pain, he would not be able to maintain his thaumaturgical equations.

He gasped and swung at her, but she skipped backward, sideways, and leaped into the air just as the leviathan's tentacle whipped beneath her legs. Now she was fighting two foes: one in front of her, one behind. Rikard lay motionless on the ground, no help at all.

From the corner of her eye, she saw a hundred shorter tentacles undulating toward her, reaching, yearning, hoping to drag her into the creature's deadly embrace. Again the longer tentacle lashed. This time it came at waist height, hoping to strike her body. She rolled beneath it, felt air being displaced as it whipped through the empty space above her.

She came to her feet in a single motion and launched her other knife at Alfadi. The thaumaturgist waved his hand, and the whirling weapon spun off to one side, as if it had hit some invisible shield. Alfadi stood still, both hands like burning coals, waiting for her to take a step out of the range of the leviathan.

Kata knew she was finished, caught between the two monsters. She dashed forward and to her left. Alfadi's hand shot out at her. She raised her arm to block it, but this time he caught her arm. She lost her momentum, fell to one knee, and screamed. Her forearm burned as if a bracelet of molten metal was clasped around it. Alfadi's other hand reached toward her face. She caught Alfadi's forearm in turn, halting his palm just before it seared her skin. She felt the heat, a little furnace close to her cheek.

Though she was quicker than Alfadi, he was the stronger of the two, and now he had the advantage. She leaned back to avoid the searing hand, but that brought her closer to the swinging tentacle behind her. At any moment either Alfadi's blazing palm would clamp her face or the tentacle behind her would whip around her leg and drag her into the pool. Hope was gone, replaced by despair.

Alfadi suddenly screamed. His hand dropped from her face. He looked down at his foot, where a sharp little gladiator sword—like a long piercing needle—had been driven between the bones. Henri scuttled away like a crab.

In an instant Kata grasped Alfadi's right wrist, which still held her burning forearm. Dropping to her back, she pulled the thaumaturgist toward her. He lurched forward. His great bulk connected with the soles of her feet, which were now pointing toward the sky. With a rapid kick, she threw him over her head.

She heard a terrible scream. By the time she hopped to her feet, Alfadi was already wrapped in a dozen tentacles, constricting around him like a writhing mass of pythons.

Kata scrabbled back as the leviathan slid its slippery and immense bulk into the water. Alfadi struggled in the monster's powerful tentacles as it descended into the depths, still looking at her with those terrifying alien eyes.

On the far side of the room, a soaked Maximilian hauled himself out of the tank, heaving and gasping.

Kata couldn't think of anything to say to the wide-eyed and staring Henri. Eventually she just stepped across to him and pulled his awkward body to her. Relief and love flooded through her. The little boy was alive, and he had saved her, just as she had wanted to save him. *He's so smart,* she thought.

"I couldn't get away," he said. "So I had to pretend I liked it here. He was going to kill me."

Rikard was unconscious, one side of his face burned black and red. His eye was closed over, or burned away—she couldn't tell. His body heaved for air.

"Come on, Maximilian. We have to get him to the Opera. We can't be sure if we're safe here, so we'll return the way we came. Who knows how many of these thaumaturgists were in Alfadi's employ? Perhaps all of them."

"We can't take him to the Opera. Ejan will have us arrested," said Max. "From what Alfadi said, he, Dumas, and Ejan formed a triumvirate."

"Rikard is my friend." Kata's voice was certain, angry. "There will be healers at the Opera who might save him, so that's where we're taking him."

They lifted Rikard over Maximilian's shoulder and headed to the secret door, which still hung open in the wall behind them.

Black-suited vigilants helped them carry Rikard through the Opera and deep into the vigilant wing. The place was quiet for once, for the action was about to begin at Technis Palace. They carried Rikard into Ejan's office, placed him gently on the table, and lit the fire for warmth. Kata had already told Henri in no uncertain terms to go home, and the boy had simply said, "Yes."

In the office, Ejan peered at the dying Rikard and turned to Kata coldly. "What have you done to him?"

Kata crossed her arms belligerently. "This is *your* fault."

Two apothecaries rushed in and quickly began to apply balms and some kind of thaumaturgical reparative. "Not even a Sortilege could save him," one of them remarked.

When they were done, Kata held out her own arm, which they treated and wrapped. She expected the vigilants to arrest her at any moment. She looked at Ejan again, prepared herself for a confrontation. She might still kill him: she judged the distance between them. *Yes,* she thought. *He's not too far.* His thuggish bodyguard Oskar stood in the corner of the room, but he wouldn't have time to react to Kata's first blows.

But before they could break into even greater hostilities, Kata looked up to see Dexion striding through the door. She immediately felt safer. Around him, twenty or so globes from the entry hall burned a steady orange. He flapped his arm at them, and they scattered.

"Kata, thank the gods, I found you here," said the minotaur. "I've been at the Arena with the other gladiators, preparing for the final spectacular. A message came from the Marin Palace about a half hour ago. All work stopped, and those asleep were awakened. Dumas is mobilizing the gladiators. They're heading for all the strategic points of the city. From what I can tell, the Collegia are moving against the seditionists. A counterrevolution has begun."

Silence reigned for a moment. Kata dropped her head despairingly. It was all over now, the city's hopes and dreams in ruin. She turned to Ejan. "So, you've succeeded. You and your friends can now divide up the city."

Ejan looked at her blankly. "What are you talking about?"

"You know what I'm talking about: Alfadi. The Collegia. You. You met with Dumas the other day, and you've refused to move against him. You placed the corrupt Georges in charge of the Criminal Tribunal. You tried to kill Maximilian. But this time you'll succeed—there's no one to stop you now."

To Kata's shock, the man grinned in disbelief. It was such an incongruous expression, she was taken aback. Even his tone had changed when he next spoke. "Kata, we may disagree on certain things, but I'm not interested in ruling the city—I never have been. I know nothing of Alfadi or Dumas's conspiracy. All I wanted was to maintain order, to defeat our enemies by any means at our disposal"

"Liar." Kata was filled with doubt. Had she misread his motives and intentions? She thought now of Rikard's denials, and how certain her friend had been that her accusations were unfounded. "You were about to attack us in the Technis Palace."

"Because you had attacked the popular power. You had killed vigilant guards and undermined the decisions of the tribunal. It was *you* who were setting yourself up as a dictator, *you* who defied the elected representatives of the Insurgent Authority. Where was your democracy then?"

Kata stood silent, dumbfounded. Only the crackling of the fire disturbed the silence.

Ejan turned quickly and opened a locked chest behind his desk. She half expected him to unveil a bolt-thrower and shoot her down, but instead he held up a folder containing a thick wad of papers. "Kata, here is your file from House Technis, containing the entirety of your history before the overthrow. Take it."

Kata reeled but took the file. "Why didn't you use it against me?"

Ejan's face regained its steely composure. "I knew you had changed. You were a seditionist. Rikard vouched for you, and I trusted him. Discrediting you would have brought no victory to me or to the movement. We fight for principles, not people. I didn't want to defeat you; I wanted to defeat your ideas."

Kata leaned against the table next to Rikard. She felt as if her legs might give way. She had been willing to believe that Ejan was a part of the conspiracy because she hadn't trusted him. She'd judged him before she had any right to. And he had stuck to his principles, even if they were crude and cold in her eyes.

"I've been so wrong. I've made so many mistakes," she said.

Ejan nodded. "We all do, you know. I should have moved against Dumas as you suggested. Now he moves against us."

The reality of the situation crashed back onto Kata. A gladiator army was marching toward them. Dumas had been right when he'd written that letter: they *would* be ready by the Twilight Observance. They had hoped to lie in wait like a snake beneath a rock, but she had provoked them into action. Would the thaumaturgists march too now that Alfadi was dead? Someone must have sent the letter from the Marin Palace to Dumas. But who, and how many thaumaturgists did that person command? Would the Brotherhood of the Hand rise to help? The questions were impossible to answer.

Ejan turned to his lieutenants. "The conflict between the vigilants and the moderates is over. Take Kata here to the Technis Palace immediately. In my absence, she is to be considered leader of all the vigilant forces there. I'll fight a rearguard action here at the Opera with those remaining."

Ejan turned back to the stunned Kata. "Save us, if you can. Go now! Go!"

Kata laid a hand on Rikard's chest. She then turned and threw her file into the fire. The flames surged, devoured the papers, and threw warmth out into the room. *At least the file was good for something,* she thought.

Kata then turned and strode through the Opera, Dexion, Maximilian, and Ejan's lieutenant behind her. They climbed onto horses reserved for vigilant leaders. Kata's mind was awhirl. She had misread everything, misjudged everyone. But now all truths had been unveiled, and the decisive clash was at hand. She would not fail this time. She would die before that happened.

Kata rode with the cool wind in her hair, possessing a calm certainty for the first time in her life.

# THIRTY-NINE

The griffins set Armand and Giselle down on the outskirts of Varenis, for the wild creatures would not approach the vast thrumming metropolis. After a train ride into the city, Giselle took Armand to a boardinghouse in the Kinarian Pocket, where she had been keeping a large room. As she led him through the door, Armand became aware of a massive figure lounging on a soft chair, one hand pointing a gargantuan modern bolt-thrower at them.

"Fat Nik! Put that down, you fool," said Giselle.

The man shrugged, leaned the chunky bolt-thrower against the chair, took a piece of fruit, and dropped it into his mouth.

Giselle collapsed into a nearby chair and reached over for the fruit bowl, but Fat Nik swatted her hand away with his other arm, which was only a stump. "Get your own."

Armand thought about his future. In the images, his left arm had been amputated, presumably to stop the bloodstone disease that even now burned within it. Was it possible to change this future without changing his later triumph? *What did it take,* he wondered, *to change history?* Wasn't it happening at every moment? Already he was anticipating the future he had seen. In doing so, wasn't he changing that very future? He shook his head, as if to clear it of these maddening thoughts.

He would stick to his original plan: to conquer Caeli-Amur at the head of one of Varenis's legions. He hoped that this would still allow him some flexibility, to save both his arm and Irik. Would the future allow his victory over Caeli-Amur together with these personal rescues? Could he change his future, altering the visions just enough to keep his victories and avoid his defeats?

He was certainly changing. The dreadful time in Camp X, the

pain of losing Irik at the Needles—these ate away at everything he had believed in. He was shedding all his former verities—loyalty, honesty, civilization—and replacing them with cold calculations. One did what one had to reach one's goals. Valentin had been right when he'd said, *You must learn to be* realistic. For the first time, Armand reconsidered Valentin's story about his grandfather's betrayal. Perhaps Valentin had told the truth.

"I thought we were receiving reinforcements," Giselle said to Fat Nik. "You're not all we're getting, are you?"

"Very funny," said Fat Nik. "Dumas sent me with a secret weapon. It's in the other room." Nik waved. "I couldn't bear to keep it in here. There's something wrong about it—you know, something unnerving."

Fat Nik picked up an odd-looking pastry from a wooden board and examined it for a minute before stuffing the entire thing into his mouth.

Through the open door to the bedroom, Armand could see a large brown book lying in the center of the bed. Armand found himself walking slowly toward it as Nik continued to talk, his mouth half full with food.

"Bound in human skin, apparently. Thaumaturgical tattoos all over it. They might have lost their potency, but I'm not taking any chances."

From up close, the book emanated unearthly power. Armand felt its force as his hand hovered close to its covers. The faded equations and ideograms drew him in, and he found himself staring at it, absorbed by the symbols, which seemed to spin before his eyes.

Excitement filled him, for he had seen this book before, during the Embrace with the Augurer. In that vision, he had given the book to the Gorgons, which was surely a step on the path to his victory.

From the other room, Giselle continued talking to Nik. "What happened to your hand?"

"I lost it fighting a dragon in a pyramid near the Teeming Cities. We passed deadly traps and crossed vast abysses before I lifted the ancient statue of some long lost god from its pedestal. Sculpted from sapphire—you should have seen it. Then the serpent slithered out of the darkness. Gods, the size of it, its awful fangs! It swallowed my hand and the statue whole!"

Then Fat Nik called out to Armand. "Leave it alone, Lecroisier. It'll send you mad."

Armand opened the book but could understand little of the contents. The language was theoretical and specialized. There were sections about the structure of Alerion's prism, the nature of the life-force within. Detailed diagrams and equations were written in spidery text, many overlapping so that the pages themselves resembled the insides of some ancient technology, all latticework, cogs, and gears of unknown design.

Armand closed the book, but he felt like something had dislocated in his mind.

That night Giselle took the couch, and Fat Nik sprawled his elephantine body over the soft chair. Fat Nik snored like an engine. Every now and then Giselle would sit up from her couch and lash out with a cushion. "Shut up, Nik. By the gods, you're lucky you're my ally!"

"What? What?" Each time Fat Nik raised his head, looked around, and quickly returned to his thunderous slumber.

In the bedroom, Armand tried desperately to decipher the book's contents. He could not understand the theoretical sections of the book, nor the mathematical ones. But, from the preface, he came to understand the prism's history. Once Aya was gone and the other gods had fled the world, Alerion—mighty and angry—had lashed out, wrecking those parts of the world not already broken by the war. When he came to Caeli-Amur, it was clear he was dying. Aya had injured him in the battle at Keos Pass. Some slow-acting, poisonous algorithm was working its way through his body.

As Alerion's soul slipped away, the Aediles found him. Taking his body into their laboratories, they captured what was left of his power and encased it in the prism, hoping the object they made might help them heal the world. Yet the world disintegrated, the works of the ancients fell, and everything was in ruin. Not even the prism could stop entropy. But it *could* ward off the poisoning effects of the thaumaturgy. It also possessed other dark powers Armand couldn't quite understand. How much of Alerion's spirit still resided in the prism was unclear, though the object seemed to possess a personality.

Without this book, it seemed, control of the prism would be at extremely dangerous at best, and perhaps impossible. And so Armand now possessed his trump card. He could approach Controller Rainer and exact his revenge on Valentin. He had been through too many trials to fail.

When Armand and Giselle entered Rainer's vast office in the Department of Satisfaction, he was already waiting on a wide couch, a chess set in midgame in front of him. He had lost weight, revealing huge and muscular shoulders, though his beard was still trimmed and sculpted into sharp and geometric edges, and his head was still shaved.

On a pile of cushions nearby lounged a slight female figure, her hair dyed a brilliant purple—a Trid-Girl. Armand remembered her from Valentin's party, when a group of them had surrounded Rainer. There was something airy and insubstantial about her, as if she might at any moment float up into the air. She stood and, placing her hands on the floor, gracefully cartwheeled once, twice, and pressed herself to Rainer. Once there, she began to croon quietly.

Rainer wrapped an arm around her. "Not now, Siki. We have visitors."

The woman continued to croon as she turned her head to Armand and Giselle, examining them curiously.

"Miracles never cease." Rainer brushed his cheek against the Trid-Girl's. "Even here in the Department of Satisfaction. Armand, my friend. Just in time, too. It's amazing how powerful a pawn can be when it finds the right square on the board."

Armand remembered Rainer's warnings at Valentin's party: *Valentin: he's not to be trusted*, the man had told him, clear as day.

"I should have listened to you," said Armand. "You warned me, but I was loyal."

"I thought loyalty was one of your precious principles?" Rainer kissed Siki. She pushed herself away and spun across the floor like a dancer. Another Trid-Girl, this one with orange hair, appeared at a nearby doorway, leaned against the frame calmly, and watched the conversation curiously.

"I have learned there is a higher principle, and that is to face reality, to make use of any means to reach your goal." Armand's voice had found a new cold and sure equilibrium.

"Ah, Realpolitik—that is the Varenis way," said Rainer.

Armand walked to the window, looked out over the plaza. A cold wind whipped between the twelve immense black towers. Huddled in the middle stood the smaller tower of the Director. "So, how is my protector, Valentin?"

Rainer laughed and walked over to stand beside Armand. "You should see him panicking in his tower, desperately trying to call in favors from Controllers who do their best to ignore him. The prism is unworkable, of course, bound with arcane sciences no one can unlock. Meanwhile, in Caeli-Amur, the seditionists are destroying the entire city, and Valentin's plans have come to naught. His support has deserted him. We need the Gorgons to call another ritual."

Armand tried to see through the windows of Valentin's tower. He imagined his betrayer hiding in there, scrabbling to maintain his power. "There is a way to unlock the prism's secrets, and I possess it."

Rainer smiled broadly. "Are there no end to your surprises, Lecroisier? It seems our pawn has made the long journey all the way to the back row. The question is, what piece are you now?"

Armand placed a hand on each of Rainer's broad shoulders. "I think you know. You didn't believe it back at Valentin's party, but I think I'm probably a Gorgon now. Shall we recapture Caeli-Amur, I at the head of the legions and you in the Director's seat?"

Rainer's voice trembled with anticipation. "Oh yes. The real Gorgons will be keen to discuss it with us, I'd say. Shall we pay them a visit?"

The passages beneath the Plaza of the Sun were labyrinthine, and Armand followed Rainer with trepidation. He had learned not to trust but to be constantly on guard. At first he controlled his emotions, but he became more anxious when they took other, older paths, deeper down. Soon the walls were made of the same black stone as the Sortileges' Towers. Armand knew this was primeval rock, rock that held secrets predating even the ancients. Down here, in the black bowels, lived the Gorgons.

A vast door loomed before them. Its surface was carved with great images from the days of the ancients. The two dragons wrapped and writhed around each other in the embrace that signaled their compact against the ancients of Etolia. For years they had wreaked havoc until Alerion faced them on the rocky island of Culia, not far from Aya. He returned victorious, but he was changed. After that, he was filled with anger—or so the myth went.

Rainer pressed the doors, which creaked open of their own accord. A single thin corridor led into the darkness. Rainer handed Armand the lantern. "I will wait here, for it is you who they want to talk with."

Armand entered that black passageway, a tightness in his chest. On it went, until, after what seemed like an age, he came out into a vast and shadowy circular hall, flickering torches on its walls. Thinking he might find the Gorgons in the gloom on the far side of the hall, he walked toward the center before realizing that three sections of the floor were in fact large circular pools of black water. Armand stopped, put his lantern on the floor, and knew where he had seen this hall before, in the Embrace of the Augurers.

The pools were shimmering. Something moved beneath the surface. An interminable rolling of the waters, and then something wriggling broke the surface: a serpent, its tongue slithering out of its mouth, its fangs bared. It was followed by another and another, writhing around one another, until finally the Gorgon's head burst from the waters.

Armand heard water streaming from the bodies of the two Gorgons rising from the pools behind him. Terrified, he stood rooted to the spot as the first creature approached him. Its pupils were vertical ellipses, like those of the mad serpents writhing on its head. Though the snakes were horrific, the Gorgon was beautiful, too, with classical features, high cheekbones, perfect skin, full lips. She tilted her head and opened her mouth. Sharp canine teeth brushed her bottom lip.

Now that all three were close to Armand, they circled him, tilting their heads, looking him up and down as if they had never seen anyone like him before.

Armand broke the awful tension. He held out the book. "In return for the Directorship, I bring you this, *The Alerium Calix.*"

One of the Gorgons stepped toward him, her face closer and closer. Her eyes fixed on his, and he trembled. Cold snakes slithered over his forehead. Her lips touched his as she took the book; she looked down upon it, opened it. Gasping, she stepped backward. Her serpents hissed in excitement. Forked tongues lashed the air. Armand closed his eyes, expected death to come quickly. When he opened them, a second Gorgon was leaning over him.

"Ah, the means to work the prism," she said.

"This is what we have . . . ," began another.

"Been searching for," finished the last Gorgon.

The first Gorgon reached out, cupped Armand's face with her hand. "You have the numbers on the council to replace Valentin?"

"We do."

She smiled a terrifying smile. "The Sortileges will soon return from their Towers, their current research complete, and they will work the magic of the prism. In return, a new ceremony will be called shortly. Feel free to dispose of Valentin as you see fit. He has lost our confidence, anyway. If you have the numbers and he can withstand our test, Rainer can rise to the position of Director."

The serpents writhed across Armand's head as the Gorgon leaned in and kissed him.

# FORTY

Armand's hands were shaky from nervous excitement as he strode along the corridor, Rainer's great bulk shifting from side to side to his right. Behind them, Giselle headed a group of ominous men who carried terrifying baglike hoods.

The group squeezed uncomfortably into the elevator, which carried them high up the Director's Tower. When they shuddered to a halt, Armand pulled the accordionlike door open, and they stepped into a reception room filled with chairs, chaise longues, and small geometric tables.

From a higher level came the voice of the Director. "Who's there? What is it?"

Armand reached the stairs first, mounted them with energy. A balcony encircled the room, and through the windows they could see the magnificent plaza with its vast Department buildings. The black towers of the Sortileges loomed closer, and Armand wondered if those thaumaturgist priests were taking an interest in these petty politics, or if they were still caught in their dark research.

Valentin sat at a desk in the center of the room, which each of the Controllers in their towers could see. He looked up from his work, irritated. "What do . . ." The irritation faded into confusion. "Armand. But . . ." Already the men from the Department of Security were encircling Valentin, and his eyes showed he was suddenly aware of them. Caught between anger and terror, he started to stand, sat down again, gathered himself.

"Friend of my grandfather," Armand said. "Valentin, whom I cared for and respected. I have so longed to see you."

Valentin's face dropped into coldness. "So you're just like your grandfather, a treasonous . . ."

Armand felt a surge of confidence. Revenge was sweet indeed. "Even if my grandfather did betray you—well, Valentin, it's you who taught me that sometimes it is necessary. Sometimes you have to lie and cheat and betray for the greater good. You are just reaping what you sowed. In one way, you are a father to me."

Valentin shifted a paper onto a pile beside him, as if work continued uninterrupted. Armand admired his calm dignity.

"Where shall we take him, sir?" asked one of the men from the Department of Security.

"To Camp X, with the political prisoners. The former Director Tiedmann will be waiting for him there," said Armand.

With a whipping motion, a bag went over Valentin's head. Straps were tightened. The man sat motionless. Just as Armand had accepted his fate, so Valentin acceded to his. He only let out a tiny burbling sob as he was led down the stairs. Sometimes the force of history was too powerful to resist.

With a feeling of contentment, Armand watched them lead the man away. Victory was his. *There is justice in the world,* he thought. *You just have to take it.*

Once Valentin was gone, Rainer sprawled into the Director's chair and looked around the room. "I could get used to this. Now, first things first. Once I'm Director, we'll need to mobilize the legions. Some will need to return from the west, I suppose. Still, Caeli-Amur shouldn't resist too much, should it?"

Armand walked to the sphere that stood before the Director's desk. He ran his hand over it. He knew the sphere's sibling was in the Technis Director's office. He remembered Autec's conversations with Tiedmann, all those months ago, and the chilling appearance of the Sortileges behind, their sheer power warping the images. Yes: once they had finished their rituals, the Sortileges would appear to them, and nothing could defeat them then.

"They're only seditionists," he said.

# FORTY-ONE

Sparks flew from the horse's shoes as they struck the cobblestones on Via Persine. As night deepened, Caeli-Amur was blanketed in its usual thick autumn fog. Kata and the lieutenant raced ahead of Max, who gripped his reins tightly. The minotaur trailed behind.

"Come on!" Dexion slapped the horse's haunch, but the creature's tongue was already lolling out of its mouth. The look in the poor thing's eyes spoke volumes: *Why do I have to carry this horned monster?*

In the square in front of the Technis Palace, the vigilant forces were already mobilized, ready to strike. Behind the walls, the moderates were armed and ready.

When he was informed of Ejan's orders, the vigilant commander stood blinking in disbelief. "But, but—"

The news broke that the seditionist conflict was over, and the vigilant forces let out a cheer. Moderates streamed from the complex. Hands were shaken; relieved conversations begun. The citizens valued unity, above all else.

But events were occurring at a frantic pace, and no sooner had the fraternizing between the forces begun than a messenger raced into the square. "Gladiators are marching down Via Gracchia!"

Max pictured the city. This force threatened to cut off the seditionist forces around the Technis Complex from those at the Opera. He knew the first principle of military strategy was to never divide your forces. But Max also knew his place. He was not the leader of this army. He was here to help Kata, just as she had helped him in his time of need. He was here as a seditionist foot soldier, doing what he thought right.

Kata gathered the captains in a circle, black-suited vigilants and

gray-uniformed moderates awkwardly assessing the new align-
ments. "I won't be isolated up here, away from our bases in the
factories and Ejan's forces at the Opera. From the Factory Quarter, Ejan should be able to retreat and join us. We can fight together,
or retreat across the wall and out of the city if need be."

She sent a screening force of mobile philosopher-assassins along
Via Gracchia to slow the gladiator's advance along the café-lined
street. As the rest of the troops marched toward the Factory Quarter, news came of vicious clashes already occurring. But the rear
guard proved successful, and before long the rest of the seditionists
were entrenching themselves among the factories and densely
packed houses. Quickly constructed barricades, built of furniture
and loose bricks, went up across the streets. Scorpion ballistae were
set up in strategic positions, their sights aimed down the largest
approaches.

The sun rose to the east, and the fog lit up like a vast sheet of
burning gold. The very air seemed overheated, as if the city had
been torn from the ground and existed in suspended animation in
some luminous underworld. Max thought of the summer before:
so hot, but giving way so quickly to a frigid autumn. Who knew
what winter would be like?

*She's mad,* said Aya. *To abandon a fortress for open streets. She could
have holed up there for a week.*

—She's not fighting only a military war; she's fighting a political one. She won't abandon the city or its citizens—said Max.

Adjutants ran in every direction, rushing to find Kata, rushing
off again with new orders. Citizens slowly emerged from their
houses and apartments. Some helped in the barricade building;
others scurried away, carrying what valuables they could.

Another messenger came, this one bloodstained, a haunted look
in her eyes. "The Opera has been overrun. Some escaped into the
Quaedian; others were hunted down and slaughtered. The dead lie
in the streets all around the Market Square. More float in the harbor. It's a massacre."

Max thought briefly about Rikard, lying unconscious in the
Opera. Kata would be upset at his death.

The Collegia's army did not press its advantage at Kata's rear, letting the rear guard of philosopher-assassins escape, fewer and bloodied, but alive. Instead they waited for their forces from the Opera to come up Via Persine. Together they would crush the seditionists in a pincer movement.

Then even worse news came, as a second black-shirted messenger staggered toward Kata's entourage. Blood stained her uniform, and the vigilant's ghastly face said it all. "The thaumaturgists are mobilizing at Marin. They have summoned the Furies."

Kata's face looked suddenly drawn. She seemed older, worn-down. Dexion let out an impressive growl. He pulled his huge hammer from his belt and swung it forward and backward ominously.

*I like that minotaur,* said Aya.

Max had seen the destruction the Furies had wrought when the Houses had loosed them on the striking Xsanthian dockworkers before the overthrow. Blackened corpses had been left strewn around Caeli-Amur's piers, stinking in the sun. The Furies had been the Houses' secret weapon: creatures summoned by the thaumaturgists from the Other Side, the land of death. Few could look at their hideous bodies as they slipped in and out of the material world without fleeing.

Max looked desperately around. He was the only thaumaturgist there. "How many?" Max asked.

The woman, exhausted and wounded, said, "A hundred or so."

Max drew a breath. Now there was truly no hope. Only death awaited them.

Kata turned to him. "Max, your friend Odile. She came to me at the Arena and warned me that you were imprisoned in the Arbor dungeons. She also said she was part of the Brotherhood of the Hand, who were loyal to the seditionists. Without those thaumaturgists, we can't fight the Furies. Can you contact her?"

Max let his head drop back slightly. "Maybe, if she still lives near the university."

"The Brotherhood: we need them, wherever they are."

Strengthened by a new sense of hope, Max dashed along the cobblestone streets, past the hastily constructed barricades. The shopkeepers on Via Persine had already closed their doors and shutters, pulling down their grates and leaving the place as empty as a ghost town. Max glanced in both directions, expecting the Collegia's forces to emerge from the fog, but the street remained cold and empty.

Max scrambled across the street and headed toward the university. A few citizens scurried from place to place: grim-faced women carrying bundles or bags, hooded students with books beneath their arms. The citizens knew violence was at hand.

*Well, it looks like we're finally going to die. It's a strange thought, after all these years. Oblivion: How do you feel about it?* said Aya.

—We're not going to die—replied Max. —Though it would be worth it for a little piece of mind around here.

*You injure me.*

—You're making jokes right now?

*When you're facing oblivion is the best time for jokes.*

Max breathed hard as he broke into a run, slowed to a fast walk along the steep and narrow streets, and ran once more down stairs until he came to a small crossroads. On one corner, a stone tower rose a couple of stories above the building it emerged from. Max had spent evenings here, drinking coffee and debating with Odile before the overthrow. Back then she had been an intellectual, opposed to the seditionists. Apparently, events had dragged her in. History had a way of doing that.

Max opened a small wooden door, ducked beneath the crossbeam, and climbed the miniature stairs up to the third-floor garret. He struck the door sharply three times—*rat-tat-tat*—and waited.

Whispered voices came from the room beyond.

"Odile," he said. "It's Max. Let me in."

The door opened slightly, and Odile looked out through the gap. Her close-cropped blond hair was ruffled, her eyes tight with anxiety. "What are you doing here? You'll get us all killed."

"Odile, the Brotherhood of the Hand. They're the seditionists' only hope."

Odile looked at him for a moment, pulled open the door, and hustled Max into the circular room. A thaumaturgist peered through one of the arrow slits that served as a window to the street below. The man turned and examined Max briefly. He rolled his shoulders and brushed his greenish face with the back of his hand. "I'm Clovis, of the Brotherhood."

Max said, "The Collegia have moved against the seditionists. A gladiator army already has control of the southern part of the city."

"We know," said Odile.

"Alfadi bought the thaumaturgists off with promises of the Prism of Alerion, and now they march on us from the Marin Palace. We cannot face them alone. We need you. We need the Brotherhood."

Clovis turned back to the window, glancing up and down the streets anxiously. "We cannot help."

Max stood there, not believing him for a moment.

Finally Odile broke the silence. "Maximilian, there are only fifty of us. Not enough to face Alfadi's thaumaturgists. Not enough to face the Furies."

Max's heart scampered like a lizard in a cage. "There is a battle happening right now, and you're choosing to stand aside? This is it, the decisive moment."

Odile smiled grimly. "There is never a decisive moment, Max. You should know that by now. It's one long struggle, and just when you think you've won, you find you weren't fighting for what you thought, and you must rise up again with new thoughts and new ideas."

"We don't have the strength," said Clovis. "Not against Alfadi or his forces. You should consider returning underground. Everything was premature. The vigilants rushed things to a crisis too quickly. They moved too fast—all of you did. People don't like change. They must grow accustomed to it slowly so they see they won't lose who they are."

"Alfadi is dead," said Max. "I saw him taken by a leviathan in Marin's palace only hours ago. We have a chance—at least, with you we do."

Clovis turned back from the arrow-slit window. "Get back to your forces. You're a danger to us here."

Max put his face in his hands. That was it. Their fate was sealed.

One hundred thaumaturgists, led by a horror of Furies. Max left the garret and stomped slowly down the stairs, black despair overwhelming him.

*Well, that went well,* said Aya.

By the time Max returned to Via Persine, the street was thick with troops. Gladiators, bolstered with the Collegia's squads and what appeared to be hired ruffians from the Lavere, moved to designated starting points for an assault on the Factory Quarter. So far, there were still spaces between the groups, so Max chose not to invoke thaumaturgy to make his passage safe. He would need his strength later.

*I'm a bit disappointed, you know. This place is starting to grow on me.*

Max pressed himself into an alcove as one of the groups marched past the alleyway, the gladiators armed with traditional weapons: bronze shields and short-swords, or pikes and nets. Many of the thin blades of the Collegia guards were rusted or notched, while the ruffians carried nasty knives, clubs, and axes.

"They'll have dug in by then, like ants in a nest," said one of the louche-looking ruffians.

"Worse if we move before the order," said another. "Attacking piecemeal would allow us to be picked off one at a time."

As soon as they passed, Maximilian dashed across the street. He heard a cry behind him and raced forward. Once he was in the warren of alleys, he looked back, but saw that though he had been spotted, no one dared give chase.

The narrow streets cut across the incline of the land, or else led down toward the Southern Headland or the Market Square. Everything remained obscured by the low-lying fog, still luminous under the rays of the faraway sun. Every now and then he glimpsed larger buildings and perhaps even the shape of the mountain before the fog deepened again.

Max glimpsed motion from the windows of one of the factories to his right. He stopped dead still, his heart beating. A man, bolt-thrower held in both hands, observed him closely. He was in a killing zone, standing at a crossroads in the line of sight of several bolt-men or archers. Suddenly he was aware of the combatants in the factories and apartments surrounding him. A scorpion stood, half hidden by rubble, along one of the alleys. The seditionists had turned the area into one great fortress.

Max scrambled over a barricade, out into a central square, over a second barricade—this one defended by two scorpions—and then up the ladder leading to an ancient ruined water tower that stood high above the buildings. Here Kata had set up her command. The tower's roof had collapsed long ago, shingles stolen away for new building work. Over its crumbling walls, the district could be seen drifting in and out of the fog.

An adjutant finished reporting that the gladiators were busy sealing up the holes in their encirclement lines. Soon the only escape would be over the city's walls at the seditionists' rear, and Max imagined the slaughter that would occur if they tried to flee that way.

Dexion stood beside Kata, a massive bodyguard. Max hadn't warmed to the great creature, who seemed too jejune for his taste, though he appreciated the minotaur's immense, almost godlike presence, which did much to raise morale. Dexion seemed to be here out of loyalty to Kata, and for the excitement of it all.

Kata dismissed the adjutant and looked to Max questioningly.

He ran his hands through his short hair. "They said no. They think we cannot win a conflict now, that we should return underground."

Kata leaned over the water tank's walls, looked out over the foggy district. "We're *not* going to surrender. Better to fight and lose than not to fight at all."

*When I fought Alerion, it was much the same. He was always belligerent, and was much better prepared than I. But I admire this Kata. She's resilient, isn't she? Even when others would have buckled, she holds firm. She's a bit like me.* Aya spoke seriously now.

—She's nothing like you—said Max.

*See, there you go again. Always putting me down.*

Dexion called out. "The enemy is moving, Kata."

A particularly thick and eerie fog rolled over the quarter. It nestled into the buildings and hovered in the squares, leaving everything ethereal and ghostly. Along several of the approaches to the square, they caught sight of bronze breastplates and helmets, pikes and swords. Only the sound of gladiators marching echoed through the thick air—the awful sound of ruin.

A cry went up, and the gladiators charged forward. Still no answer came from the defenders.

Max's eyes fixed on the main column as it charged along the largest street, directly toward the square. It had almost reached the first line of barricades, yet still the defenders did not strike. Closer and closer the gladiators came, until their leading members scrambled up the obstruction like a deathly wave. The street behind them was awash with the Collegia's army.

The defenders answered with their own desperate but unbeaten cries. Bolt-throwers appeared at windows. Doors were thrown open. Guards leaped to their feet behind barricades. Scorpions drove giant missiles through the massed gladiators. The sound of a thousand bolts being loosed carried through the heavy air, followed by the ring of steel striking steel. Philosopher-assassins danced among the melee, throwing knives and stars, swinging chains and lassos. Then came the ghastly screams of dying men and women. The seditionists fell upon the Collegia like the great enveloping mist itself. For all the training the gladiators had done, they were not ready for this. Hundreds went down in the first minute, many more afterward.

*The little people of history. They're always the ones who are forgotten. Yet they're the ones who make the difference,* said Aya.

A wave of fog drifted across Max's line of sight. By the time it passed, the Collegia's forces had fled.

"Come," said Kata. "Let's go to the ground. We're no use up here."

*How long before the thaumaturgists arrive with the Furies? Not long,* thought Max.

# FORTY-TWO

Vicious fighting began all along the line. The seditionists had prepared their emplacements well, and citizens from the district, armed with kitchen knives, rakes, and wood-cutting axes, joined them in short brutal engagements before falling back to their next line of defense. Kata had known what she was doing, retreating to the area where the seditionists had their base.

Cries and screams echoed dully through the fog. The dead were left where they fell; the injured fought on until they were brutally dispatched. Citizens who did not join the fighting retreated in groups across the squares. Children cried as they scurried along with them.

Kata and her entourage formed a kind of mobile headquarters, racing through the thickening fog from crisis point to crisis point. Again and again they threw themselves into the fray at decisive positions, beating back breakthroughs, reestablishing defenses. Then they charged off to the next pivotal confrontation. With inhuman strength, Dexion fell upon the enemy, his huge hammer crashing down onto bodies, shattering bones, crushing skulls. Wherever he joined the battle, the enemy was routed, eyes filled with terror at the colossal creature facing them.

Max joined, helping where he could, his stomach lurching at the sight of the critically wounded. Here a man, his head caved in; there a man skewered by a trident, its three points horrid wounds. Many of the seditionists had been trapped in the gladiators' hooked throwing nets and, once incapacitated, the gladiators found them easy to dispatch.

Max made himself invisible and struck stealthily in the fog, a silent killer using one of Kata's knives. But his strength soon wavered, the feeling of the Other Side seeping into him like water into a sponge, weighing him down, soaking him with its alienness.

After a particularly vicious engagement, Max followed Kata back to the square in front of the water tower, to a barricade built from loose bricks and furniture—a final line against the oncoming army.

An adjutant scurried toward them, his face streaked with dirt and blood and tears. "Kata! Kata! The thaumaturgists. They've loosed the Furies down at the steel factory. The line is broken."

Kata stared for a second, grim-faced. "Sound the retreat, to back here at the water tower. We'll try to re-form the line here."

But Max had little confidence in the plan. When the thaumaturgists arrived with their pitiless Furies, they would shatter the seditionists' front, sending the survivors screaming through the alleys, only to be caught in cul-de-sacs, trapped up against the wall. The massacre would be terrible. Grief pressed down on Max at the thought of it: All their dreams for a better world smashed. Did this world allow no hope?

Then Max saw a way to face the enemy: he had glimpsed Aya's mastery of the Art, his skill with the prime language. If he could somehow appeal to the ancient mage . . . But how?

—Help me—Max begged Aya.

*I'm enjoying watching this. Why would I choose sides?*

—You've lost all connection to the human race.

Aya settled back calmly in Max's mind, like an ancient lounging in one of the pleasure palaces. Max's thoughts roved desperately for a solution.

More messengers told of the seditionists retreating from the gladiators near Via Gracchia. The defense was collapsing like a deflated balloon. Kata stood nearby on the barricade, seemingly unfazed.

Max knew there was one last, desperate action he could take.

—What if I gave you control? You could do so much. You could change the outcome.

Aya laughed, a strange echoing thing. *You are doing fine.*

Max lay on the barricade and released his inner control. His arms dropped to his sides, his head pressed heavily against a wooden table. Something jutted into his back.

—Here, Aya. It's yours. I'll not challenge you for this body. It's yours forever.

*Don't you think you'd better get up? I think the Furies are coming. I really want to see them.*

Resigned, Max settled back into his body and raised his head, ready for the end. He put aside the knife, took a short-sword from a dead guard, and held it inexpertly in his hand.

The remains of the seditionist forces came running, half mad, screaming, and wild-eyed. It was unnerving to see how many leaped the barricades and fled toward the city walls. The terror was infectious, and others broke along with them. Then the last stragglers dragged themselves across the square. These were wrecked men and women. One held his arm against his stomach, holding pinkish entrails in; another crawled on all fours like an animal, emitting a low moan; a woman helped another whose lower leg had been shattered by some blunt instrument. Others didn't make it to the barricade, but fell in the square, dead or dying.

Chills rushed up Max's back as he stared into the rolling fog. A strange silence came over the area. For what seemed an eternity, the defenders stared out into the thick murk, expecting enemies to burst forth at any moment. They waited and waited, their nerves fraying. Every now and then a seditionist guard let out a low moan of fear.

Finally a shape began to emerge: first its snout—somewhere between that of a hound, or perhaps a fanged goat—then the rest of its shadowy form. Wiry limbs with tight thin muscles roiled out of the darkness, then disappeared, appeared once more in impossible places. Elsewhere a torso resembling a skinned cat's, dripping with blood and ooze, emerged, then sunk back into the black.

A leash held the creature back, but it strained, its demonic eyes burning black.

Something dislodged in Max's mind, came free. He thought he might be going mad. He felt his tongue bleeding, for he had bitten it. Strength drained from his limbs. Whines came from the guards around him. Others closed their eyes, buried their faces in the ground, or into the makeshift barricades.

*Oh yes,* said Aya. *Oh yes. I'd forgotten how beautiful they are.*

The creature strained against its leash, strode forward, reconfigured itself in some impossible way, pieces of it shifting and moving. More of the creatures appeared to its left and right.

The handler of the first creature emerged, at first only a silhouette. Then the outline became material, a black suit and death mask carved in the shape of a horse's skull.

Max looked around in desperation. He could make himself invisible, but he knew that would not fool the Furies. They were creatures of the Other Side; his invisibility only affected those in the material world. He didn't know the sciences of the dark lands.

All around him, seditionists broke and fled. Dexion roared, but it seemed to come from far away.

Max looked inward at himself, at Aya, at his life. What was it? What had it become? He laughed at his youthful arrogance, at his self-centeredness. He had been prepared to sacrifice others on the altar of his own certainty. He thought now of Markus, his mentor, who he had so easily sidelined from the movement. He looked into the darkness that was his mind, where Aya lay, self-satisfied, content. Neither of them deserved to survive, for they were alike in some terrible way Max now recognized. The thought rattled in Max's mind. *Neither of them deserve to live,* he thought.

At the center of the approaching thaumaturgists stood a tall cruel man, his face obscured by a long death mask, a stretching, leering thing that looked like it might have melted. This dark captain reached up and pulled his mask away, revealing a horrid, ruined face. Bloody and swollen, torn and bleeding, only the malevolent white eyes made him recognizable. Alfadi had survived the leviathan.

The Furies were loosed.

Max knew what he had to do. In truth, he had known it for a long time but had kept the knowledge from himself, for it had frightened him. Now he withdrew into himself, gathered all his forces together, and looked down onto the landscape of his mind, at all the features he had once been so proud of: at his intelligence, like some great monolith towering over a plain; his talent with the Art, which lit that landscape up; at the dark valleys and chasms of his hurts, the places where he had taken blows. He looked down on that landscape and at the creature he had once thought of as a god: he gazed down at Aya.

Max let himself plunge down over that landscape like a flood. In that instant Aya realized Max's intention.

*No!* The mage screamed and lashed out, trying to force Max back.

Max offered no resistance to Aya, but engulfed him like water. He kept no barriers to his mind. Aya lashed out, but with each blow he only sunk deeper into the formlessness that was Max.

Sudden flashes of memory came to Max then, as he lost himself. He did not know who he was, or where he was. Now he was a maelstrom, a seething mass, twisting and turning. Pieces of him broke off. Pieces of Aya joined him. Knowledge flooded into him; other things he forgot, remembered again. All aspects of his life were reconstructed, seen anew, so that they seemed like different events, events that took place beneath a different sun. Pieces locked together in new ways. New emotions came into being. He felt a great distance—an isolation—enter him, along with snatches of the language, the prime language, which he came to know and understand. Aya cried a terrible, lonely cry as his personality finally dissolved. The maelstrom quieted, the water settled, and he came back into consciousness, as Max, as Aya, as some hybrid of the two of them. No: as Max, but terribly transformed, a Max barely recognizable.

The dull light pierced his eyes, and he came up. He glimpsed movement: a mask, white and deadly; whips; something coming at him with fearsome rapidity. Bloody ropy muscles and tendons, yellowed fangs from red gums. Not a dog; a horse. Not a horse; some exotic creature moving at unnatural speed. An unnatural creature. It was almost on him now, and two fragments of his memory came together as it did. He was not whole, but he knew this thing should not be here. It belonged on the Other Side, and it planned to take him with it. He slowed down time, so that the creature seemed to float through the air.

He stood up, and the equations rose up to him. His head tilted back and his arms reached out as he channeled the universe's power.

He—whoever he was—set the universe's awesome power loose. The air was rent. A blinding light shone forth.

# FORTY-THREE
#### 〜⦿〜

The Furies descended on the remains of Kata's forces. There was little she could do now except die with the rest of them. Across the square, Alfadi smiled cruelly, his ruined face hitching itself up like some ship's ragged and torn sail after a storm. She looked into those pale and empty eyes and saw only bleakness and violence. He had bested her, just as he had bested Aceline.

The Furies flew through the air, their speed unnatural and frightening. As Kata's guards broke and ran around her, or pressed themselves down on the barricades, as if they might somehow melt into it and disappear, she stood tall, her head held high. Time seemed to slow, movements delayed, sounds stretched out. The calls and cries of the seditionists beside her seemed to yawn through space. Two of the Furies came at her, racing each other.

On they came, first thirty feet away, then twenty. Bolts were loosed from the scorpions behind the barricades and bolt-throwers held by desperate guards. Time itself seemed to distort. The bolts seemed to fly forward, hover gracefully in midair as if halted by some unseen force, then speed on to their targets. Some flew past the creatures; others disappeared into the darkness surrounding them. One of the Furies skidded across the cobblestones, rolling and twisting in pain, disappearing into the darkness. For a moment Kata thought it might be sucked back to the Other Side. But no, it recomposed itself and sped on.

Now ten feet away, the other Furies flew toward her. Still, she seemed to see every movement, every tiny detail as death came at her. She prepared herself for the creatures to smash into her and rend her with their teeth.

With one giant leap, Dexion brought his hammer down onto

one of the creatures' heads. It crumpled to the ground, and an instant later the two of them were at each other, spinning and lashing out, like wild dogs fighting.

A light gleamed to Kata's left, like a powerful lamp. Kata realized she had been vaguely aware of it for a while, but now it burst into a glowing brilliance. She looked to the side and saw Maximilian there. A blinding ray burst from the radiance surrounding him, and then another and yet another, until it seemed that a white sun burned. Only the silhouette of Max was visible; the rest of him was a bulb of incandescence. Kata averted her eyes, looked back and away once more.

Ahead of her, the Furies cowered and scrambled away sideways, having forgotten their prey. Like dogs that had been kicked, they scratched and scrambled farther back, their bloodshot eyes fearful, terrified.

Alfadi's thaumaturgists held their arms to their eyes and crouched, as if expecting a blow.

Only Alfadi faced the brilliance uncowed, but his cold white eyes were filled with a desperate anger and surprise, his ragged face grimacing under the beams of blinding light. The thaumaturgist rushed forward, his hands burning red with thaumaturgical power. He raced up the barricade directly into the globe of light, intent on attacking Max. But as he entered the searing globe, Alfadi's body seem to shrink, as if it had aged rapidly. His suit emptied itself and fell down. A bundle of rags tumbled from the barricade and onto the ground, nothing more than a ruin.

One by one the Furies screamed, terrible unearthly cries, as they were sucked back into the Other Side like water down a hole.

The enemy thaumaturgists cowered. Some crawled away over the cobblestones, the white light of some new form of enchantment bearing down on them with a terrible weight. Others lay prostrate, clamped down to the ground by the relentless force.

When they saw the thaumaturgists turn and flee, the gladiator troops behind them broke.

Dexion staggered to his feet, his skin torn and blackened, and his voice rang out. "A mage. It is a mage of old!"

Kata's troops pursued their enemies down the streets, toward Market Square. Leaving Dexion with a now unconscious Maximilian, she staggered after them. Bodies lay strewn along Via Persine, cut down from behind. The seditionist guards were not inclined to forgive, it seemed.

Around the Opera, corpses lay scattered like rag dolls in a nursery, their arms and legs at unnatural angles. Blood lay in pools beside the bodies, entrails held in place by stiffened hands. Most of the bodies were vigilant guards. Though they had defended the building resolutely, they were no match for the trained force of the gladiator army. Here and there a gladiator lay fallen, a trident or short-sword by his side.

Already a slightly unpleasant odor hovered in the front hall. Here she found seditionist guards rummaging through the bodies for valuables. The Opera's mobile lights pulsated an intense, angry red and refused to come down from the ceiling.

Kata rushed into the southern wing, looking for Rikard. She could feel the hope inside her, a little spring emerging from the rocks of her heart, even though she knew it was misplaced. The wing resembled a bloody harvested field: nothing remained standing; there were only stray stalks of wheat scattered on the ground. Corpses were strewn in the corridors and jammed up in the corners of rooms.

Kata came to Ejan's former office. Across the room lay a dark-haired man, facedown. Rikard! She ran to him, noticing as she did the pool of red and black blood that lay beneath him. The spring in her heart dried up. She turned the man over. His middle-aged face had been smashed in, his stomach slashed with a hundred cuts of a sword. It wasn't Rikard.

Numb with the horror of it all, she continued to an open courtyard. Here some moderate guards were piling the bodies up on a hastily constructed pyre, built from ruined furniture and paper from the printing presses.

"We won't be able to bury them all." One of the seditionists looked around despairingly.

"Ejan's lieutenant Rikard. Have you seen him?" said Kata.

"He's in one of the rooms off the corridor. We moved him there so he'd be more comfortable." One of the men threw a broken lamp onto the pyre, which began to burn quickly.

Kata stumbled back, moved from room to room until she found one filled with injured seditionists. Some groaned. Others lay pale-faced and grim. A good-looking bearded man moved from patient to patient, offering water and words of comfort.

Along one wall lay Rikard, one side of his face burned horribly. He held one hand against a deep wound in his stomach. His smile was part grimace.

Kata dropped to her knees beside him.

"They got me," Rikard said. "Made sure of it."

Kata looked around for healers or apothecaries, but there were none. "I'll find someone to help you."

"Kata, it's not good. Look at the wound. No one can save me. Stay here with me. I don't want to die alone."

It had been a long time since Kata had cried, but now the tears came, and she didn't try to hold them back.

From across the room, the bearded man smiled gently, nodded with compassion, tended to more of the injured.

"It's better this way, anyway," said Rikard. "Look at me. Look at my face."

"There's nothing wrong with your face," said Kata.

"Will you tell my mother? Tell her it was quick, though, won't you? Tell her I didn't suffer much."

Kata got to her feet. She would find that apothecary. But Rikard grasped her arm. He spoke in short breathless gasps. "No. Stay here, Kata. It won't be not long now. I wanted to thank you. You've got a good heart, underneath it all. Remember that history isn't kind. When great events come, hard decisions must be made. Of course you know that. I'm not sure why I'm saying it. And you alerted me to the dangers of hasty decisions, easy solutions. To the dangers of believing *we* know those solutions, that we are the ones with the right judgment. Thank you for that. It's a pity I haven't been able to make better use of it."

Kata tried to think of something to say, but there was nothing. Instead she wiped her tears from her eyes.

"All those things I'll never experience. I thought one day I might have children, you know."

Kata was shocked. "What?"

"Yes. A long way off, but why not? Life can be about the little things, can't it? You never saw that in me, did you?

"I associated you too much with Ejan," said Kata. "And I associated Ejan too much with . . . I don't know, things I wanted to believe about him."

Rikard groaned, and his words came more breathlessly. "That's it, Kata. It's coming now. I can see the Other Side, I think. I'm scared. See all those figures, walking soundlessly through the field. They're all dead, Kata. They're all dead. Can you see it? The black stairs, leading up to the long black field. Can you see it, Kata? I can see the Dark Sun. Those black rays are cold. The Dark Sun. It's magnificent, isn't it? Terrible and magnificent."

"I'm here. I'm here." She kept repeating it again and again as Rikard's breath came quick and ragged. He began to shudder, as if he were awfully cold. Then the shudders became spasms. His chest thrust forward. He stopped breathing, burst into three ragged breaths, stopped breathing once more, and was dead.

After Rikard's death, the bearded man came to her and she sized him up for the first time. His name was Irik, and he was from Varenis. His clothes were ragged and worn, and he had the lean look of a man who had been through hardship. Yet there was a softness about his manner and movement. He touched everything as if he were a gardener, tending to fragile flowers. He placed one hand on her shoulder, gently. "I'll look after him now. You don't need to worry. He's safe now. He's safe."

So Kata left them both. Her tears dried as she walked blindly from the Opera. She wanted revenge on those who had killed her friend. She wanted Dumas's head on a pike.

Others had the same idea. On the balustrade, guards of both factions—moderates and vigilants—were carrying out executions. A line of prisoners kneeled, heads bowed, before a pile of bodies on the cobblestones beneath them. Behind the captives stood seditionist guards, bloodied swords in hand. In the square nearby stood even more guards, encircling the remaining miserable-looking prisoners.

Blades hacked into necks or drove through bodies. The line of captives fell forward, over the balustrade and onto the pile of bodies nearby. Another line shuffled to take their places. They quivered and whimpered as they waited for the final blow.

At the head of a battered group, Ejan emerged from the Quaedian, his bodyguard Oskar covered in another dozen bloody cuts that would one day add to his scars. Seeing the executions, Ejan called out, "No! Stop this immediately."

The fragile-looking Elise stepped forward from behind the prisoners. Apparently she had been overseeing the killings. How things had changed. Everything had turned upside down: vigilants calling for mercy, moderates organizing a massacre. "They're traitors. They would have done the same to us."

"You're right—they would have," said Ejan. "But that's one of the things that separates us from them. There will be trials. They must have a chance to defend themselves. There will be justice, but no executions now."

"Wouldn't it be easier if we kill them?" said Elise. "Wouldn't it be easier to cleanse the city of those who will destroy us?"

"They're no threat to us now," said Ejan. "Take them to the dungeons in the Arbor Palace."

Elise and the others grumbled and led away the prisoners, whose shocked faces were softened with relief.

Elsewhere there were more massacres. Kata came too late, finding only bodies piled up, seditionists loitering around or gone to pursue more enemies. At other times the seditionists had already lined up the exhausted enemies and were leading them slowly to the Arbor dungeons. Kata followed the devastation to the great metal structure of Collegium Caelian.

There she found her veteran captain Terris looking up at Caelian's huge building. In another time, Terris might have been an architect or a teacher. His lack of personal ambition made him a perfect captain. In fact, Terris was one of those seditionists who just wanted it all to be over so he could return to real life.

Seeing her approach, he said, "They're not answering. They're deciding what to do, I guess."

Kata approached the door, looked for some kind of opening above.

A panel slipped open, and a head poked out. "If we give you Dumas, will you allow the rest of us to go free?"

"We should send them all to the dungeons," said Terris. "They all deserve the Bolt."

Even Terris wanted a reckoning. Many of the seditionists grumbled their agreement. Others waited to see what Kata had to say.

If she accepted the deal, she would have Dumas. There would be no more bloodshed, here at least. But then the rest of the Collegia hierarchy would escape justice. How could they continue to build a new Caeli-Amur when they had enemies in their midst, saboteurs who could strike at any moment? How could they build a new world, when justice had not been served?

"I don't think you're in any position to make demands," she said.

The man said, "These walls are impregnable. In any case, the Collegium is a network, not an organization. Most of us had no idea about Dumas's plans. We were as surprised as you."

What he said may well have been true, but Dumas was still the Collegia's leader.

Kata agonized before finally saying, "Give us Dumas. The rest of you are free for the moment. But we will require your identities before you may leave. You may yet face recriminations."

There was a grumble of discord among the seditionists and she sensed Terris's dissatisfaction as he shifted on his feet nearby.

The doors slid open, just enough to allow Dumas's heavy figure to be shoved out. Dumas's bloodhound cheeks seemed even more saggy, the reds of his eyelids clear for all to see. He looked exhausted, broken. Kata felt a flush of power run through her. The man was in her hands, and she could do what she wished with him. The feeling was seductive, overwhelming. She liked it and was disturbed that she did.

Kata strode toward Dumas, who raised his arm to protect

himself. But she was already behind him. One hand grasped his forehead, pulling it back, as the other pressed her knife to his neck.

But she couldn't do it. She tried to think of something fitting to say, something that would make the new relationship clear, make sense of the situation, capture the moment, but words were not enough. Finally all she said was, "To the dungeons."

She pushed Dumas forward, and he fell to his knees. Two seditionists took him by the arms and led him toward House Arbor.

# FORTY-FOUR

Armand would never become used to the feeling of being watched. Through the Director's windows, the Sortileges' Towers loomed around their building, like cruel adults encircling a child. The Sortileges had emerged from their researches and looked outward. A cowering consul had come scuttling across to the Director's office, face pale, voice quavering, to explain that the Sortileges were very unhappy. They were set to intervene themselves, he squeaked, if the situation in Caeli-Amur wasn't resolved.

From where Armand stood in the center of the office, each of the Department buildings' ninth-floor windows could be seen clearly. Armand thought he could see Controller Dominik looking down on them from the Department of Benevolence.

Behind his desk, Rainer shifted uncomfortably in his seat. Giselle stood before the sphere and looked at Armand. It was time. The seditionists had contacted them a day before and agreed upon this meeting.

Giselle ran her hands over the ball. A small point of light emerged, grew to engulf the sphere, transcended its boundaries, and a second three-dimensional room was superimposed on the material one.

A group of figures sat before them. At the front sat the Northerner Ejan and the thaumaturgist Max. Lounging beside them, her face steely, was the former spy Kata. News had come that she was now one of the leaders, which was typical of the seditionists: their leader was a murderer and a liar, and a woman to boot. A magnificent minotaur sprawled over two seats at the very rear. What a motley bunch they were, a ragtag group of scum.

"The Caeli-Amur Insurgent Authority," said Rainer. "We will

give you one chance for unconditional surrender. We have everything now: the Prism of Alerion and the book, *The Alerium Calix*. The legions are mobilizing. Five battle-hardened legions are returning from the west, where they've been pacifying barbarians."

Kata ignored Rainer. "Armand, we know about your plans. You might not have heard, but your allies in Caeli-Amur have been . . . disarmed."

"What allies?" said Armand.

"Alfadi and Dumas," said Kata. "I saw Alfadi go down, crushed into nothingness. Dumas will not survive the justice we are meting out either."

"Well, that makes you a bloodthirsty ogre, doesn't it?" Armand spat back. But he knew this was the world he was in for: the world of Realpolitik, as Rainer called it, the world of cold calculations and maneuvers, of the will to power. There was no room for sentiment.

"What does it matter, now that the legions are mobilizing?" said Rainer. "You don't stand a chance, so it would be better if you negotiated now. We can bring this little adventure to a peaceful end."

But Kata seemed intent on pressing her advantage. There was a cruelty to her, apparently. She gestured to the figure hiding in the darkness nearby.

Irik strode into view. The handsome cheekbones, the way he leaned forward slightly as he walked, the calmness, as if no event overwhelmed him—all this was like a dagger in Armand's gut. The pressure was too much. Armand's face cracked, like that of glass under too much pressure. "Irik?"

"I'm sorry, Armand," said Irik.

"You see," said Kata. "We know all about your plans. You intended to use the tunnels beneath the city as a secret entranceway, didn't you? While our troops concentrated on the walls, you hoped to storm the city easily. That's what you told Irik, isn't it?. But your armies won't surprise us. Not now."

Armand stood up and strode toward the ethereal figures until he was almost on top of them. "There is no loyalty in this life. Know this, Kata: you will not be spared. I have visited the Augurers, and I have seen the future. You will end your life, crawling away on the dirt like a dog! Your minotaur will have his horns cut off. Your friends will be strapped on our machines and broken, driven into half-life by our thaumaturgists. They will live in the zone between us and the Other Side, become our perished slaves, dead yet not dead, living endlessly in torment."

Kata looked at him coldly. "The future is not something set, Armand. We make it every instant. We change it every step we take. The future is fluid. Surely, the Augurers taught you that."

"And yet," said Armand, "everything I've seen has come true."

"There's still a chance to stop this, Armand," said Irik.

Armand turned to Irik. "And you. You will not be spared either."

Irik drew a deep harried breath and looked away in pain.

Armand felt the bloodstone in his arm, burning with unnatural fire. He knew what he needed to do to save himself, and to keep the future on track. He was determined now to ensure he became ruler of Caeli-Amur, whatever the cost. If that meant he ended up carrying a dead Irik through empty halls, then so be it.

The Department of Devotions was housed in a gargantuan building, like the rest of the Departments. Unlike the others, it was filled with comforts of every kind. The air was warmed to a perfect temperature. In every corner sat long couches and cushions, fountains sprouting fresh water.

The surgeries were upstairs: a small select place where the officials of Varenis might reconstruct themselves, rebuild their faces, straighten their noses, hitch up their skin so it was tight as a drum over their bones.

Armand followed one of the surgeons down a wide corridor. It was lit a comfortable red, as if the place were a womb.

A door opened not far along the corridor, and a long thin woman shuffled out. She seemed to have some kind of plastic wrapped around her face, and bloody scars could be seen beneath it, half healed through some grim thaumaturgical science. Her skin shone with a sickly, unnatural glow.

"Armand! Armand, my dear, look at you. Oh, how lovely to see you." Olka Valentin reached out to him. "What are you doing here? You're already so beautiful! Oh, you will come and see me, won't you? I'm all alone now, you know."

Armand nodded stupidly, though Olka did not seem at all upset that he had betrayed her husband.

She leaned toward him, lecherously. "I want you to come and *visit me.*"

Armand nodded and backed away with horror. "Of course. Of course."

As quickly as he could, he followed the surgeon into the operating room and sat on a long reclining chair. The walls, the fittings, the light globes—everything was curved and smooth and sleek, designed to relax the mind.

The surgeon looked down at him. "Show me your arm, Controller Lecroisier."

Armand pulled up his shirt and revealed the red spider's web creeping up his forearm. "The only way to save me is to cut it off."

"Yes, yes, I've seen this before. Rare, though. Only thaumaturgists suffer from this, really. I can't imagine how you contracted it. Anyway, lie back and relax. It's all going to be fine." Armand felt a sharp prick in his elbow and a soft warmth spread through him. As he started feeling groggy, he began to panic.

"There will be a lot of blood," said the surgeon to someone beside him. "Prepare for that."

Armand tried to sit up, but something held him down.

"It's all right. It's going to be all right," said the surgeon.

"Nnn. Nnnn." Armand tried to speak, but the roof blurred and he lost all strength. The last thing he heard was the sickening sound of an engine starting, and a saw whirring and whining in the background.

And so it was done. Armand awoke and looked down at the stump of his arm. The pain was terrible, but he refused the opium they offered him. He wanted to endure it, to cleanse himself. He wanted to feel the consequences of his decisions. He wanted to face up to the pain.

After a few days recovering in the Department, he made his way back to the Director's office, where Rainer had already arranged himself. On the balcony surrounding the building, two Trid-Girls stood, arm in arm, looking out over the plaza. Both wore bright dresses that moved and shifted over them, here showing off the fractal tattoo on one girl's back, there curling around the other girl's neck. One dress was orange, the other green—each of them the same as the girls' hair.

Rainer glanced at the soft white bandages wrapped around his stump. "We all cut things off. It hurts, but it's necessary."

Armand thought of Irik. "We do. We do."

"It won't be long before the legions will be ready to march south," said Rainer. "Don't make a mess of it, or we'll both be sent after Valentin. I can't imagine you want to end up back at Camp X, do you?"

Armand looked out at the magnificent plaza and the towering Department buildings. He looked at the Sortileges' Towers, black and omnipresent. He looked further out between the buildings, to the Kinarian pocket and beyond. He hated this city. He could not wait to go home. He could not wait to return to Caeli-Amur.

# FORTY-FIVE

Kata stood beside Max at the Standing Stones. Around them waited hundreds of people, now quiet. The composition of the crowd had changed. Fewer now came from the Lavere. More men and women from the factory district and students from the Quaedian circled the ancient monument. This mass stood silent, quieted, even as the cart rattled along the road from the Arbor Palace. Seven haggard-looking men clung to the bars, stared out into the multitude bitterly.

"How could we have sanctioned this?" said Max.

"What can we do, otherwise?" said Kata. "The citizens control their lives for the first time. There is an Assembly. There are open debates and discussions. People make their own choices, free from an oppressive power. But our power hangs by a thread. We must have deterrence, to stop the next group of Dumases and Alfadis."

"Deterrence never works," said Max. "There will always be opponents."

Dumas was led from the cart, his great bulldog head staring at the very machine he had designed.

A new guard called out. "Guillam Dumas of Collegium Calian, sentenced to death for conspiracy to overthrow the Insurgent Assembly."

Still the crowd was silent. Max was right: if the liberation had brought joy across the city, in the bars or the alleyways, in the avant-garde plays held in the Quaedian, in the agitprop on the street corners and the never-ending parties in the universities, that joy did not make it here.

"The legions have already begun mobilizing," said Kata.

"So that is the end of opposition," said Max. "That is the end of discussion. That is the end of debate. You think you're allowing the citizens to choose their lives, but how can that be when they can't speak their minds?"

The guard turned to Dumas. "Any words, Dumas?"

Dumas looked up. His voice came roughly and angrily. "Are you any different from the Houses? You have your Bolt. You have your dungeons. Where is this new world of yours?"

The words rang in Kata's ears. Not long ago she might have made the same argument. She might have agreed with both Max and Dumas. In fact, she still did. Yet events had a logic of their own. She had chosen to become a leader and now she was responsible for *this*.

No one responded. Instead, a sense of melancholy resignation hovered over everything. This was no celebration. In a sense, it was a defeat. The crowd understood that.

Dumas was strapped into the machine. The Bolt burst through his chest. It was over.

Kata looked away. "We didn't choose this. It was forced upon us."

"What other horrors will be forced on us before this is all over?" Max took her hand and held it in his own. He looked at her, his eyes questioning and uncertain. He had changed terribly in these last days. He looked on as if from an Olympian height. He held her hand tighter. "I feel like I'm slipping away from the world. I can't feel anything. I . . . I . . ."

Kata leaned against him, the weight of her body pressing into his, the weight of events pressing on both of them. History—life—was exhausting. It ate up people, places, dreams, and visions. It offered happiness, took it away, offered it once more, then wrenched it out of sight.

Max's hand pressed hers even more tightly. "Don't leave me now. I need you. I need you more than I ever did."

Kata squeezed his hands back, then pushed him gently away. Too much had changed, in her and in him. "We can't, Max. Not like that." They were different people now, new incarnations of

themselves. "Actually, that's not what I meant. I meant that *I* can't."
She thought of Dexion. She was drawn to that magical creature's
power, his love of life, his growing maturity. "I have to go now."

As she left Max, Kata looked at the ruined city before her. They
had hoped to be fully human, but it had turned them into . . . what,
monsters? She headed across the city, to the only monster she really
knew, the creature who was more fully human than any of them.
She knew where she would find him.

# FORTY-SIX

Max stared at the Standing Stones, oblivious to the crowd and the events surrounding them. A symbol for so much, the Stones had always stood there, mysterious, implacable. They had been there since before the time of the ancients, would last longer than any of them. What did his little life matter in the face of such vast expanses of time? Why had the seditionist movement mattered to him when it would pass out of history in a decade or a century? When in a millennium Caeli-Amur itself might be forgotten?

Max shook his head. He knew those were not his thoughts. They were Aya's, or those parts of Aya he had absorbed. The mage who had existed in Max's mind had been only a fragment of his original self, and so Max was still himself for the most part. He was disappointed to discover he knew only parts of the prime language. Aya himself could not recall it all. It would take decades of study to recover it, if it could be recovered at all.

Max turned away from the Stones and made his way down to where the water lapped against the headland below. He found a rock on which to sit. A cold wind came off the ocean, and Max crossed his arms against it. Winter would be on them soon.

Max had absorbed more than Aya's thoughts: he had absorbed the distance that came with practice of the prime language. He would have to strive desperately to connect with the world. That was why he needed Kata: to keep him human, to save him from the coldness that swallowed up all Magi in the end. But she didn't need him. And so he would have to return to his first love, the seditionist movement. It was a love that never ran away, was always there when you needed it, a trusty companion.

He would work for humanity and the future. Yes, their lives

were only brief gusts of wind in a summer storm, but that did not mean they didn't matter. Yes, each of them would be forgotten; the movement would be surpassed; the city would be torn down and rebuilt. Nothing would survive. If he were one of the stars in the sky, he would look down impassively on these tiny people. But he wasn't some distant sun burning in the vast firmament. He was a man, alive. He was a thaumaturgist. He cared for people—not just those close to him, but the people he'd never met and would never meet. He cared for the generations to come. He was Max.

# FORTY-SEVEN

Kata wandered through the abandoned baths. The air was cold and dry, not steamy like so many times before. Some of the waters were blackened, filled with refuse. Others looked clear and icy. She passed the long corridor with private rooms and stopped at the one with the broken door. She looked into the gloomy room. A bath still stood in one corner, and the wonderful mosaic was barely discernible in the gloom.

Kata stood there for a long time, thinking of Aceline. Perhaps the woman had died at the right time. She had missed the bloody conflicts that had wracked the city, conflicts that had nearly engulfed them, that had taken Rikard away, and many more. Yet they had survived. The seditionists had defeated the enemy within. The city was united for the first time in its history. The citizens marched together in a common front toward the future.

But even if the seditionists were in control, what were they in control of? A city in desperate trouble, its industries grinding to a halt, its supplies barely enough for a hungry population, that population itself cowed, quiet, waiting and watching, getting by the best they could. Where the city had been so full of life, now the nights were characterized by an eerie quiet. Even the Quaedian was a shadow of its former self.

And yet the seditionists *were* in charge. If they could get the farms working, the fishing boats out to sea, the industries running, then life would spring back. The festivals would be full of color, the bars full of flower-liquor, the home fires full of warmth.

But they had no time. That was the tragedy of it all: as soon as one crisis was averted, another descended. Varenis's legions were on the march. Their Auxiliary troops, comprised of Cyclopses or other giants, had already made it south of the Palian Wall.

What hope did Caeli-Amur have?

Kata walked until she came to a wide clear bath. In the niches of the wall, someone's unusually large clothes were jammed in without care. The lamps hanging on the walls threw off a warm yellow light. Cutting down at an angle, a shaft of white natural light complemented them.

Floating on his back, in the center of the pool, lay Dexion. The giant minotaur's arms drifted out from his body in the shape of a cross. His eyes stared at the lovely mosaic above. For a moment he appeared dead, but in a surge of energy he burst to his feet, the water streaming down his powerful physique. He shook his head, the beaded braids of his mane whipping about, sending water flying.

"Kata! You must come in. It's cold and clear. It will refresh you."

Kata looked around at the empty complex. "This place is empty. It's lonely."

Dexion laughed, splashed water up at her. "There's no one around. That's better!" He dove under, came up again, and drenched Kata with two powerful rotations of his arms. The coldness hit her. She laughed and backed away, but he was already out of the bath. Two mighty arms wrapped around her. She squealed like a little girl as more cold water engulfed her. Then she was off her feet, suspended in the air.

With Kata still in his arms, Dexion leaped backward. Kata felt air rushing by. She squawked again, like a bird, but there was laughter mixed with it. She was suddenly afraid of the powerful creature. She had lost all control. Her heart raced. He could do anything he wanted to her. Then a sudden shock, and she was under the cold water, eyes closed.

Dexion let go and she came up spluttering, the shock of the cold coursing through her. "Dexion! No!"

She turned to face him in some confused mixture of anger and laughter. "Dexion, I didn't *want* to come in!"

The minotaur was already floating on his back away from her.

He laughed again, kicked backward. "You wanted to come in. You love it in here."

Kata, still confused, said, "If I . . ." But she gave up. She was having too much fun, even if Dexion was *maddening*.

"Take your clothes off. It'll be easier to swim," said Dexion.

Kata pulled off her shirt, looked down at the two knives she kept strapped to her, and unbuckled them. A moment later her boots and skirt and undergarments were lying by the side of the pool.

Kata kicked back. It was true: she was less constricted without her clothes. She floated on her back near Dexion. She became suddenly aware of his massive naked body next to her. Fear and excitement ran through her. She turned her head, looked at him.

His inky black eyes met hers. She fell into them, and they seemed to grow and fill the room. Everything else dropped away. For a moment the atmosphere of the bath changed. Then Dexion reached over and gave her a quick push that sent her spinning and reaching for the bottom.

His laugh filled the baths, echoed down the corridors. "See, it's not so bad in here."

Kata looked up at the mosaic above her. On one side lay a mythic city from Old Aerth. A grand river ran through its odd square-shaped buildings. On the opposite wall lay a flat sea, an island city in the center, as Caeli-Enas had once sat in the sea off the coast of Caeli-Amur. Above was a mosaic of sky, filled with stars and constellations Kata did not recognize. *Another world*, she thought. She wondered what it might be like, this strange place. She wondered about the hopes and dreams of its inhabitants. She imagined lives and deaths that she would never know about. She would be separated from those people forever, and yet some part of her cared for them even so. She looked up again at the mosaic above her, depicting the strange faraway city, and that deep black night with its stars askew.

# ACKNOWLEDGMENTS

To my editors, Julie Crisp and Liz Gorinsky, without whom *The Stars Askew* would have been *very* askew; my agent, John Jarrold; the fine folk at Pan Macmillan UK, especially Bella Pagan and Louise Buckley; Tessa Kum, Ben Chessell, Jeff Sparrow, Alex Hammond, Patrick O'Shea, Andrew Macrae, Peter Hickman, Matthew Chrulew, Keith Stevenson, Jason Nahrung, Morgan Grant Buchanan, Maryellen Galbally, Francesca Davidson, and Leena Kärkkäinen.